Myrddin's War

B J Burton

The sequel to

Dartmoor ...The Saving

MOORHEN PUBLISHING LLP

First published in Great Britain in 2008 by
Moorhen Publishing LLP
1 Hazelwood Close, Windmill Hill, Brixham, Devon, TQ5 9SE
www.moorhenpublishing.co.uk

A CIP catalogue record for this book is available
from the British Library.

ISBN   978-1-905856-02-2

Cover photo by Miles Herbert
Cover design by Deep Red Designs

Printed and bound in Great Britain by
SRP Limited, Exeter, Devon

Dinication

This book is dinicated to all the readers who were kind enough to
write telling us how much they had enjoyed
Dartmoor ...The Saving,
to Auntie Barbara for her enthusiasm and
Cheryl for forty years of fun.

CHAPTER 1

Celtic treasures

Extract from *The New York Times*

Celtic treasures sold

Six ancient artefacts were sold yesterday for a total of nearly $4m. The items are believed to be almost 2,000 years old and included gold bowls and a large gold plate, all engraved with pre-Christian Celtic designs. An excited Sotheby's spokesperson said, "We expected a lot of interest and we weren't disappointed. Incredibly, these items had remained in the ownership of the same family for hundreds of years and provenance is sound. What is really exciting is that we understand that more wonderful objects will be coming to the market from the same source."

Three of the items were bought by museums and three were sold to private buyers. The seller did not want to be identified.

CHAPTER 2

A little place in the country

Extract from *Bridport and Lyme Regis News*

Farm sold to mystery buyer

Coast Farm, a 300-acre arable and livestock farm that lies along the cliff top between Seaton and Lyme Regis, has been sold to a mystery buyer. Farmer Ben Brown, 47, said, "We hadn't thought of selling, but we were approached with an offer that we just couldn't refuse." Mr Brown says that whoever has bought it clearly doesn't intend farming the land in the way that it has been farmed as he has been asked to sell off all the livestock and deadstock. The auction will take place next Wednesday starting at 10 a.m.

"Contractors have already been to measure up for a high fence all around the boundary of the farm. From the height of it, my guess is that a deer farm could be planned, but you'd need tractors and trailers for that and we're selling those – so I could be wrong," said Ben.

He's clearly a happy man. When asked what he is going to do next, he said, "Probably nothing," with the big smile of someone who will no longer be getting up at 5 a.m. and worrying about the price of milk.

CHAPTER 3

Life with the Johnsons

"One day, Arthur my boy, all this will be yours." Bob gazed at the damp patch on the ceiling. It was definitely growing: the patch was looking darker and there were signs of sagging. Bob sighed. It was July, but summer didn't seem to have got going. The driving winds and rain of the previous winter had continued through the spring and on into the summer. The old house was suffering. It needed a lot of money spending on it, and a lot of money was just what Bob didn't have.

He sighed again, but this time the sound had an echo. He looked down at his five-year-old son who was looking towards the damp patch with a doleful expression on his face that Bob realised was a pretty good copy of the way his own face was looking.

As soon as he knew that he had his father's attention, Arthur chuckled. Bob looked into the bright blue eyes beneath the thick thatch of unruly blonde hair and burst out laughing.

At that moment Jane appeared in the doorway of the bedroom. "And what's so funny in here?" she asked.

"Nothing much," said Bob, "just the house falling down." Father and son both laughed as if this was a wonderful joke.

"Nothing new then," said Jane. She looked at the happy faces of the two men in her life and couldn't help smiling. "You two are impossible! Anyway, I've got to go now."

Immediately the two faces assumed an expression of abject misery and it was Jane's turn to laugh. "Just stop it the pair of you. I'll be back as soon as I can, but it will be well after Arthur's bedtime so I'll expect you, young man, to be asleep."

Bob and Arthur followed Jane downstairs, along the hall, out of the front door to the drive where they waited until Jane got her old Ford Fiesta started and drove out onto the road in a cloud of blue smoke.

"That car," said Bob, "sounds like someone kicking a biscuit tin of spanners down the road." He shook his head. He had an afternoon to spend with his son. This wasn't the time to get depressed about money. "Well, young Arthur, what shall we do with ourselves?"

"I know," cried Arthur. He ran back into the house, disappearing into the lounge.

Bob followed slowly, knowing exactly what to expect. As he stepped through the lounge doorway he received a whack on the knee from a plastic sword. He gave a roar of mock pain and surprise.

"That's not fair! I wasn't ready. Where's my sword?"

"On the settee." Arthur grinned at his father over the top of a plastic shield.

Bob picked up the sword. The blade flopped over.

"Why do I always get the wobbly one?"

"Because you broke it," said Arthur, launching a furious attack.

The battle raged all over the house for an hour and only finished when Bob begged for mercy and called for a truce.

They recovered from their exertions sitting companionably side-by-side on the lounge settee, each sucking noisily on ice lollies. When they had finished, they remained sitting there, both staring up at the chimneybreast in front of them.

Firmly secured to the oak panelling above the granite fireplace was The Sword of Power. Initially it had simply rested on the point of the blade on the mantelpiece, made secure by its own massive weight, but as soon as Arthur was born Jane had insisted that Bob make sure that there was no risk of it toppling. Despite his grumbles about the damage he was doing to the woodwork, he had secured the sword with two brass brackets.

Bob was thinking back to the moment when he had first seen the sword as it rose from the sea near the tiny Scillies islet of Great Arthur. His thoughts were interrupted by his son speaking.

"Daddy, I want to touch my sword."

"Sorry, what did you say?"

"I said that I want to touch my sword."

Arthur slipped off the settee, stepped into the tiled hearth of the fireplace, pointed up at the sword and stared into his father's eyes.

A pair of equally blue eyes stared back.

"Did you just say that it's *your* sword?"

"Yes, of course it is, Daddy – you know it is." Arthur spoke with total assurance, his young face calm, but expectant.

Bob felt the hairs rise on the back of his neck. The room felt suddenly cold and a shiver travelled down his back.

Arthur had shown great curiosity about everything with which he came into contact. He had questioned his parents about every object in the house – except for the sword. Bob had often seen Arthur staring at it, but never once had the boy spoken of the mighty weapon. Now he was not only speaking of it, but he was claiming it as his own – and he wanted to touch it.

When Bob had first handled the sword he had experienced visions that had left him terrified, but exhilarated. Later, Myrddin had held Bob's hand to The Sword of Power to show him visions of the wrongs in the world that Myrddin had returned to put right. Almost six years had elapsed since Myrddin had disappeared with Gilda. Bob's conviction that he would be called upon to play his part in Myrddin's war had occasionally weakened. Whenever he had felt that happening he had touched the great sword and, feeling its power flow through him, his faith was restored.

In all the time that the sword had been with them, Jane had refused to touch it, frightened of the effect it might have on her.

Now their son wanted to touch it.

"Come on, Daddy, hold me up." Arthur was still pointing up at the sword.

Bob slowly rose from the settee. He stepped forward, put his hands to his young son's waist and lifted him. He moved Arthur towards the sword, but it wasn't the blade that Arthur wanted.

"Up," he insisted, stretching up towards the hilt.

Bob straightened his arms and Arthur reached out. His small fingers went to the leather binding on the hilt. Bob held his breath, anxiously looking for his son's reaction. Arthur seemed to pick at an end that Bob couldn't see and the leather came loose. As Arthur pulled his hand from the sword he took with him a broad strip of leather that snaked away from the hilt.

Bob gasped. For years he had looked at the sword and had grown accustomed to the dull leather binding. Now the hilt shone like gold and a yellow light brightened the room.

Bob lowered Arthur and changed his grip so that his son sat on his arm, their faces level and close together. The faces were so alike, but the young face was calm while a range of expressions flowed over the other. Then father and son smiled broadly and hugged each other.

*

That evening, after Arthur had gone to bed, Bob again sat on the old leather settee, a glass of beer in one hand and a strip of ancient leather in the other. He stared at The Sword of Power as his thoughts carried him back over the last six years.

Six years ago Jane had been a primary school teacher. He had previously given up a profitable career as an accountant to take the job as a Dartmoor National Park ranger and, despite his reservations about the big drop in his income, they had been comfortable enough with the two salaries and he had loved his new job.

The only source of unhappiness had been the lack of children in their marriage. After years of trying they had come to accept that it just wasn't to be. That had been difficult enough for him, but for Jane, who spent her working life with other people's children, it had been much harder to bear.

Their lives had been turned upside down when he had discovered a tribe of tiny people living on Dartmoor. They called themselves Dini, and The Droller, the storyteller of their tribe, had told him and Jane the history of the tribe according to their folklore. They were the descendents of the Celtic Votadini, great warriors and horsemen who fought alongside their kinsman warlord, Artos, in the battles against the Saxon invaders. Artos, now remembered as Arthur, had wielded a great sword fashioned by fusing together the swords of the Celtic kings in whose name he fought – the sword that for the last six years had been mounted on his chimneybreast. As Bob gazed up at the sword he could remember vividly the sensations that had swept through him when he had pulled the sword from the sea.

According to The Droller's story, Myrddin had been found sealed in a lead box where he had lain for fifteen hundred years. When Myrddin had been with them there had been moments when he and Jane could just about accept that the Merlin of legend had returned. Myrddin had been unlike anyone they'd ever met and there was no denying that the old man had seemed to radiate some sort of energy that swept people along.

But now his every rational thought rejected the idea that Arthur and Merlin were somehow playing a part in the twenty-first century. But he had no doubt that the sword was the source of a power that he couldn't explain – and the fact that his son felt a strong connection with the sword was unsettling.

Myrddin had told them that he had been restored to stop the poisoning of the Earth, to fight the causes of the floods and famines plaguing the planet. Whatever they believed about his background, it was a cause that they could believe in and he and Jane had accepted that they had a role to play. But then Myrddin had disappeared with Gilda, the witch of the Dini tribe, leaving them with the problem of protecting the Dartmoor Dini.

He chuckled to himself as he recalled his first troublesome meeting with HRH The Duke of Cornwall as he sought his help. But the help had been forthcoming and the Dartmoor Dini were now living on a remote royal estate in Scotland.

Shortly after that Jane had found that she was pregnant and, to their enormous delight, Arthur was born. Jane believed that Gilda had worked a miracle with one of her potions, but he had felt sure that it was the influence of The Sword of Power.

Jane had decided not to return to work. She had waited too long for a family and now that she had a baby of her own she wasn't going to let anyone else care for him.

He had been happy with that decision, but he was still a Dartmoor ranger and living on his income alone was difficult, especially when the persistent foul weather battered their old house. It seemed that almost every month money had to be found to pay for repairs. Their savings were practically exhausted.

A frown settled on his face as he once again told himself that they really ought to sell his family home. He had grown up there and Arthur was enjoying the house and garden just as he had done, but reality had to be faced.

Driven by the belief that Myrddin had instilled in them, he and Jane had become active in environmental campaigning. With the extra time available to her after giving up her job, Jane had been particularly energetic becoming a committed member of the Green Party. Her involvement had been such that she had now been selected to stand as a Green Party candidate in the next General Election. Six years ago she would have stood very little chance of being successful, but she said that times were changing. The change in weather patterns around the world were there for all to see and concern was rising within the people of Britain. He had his doubts: the concern may be there, but he saw little evidence of enough people being prepared to make major lifestyle changes.

The thought of Jane possibly being elected did not remove the frown from his face. A MP's salary would be very useful, but Jane would be away from home a lot. Arthur would be starting school soon: maybe they could cope with her absences, but it wasn't a prospect that he relished.

The sound of Jane's car on the drive brought Bob fully alert. He looked up at the shining hilt of the great sword – he had some explaining to do.

The front door opened and Bob heard Jane call, "It's me – I'm home." He knew her so well that he could tell from the sound of those few words that the meeting had not been a good one. Jane went straight to the kitchen and by the time Bob joined her she already had the kettle on and was standing with both hands resting on the tea caddy, staring unseeingly into the sink.

Bob stood behind his wife, put his arms around her to give her a squeeze, kissed the back of her neck then moved away to drop the blinds, take two mugs from the cupboard, a spoon from a drawer and the milk from the fridge. Then he returned to rescue the caddy.

"Go and sit down and tell me all about it while I get the tea."

Jane sighed, but smiled at him and sat at the kitchen table.

"Not much to tell really: it was just a bit of a waste of time."

"Many turn up?"

"No. It started to rain about an hour before we were due to begin, which probably put some people off coming. We'd set out seating for a hundred and fifty and about fifteen turned up. Most of those were Party members and their families."

"Biscuit with the tea?" Bob reached for the tin.

"Yes – no, hang on; there's that chocolate cake in the fridge, I could do with a big chunk of that."

Bob got out the cake and cut off a slice. He chuckled. "You'll have to explain yourself to Arthur. He knows exactly how much was left."

Bob took the tea and cake to the table and sat down. "So, as usual, you were preaching to the converted."

"Not quite. There was a handful there who seemed to have come just to enjoy an argument."

"There can't still be people who don't believe that the climate is changing!"

"No, probably not, but there are plenty who don't see why it's up to them to do anything about it. You get the 'When China stops building coal-fired power stations I'll use my car less', and 'The Earth's climate is always changing and you can't *prove* that the current changes are anything to do with mankind', not to mention the totally selfish 'I'll be dead before there's any real disaster, so it's not my problem' – we had them all tonight."

Jane filled her mouth with cake and her eyes closed for a few moments, "That is delicious. Anyway, that's enough of the Green Party and me saving the world for an ungrateful mankind for one day – what have you boys been up to?"

"Aah. When you've revived yourself with tea and cake, I've got something to show you."

"That sounds ominous. What's fallen off the house now?"

"No, it's nothing like that. It's just something, well, er... *interesting*."

*

Bob and Jane were sitting on the settee in front of the lounge fireplace staring up at The Sword of Power. Jane had reacted exactly as Bob had expected. Initially anger with him for allowing Arthur to touch the sword had combined with concern at any effect on her son, but that had given way to a feeling that was a mixture of bewilderment, excitement and fear.

As Bob gazed into the golden glow of the sword he felt a conviction that their adventure was at last moving into a new phase.

CHAPTER 4

Scotland

Carn eased from the bed, dressed as quietly as he could and closed the door behind him trying, without success, to prevent the loud click of the door latch.

Still in bed, Eppie, who had been waiting for that click, smiled to herself and went back to sleep.

In the kitchen, Carn pulled on his coat and his boots and went outside. Dawn was some way off and there was no moon. Carn moved confidently through the darkness: he was used to it after a lifetime of travelling across Dartmoor when the Dini had been mainly restricted to moving about at night.

He followed the track across the corner of the conifer plantation to the small stand of oak and beech that stood at the edge of the meadow. He had placed a log at the foot of one of the oaks to act as a seat and he settled down with his back against the tree.

This was his favourite time of day. He loved the feeling of the Earth being reborn each day as the sun rose, bringing its life-giving light and warmth. Before the first lightening of the sky in the east, the first bird song began. It was a robin – he knew it would be. And he also knew that the robin would begin its song from the branch above his head. Carn had noticed that there didn't seem to be as many robins in Scotland as back in Devon, and they were less bold. But the bird now singing its beautiful, if rather melancholy, song above Carn's head had grown used to the Dini and now sought them out looking for scraps of food.

The robin's song acted as an alarm call for the other birds and as the sky grew lighter the dawn chorus filled the wood behind.

Long before full daylight he could see clearly the Shetland stallion in the smaller of the two pony paddocks on the meadow. The stallion's mane and tail shone a pale gold. Carn watched with pride and pleasure as the pony launched into a gallop around the paddock, tossing his head and flicking his tail. The pony stopped at the point nearest to where Carn was sitting, thrust his head over the top rail and whinnied.

Carn smiled and got to his feet. As he walked towards the pony he called, "Morning, Sunshine. There's no hiding from you, is there?" When Carn reached the fence the stallion pushed his head between the top and bottom rail and snorted into Carn's face.

"And how are you today? Full of life, by the look of it." As he spoke Carn fondled the soft muzzle, but then he spotted something in Sunshine's paddock. "A bit *too* full of life, by the look of it – I see you've kicked your water bucket over again."

Carn stood the metal bucket back upright in the shallow hole he'd dug for it and made three trips with two much smaller buckets to the nearby water tap. As the pony drank noisily Carn groomed him. The honey-coloured summer coat was as smooth as silk and glowed in the early morning sun. He stood barely thirty-six inches high at the withers, but at only two feet high himself, Carn had to stand on the bottom rail of the fence to brush the pony's back.

Satisfied with his work Carn moved to the adjacent larger paddock where three mares, each with a foal, and two geldings stood watching him expectantly. He groomed the mares and foals. The geldings would be working during the day and he would groom them in the evening. Carn climbed onto the top rail of the fence. It was a fine-looking group of ponies that stood looking back at him.

He heard the cackling of hens: Eppie must have gone to the run and opened the door to the hen house. He could picture her standing warily at the door, large stick in one hand. The cockerel unnerved her; when he stretched up, threw back his head to crow and flapped his wings he was intimidatingly large and Eppie didn't like the look of the sharp spurs on his legs. Carn smiled at the image of Eppie shooing the cockerel away, before looking for eggs. He allowed himself a little longer, enjoying the first suggestion of warmth from the early morning sun, before climbing down from the fence and heading back.

In the distance he saw Bran and Enid returning after milking the dexter cow kept in a small paddock behind the McDonalds' house.

When he got back he found most of the others noisily enjoying breakfast. The only one missing, as usual, was Tegid.

Carn washed his hands and pulled a tiny chair up to the low table, sitting next to Erbyn. Eppie and Issel were trying to keep up with the demand for scrambled eggs, toast and tea. Carn joined in the laughter at the amount of food piled up in front of Erbyn, who was taking the ribbing with his customary good humour.

"I'm a growing boy," he said, patting his ample stomach, "and I've got a lot of work to do today, so I need fuelling up."

"Quite right, too," said Carn, playfully nudging Erbyn's elbow so that the egg fell from his fork just before it reached his mouth. "What have you got planned?"

"Nudd and I are cutting wood. We thought we'd get the woodshed filled and give the logs some time to dry out before winter."

"Good idea," said Bran, "but Nudd doesn't seem to be fuelling up to the same extent."

They all laughed again but, unabashed, Erbyn carried on shovelling scrambled egg into his mouth and wiped a trickle of butter from his chin with a piece of bread.

"We're going to pick fruit," said Enid, putting an arm around Bran, "aren't we?"

"Yes, we had a look yesterday evening and there seemed to be a lot ready for picking."

There was a snort from Erbyn and he swallowed his mouthful of food. "Talking about people eating a lot, when you two picked strawberries the other day you were picking for hours, your faces and hands were stained pink, but very few strawberries arrived here. When they were shared out I only got four!"

There was more laughter and when it died down Eppie asked Carn, "What about you, what have you got planned? Or have you already done a day's work?"

"Yes, Carn," said Bran, leaning over to give him a dig in the ribs, "what time were you up this morning? Eppie kick you out of bed again?"

"No, I haven't done a day's work. I just groomed Sunshine, the mares and the foals…"

"Sounds like more than a day's work to me," Erbyn interrupted with a smile.

18

"…I thought I'd spend the rest of the day in the vegetable garden. I suppose you two will need the cart for the logs."

"Yes," said Nudd, 'we think there's room for about four more cartloads in the shed."

"I'll give you a hand getting the ponies harnessed," said Carn.

Erbyn and Nudd exchanged a look. They were quite capable of handling the ponies, but if there was any chance of working with the Shetlands there was no keeping Carn away.

"And what's Tegid up to? Anybody know?" It sounded like a question addressed to them all, but he knew it would be Nudd who answered.

Nudd flushed with embarrassment; it didn't matter how often the others tried to reassure him, he still felt responsible for the actions of his brother.

"He didn't come in until nearly dawn – it may have been the noise he made that woke you up, Carn." Nudd looked apologetic, but Carn shook his head.

"I don't think so – but even if it was, it wasn't your fault. Any idea where he'd been?"

"No. But he was drunk – again. He's getting worse and I don't know where he's getting it from. Ever since Mr McDonald caught him stealing his whisky, they've made sure he can't get into the house and Erbyn hasn't made any beer for a while – but Tegid's still finding drink. What can I do? I can't lock him in."

"He must have hidden some away. It can't last much longer at the rate he seems to be drinking it." Enid put a sympathetic arm around Nudd. "Don't worry; I'm sure he'll settle down. Somehow we've got to find him something useful to do – and that's a problem for all of us, not just you, Nudd."

After breakfast Carn headed back to the pony paddocks. He made a fuss of the two geldings, fed them a few carrots and then led them to one of the storage sheds where they stood patiently while he put on the harness. Erbyn and Nudd pushed from the shed the little four-wheeled cart that Mr McDonald had found for them. Carn backed up the ponies and secured the harness to the cart.

Erbyn and Nudd loaded saws, axes and rope, then they each took hold of the leading rein of one of the ponies and set off for the part of the conifer plantation where Mr McDonald had used a chainsaw to fell some trees where thinning-out was needed.

Nudd shouted, "We were on our way back and decided to run for it, rather than hide in the trees." He looked around and bawled, "Where's Tegid?"

The alarm bell stopped, the sudden silence being almost as startling as the noise itself. No one spoke for a few seconds, then the door that led to the bedrooms opened and Tegid came into the kitchen.

"By all the gods, why do we have to suffer that infernal din?" He slammed the door behind him.

Nudd looked relieved to see his brother. The others, accustomed to Tegid's tantrums, ignored him.

To help keep the Dini secure, HRH had had an electronically-controlled gate installed where the entrance lane left the road, together with a closed circuit television system. Anyone wanting to enter had to press a button on the gate that sounded a buzzer in the farmhouse. Mr or Mrs McDonald would check the identity of the caller on the screen in their kitchen and, if they were happy to let the caller in, they would open the gate by pressing a button. Before opening the gate they sounded the alarm bell on the roof of the Dini's house for twenty to thirty seconds to give the Dini time to get out of sight.

Enid cautiously moved a curtain to one side and looked towards the farmhouse.

Tegid, irritated by being ignored, dragged a chair noisily to the table, sat down and demanded, "Any food ready?"

Carn looked at him – it wasn't a pretty sight. Tegid had been refusing to allow Enid to cut his hair and it hung around his face in greasy, tangled lengths. He had a dirty sock pulled over the stump where his left arm ended at the wrist, he had slept in his clothes and his eyes were red. No matter how they tried to hide the beer that Erbyn brewed, Tegid found it.

Carn thought of a number of biting retorts all suggesting that only those who had worked for the food should expect to receive any, but he'd been making that kind of comment for years and he knew it was a waste of breath. The others clearly thought so too, for still no one spoke to Tegid.

"It's a big white van," Enid said.

"Well I'm not hiding away anymore," cried Tegid, jumping up and making for the door.

Nudd quickly stepped across and blocked Tegid's way. "Grow up! Stop being stupid. Sit down and keep quiet," he said, giving his brother a shove back towards the table. Carn tried to hide a smile. One thing that had changed in the years they had been in Scotland was the relationship between Tegid and Nudd. The feeling of security had increased Nudd's confidence and Tegid no longer controlled his brother.

"You lot sicken me!" shouted Tegid. "Why *should* we hide away like this? At least on Dartmoor I used to have some fun." He sat down again and banged on the table with his fist.

They were all quiet for a few seconds and Carn heard Eppie sigh. He looked at her face: it was wearing an expression that he had seen increasingly often over the last few years. He knew just what she was thinking. Most of the time Carn was happy with his new life and when the doubts assailed him, throwing himself into his work got him through. He knew that the rest of the group tried to cope in the same way – except for Tegid.

Following the appearance of Myrddin in their lives they had made the move to Scotland and their lives were undoubtedly better. They had a house to live in, rather than cold, damp caves; the house had the luxury of hot water, television and a telephone they could use to speak to the Johnsons; they had plenty of food to eat and the McDonalds, encouraged by HRH, did everything possible to provide whatever the Dini felt they needed.

But there were still occasions when they had to hide away and those occasions, contrasting so sharply with their freedom to be out on the land in daylight, rammed home their disappointment with what Myrddin had achieved for them. They had clung to hopes that he might somehow use his powers to restore the Dini to normal size, so that hiding away would never be necessary.

And they had had no contact with The Droller since their move. No contact meant no news of the other groups of Dini; no news of Gilda or of Myrddin himself.

Most important of all, Myrddin appeared to have done nothing about their biggest problem; no baby Dini had been born; the Dini were dying out. Carn looked across the room to the young couple of their group. Enid stood peering out around the curtain and Bran sat with an arm affectionately wrapped around one of her legs. The odds were that, all too soon, either Enid or Bran would be living on their own – the last of the Dartmoor Dini.

Eppie broke the short silence. "Bob and Jane will be visiting soon. I wonder if they will bring Arthur." She paused. "I expect he's much taller than any of us now."

As much as they were grateful to Bob and Jane, their visits left the Dini unsettled. Arthur's birth just emphasised that Myrddin and, or, Gilda, had given that previously childless couple the child for which they had longed. Why couldn't they do the same for the Dini?

Tegid snorted derisively. "Wonderful! Just what we need. I can't wait to see them. I hope they're here soon – I'm so excited I won't be able to sleep with the excitement of it all." He banged on the table again. "I'm starving!"

Eppie ignored him. "Do you think they'll have heard any news?" she said, quietly.

It wasn't really a question. She knew the answer. Carn waited a moment and then said what one of them always said, "They would have phoned if they'd heard anything."

Enid held up a hand. "The driver's getting back in the van… he's going…we're all right now – he's out of sight."

The alarm bell sounded the all clear.

CHAPTER 5

Jane and Arthur

"Yes, I quite understand. I'll have it sorted out in good time for the meeting next week. If you could just email that article to me...? Great. See you soon. Yes, of course. Bye now." Jane hung up the phone and, with some satisfaction, crossed the last item off her list of tasks for the morning. She added one item to her new list of jobs for that evening, and resolutely closing the old roll-top desk sat back in her chair.

The room lightened as bright sunlight suddenly flooded in. She looked out of the window and could see blue sky.

"That settles it – it's some fresh air for us this afternoon." She listened, but the house was silent. "Arthur! Where are you?" When there was no reply she called again, "Where's my big man?" Jane stood and moved towards the door. Glancing out of the window she spotted Arthur.

He was lying on his stomach on the patio, legs bent at the knees so that his feet were in the air. His feet were tapping together to some rhythm in his head. In one hand he held his favourite present from his fifth birthday, a large magnifying glass. In the other hand he held a small stick that he was poking into a gap between two paving slabs. Something he had spotted was being studied intently.

Jane leaned against the window frame, content to watch her son. Even after almost five years, she still could hardly believe that she had a child. The words 'my son' were so sweet to her that she savoured the sound to the extent that, sitting at her desk, she would find herself saying, 'My son', and she would have to fight back the prickle of tears.

Since Arthur's birth there had been no sign of any more children. It was as if this one, very special child, was meant to be. As the years slipped by they were finding that they repeated their theories about whether The Sword of Power or Gilda's potion had finally brought about his birth with increasing embarrassment. If it hadn't been for their visits to the Dini in Scotland the whole adventure of five years ago would have become hard to accept.

"Well, Arthur, my son, whatever happened there was something magical about your birth and there's something magical about you," said Jane, smiling contentedly and speaking out loud to the window.

Arthur was still in the same position. The patio was wet from the morning rain and his clothes would be filthy, but Jane had been determined from the outset that they were just necessary to keep little boys warm. No activities should be restricted by worries of damage to clothing.

He was still captivated by whatever he was studying. Jane wondered how long he had been lying there. She'd checked on him from time to time through the morning and found him happily occupied in the lounge, sometimes reading, sometimes watching the television.

She still had a smile on her face, but she gave a little, bemused shake of the head as she looked at him. He had slept through the night from the first day they had brought him home. If he woke early he would lie quietly in his cot until Jane or Bob appeared and would greet them with a big smile. He had walked well before he was twelve months old, could read before he was two, had never had a tantrum. He could be noisy and excitable, but never bad-tempered. His taste in television programmes fascinated Jane. Arthur watched any nature programme with rapt attention, but she would find him gripped by something unexpected. She had found him silently watching an episode of *The World at War* with tears trickling down his cheeks.

But he was still a child and he loved some of the children's programmes, especially those with music. He would bawl out the words at the top of his voice, beating time with whatever satisfyingly noisy objects he could lay his hands on.

Jane had wondered if they should seek out some sort of music lessons for him, but had dismissed the idea. They just couldn't afford it. In recent years the house had been a pit into which they had poured large sums of money: the new heating system, the new windows, the re-wiring, a new roof on the front – with the back now in urgent need of attention. Then there had been the new damp-proof course, the collapsed drain and the new septic tank. Jane's smile changed to an anxious frown.

Arthur, sensing eyes upon him, turned to look at the window. He gave Jane a frantic wave, jumped to his feet and rushed into the house.

Jane met him in the hall where he threw his arms about her legs.

"Have you finished working, Mummy? Can we have some fun now? We haven't had lunch. Can we make a picnic and take it onto the moor? I'd like to go to a river. There'll be lots of water after the rain." He paused for breath, pushed back from her legs and looked up at her. "Can we?"

"Of course we can." She bent over and scooped him up into her arms. "First job – make the picnic."

Jane carried Arthur into the kitchen and held him up to the sink while he washed his hands. Then she sat him on a stool at the kitchen table.

"What shall we have in our picnic?"

He thought for a moment. "Honey sandwiches and crisps." When Arthur spotted his mother giving him a disapproving look he added, "And an apple."

"O.K. Sounds good to me.' She got out the loaf, butter and the jar of honey; cut slices off the loaf, buttered them and passed them to Arthur. With a frown of concentration on his face he struggled in vain to spread the thick honey without the bread tearing into small pieces.

"I like honey," he said.

"Yes, I know you do. So do I."

"Bees make it."

"Yes they do."

"When I went into the garden I saw a big spider's web. There were lots of shiny raindrops on it."

"Bet that was pretty."

"Yes, but as I was looking at it a bee flew into the web and got stuck."

Jane could tell that Arthur had something on his mind.

"What happened?" she asked gently.

"The bee buzzed very loudly and made the whole web shake. I thought it would break free – but it didn't."

Jane put the broken, sticky fragments of honey sandwiches into a plastic box while she waited for the rest of the story.

"The spider rushed at the bee and they had a fight. Who do you think should win in a fight between a spider – a big spider – and a bee?"

"Hmm. I'm not sure. I imagine that the bee is stronger and has a sting, but the spi…"

"No, I don't mean who *would* win in a fight, I mean who *should* win. The bee makes honey for us so I didn't want him to die. I got a stick and thought I'd set the bee free; but the spider must have worked very hard to make that big web and he needed the bee for food. Maybe the spider would die if the bee got away."

Arthur waved very sticky fingers at his mother and Jane lifted him up to the sink again. When she put him down he shot off to the cupboard where the crisps were kept and pulled out at a variety pack. He brought the pack to the table and held up his arms for Jane to lift him back onto the stool. He emptied the pack onto the table and started checking on the flavours that were left.

Jane prompted him. "What did you do about the bee?"

"I got him out very carefully so I didn't break much of the web. Then I came in here where I'd seen a dead bluebottle on the floor by the door. I took it out and dropped it onto the web. So the bee can go on making honey and the spider got some food. I think that was fair."

Jane looked at her young son as he sorted through the crisps, pulling faces at the flavours he didn't like. She should not be having conversations like this with a boy who had had his fifth birthday only last month. In her years as a primary school teacher hundreds of first year intake children had passed through her hands. Not one of them had been like this extraordinary child – her son.

At the thought of school a sadness came over her. Arthur was due to start in the autumn and she hated the idea. The thought of handing him over to someone else to look after him, to teach him, horrified her. And she would really, really miss their time together.

"Why are you sad, Mummy?"

"I'm not sad, just wondering where we should go."

"You were sad – I know when you're sad."

"O.K. I was sad – but only because I thought you were taking the best crisps." She grabbed Arthur and tickled him as he squirmed about on the stool, giggling. She let him tumble gently to the floor. "I'm starving. Let's get everything together and go as quick as we can. Where shall we go?"

"On that nice grassy bit by the pub."

"Right – let's go!"

They soon had everything packed into the Fiesta and, in a cloud of blue smoke, they set off.

Jane parked near the Warren House Inn. She changed her trainers for walking boots and helped Arthur pull on his wellies. She hefted a large rucksack onto her back. Arthur pulled on his own small rucksack then, with a fishing net in one hand and a plastic bucket in the other, he walked with his mother down the track to the stream.

Jane spread their waterproof picnic blanket on the lush grass near the water. They settled down to eat their food, afterwards washing their sticky fingers in the stream.

"What are you going to do now?" she asked, already knowing the answer.

Arthur rummaged in his rucksack and pulled out his magnifying glass. "I'm going to see what I can find to have a good look at." He dipped his bucket into the stream, placed it on the edge of the stream bank, grabbed the cane of his fishing net and stepped into the water.

The stream was so high and the current so strong that the water immediately flooded over the top of his boots. Jane looked on anxiously, but Arthur seemed unconcerned as he moved about the stream planting his feet firmly and pushing his net into the gravel. He regularly inspected the contents of his net and if there was nothing of interest he tipped the stones back into the water. From time to time he moved to the bank and carefully slipped something into his bucket.

Eventually he left the stream and lay on his back next to Jane with his feet in the air so that she could pull off his boots. She also removed his socks, dried his feet – tickling the soles while he squirmed and chuckled – then put on dry socks.

"Let's leave those wet boots to dry off for a bit. Stay on the rug for a while. Now, what exciting things have you got to show me?"

"Not sure yet. I'll show you when I've had a look." He scrambled over to the bucket and sat crossed-legged with it trapped between his legs while he dipped into the water it contained.

He looked as if he would be happily occupied for a while, so Jane took her binoculars from her rucksack and then made herself comfortable sitting with the rucksack as a backrest. Although the sun was still shining, it looked as if it wouldn't stay dry for long. There was blue sky overhead, but cloud cover was increasing; the nearer clouds looked white and fluffy, but in the west the sky looked dark.

She sighed. This was supposed to be the height of summer, yet week after week the rain kept coming. Doubts were growing in Jane about whether she was ever going to achieve anything meaningful through her Green Party activities. The changes were plain for all to see. In four years out of the last six summer floods had surged over the flood plains causing vast amounts of damage and misery. Thousands of homes had been permanently abandoned where flooding had re-occurred before the damage of previous floods could be repaired. The insurance companies had produced maps of the country with the areas marked where they were no longer prepared to offer cover. Chaos in the housing market had ensued with thousands of people left owning unsaleable properties; many of them had mortgages secured against houses that were impossible to value.

Food crops either failed to ripen or were left to rot in fields that had become oceans of mud. For the second time in three years the tennis championships at Wimbledon had been abandoned; last year the cricket county championship had been abandoned and this year's appeared to be heading the same way. And it wasn't just in Britain – the whole of the developed world was suffering from similar disruption of their weather patterns.

It's as if, thought Jane, *Earth herself has lost patience with mankind and is trying to wash us away. And still most people won't accept that they have any personal responsibility for what's happening. The Government should have had the courage to enforce changes in behaviour. No, it's the fault of the Democratic system – no Government would force through such unpopular measures as they wouldn't get re-elected. Now, if we'd had a dictatorship with me in charge, we wouldn't be in such a mess.*

Jane smiled at the idea.

"Why are you smiling, Mummy?"

"I was just thinking what I would do if I were the boss of the whole country. Why stop there? I should be boss of the whole world."

"Can I be the boss, too?"

"Hmm, well, maybe. It depends on what you'd do if I made you joint boss."

"I'd make everybody happy."

"Sounds like a good plan. How would you do it?"

Arthur looked back into his bucket. "Don't know. I don't know why they're not happy now."

"Aren't people happy now?"

He looked back at her. "I don't think so. When we go into the village everybody seems sad."

Jane was taken aback. When they went into Chagford she chatted to various friends and shopkeepers and they all made a fuss of Arthur. He loved climbing onto the red leather sofa in the bookshop and looking at books from the children's section. It came as a shock to Jane to find that her son thought that his world was full of sad people.

"Maybe they could all do with some sun. Anyway, no need for us to be sad, is there? What have you got to show me?"

Arthur placed his bucket by Jane's legs and sat on her lap. "Hold out your hand."

She did as instructed and Arthur carefully took something from the bucket and placed it in her palm. He offered her the magnifying glass. "Take a look at that."

She took the glass and looked at the caddis fly larva, the long thin body covered in tiny fragments of stone. "Do you know what it is?" she asked.

"It's a caddis fly larva."

"Clever boy! How do you know that?"

"Daddy showed me one last week. I've got three more. They use the stones to make it hard for fish to spot them – but how do they stick the stones on?"

"They make sticky threads – like the ones that spiders use for webs – and they sort of tie the stones on. You can see the strings through the glass."

"Let's see." Arthur took back the magnifying glass. "Oh yes."

"What else have you found?"

"A mayfly larva."

"I suppose Daddy has showed you those before, too."

"Yes, they have three long tails."

CHAPTER 6

A Ranger's life

"What a mess. What an absolute eyesore," Bob muttered to himself.

He was far from pleased with his morning's work. His eyes followed the long length of fluorescent orange tape snaking its way from post to post across the eastern slope of Water Hill on towards Hurston Ridge.

The tape marked a small section of the route of the popular long distance walk, the Two Moors Way, which crossed both Dartmoor and Exmoor. The combination of all the human feet, the livestock and the exceptionally wet weather had resulted in serious erosion. The Rangers were trying to protect the moor by restricting walkers. No one was happy about it – least of all the Rangers.

Bob shouldered his sledgehammer and the unused poles, picked up the reel of tape and set off back down towards the small car park on the B3212 where he'd left his Land Rover. He'd stowed the gear in the back and took out his sandwich box. He leaned against the back door and took a large bite of cheese and pickle. Should he pop into the Warren House Inn for a swift half, just to wash down his lunch?

"Is that Mr Johnson?"

Bob turned towards the voice and found a white-haired lady looking at him. In the few seconds it took him to clear his mouth Bob tried unsuccessfully to put a name to the face.

"Yes, it is, Mrs … er …"

"Oh, you won't remember me. My husband and I have been to a couple of your talks. I'm Betty Browning." As she spoke she looked rather anxiously over her shoulder towards Water Hill.

"Well, Mrs Browning, is there something I can do for you? If it's about all the tape, I know it looks ghastly but…"

"Oh no, it's not about the tape. I saw you come down from Water Hill and I wondered if you'd seen my husband."

Bob thought back. "I think I only saw three groups of walkers this morning, all head…"

"No, no, he wasn't in a group. He set off on his own on a walk, but he's well over an hour overdue and he's usually very accurate with his estimates. I expect I'm just being silly, but it's just not like him…" Her voice cracked and she bit her bottom lip.

"I expect he's fine," said Bob. "He's probably enjoying himself and just gone further than he intended. Do you know where he planned going?"

"He always leaves me with his route. It's in the car." She pointed in the direction of a Honda Civic.

"Let's have a look, then. What's he wearing?"

They moved to the Honda; Mrs Browning reached in and produced a spiral-bound notepad.

"A green waterproof jacket, beige trousers and a red hat."

"What's he got on his feet?"

"Proper walking boots. He's very sensible about things. He's got a rucksack that I'm sure is full of everything he's supposed to have."

"Well, it sounds as if he can't have come to much harm."

Mrs Browning opened the notepad and pointed. "See, he always writes down exactly where he's going."

The pad was well over half full. Bob read out the last entry. "Up to Hurston Ridge. North to the stone row. West to the wall around Fernworthy forest, through the gate, down the track to the road. Follow the road west until it ends. West along the track passing the stone circle, on through the forest to the gate out onto Long Ridge. South-east along the forest boundary wall. Leave the wall at the south-east corner and straight back to the car park."

Bob mentally totted up the distance. It was the sort of walk that didn't look far at a glance at a map, but it could easily add up to seven or eight miles. Less than half the distance was on good forest tracks where three miles an hour would be reasonable. The rest was over open moorland where two miles an hour would be more like it. If Mr Browning, like his wife, was in his seventies, that could take three-and-a-half to four hours, allowing for the occasional stop to take in the view.

"How long did he think it would take him to get back here?" he asked.

"Four hours."

Bob smiled. "It sounds to me as if he knows what he's doing. He's well-equipped, obviously used to walking on the moor and he's left details of his walk with you."

"But he's been gone since eight o'clock."

Bob glanced at his watch. Twenty-past one.

"Have you been sat in the car all this time?"

"Oh, no. I've been to Princetown to see my sister." She was staring anxiously into the distance. "He has a mobile phone, but there's no signal in a lot of places around here."

Bob thought for a moment. "All right. Here's what we do. I'll set out doing his walk in the reverse direction. You wait here. If he turns up, no need to hang around, just leave a message for me at the pub."

He didn't have to walk far before spotting his target. From the southernmost point of the wall surrounding Fernworthy Forest, Bob could see a figure in a red hat moving slowly along the wall near the bottom of a shallow gully. As Bob approached, the figure sank to his knees before using the wall to pull himself back to his feet. Bob hurried towards him as best he could, his progress hampered by the soft ground. If he stepped between the tussocks his boot sank deep into the wet peat.

The man had seen him coming and was leaning against the wall waiting for him.

"Dr Livingstone, I presume," said Bob. "Or should that be Mr Browning?"

The man was looking all of his seventy-odd years, his face pale and deeply lined, but he managed a smile. "Browning it is. And you're Bob Johnson, commonly called Ranger Bob, I believe. I imagine that you've just seen my wife."

"So I have. She tells me you're a bit overdue."

"More than a bit, I'm afraid. It's this wet ground. It's such hard work moving over it – especially in these gullies.' He looked ruefully at his trousers, plastered in black peaty mud. "The ground shouldn't be like this in July."

"You're right. It shouldn't be like this – but unfortunately it is. The important thing is that you had the good sense to give your route to your wife and stick to it. Better let me have that rucksack." Bob swung it onto his own back. "Right, follow me. Put your feet exactly where I do – unless, of course, I suddenly disappear."

After returning Mr Browning to his relieved wife, Bob hurriedly ate the rest of his sandwiches thinking that it might even be possible that the National Park Authority would have to close the whole moor. It was really becoming unsafe to venture out of sight of a road.

He was now running late and he suffered a further delay. On his way to Princetown he spotted a silver Ford Focus that had been driven too far from the road onto the moor. The NPA had created parking areas where tons of stone had been deposited and then compressed into the ground to produce a surface firm enough to take the weight of cars. At each of these sites warning signs told motorists the maximum distance they should drive from the road. From time to time cars were driven too far, at best churning up the soft ground and, at worst, becoming stuck.

Bob parked near the Focus and walked over to it. The sole occupant was a man, his seat partially reclined and a cigarette in his mouth. Bob tapped on the window. The window wound down and a face turned towards him.

The combination of the cloud of tobacco smoke and the sight of the face made Bob take a step backwards.

*

Nigel Sligo was forty years of age. He'd had a miserable, friendless childhood, mainly because he'd been a thoroughly unpleasant little boy – the sort who enjoyed pulling wings off butterflies and inflating frogs with drinking straws. He had eventually scraped the A-Levels needed to get him into a third rate university and when even that institution couldn't bring itself to give him a degree (not because he wasn't bright enough, but because he couldn't be bothered to apply himself) he had found himself with nothing to show for his three student years except for a load of debt and a great deal of contempt for his fellow students.

He soon discovered that what he perceived as weaknesses in his fellow man could make a useful source of income. A job with a firm of bailiffs opened his eyes to just how weak people could be. His next job with a firm of private investigators completed his education. Now he called himself a freelance reporter.

Sligo specialised in seeking out unsavoury aspects of human behaviour. There was no doubt that he had a talent for what he did. He had developed a sensitive nose that could detect the faintest whiff of corruption or indiscretion. He had developed his own list of targets prioritised in terms of how much a story would be worth. Top of his list came film stars, then TV stars; then sports stars (particularly high-earning footballers), then politicians, then police officers, then the 'celebrities' who achieved a temporary fame by appearing in a 'reality' TV programme, then a member of any religious order and, finally, teachers. He was always hoping to get the Royal Family onto his hit list, but editors were still reluctant to carry his sort of story with a royal target; he assumed it was because editors and proprietors were hoping that some sort of honour might come their way.

Over the years Sligo had built a network of useful contacts – people who, in return for a cash payment, could supply useful information. He could trace vehicle owners from registration numbers; obtain credit ratings; receive photocopies of bank statements; trace family members and 'friends' of victims who would be happy to talk in return for cash. He also had connections who provided the starting point for his scoops – staff at supposedly discreet luxury hotels and restaurants, backroom staff in football clubs, actors who were permanently bit-part players and jealous of others' success.

Given the vaguest details he could concoct scandalous stories that usually had just about enough truth in them to avoid legal action. Digital photography had been a boon to Sligo. He didn't need top quality photos, just an image good enough to be recognisable. He could take adequate photos on a tiny pocket camera or even on his mobile phone – and so could his contacts. Thanks to the technology he was able to email a summary of his story and one or more photos to the editors of the tabloid newspapers and then effectively carry out an auction sale to determine who should receive his richly embroidered and grossly exaggerated version of events.

He'd been doing it for years, but he still got a thrill whenever he opened a newspaper to see one of his stories. He savoured the thoughts of the effect that he must have had on the victim – and he enjoyed receiving the cheques.

But there were downsides and he'd just experienced one. He had come up with a juicy story that had destroyed the marriage of a Premiership footballer. He'd got good photos and, for once, his story was largely true. But the footballer came from the East End of London and had grown up with some interesting characters.

A call from the footballer's agent to a sports reporter on the paper obtained Sligo's contact details in return for promises of exclusive tip-offs in the future.

A couple of weeks later, Sligo opened his front door at ten o'clock at night expecting to see a pizza delivery boy. As soon as he released the Yale lock the door slammed into him dislocating two of his fingers and sending him crashing into the wall. The front door closed and he found himself in the company of two large gentlemen whose lack of hair was more than compensated by an abundance of tattoos.

By way of introduction one of them punched him solidly on the nose. His head snapped back and bounced off the wall. To prevent Sligo sliding to the floor, his other visitor thoughtfully supported him while his colleague landed another ten blows. Before they left, a barely conscious Sligo heard the puncher hiss in his ear, "I enjoyed that. I think I'll be coming back for some more."

When the pizza delivery boy arrived he found the door ajar and his customer sprawled in the hall. He took the £10 from Sligo's wallet. Before he left he phoned for an ambulance.

The ambulance crew called the police.

The two police officers watched as Sligo was loaded into the ambulance, then they ate the pizza and shut the door behind them as they left. They knew Sligo. It wasn't the first time they'd been called to the address.

When Sligo was released from hospital he decided that his four cracked ribs, broken nose, split eyebrows and collection of bruises could do with a holiday: an extended one – a long way from London.

A few minutes on the internet was all he needed to find out that, thanks to continuing wet and windy weather, all over the country there were holiday cottages available, despite it supposedly being the peak holiday season. When he saw Dartmoor mentioned he paused. One of his previous attackers had been sent to Dartmoor prison – he had set about Sligo in a pub and had been detained by other drinkers until the police had arrived. As far as he knew, the man was still there. The idea of standing outside the prison, knowing that his attacker was locked up inside, appealed to Sligo.

A phone call to a property-letting agent secured him a two-bedroomed terraced cottage in Princetown for two months.

CHAPTER 7

Mike's Gal

The driver brought the white van bearing the name 'Mike's Marine Electronics' to a halt on Newlyn quay, close to where the boat that also bore his name was tied up. Mike Trevean climbed out of the cab and opened the rear doors. He dragged out a large, grey, plastic tank and carried it down the steps and onto *Mike's Gal*.

The tank contained about two hundred live sand eels crowded in only a few centimetres of water. Using a bucket, Mike scooped water from the harbour and topped up the tank. He fitted his aerator and turned it on. He waited for a few moments to check that there was enough air flow to keep the sand eels alive before returning to the van to bring down a coolbox containing the rest of the bait and a four-pint container of milk.

He had filled the diesel tank the night before, so all that remained for him to do was to carry out a final check to make sure that Mike's Gal was looking at her best.

The angling party still wasn't due for twenty minutes so Mike lit the gas under the kettle and while it boiled he checked the tide timetable and the waymarks entered on the GPS. He tuned the VHF radio to the weather channel and drank his tea as he listened to the forecast. He felt that he needn't have bothered. The forecast seemed unchanging: for day after day, week after week, it just repeated the warning of heavy showers blowing in from the west, with winds gusting to force 8 or 9. He switched back to Channel 16 and settled down to savour the rest of his mug of tea.

The group of eight anglers arrived on the stroke of eight o'clock. The early start hadn't dampened their enthusiasm and the loud cheerful banter in their heavily-accented Birmingham voices meant that Mike could hear them coming along the quay when they were still some distance away.

Mike smiled. It constantly amazed him how enthusiastic Brummies were about fishing. Their city was the best part of one hundred miles from the sea in any direction, had no significant river flowing through it and yet a large part of the population seemed to have a passion for all forms of angling. Quite a few of his charter clients had been proud to tell Mike that the Birmingham Anglers Association was one of the largest in the world with many thousands of members. The noisy group on their way to *Mike's Gal* were regulars. Twice a year they had a few days in the Westcountry going on daily fishing trips from ports on both the north and south coasts of Cornwall. They always booked a trip with Mike.

Dave Cooper, the one who had phoned to make the booking, appeared at the top of the steps. "Morning! How's our Singing Skipper, then?"

Mike returned the greeting with a quick burst of *Oh What a Beautiful Morning,* sung in his broad Cornish accent, before taking aboard all the rod bags and boxes of tackle passed to him from the steps. Then he shook hands with each of the men as they stepped aboard, surreptitiously looking them over as they reminded him of their names. They were all in good humour and although Mike learned that they had sunk a few pints the night before and not got to bed until well after midnight, none of them seemed the worse for wear – which was just as well as it wouldn't be a day of smooth seas.

Usually with a party as large as eight, Mike would have taken along a deckhand, but cash was tight and he had decided to do without any crew. All of this party had sailed with him several times before; he had seen them confidently standing as the boat wallowed in heavy seas, both hands busy with rods and reels, their legs flexing like those of experienced seamen to adjust to the movement of the deck beneath their feet. He was also confident that they knew how to handle fish; there would be no hands gashed on the razor sharp gill covers of the bass they would catch.

Mike slipped the lines and took his boat smoothly away from the quay. Even within the harbour he could feel a swell lifting her; it was an ominous sign.

"So, Skipper, what have you got lined up for us today?"

"We'll make it to a sandbank and drift over it while the tide's running, then we'll move to a wreck for slack water and after the tide has turned we'll head back to the sandbank."

There was a cheerful chorus of approval.

"What's the fishing been like, Skip?"

"When we've been able to get out, it's been good. Plenty of good bass on the sandbanks and big pollack, ling and conger on the wrecks – but the weather's been difficult."

"Yeah, we know all about that. Most of our trips over the last couple of years have been cancelled or cut short. What's the forecast for today?"

Mike gestured at the overcast sky. "Not good. Frequent showers, some heavy, wind gusting to force 8 or 9 later in the day."

"No need to worry about slappin' on the factor fifty today, Chalky!" Dave used both hands to enthusiastically slap the bald head of a colleague who was utterly unperturbed by the rough treatment.

"You should have seen him in May. We went out from Weymouth and got a rare fine day. Chalky's head looked like a snooker ball – bright red and shiny it was. A couple of days later he didn't half peel – when he pulled his jumper off we all thought it was snowin'!"

Mike joined in the general laughter as he directed *Mike's Gal* across Mount's Bay towards the sandbank that he'd waymarked. It wasn't far, about forty minutes away, and the wreck he'd chosen was pretty close to it. This wasn't the sort of day to set off for a mid-Channel mark.

There was a four-foot swell and the wind was whipping the tops off the waves. Mike could see that the sea on the horizon was very lumpy.

"Right then, lads. There'll be quite a tide running. I suggest weights of at least four ounces, eight-foot traces and live sand eels – you'll find plenty of them in the tank."

His passengers busied themselves tackling up as *Mike's Gal* powered on.

Mike kept his eyes on the GPS and the echo-sounder. As they reached the sandbank he swung the boat about so that she pointed up-tide and he adjusted the revs so that she would slowly drift across the sandbank below.

"O.K. boys – in you go! Good luck!"

With a loud cheer and some last minute bets being placed, eight sand eels were lowered into the water. Three were taken by mackerel before the lead weights had hit the bottom. The mackerel were quickly removed and the hooks re-baited. On the first drift six bass were caught, but five were too small and were immediately and carefully put back.

44

As they reached the end of the sandbank Mike called, "Tackle out!" When he was sure that all the lines were clear of the water he powered *Mike's Gal* back to the starting position and repeated the drift.

On the third drift the first shower hit. Heavy rain swept across them and the wind gathered strength. No one seemed to mind.

A good thornback ray was brought aboard.

"I've got a feeling I'm going to pull in something massive today!" one of the anglers shouted.

"You ain't pulled anything massive since that blind date when you met your missus!"

The banter and the fishing continued until the tide began to slacken.

"O.K. boys, we'll hit this spot again later. Let's move on to a wreck!"

Mike set the new waymark. They were about twelve miles south of Penzance, due west of Lizard Point. Their new destination was a wreck only three miles from the coast at the western end of Mount's Bay. *Mike's Gal* powered through the increasingly heavy seas heading towards Gwennap Point.

"Better put lifejackets on, gents. You'll find them in here." Mike used a foot to indicate a storage locker.

Another squall of rain hit them. Mike called out, "Anyone wanting to get out of the rain is welcome here in the wheelhouse – but they have to make the coffee!"

There was no shortage of volunteers. Half-filled mugs of hot coffee were passed around and attempts to drink it in the plunging boat caused a lot of good-natured cursing.

Mike was enjoying himself. The bad weather had kept him in harbour too often: it was good to get out. The waves were now close to six feet high. He had complete confidence in his boat and in his own ability. From their continued good humour it was clear that his passengers shared that confidence. Mike had been hoping that the seas would ease at slack water, but it hadn't happened. It was far too rough for sensible fishing, but he thought that it should be calmer nearer the land and he pressed on towards the wreck.

His passengers seemed to be regarding the whole trip as an extended fairground ride and he heard a shout of, "Come on, Skipper! You're much too quiet. Give us a song!"

He didn't need any more encouragement and he roared his way through *Irish Rover, Gypsy Rover, All for me Grog* and *The Shoals of Herring,* with the angling party joining in with the choruses and anywhere else that they thought they knew the words.

As *Mike's Gal* crested another wave, Mike caught sight of a sail ahead of them. At first Mike only got glimpses of the other boat as the waves were now high enough to block his view when they dropped into the troughs, but when they got closer he recognised it as a Hardy motor-sailer. They were sturdy boats and perfectly sea-worthy, but at only eighteen feet long Mike thought that its crew must be having a tough time. The mainsail was only half raised and she was making way largely from the small inboard diesel.

He took *Mike's Gal* as close as he dared and as the two boats slowly passed he saw a man in his thirties and a woman of the same age. The adults were in the cockpit. Mike spotted a young girl in the cabin with her face pressed against the window. The anglers spotted her too, and waved. She scrambled out into the cockpit and waved back. The woman looked very anxious, but the child looked perfectly happy. She was aged about six with blonde hair showing under the hood of her yellow waterproof. She wore a red lifejacket and a big smile. Mike noticed a thin rope around her waist.

"Everything all right, Skipper?" Mike called.

"Just about. We've been trapped in the Scillies for ten days, but I had to get back. The weather didn't seem too bad when we set out, but we've had a really rough crossing. Where are you headed?"

Dave Cooper called out, "We're doing a bit of fishing and having a good old sing-song!"

Mike saw the woman relax and she smiled back. It was obvious that she was re-assuring herself that if the sea was calm enough for a social outing, it couldn't be too bad.

As the boats moved apart, Mike shouted, "You're only three miles from sheltered water! You'll be O.K. close to the coast!"

The rain had eased off, but it hit them again with sudden fury. Mike could see very little through the front window of the wheelhouse, despite the action of the wiper blades. He could make out the next wave looming in front of them just before *Mike's Gal* climbed the face of it and slammed down into the trough behind.

Suddenly Mike was aware of something different. The wave a few yards in front of the boat filled his entire view. It must have been fifteen feet high.

Mike just had time to bellow out a warning of, "HOLD TIGHT!" before *Mike's Gal* lurched up the wall of water. She seemed to pause at the top before diving into the trough with a stomach-churning free-fall. The next wave was as big and for a moment Mike thought they wouldn't make it. Her bow dipped into the foot of the wave, but then she broke free and she slowly climbed to the top.

Mike caught sight of the next wave. The third one was a monster nearing twenty feet. "HOLD ON! WE'RE GOING AGAIN!"

This time she couldn't manage the climb. Half way up the face of the giant wave the wall of water swept over the boat and crashed down upon her. She shuddered and all forward motion stopped.

For a moment Mike wondered if she was sinking, but the wave rolled by and *Mike's Gal* was still afloat.

Mike was knee-deep in water. The wheelhouse doors had disappeared. He stood in the doorway and did a quick head count. All eight anglers were still there; all of them on their knees and clinging grimly to the rail. The big tanks that had held the catch and the sand eels had gone.

The boat was dangerously low in such rough seas. The engine was still running and Mike could hear the pumps working. He roused his passengers, "Quick! Grab anything you can and start baling!" Pumps are all very well, but they don't shift water as quickly as a worried man with a two-gallon bucket.

He checked the electrics. Everything seemed to be working.

He moved onto the deck area to take a better look at his clients. "Everybody O.K.? Any injuries?"

One of them had been hit by a wheelhouse door and had a bump on his forehead that was already the size of a golf ball. Another had a fish hook embedded in his arm. Otherwise they were unharmed, but shaken.

The sea seemed to feel that it had done its worst and the waves were back to about five feet.

Mike had a sudden thought. He climbed around to the foredeck to gain some height and looked in the direction where he

boathook and pulled Becky alongside. Willing hands seized her, lifted her aboard and laid her gently on a blanket on the deck.

"Give us a bit of elbow room, boys," said Chalky, pushing them back. The paramedics quickly checked her over, moving her into the recovery position. "She's still alive. But having difficulty breathing."

Mike passed them his first-aid kit. Chalky looked at it. "Can't do much with that, Skipper. We can dress the wound, but it's her breathing that's the real problem."

Mike powered his boat towards the harbour.

"Lifeboat's coming!"

In the distance the re-assuring bright orange shape of the Penzance lifeboat was charging through the sea towards them. He moved towards the radio.

"Chopper coming, too!"

The Search and Rescue helicopter from Culdrose was coming, fast and low.

"Falmouth coastguard. Falmouth coastguard. Falmouth coastguard. This is *Mike's Gal*. We have recovered the little girl. Repeat – we have the girl onboard. She is alive, but breathing with difficulty. Medical assistance needed urgently. I have two paramedics onboard so this isn't just my opinion. We are also concerned about the mother. She is in deep shock. Over."

Mike knew that the crews of both the lifeboat and the helicopter would have heard the message.

The Sea King clattered overhead; the fierce downdraught battering them like a vertical storm-force gale. One of the two pilots came through on the radio. "Skipper – you're looking a little crowded down there. Got room for one of us?"

Mike cleared everyone away from the stern of the boat and kept *Mike's Gal* moving steadily in a straight line while the pilot and winch operator cooperated expertly to lower the winch man onto the small deck space.

He briefly conferred with Chalky and then made his own assessment of both Becky and her mother. He spoke to the chopper on his own radio and then the pilot came back on the boat's radio.

"Skipper, we'll take the girl now. Mother can wait a while, but the girl can't. We'll fly her straight to Treliske Hospital. Just keep your boat on this heading and we'll have her off in a jiffy."

Within five minutes Becky was on her way to hospital. Her father sat with his arm around the still silent mother.

The lifeboat approached and stood off at about thirty yards. The coxswain used a loud hailer. "Hello Mike. Caught more than you bargained for, eh? Some might say that it's not fishing weather – but it looks as if it's a good job you were here."

Mike picked up the radio handset. "Hello George. How about Channel eight? Over."

"O.K. Mike, Channel eight it is."

They both switched their radios to Channel eight.

"George, the girl's mother is in a bad way. Deeply shocked. She's not saying a word. And we've got a couple of minor injuries – one of my clients has a lump the size of an egg on his forehead and another has a hook stuck in him. Can you take them all in? We've also got a paramedic who can keep an eye on them. Over."

"Will do. Is the other boat still afloat? Over."

"Was last time I saw her. Over."

"In that case, can we give you a couple of marker buoys? We'll take the casualties in and then come back to see if we can recover her. If you can attach the buoys to the boat we'll spot her a lot easier. Over."

Mike sighed. He suddenly felt very tired, but he said, "Yeah, why not. Over."

Mike stopped his boat and the coxswain expertly moved the lifeboat alongside. The father, mother, the two injured anglers and Billy were moved to the lifeboat and Mike accepted the bright orange marker buoys.

The lifeboat powered away, creating a big bow wave.

"O.K. gents. Let's see if we can find *Sea Frog*. If we let her drift away, some other boat doing twenty knots in the dark will probably find her."

They found her easily enough and after fixing the buoys Mike turned for home.

The anglers were silent on the way back, quietly trying to sort out the tangled remains of what was left of their tackle. Dave Cooper put into words what they were all thinking.

"If we hadn't waved at her she would probably have stayed in the cabin and been all right."

Mike pulled alongside the Newlyn quay and was making *Mike's Gal* fast when the radio crackled into life.

"*Mike's Gal. Mike's Gal. Mike's Gal.* This is Falmouth Coastguard. Falmouth coastguard. Are you receiving? Over."

"Hello coastguard. *Mike's Gal* here. Receiving you loud and clear. Over."

"Falmouth coastguard here. Thought you'd like to know. Becky is going to be fine. Over."

There was a loud, relieved cheer from the boat.

"Thanks coastguard. Appreciate your letting us know. Over and out."

*

For a while after the anglers had left him, Mike sat at the stern of his boat, deep in thought and unaware of the rain.

He had tried to ignore the changing weather over the last few years and simply soldiered on struggling to earn a living in the same way, but it just couldn't go on. There were two sides to his business, the marine electronics and the fishing trips: both were suffering. For the last two years the income from the fishing charters hadn't even covered the cost of running *Mike's Gal* let alone provided an income.

He would have to sell his boat – if he could. That was easier said than done; half the boats in the harbour were for sale and they weren't selling. He would be lucky to raise enough from a sale to clear what was left of the loan he had taken out to buy her.

The electronics business was suffering, too. People just weren't prepared to spend money on their boats when they were getting so little use out of them.

He was making no money to support his family. They were living on Louise's income as a teacher. Things would have to change. He needed to talk.

And the people he needed to talk to were Jane and Bob.

*

When Mike got home he was surprised to find Louise's car on the drive. She was supposed to have taken their daughters to their grandparents' home in Taunton for the first week of the school holidays.

He let himself in and found the girls in the lounge watching television. "Hello you two! What are doing still here? I thought you were off on your hols."

Neither of them looked away from the television screen. The older one gave him a vague wave and said, "Hi Dad."

The younger one said, "Hi Dad. Mum's got one of her migraines. She's in bed."

Mike made his way upstairs and, as quietly as he could, slowly opened the bedroom door a little and peered inside. The heavy curtains were drawn together.

"It's all right, I'm awake."

He eased into the room leaving the door slightly ajar. "How are you feeling?"

"Rough."

Mike sat on the bed. Louise lay with one hand over her eyes. He took her other hand in one of his and gave it a gentle squeeze. "Can I get you anything?"

"No, thanks. The girls have been looking after me." She took her hand off her eyes and waved it in the direction of the bedside cabinet where Mike could see an uneaten sandwich, a slice of cake and various drinks. "What's the time?"

"Half-past two."

"You're back early."

"Yeah. Weather. I'll have a quick shower and take the girls to Taunton." He paused. "I'll call in on Jane and Bob on the way back. That means I'll be very late getting back here – is that O.K.? Would you rather I stayed here?"

"No, off you go. You know how it is – I just need to stay quiet for a while. I expect I'll be fine tomorrow."

*

Bob and Arthur were busy in the kitchen. Jane broke off from working on her laptop in the lounge to check on the progress of her dinner. As she walked into the kitchen the phone rang. Bob reached out a hand that was covered in flour and pastry, but Jane grabbed him by the wrist.

"Oh no you don't!" She picked up the phone and in exaggerated tones of refinement said, "The Johnson residence, who is calling?"

Arthur giggled. He had flour and scraps of pastry up to the elbows, over his face and in his hair.

"Oh, hi Mike! … Yes, yes, that would be great. You're in luck – Arthur and Bob have been baking. The pasties should be

53

ready by the time you get here … Yes, that might be wise. See you soon.

"That was Uncle Mike. He's on his way to see us." Arthur cheered. "When I told him you'd been baking, he asked if he should bring fish and chips."

Arthur and Bob exchanged looks of outrage.

"Right, then. You two had better get yourselves cleaned up while I try to stop the kitchen looking like the scene of an explosion in a flour mill."

*

Mike looked down at the large, misshapen lump on his plate and nodded approval.

"My, my – doesn't that look 'ansum! That's a real proper job of a pasty and no mistake."

Arthur looked at it with a puzzled expression on his face. "It's got all the same things in it that Mummy puts in, but it doesn't look like one of hers."

"Mebbe not – but I bet it tastes just as good." Mike enthusiastically tackled his dinner and was easily persuaded to have a second, somewhat smaller, pasty to follow.

Over dinner they talked light-heartedly of family matters. Somewhat later than his usual bedtime, Arthur went up to bed. Jane gave him fifteen minutes and then went up to make sure that he wasn't still reading and to say goodnight.

When she came back down Bob and Mike were in the lounge, Bob pouring beers. Mike had brushed against her laptop mouse, bringing the screen to life. Something on it had caught his attention.

"What's this, Jane?"

Jane glanced at it. "I don't really know what to make of it. I keep coming across links to it from environmental sites. It's a bit strange. It seems more religious than the usual environmental sites. As I say, I keep coming across links to it, but I'm usually looking for some specific facts to back up my arguments and I haven't really studied it."

Mike took the beer offered to him, but carried on reading for a couple of minutes. "I see what you mean. It *is* strange. Just reading it has a …I don't know…a calming effect."

Mike picked up the laptop. Jane and Bob moved alongside him. All three looked at the screen.

"Yes, I noticed that," said Jane. "It must be something to do with the rhythm of the way it's written. The content seems to have a gentle, caring message, but it's very cleverly done. It flows serenely along with a sentence structure that's more poetry than prose."

Mike glanced at the top of the screen, "What's the site called?"

"themessagenottheman.com," Jane told him. "The web address is memorable, if not too easy to read. I was looking at it tonight because there's an environment conference coming up in Bristol. The Green Party is running one of the sessions. I got the programme today and I noticed that one of the sessions is called, *The Message not the Man* – aren't there some lovely photographs?"

"Yeah," Mike pointed to a scene of the Isles of Scilly with the sun just appearing over the horizon, the sea and sky a warm fusion of pink, yellow and silver, "that's what caught my eye." He paused and then added, ruefully, "I can hardly remember when I last saw the sea that calm – which brings me back to why I wanted to have a chat."

He put down the laptop and they all sat down, Bob and Jane on the sofa and Mike in one of the armchairs. Out of long habit Jane swung her legs up so that her feet were in Bob's lap: out of equally long habit he unconsciously began massaging them.

Mike quickly gave them a brief summary of the day's events and followed it with an even briefer summary of the state of his finances.

"Look, I'm at my wits' end – and I know I'm not the only one in that position. I need someone to tell me what's happening. Is the weather going to stay like this? Is it going to get worse? Or … or … or what?" He paused while he gathered his thoughts. "I know the television, radio and newspapers are full of it. They report all the disasters all right – even seem to enjoy doing it – but when it comes to telling us what's really going on, or what we can do to stop it happening, I don't think any of them really has a clue. We get endless discussions with some experts telling us one thing and then they wheel someone out who says the opposite.

"Jane, you're involved in all this – just what *is* happening? Where will it all end?"

He was clearly close to tears and Bob was shaken to see big, loud, confident Mike in such a state. Before Jane could start to answer Mike's questions, Bob asked, "Mike, have you seen the news today?"

Mike shook his head. Bob eased Jane's legs aside and moved to turn the television on. He returned to his seat and picking up the remote control selected the news channel. The weather and its effects were the focus of attention. A band of torrential rain had moved across the middle of the country. The Thames, Severn, Avon and Wye had again burst their banks and widespread flooding had resulted. After a couple of minutes of looking at scenes of streets under water and hearing forecasts that water levels were still rising, Bob turned the television off.

"Down here we've missed the worst of this lot. It seems to answer one of your questions – it *is* getting worse."

"I'm not sure that I have any answers for you, Mike," said Jane, shaking her head. Bob looked at her in surprise: he'd been expecting a passionate re-statement of the Green Party policy, but Jane simply looked sad and defeated. She caught his look.

"I know, I know: I've been going on for years about what's happening and what people should do about it, but now I'm thinking that we've all been too selfish and too stubborn and now it's probably too late." She paused for a moment and then continued.

"Mike, think about it. You're all shaken up because today you saw a little girl, a little girl who probably reminded you of your own girls…" Mike nodded, "…nearly die because of the sort of weather that just shouldn't be happening in July. You saved her – but why were you out there? You were there because a party of eight anglers from Birmingham were trying to carry on doing what they've always done.

"Eight of them, means two carloads. So two heavily laden cars travel the best part of three hundred miles to Penzance and then back again. That's twelve hundred miles. Add on the extra mileage driving to the other ports they planned fishing from and we're probably up to fifteen hundred miles – about fifty gallons of fuel burned. And there's the fuel burned by your boat.

"It may not sound like planet-damaging stuff, but the majority of people are doing it; they're all just going on doing what they're accustomed to doing – each of them thinking that *they* aren't doing any significant harm and they don't see the point of making big changes to the way they live – if nobody else is. We are bringing it all on ourselves."

There was silence for a few moments, and then Mike nodded. He spoke slowly and sadly.

"I think you're right. Those were exactly my thoughts. I needed to hear someone else say it. Whatever the causes, *Mike's Gal* has to go – I just can't afford to keep her. But for the life of me I couldn't see what is going to happen that will make people change their ways. But when I was out at sea today I was reminded of our trip to the Isles of Scilly – not that there are many days that I don't think about that day. I remembered that Myrddin chap standing at the bow waving me on to Great Arthur. I remembered you lifting that sword from the sea," he nodded at the Sword of Power on the chimneybreast and stopped. "There's something different about it. It's the hilt! It used to be covered with leather. What was I saying? Oh, yes, and I remembered what you told me about what happened afterwards; about Myrddin believing he had returned to fight against all this. I know what *I* saw and I know what you said happened later. There *was* something magical about him. But you haven't heard anything from him or about him in all this time?" he looked questioningly at Bob and Jane and they both shook their heads.

"Well, if ever there was a time when we needed a bit of magic, it's now." Mike turned to look up at the sword.

The three of them stared at The Sword of Power for a few minutes without speaking. The hilt seemed to be glowing brighter.

Bob spoke, his voice clearly showing a mix of anxiety and exasperation.

"Myrddin – where the hell are you? We're ready to help, but we need some direction here. We've been waiting long enough: it's time we heard from you."

The door behind them slowly opened. They all turned to look.

Arthur was standing in the doorway, his magnifying glass in one hand and the handset from the hall phone in the other.

He looked up at The Sword of Power and said, "He's coming."

He came into the room and offered the phone to Bob who, after a baffled look at Jane and Mike, accepted it.

The phone rang.

CHAPTER 8

The phone call

Bob, Jane and Mike all stared at the ringing phone in Bob's hand until Arthur prompted him.

"Answer it, Daddy."

Bob pressed the green button and held the phone to his ear. "Hello?"

He heard a voice that he recognised instantly.

"Good evening, Robert Edgar Johnson."

Bob cleared his throat and spoke loudly enough so that Jane and Mike would be sure to hear what he said. "Hello, Myrddin. We have been hoping to hear from you."

So many questions formed in Bob's mind that for a moment he hesitated, not sure how to begin. The voice at the other end of the phone spoke again.

"I trust that the good Lady Jane and young Arthur are well?"

"Yes, yes... hang on! How do you know about Arthur? You disappeared before we even knew that Jane was pregnant."

Myrddin chuckled. "Oh, I know all about Arthur. And I expect that he knows about me – does he not?"

"Er, well, yes, he does seem to know something about you."

"You will remember Joe Morgan. Most people know him as Trader Joe."

"Yes, of course."

"I have need of The Sword of Power. Only for a short while. It will be returned to you – The Sword must be with Arthur. Joe will contact you and arrange to collect it."

There was a click and the line went dead.

"Myrddin! Myrddin!" Bob looked helplessly at the others. "He's gone."

"I'm going back to bed," Arthur calmly announced and left the room. The three adults watched him until he had closed the door behind him.

Mike was still staring at the door when he said, "Am I imagining things or did Arthur really pass you the phone before it rang?"

"Yes, he did," said Jane. Then, turning to Bob, she said, "Come on then. What did he say?"

It had been such a short conversation that Bob was able to recount it word-for-word.

"And that's it?" Jane cried, incredulously. "He disappears for six years; leaves us wondering for all that time – and now he's just sending someone to collect his blessed sword!"

"Yes, that's it," Bob nodded. "No news about where he's been or what he's been doing; no news about Gilda, The Droller or the Welsh Dini – except, of course, if he was here he'd be telling us to call them Gododdin." Bob angrily tossed the handset across the room onto the unoccupied armchair. It bounced into the air and tumbled onto the floor.

Mike put a hand to his forehead and slowly drew it down over his face. "He said he knew about Arthur and that Arthur knew about him?" Bob nodded agreement. "So, apart from that funny business just now with the phone, has Arthur said anything about Myrddin?"

"Yes," said Jane. "The other day when we were on top of Birch Tor he suddenly announced that Myrddin was coming back."

"It was Arthur who revealed the hilt of the sword," Bob said, pointing up at the hilt that was glowing a rich gold. "He's never mentioned the sword before, but last week he announced that it's his and insisted that I lifted him up. As soon as he touched it, the leather just peeled away."

Mike just sat shaking his head. Then he caught sight of the time. "I must go. It will be well after midnight by the time I get home."

"Stay the night," Jane urged.

"No, but thanks for the offer. I must get back. I don't like leaving Louise when she's got one of her heads, but I just had to see you – and I'm glad I came."

As they saw him out of the front door he stopped to kiss Jane and shake Bob's hand. "Don't forget, I want to hear all about the next crazy thing that happens around here."

Bob and Jane went back to the lounge. They sat without speaking for a while. Bob picked up the remote control and turned on the television. They stared, without seeing, at the images of boats moving along city streets; people standing in their homes knee-deep in water and others, at the edge of the flooded areas, anxiously piling sandbags against their front doors.

Eventually, Bob turned the set off again and looked at his wife. "What are you thinking?"

Jane sighed. "The same as you, I expect. I've been looking back over the last five happy years – and wondering what is happening to our son."

*

The Johnsons sat around their kitchen table at breakfast time the following morning. Bob and Jane had agreed not to mention the call from Myrddin until Arthur had had a chance to mention it first – but he didn't. Arthur simply ate his breakfast as normal, keeping up a flow of chatter about what they were all going to do with the day.

Eventually, Bob had to break into the flow. "Do you remember that we had a telephone call from Myrddin last night?"

Arthur looked up at him. "Yes, Daddy."

"Er, well, you know the big sword – your sword?"

Arthur chuckled, "Of course I know my big sword, silly."

"Well, the only reason Myrddin phoned is because he says he needs the sword."

"Did he say he would send it back?"

"Yes."

"That's all right, then." Arthur continued with his breakfast.

Bob and Jane exchanged looks.

"Trader Joe is coming for it," Jane said.

For a moment Arthur looked puzzled, then he asked, "Is that the man you told me about who used to help the Dini?"

"That's right. He had a big van and he went around the country selling things."

"I see. Do you have to work *all* day, Daddy? It's not raining – we could do something nice."

"Sorry, it's all day – but I'll get back as soon as I can and we'll do something fun this evening."

60

"Hooray! What about us, Mummy, do you have to work, too?"

"Yes, but only for a couple of hours. And I mustn't forget to phone Carn and the others to let them know that we've heard from Myrddin – even if we haven't got much news for them."

"Oh, may I speak to them?"

"Of course – is there any one of them that you'd particularly like to talk to?" asked Jane, winking at Bob because both of them already knew the answer.

"Enid," said Arthur without the slightest hesitation. "I wonder how much taller than Enid I'll be this time." He thought for a moment. "Do you think Tegid is still being naughty?"

Bob laughed. "I wouldn't be at all surprised. Anyway, it's time I was on my way." He went around the table to kiss his wife and son. "See you tonight. Have fun!"

Bob was heading towards the front door and they were all still shouting their goodbyes when the telephone rang. He hesitated while Jane answered it.

"Hello, Jane Johnson here. Hello, Joe. I understand you're coming to see us. Tonight? Yes, that should be fine. What sort of time? Yes, I know, what with the weather and the traffic it's hard to be precise. Let's just say sometime after 7.30. No, don't worry, we don't have to go anywhere. Yes, O.K. Bye."

She called up the hall, "Did you hear that?"

"Yes, I did. Someone's in a hurry! See you later!"

*

Nigel Sligo was waiting impatiently in Princetown Post Office to buy cigarettes. The only person in front of him was an old woman who was clearly in no hurry. She moved the items she was buying from the counter to her shopping basket one at a time, pausing between each one to exchange more than a few words of conversation, mainly about the prices and how it didn't seem more than a few weeks since everything cost half as much.

She eventually paid, carefully checked her change, and slowly moved towards the door. Sligo quickly handed over the correct amount for his forty cigarettes and tried to overtake her before she reached the door. Just as he hurried into the doorway he found it blocked by someone coming in. Anxious to avoid a collision that his battered face wouldn't appreciate, Sligo stopped abruptly and moved to one side.

Scotland, takes Gilda off with him, does something so that we don't get any news of The Droller or any of the Welsh Dini for years and then he just phones up with no warning and says he wants something. What sort of man is he?"

"That's a very good question and I don't know the answer to it. As you can imagine, Bob and I discussed it until very late last night. All we could think was that there is so much news, so much to tell us about, that he didn't want to do it over the phone – but that's pretty lame. And actually there was no mention of us seeing him at all, just a vague comment that the sword would be returned to us soon – and he didn't say that *he* would be returning it.

"All we can do is wait to see what Joe has to say tonight. We'll pump him for every scrap of news we can get and I'll phone you to tell you all about it. So I'll phone either tonight or tomorrow morning…"

"Please make it tonight – no matter how late it is. We'll be desperate to hear the news."

"O.K. Eppie, I'll do it tonight. Oh, hang on, Arthur wants to speak to Enid." Jane glanced down, but Arthur had gone. "Arthur! Arthur!" There was no reply. "He's disappeared, Eppie. Never mind, he can talk to her next time. Ring you tonight. Take care."

Jane rang off and went in search of Arthur. He was in the lounge standing in front of the fireplace, staring up at The Sword of Power. The golden glow seemed very bright.

He turned and smiled at Jane. "Don't worry, Mummy; we *will* be seeing him soon. What shall we do now? Shall I do some drawing while you do some work? I could look at an ant through my magnifying glass and draw a picture of it."

*

Bob had found it difficult to concentrate all day. Whatever he tried to do he found his mind drifting away to thoughts of Trader Joe's visit. There were just so many questions to which he needed to know the answers: where had Myrddin been and what had he been doing; what had Trader Joe been up to; what had happened to the Welsh Dini (and the Cumbrian ones, for that matter); what had happened to Gilda; why had Myrddin got the Johnsons fired up about tackling the problems threatening the planet and then vanished, leaving them with no guidance; why did they have The

Sword of Power and, most importantly, what was happening with Arthur?

He was glad when it was time to go home, where he found Jane in the same state of unrest and confusion. She confessed to having done no useful work all day. As soon as Bob had changed out of his Ranger's uniform, she ushered the two men in her life out into the garden to 'have some fun' while she prepared dinner.

Arthur, apparently completely unaware that anything unusual was going on, led his father around the garden showing him interesting things that he'd spotted through the magnifying glass. Together they looked at flower petals, woodlice, worms and pieces of rock. Arthur was holding the head of a daisy on the palm of his left hand when a large bumble bee droned ponderously about them and settled on the daisy. The boy simply raised the magnifying glass in his right hand and studied the bee intently.

As the bee walked off the flower onto Arthur's hand, Bob made to brush it away, but his son stopped him with a shake of his head and proffered the glass. "Take a look at those eyes, Daddy."

Arthur calmly watched the bee walk across his hand, over his wrist and up his arm as far as the elbow before taking off. He watched it fly away. "I knew it wouldn't sting me – they never do."

He took back the glass, slipped it into Bob's trouser pocket and said, "We won't need that to see what I've found. Come and have a look!" He led Bob by the hand to the compost heap at the bottom of the garden. There was a sheet of plywood on top of the pile of rotting leaves and grass cuttings. He put a finger to his lips and whispered, "Shh! We have to be very quiet."

Arthur put both hands to the edge of the plywood. Very slowly and carefully he raised one edge. Bob bent down and looked underneath. As the wood went up he could see a slow worm; fully thirty centimetres long, it lay in a figure-of-eight shape. It was beautifully shiny; a rich brown with a black stripe along its back.

"She's lovely," he whispered.

"Yes," Arthur whispered in return. "And she's useful to have in the garden as she eats slugs and snails."

Bob smiled: Jane had evidently been on the same tour.

Arthur gently lowered the wood and they moved quietly away.

"What shall we do now?"

"Cricket!" Arthur cried and scampered away to the shed, returning with a plastic bat, a ball, a stick and a bucket. He set the bucket upside down on the grass to act as wicket, counted out twenty-two steps and pushed the stick into the ground as the bowler's mark and then announced the usual rules. "Two innings each; the hedge or the vegetable patch is a four; hit it into the shed for a six; knock petals off Mummy's roses and lose two. Have you got a coin to toss?"

Bob had a coin and he tossed it. Arthur called correctly and chose to bowl first. Bob hit a four, ran some singles and then played the ball straight back to Arthur who caught it with a triumphant, "'Owzat!"

With a "Good catch!" Bob handed over the bat.

Before he could bowl his first ball, Jane called, "Dinner in five minutes!"

"Have to make it just a one innings match," Bob said. "How many do you need to win?"

"Eight."

Bob bowled the ball a few times, just wide of the bucket. Arthur hit most of them and scampered up and down the wicket accumulating his runs in ones and twos. He reached a total of six.

Bob glanced at his watch. Joe could arrive at any time. What news would he have for them? He bowled the ball and Arthur hit it solidly back, just over Bob's head. He instinctively put up a hand and caught it.

"Good catch!" said Arthur. "You win." He picked up the bucket, put the bat and stick into it, collected the ball from his father and put them away in the shed. "Better wash our hands," he said.

When they walked into the kitchen, Jane asked, "Who won?"

"Daddy did."

"Did he really?"

"Yes. He usually drops the ball to let me win, but this time he forgot to drop it."

Bob looked helplessly at his wife, bemused that his past actions had been so transparent – even to a five-year-old. Jane turned away to hide her laughter.

After they had eaten dinner and tidied away they went back into the garden, but dark clouds were piling in the sky. It felt warm and humid. There was a flicker of lightning and ten seconds later a rumble of thunder. They hurried back into the house as large raindrops began to fall.

They settled down in the lounge and began to play cards. Bob and Jane looked at the clock every few minutes and twice Bob got up to look out of the window. The storm built in fury; the lightning lit the room continually and the thunder crashed directly overhead. There was so much noise that neither Bob nor Jane heard the doorbell ring, but Arthur did.

"Someone at the door," he declared.

Bob got up and looked out of the window. There was a car he didn't recognise on the drive and he hurried to the door. Jane and Arthur followed him. When Bob opened the door a large man, who had been pressing hard against it seeking shelter from the rain, staggered into the hall. Bob quickly shut the door and looked at the new arrival.

He was in his shirt sleeves. The shirt was soaked through and his dark hair was plastered flat on his head. He looked at them rather sheepishly and spoke in a quiet, Welsh voice.

"It's like this, see, I'd put my coat in the boot and I thought I'd get wetter getting it out rather than running to the door. I may have been wrong."

"You're ever so wet," Arthur giggled.

"I'm as wet as a fish, to be sure. And you must be Arthur." He stepped forward, bent towards Arthur, extended a large hand and gravely shook the very small one offered to him. "I'm Joe Morgan, that many round here remember as Trader Joe. Pleased to meet you."

As he straightened Jane said, "Good to see you again, Joe. I'll get you a towel – or should we try to find some dry clothes that will fit?"

"A towel will do just fine – as long as you're happy to have a damp fish sitting on your nice dry furniture."

Arthur giggled again and Joe bent down to talk to him. "I've been hearing all sorts of things about you – but they didn't tell me what a handsome, big fellow you are. You must be at least, er, ten years old."

"No, I'm only five."

"Only five! Well I never. Whatever are they feeding you on?"

Jane returned with a towel and Joe vigorously rubbed at his hair, wiped it over his shoulders and then passed it back.

"Thank you, Jane, that will do nicely."

"Well, why are we standing in the hall?" Jane turned and led the way into the lounge.

Joe followed her and looked quickly around the room before his eyes came to rest on the sword. "It's been a time since I was in here."

"Too long" said Bob, speaking for the first time.

Joe nodded. "I can understand you thinking that."

"Well, before we start chatting, can I get anybody a drink?" asked Jane.

Bob shook his head, but Joe said, "A cup of tea would be nice, indeed it would – and if came with milk and two sugars it would be perfect."

Before Jane reached the door, Arthur said, "It's my bedtime." He kissed his father and mother and shook hands with Joe. "Bye, Mr Morgan," he said and took himself off up the stairs.

Bob and Jane exchanged puzzled looks. While Jane made the tea, Bob commented to Joe. "Arthur keeps saying that the sword is his. He knows you've come to take it away. We were expecting him to make a fuss over it, to moan about it going, but he hasn't. Not a word."

Joe made a helpless gesture. "There are things going on that are beyond me, indeed there are. I know I was having a bit of fun with him just now about his age – but it's hard to believe he's only five."

While Jane was out of the room Bob stared out of the window. There should still have been a couple of hours of daylight, but the storm had brought a gloomy darkness that was fleetingly shattered by brilliant flashes of lightning.

"What sort of car is that, Joe?"

"One of these new-fangled electric jobs. Real creepy it is, starting off with no noise. Gives folks in town a bit of a turn when they just don't hear me coming."

Jane returned with three mugs of tea and a plate of biscuits. Bob accepted his mug having apparently forgotten that he'd declined the offer.

"Take a seat, Joe." Jane sat on the settee with a notepad in her lap. "I'm going to have to make notes – I've got to pass on all the news to Carn, Eppie and the others."

Joe looked uncomfortable. "I may not be able to give you much news."

"What do you mean?" demanded Bob. Ever since Myrddin's phone call his irritation had been growing. He was feeling that Myrddin had been less than fair with them. He had a lot of questions, and he wanted answers.

Joe sipped his tea nervously. "Well, we may be all right. It all depends on what you want to know."

Sensing the anger that was quickly building in Bob, Jane got in first. "We want to know everything! Everything that's happened since you drove away with The Droller. What have you been doing? What's happened to the Welsh Dini? To Myrddin? To Gilda? Why were we left with the sword? Why does Myrddin want it back now? We want to hear it all."

Joe squirmed in his seat. "I knew you would. It's probably best if you ask me simple questions and I'll do the best I can to answer them."

Bob and Jane exchanged a baffled look and Bob started with the questions.

"How are The Droller and the Welsh Dini?"

Joe opened his mouth to reply, an expression of intense concentration on his face. "They are very well." Joe looked pleased with himself.

"Where are they? Are they still in Wales? Are you still helping them?"

Joe grimaced. "Can we go one at a time?"

Bob snorted and Jane said, "Are they still living where they used to live?"

There was a pause. "No." Joe smiled.

"Where are they?"

Joe's face contorted with effort. Then he said, "Can't say."

Bob made a spluttering noise and Jane turned to him with a frown. "Wait a minute. We need to find out what's going on here." She turned back to Joe. "Joe, are you all right? Forgive me for saying so, but it's like talking to somebody with Alzheimer's; you seem to be struggling to come out with words."

Joe nodded. "It's not that I don't want to tell you – I just can't."

"But you seemed to be chatting away O.K. when you arrived."

"Oh, yes. It's not a problem with me, really. When I say I can't tell you something, I mean that he won't allow me to."

"Myrddin won't let you talk to us?"

"Not about some things, it seems."

"But he's not here!" cried Bob. "Surely you can see that we need some answers. It simply isn't fair to leave us in the dark."

Lightning lit the room and thunder shook the house.

Joe struggled to explain. "Myrddin has some sort of power. He takes control over everyone he meets – if he wants to. It's like one of those men you see on the telly that get people doing what they tell them to do. If I can't tell you something, it's because he's stopping me. Not that it's just you that I can't talk to about the Dini – it's everybody."

Bob was moving his head about, trying to relieve the tension in his neck.

Jane had an idea. She held out the notepad and pen to Joe. "What if we ask the questions and you write down the answers?"

Joe brightened for a moment. "Might work, that." But then he frowned again. "But it wouldn't be right, would it. If he doesn't want people to know these things, then I shouldn't tell them – by any method. After all, he *is* my employer."

"Is he? Well, it seems it's all right for you to tell us that." Jane smiled encouragingly. "What sort of work do you do? Are you still trading from the van?"

"Oh no, not me. The missus and our son use it some of the time. They still run the market stall back home." Joe smiled back, pleased to be able to reply properly to a question.

"And you," she prodded, "what are you doing?"

"When I said I work for Myrddin, that's not strictly true. I work for the Trust." Joe spoke the last few words very slowly as if expecting to find difficulty at any moment. When he had delivered them, his smile broadened.

"And what do you do for this Trust?"

"All sorts of stuff," said Joe, now looking really pleased with himself. "I drive Myrddin about; I do buying and selling – some of my old contacts have been quite useful."

"That's good. And what is this Trust called?"

Joe opened his mouth but no sound came out.

Jane quickly moved to another question.

"And Gilda – how is she?"

"Oh, she's well. At least I think she is. How would anyone know how she is? She usually has that scowl on her face and she never was one for small talk."

70

"Where do you drive Myrddin?"

"All over the country. He's been to Spain a couple of times, too." Joe looked surprised that he'd been able to say that.

But that was the last of their successes. All further questions resulted in Joe failing to get an answer out, despite the pulling of faces that showed the effort he was making.

"I'm sorry folks. Everything else will just have to wait until Myrddin tells you himself."

"And are you allowed to tell us when that might be?"

"Oh yes. He gave me a message to pass on to you. He said he'll return the sword when he sees you in Bristol."

"Bristol! Why Bristol!" groaned Bob. "And when?"

"I'm going to that conference in Bristol just after we get back from holiday," Jane pointed out.

"Holiday? Going anywhere nice?" asked Joe, seizing the chance to talk about something as ordinary as holidays.

"Scotland."

"Scotland? That's a long way. Like it up there, do you?"

"We go at least once a year."

"Really?"

"Yes, really. Do you not know why we go there?"

"No. Why should I know why you choose Scotland for your holidays?" Joe looked genuinely puzzled.

Jane looked at Bob. "Is it possible that Myrddin doesn't know? I've always assumed that he knew; but, thinking about it, I had no reason to make that assumption."

Bob smiled for the first time that evening. "Well, that can be our little secret. Two can play at this silly game."

"How are Carn and the others? O.K. on the moor are they?"

"That's another secret."

Joe shrugged. "I think I'd better take the sword and get off. The storm's blowing over, but it's still raining."

"Got far to go?" Bob asked disingenuously.

Joe struggled to find an answer and finally said, "Far enough."

They all stood up and looked at the sword.

Jane said, "I'll get an old blanket to wrap it in. It'll protect the sword and your hands." She hurried out of the room.

Bob didn't speak while she was gone. He stood staring at the sword. He hadn't taken the weight of The Sword of Power

71

since he had lifted it into its present position and secured it with the brass mounts. When he had drawn it from the sea it had taken all his strength to lift it into the boat. Something had happened after that and he didn't understand it. Somehow power and belief had flowed through him. He had felt the power of the sword and savoured it – been energised and uplifted by it. When Jane had told him she was pregnant he had waved the sword one-handed above his head. Since then, whenever he had felt his belief faltering, he had touched the sword and felt its power anew. He had lifted it to its present position without difficulty.

But now he was feeling angry and disappointed. In this mood, would he still manage the weight?

Jane returned with a blanket and a kitchen stool. Bob climbed onto the stool and wrapped a part of the blanket around the blade just below the golden hilt. As his fingers brushed the metal of the blade he felt a tingle run the length of his arm. He took a firm hold, hesitated a moment, and then lifted the great blade upwards and free from the mounts. It moved easily. He scarcely felt the weight.

Bob stepped down from the stool. He laid the sword on the floor and carefully wrapped it in the blanket. He stood up straight, lifted the sword into a vertical position and offered it to Joe. "Be careful – it's very heavy."

"Yes, I can see that," said Joe looking down at the smaller man and giving him a funny look. He reached out and grasped the blanket-wrapped sword, one hand on the hilt and the other on the blade.

"Have you got it?" Bob asked. "It *is* heavy."

"Oh I've got it all right," said Joe, looking at Jane with raised eyebrows.

Bob took his hands away from the sword. For a split second Joe held it, then the sword fell to the floor, the point of the blade slicing through the blanket and the carpet to embed itself in the floorboards between Joe's feet.

Joe gasped and belatedly moved his feet apart. He grasped the blade through the blanket and worked it out of the floor and, with a grunt of effort, heaved it up onto a shoulder.

"I don't know how you did that, Bob, but if I've learned anything over these last few years, it's not to be surprised by anything I see. I'd best be on my way. I hope it won't be so long before we meet again." Joe moved to the front door. Bob grabbed an umbrella and walked with Joe to the car. He waited while the great sword was laid in the boot and then sheltered Joe as he got into the driver's seat. Joe wound down the window.

"I'm sorry if I seemed hostile earlier, but strange things have been happening with Arthur that we haven't told you about. It's got me wound up."

"Don't give it a thought. It seems to me that you should have been told a lot more: you're entitled to feel angry about it. You take good care of that boy now." The car slid silently away and a hand waved briefly before the window was wound up against the rain.

Back in the house Bob found Jane looking at the chimneybreast. "Look," she said, "it's as if it's still there."

Where the sword had hung the colour had been taken from the dark oak panelling. The shape of the sword was clearly shown in pale wood.

"Well, what did you make of all that 'I'd like to be able to tell you but I just can't' stuff?" she asked.

"I don't know what to make of any of it. I do remember Carn telling us about being in the woods with Myrddin when a man walked past. Carn swears that the man looked directly at them, but didn't see them. He reckoned that was because Myrddin was able to exert some sort of control over the man's mind."

Jane sat down again. She waved her notepad. "This is going to be a much shorter phone call than I was expecting." She looked at her notes. "What it boils down to is: The Droller and the Welsh Dini are O.K. but no longer living where they used to; Joe is employed by some sort of Trust and does various things for Myrddin; Gilda is O.K.; Myrddin travels around the country and has been to Spain; we'll get the sword back (why we don't know) and see Myrddin in Bristol, presumably just after we return from Scotland. And that's it. The Dini will be very disappointed."

"Not as disappointed as me! But I suppose we've been waiting for six years for his return, another week or two won't make much difference. At least we've had contact."

While Jane made the phone call, Bob stood at the lounge window. The storm was in the far distance. He could still see the flare of lightning, but he couldn't hear the thunder through the new double-glazing. Rain spattered against the glass.

When Jane had finished, she stood behind him, her arms around his waist. "What are you thinking?"

73

"That I don't fancy camping in Scotland next week."

A fresh flurry of rain swept over the window. Jane shivered. "Nor me," she said.

"Nor do I fancy the chances of your car making it all that way – and back again. I've just been keeping my fingers crossed that it will limp along to the next MOT before it gets consigned to a motoring graveyard, but I have a strong suspicion that that amount of motorway driving will finish it off."

"Do we have an affordable alternative?"

"We could hire a car, but that would still mean camping. I know we decided that we couldn't afford to rent a motor home this time, but I was wondering if, with all this rain, they might not have been able to rent them all out. At this late stage we might get a decent discount. I'll phone them in the morning."

He gently unwrapped her arms from around his waist, turned to stand behind her and wrapped his arms around her, pinning her arms to her sides.

"I was also thinking that you'll soon be an MP. Then you can fiddle your expenses like they all do and our financial worries will be over."

She wriggled furiously until she broke free and punched him, non too playfully, in the ribs.

CHAPTER 9

Tegid's secret

The Dini had gathered together to await Jane's phone call. Even Tegid, who usually sought to isolate himself and claimed to have absolutely no interest in anything that the others were doing, had joined them.

They waited impatiently, full of ideas about the news they were about to receive. The ideas grew wilder as they waited.

"Myrddin has found a way to restore us to full size."

"Myrddin has already restored the Welsh Dini and now that he knows it really works, he is coming for us."

"We will be able to live among the Biguns without hiding away."

"We will *be* Biguns."

"We will have children!"

That last claim had come from Enid and it silenced the group. They all knew the vital importance of the news they were about to hear.

When the call came and they realised what little news there really was, they were crushed; all of their good spirits evaporated.

"So, what have we got?" said Carn. "All it amounts to is that Gilda and the Welsh Dini are unharmed, but we don't know where they are; and Joe is no longer Trader Joe, but is working for Myrddin – who for some reason wants that big sword that came out of the sea. And Bob and Jane hope to see him after they get home from visiting us. And that's it."

Tegid gave a loud derisive laugh and left the house, slamming the door behind him. Carn knew just what feelings lay behind the outburst. Tegid, having allowed himself to get excited about the possibilities, didn't want his disappointment on show in front of the others.

Carn was feeling something similar and announced that he was going fishing. As it turned out, he didn't get to go alone as Erbyn and Nudd promptly said they would go with him.

The light was fading, but it was dry and warm. They collected from the shed the metre-long willow wands that they used as fishing rods and set off for the stream that ran through the next valley.

They walked in silence at first, each occupied with his own thoughts. Eventually, Carn summed up his feelings, "We mustn't let ourselves get that excited when we're waiting to hear about the Johnsons' meeting with Myrddin. It's too big a let down afterwards."

The others nodded in agreement.

"After all this time," he continued, "my memories of Myrddin are fading a bit. For some reason I still think that he has powers we'll never understand, but I wonder if we're expecting too much."

"At least you and Eppie spent several days with him," said Nudd. "You saw that sword come out of the sea and you've told us other things about him – like calling a raven out of the sky. I hardly saw him at all."

"And I've never laid eyes on him!" Erbyn chipped in. "So it all just seems like one of The Droller's stories to me."

"It would be good to see The Droller again," said Nudd. "I miss our gatherings around the fire in Bush Down Mine, listening to his tales. Sitting watching Biguns' television just isn't the same."

"It certainly isn't," Erbyn agreed. "I can't make any sense of it. It gives me the feeling that all Biguns are crazy, living crazy lives. I know we keep on about Myrddin making us the same size as the Biguns so we don't have to keep hiding away, but I really don't think I want to live among them – they're so strange!"

Carn laughed and patted Erbyn on the back. "I know just what you mean. Bob and Jane seem all right, and so do the McDonalds, but if the rest of them are like their television programmes, we're better off keeping well away."

"You know," said Nudd, rather wistfully, "I often think about our life on Dartmoor. It's the little things that set me wondering. Like where you lived, Erbyn, in Brimpts Mine, and that cave in Wistman's Wood where you and Eppie lived, Carn, and Bush Down Mine –we left some of our stuff in all of them. I often wonder if Biguns have found any of it – and what they've made of it if they have. Do you remember those funny boots you had, Erbyn? We *did* have a good laugh that time Tegid and I stayed with you. My sides ached for days."

Nudd did his best to describe to Carn what had happened and in much improved spirits they walked on along the track through the conifer plantation. As they dropped down the hill towards the stream they passed out of the conifers and into the broad ribbon of deciduous wood that ran along the banks of the stream. Instead of the bare forest floor that lay under the pines, they were now among lush undergrowth of ferns, brambles and flowering plants.

"Fishing should be good tonight," Erbyn enthused. "All the rain we've had should mean there's lots of water coming down and that could mean that sea trout will be running."

The rain also made bait easy to find. Near to the stream they pulled up clumps of grass and found plenty of worms close to the surface. It was getting dark and they had to use torches while they tackled up – which was a simple procedure. Each tied a length of nylon line, the same length as the rod, to his rod tip and tied a hook to the other end. After baiting the hooks with worms, they were ready.

They moved to where the stream formed a deep pool about eight metres long and spaced themselves along it. Erbyn took the head of the pool, Carn the middle and Nudd the tail. Three worms plopped into the slowly moving water and the anglers moved their rods just enough to keep the bait rolling along the stream bed.

Clouds moved away from blocking the moon. It was nearly full and directly overhead. Enough light filtered through the trees for Carn to be able to see the faces of his companions. It was a comfortably warm evening; the only sounds he could hear were the gentle murmuring of the stream in the shallow runs above and below the pool, the distant cries of a pair of tawny owls and the occasional plop of a worm hitting the water. He sat down and leaned back against a tree. He was very glad that he'd gone fishing. He was sure that those still at the house would be endlessly churning over the developments. He yawned.

The next thing he was aware of was the rod being snatched from his hand and landing with a splash in the stream where it tore about the surface of the water, zigzagging all over the pool.

"That's a BIG one!" shouted Erbyn, jumping into the shallow water at the head of the pool. "Nudd! Don't let it escape that way!"

Nudd splashed into the middle of the shallows at the tail of the pool, anxiously following the movements of Carn's rod.

Carn knelt on the bank, trying to grab his rod each time it looked as if it was within reach. Eventually the rod passed directly beneath him and he grabbed it with both hands. He hung on grimly as the rod arched over, but when he felt certain that either the line or the rod would snap, he was forced to let it go. Twice more he seized the passing rod and had to let it go again. On his fourth attempt he felt that the fish was tiring and that he might at last be able to land it.

"I think this is it! I'll bring it to the shallows at Nudd's end!"

Erbyn rushed to join Nudd and the two of them prepared to grab the fish as Carn worked it towards them. Carn kept pressure on the fish and gradually moved towards his friends. But the fish wasn't ready to give in. It suddenly powered towards Nudd and Erbyn with such expected force that Carn was pulled off his feet and plunged headfirst into the pool.

Distracted by the splash, Nudd and Erbyn were late spotting the fish coming towards them. They saw it heading for the gap between them and both bent towards it. Their heads came together with a loud clunk and the fish passed between them. The towed line took one of Erbyn's feet from under him and he toppled over, although he did have the presence of mind to grab the rod. The hook pulled free and the large sea trout disappeared downstream.

Carn, up to his chest in water, waded to the bank and climbed out. The others joined him and they peered at each other in the moonlight. Carn felt in a water-filled pocket and pulled out his torch. To his surprise it still worked and he used it to inspect his friends. Erbyn reached out, took the torch from him and shone it on Carn's face.

"You're looking very fine, Carn," Erbyn said and began to chuckle.

Nudd broke off from squeezing water from his clothes and looked at Carn's head. "Yes, that's very nice."

Carn raised a hand to the top of his head and found a mass of slimy weed that was hanging down as far as both ears. He scraped it off and tossed it back into the stream.

"Next time," said Erbyn, "could you go for fish that are a bit smaller?"

They all burst out laughing.

As the laughter subsided, Carn said, "At least it's a nice warm night. A brisk walk back to house will dry us off."

They gathered up their fishing rods and were about to set off when Nudd hissed, "What was that?"

"What?" Carn whispered. Nudd was a lot less nervous than in their Dartmoor days, but was still liable to get alarmed over nothing. "I can't hear anything."

"It was something on the track," Nudd whispered. "There it is again!"

This time they all heard it. Someone, or something, was coming down the track, the noise of stones being kicked against each other carrying clearly through the still night.

They crept through the undergrowth to where the deciduous trees met the conifer plantation and then crouched behind a clump of ferns. They didn't have long to wait. In the bright moonlight they could clearly see a tiny figure coming down the track.

"It's only Tegid," Nudd said with relief and made to stand up.

Carn grabbed his arm. "Wait," he whispered, "this could be our chance to find out where he goes."

When he reached the edge of the conifers Tegid turned right and headed downstream. As he passed them, they saw a well-filled rucksack on his back. They watched silently until he was fifty paces away and then Carn whispered, "Come on!"

"But we're all soaking wet," Erbyn pointed out.

"It's a warm night; we'll be all right – but do you want to take the rods back to the house while we follow him?"

"No thanks! Let's leave the rods here. Come on! He's getting away!" Erbyn led them in pursuit of Tegid.

They closed the gap and followed, staying off the stony track and moving noiselessly over the thick bed of pine needles. The caution wasn't really necessary. Tegid was moving quickly and noisily along the track.

They followed him for two miles before Erbyn clutched at Carn's arm.

"Hang on! I've got a pain in my side. I just need a minute's rest."

"Have either of you ever been this far along here?" Nudd asked, breathing heavily.

Carn shook his head. Erbyn said, "Not quite. I've followed the stream almost this far, but there don't seem to be any better fishing spots than further up." He groaned and bent over clutching his side. He soon straightened, "That's better. Must press on or we'll lose him."

They hurried on and just had Tegid in sight when clouds drifted across the moon and they were plunged into near total darkness.

"Better get closer or we'll lose him," Carn whispered, but with his next step he trod on a dead pine branch that snapped with a sharp crack. They froze. Tegid must have heard it.

One minute; two minutes; three minutes they waited, but they didn't hear Tegid moving on. Eventually, Carn whispered, "This is silly. It's only Tegid after all. It doesn't really matter if he finds us following him."

"Oh yes it does!" Nudd hissed. "He'll be furious!"

"Well, we can't stand here all night. Come on!" Carn moved on, barely able to make out the trunks of the trees. There were no sounds of Tegid. Suddenly Carn realised that he'd come up against a wooden fence. They crept along it until they reached the track and found that the track had ended at a wooden gate.

As they stood peering between the bars of the gate the clouds cleared from the moon and the scene in front of them appeared. They had reached a lane. Two hundred paces to their left, and on the opposite side of the lane, they could see the moonlight reflecting from the slate roof and windows of a large house.

Carn nodded towards it. "I bet that's where he's going."

Nudd sighed. "Oh, brother, what trouble are you looking for now?"

They climbed through the gate onto the lane, crossed the bridge over the stream and headed for the house, keeping in the moonlight shadow of the hedgerow. They hesitated opposite the house. There was a curved drive leading off the lane, to the front door and back onto the lane. Standing out in the moonlight was a name painted in white on a dark slab of slate.

Carn read, "Apple Tree Farm."

They crossed the lane and looked up at the house. There were no lights on, no windows open, no cars on the gravel drive. It looked like a large, intimidating fortress.

Erbyn nudged the others. "Look." He pointed to the left of the house where the drive led to a farmyard.

No matter how lightly they tried to tread, the gravel crunched beneath their feet. Nudd froze. "I don't think I can do this," he said in a trembling voice.

"Yes, you can," Carn urged. "There doesn't seem to be anyone about." He and Erbyn each seized one of Nudd's arms and gently pulled him on.

Once past the front corner of the house, the gravel gave way to cobbles and they were able to move freely. A barn ran along one side of the yard and a row of stables along another. A tractor was parked in the corner where they met. There was still no sign of life.

Erbyn looked about. "Apart from the McDonalds', I haven't been this close to Bigun buildings since we left Dartmoor. Just looks like a farm. I wonder what Tegid wants here – if this is where he came."

They moved across the yard to the barn. The big double doors looked securely closed, but as they got closer they realised that there was a gap at the bottom: not a very big gap, but one that a particularly small Dini could slide through without much difficulty. Carn dropped to his knees, crawled quietly to the doors and looked into the barn. The other two joined him. They could see nothing – but they could hear liquid flowing and small sounds of movement.

Carn and Erbyn pulled out their torches, but Nudd shook his head and whispered, "No! Don't! It could be anything!"

A voice made them all jump. "You've come this far. Come in and make yourselves useful."

Carn and Erbyn flicked on their torches to reveal Tegid standing at the tap on an enormous wooden barrel, calmly filling a plastic bottle. Carn and Erbyn rolled onto their backs and slid under the door. After a last anxious look about, Nudd followed them.

"Took you long enough. Thought I was going to have to carry all this myself."

"You knew we were following you?" asked Erbyn.

"You weren't following me – I was leading you! *I* followed *you* to the river. I did enjoy your splashing about – but you didn't seem to catch many fish. Then I came down the track making so much noise that even you lot would hear me. I knew you'd follow. Now you're here you can help with this lot."

"What is it?"

"Cider. There's two more barrels as big as this down there."

Carn shone his torch in the direction that Tegid indicated. Two more of the giant barrels stood on wooden frames and beyond them was an apple press.

"They're all full," said Tegid, "but I like this one best."

"How long have you been coming here?"

"Look," said Tegid, "do you really think this is the best time for a chat? Let's get these bottles filled and we can talk on the way back." He gave his rucksack a kick. "You'll find the bottles in there."

Carn hesitated and Tegid noticed. "Got a problem, Carn? Sampling a little taste of Bigun cider too wicked for you?"

Erbyn was shining his torch over the nearest barrel and looking at it in awe. "That is so *big*; I could live in it – bed, table, chairs, the lot – and they have *three* of them. How much cider can these Biguns drink?"

"Will you just stop talking and get on with it! Here!"

Erbyn saw the rucksack kicked in his direction. He bent to pull out a bottle and moved quickly to the next barrel.

Carn saw Nudd standing looking anxiously at the doors. He could either have the argument there in the barn or get the bottles filled and get them on their way home as quickly as possible. He grabbed a bottle and got on with it.

Tegid packed three full bottles into his rucksack. The others had a bottle in each hand. Tegid pushed the rucksack under a door and followed it. The others slid under the doors, bottles in hand. It had started to rain while they were in the barn. They were about to set out across the yard when a light in the house came on. They pressed back against the barn. A second light came on and a dog started to bark. It was too much for Nudd who ran panic-stricken across the yard. When he hit the gravel the loud noise increased his panic and he sprinted across the drive and straight onto the lane. There was the squeal of tyres leaving rubber on tarmac and the headlights of a car lit up the lane.

"Come on!" urged Carn. They followed the wall of the barn and plunged into the border of shrubs. They pushed through the foliage until they reached the hedge that ran along the lane. A car had stopped, angled across the lane, and the driver was out checking around the car. The rain became heavier.

A woman put her head out of the passenger window and called, "What can you see? Whatever it was I'm sure we hit it."

Tegid groaned. Carn muttered, "Oh, no."

The man stood in the beam of the headlights and held something up. "I haven't found anything – except this."

"What's that?"

"It's a squashed plastic water bottle that was filled with what smells like cider." He moved to the passenger window. "Pass me the torch." He had another look around and under the car. By the light from the torch Carn could see that the car was red and had a jagged, rusty hole in a rear wing. One of the rear lights wasn't working.

The passenger called out, "Come on! You've had a drink and you don't want the police taking a look at this car. Let's go!"

The driver got back in and the car moved away.

Carn squeezed through the hedge and out onto the lane. The others followed him. They moved slowly along the lane shining torches into the hedge and quietly calling, "Nudd! Nudd!"

They had worked their way right back to the bridge over the stream before they received any response. From under the bridge a weak, trembling voice called, "Down here!"

Tegid slithered down the bank into the shallow water. Carn and Erbyn followed him. By the light of their torches they could see Nudd sitting in the water, his back pressed against the bridge. He was trembling violently. His face was covered in blood from a cut on his forehead and ripped clothes revealed more cuts on his arms and legs.

Tegid eased alongside his brother and asked gently, "How are you, brother?"

Nudd didn't reply for a moment, then he said, "I think I'm all right. Nothing serious, anyway." But he didn't sound all right.

"Thank Cernunnos for that!" breathed Tegid. "I thought that car hit you."

"It did. But it just clipped my leg and tumbled me over. I somehow found myself back on my feet and kept running." He held up his left hand; it still clasped a bottle. "Sorry. I lost the other one."

The bottle he was clinging on to had a big split in it and was empty – but no one told him. Tegid eased the bottle from his brother's grip. "Let's get you of this water. That's two soakings in one night. Can you stand, brother?"

With Carn on one side and Erbyn on the other they raised the still trembling Nudd to his feet, but when they tried to get him moving over the slippery stones they found that he could barely walk. They eventually got him out from under the bridge and a few yards upstream to where he could sit in the dry and be reasonably well hidden. Carn checked him over. The cuts were superficial; he'd have quite a collection of bruises, but his main problem was a sprained ankle that was swelling rapidly.

"Well, you certainly can't walk on that. I suppose we could try carrying you back," said Erbyn, doubtfully.

Carn shook his head. "Too far."

'It's not much more than a mile," said Tegid, "if you go by the lane."

"Surely it's further than that."

"No. This is the lane that passes the entrance to where we live. We came the long way around coming through the woods and following the river. I know how far it is – I've been here two or three times a week for the last couple of months."

"I still don't like the idea of carrying Nudd that far. What do we do if a car comes? We can get out of sight quickly, but I'm not so sure that Nudd could."

"No lane! No more cars!" Nudd wailed.

"Right," Carn said, briskly. "Erbyn and I will go back along the lane and ride two ponies back here through the woods to collect you two." He had a sudden thought. "The geldings weren't worked today, were they?"

Erbyn shook his head.

Nudd was still shivering through a combination of shock and cold.

"Tegid, have you got matches on you?" Carn asked.

Tegid took a box from his rucksack and rattled it.

"Good. Let's get Nudd further from the road and get a fire lit."

They got him fifty paces from the road and settled him down. Tegid took off his dry coat, wrapped it around his brother and then set about digging a hole to hide a fire while Erbyn gathered sticks. Carn took the straps off the rucksack and used them to bind Nudd's ankle.

Satisfied that they could do no more, Carn and Erbyn left the brothers together and set off along the lane. No cars delayed them and they made good time. Tegid was right about the distance. Back home, Carn went to get the ponies while Erbyn went into the house to tell the others what was happening. Only Eppie was still up and she bustled about finding blankets and warm clothes for them to take.

Carn and Erbyn rode as quickly as they dared through the conifer plantation, down to the track that followed the stream and on towards the lane.

Erbyn gasped, "I hope he's going to be all right. We couldn't have got here any quicker."

As they approached the area where they had left their friends they heard loud voices. They stopped the ponies and listened. It sounded like raucous shouting.

"What's going on?" Erbyn peered into the distance where he could just see the flickering light of the fire. They slid from the ponies and moved cautiously towards the sound. They were quite close before they realised that the noise wasn't shouting but tuneless singing.

Tegid and Nudd were sitting with their arms around each other, eyes closed, bawling out an unidentifiable song. At their feet were several empty bottles.

*

Jane was sitting at her laptop while Arthur was playing in the garden. She had gone through the programme of the Bristol conference checking out every speaker looking for any possible link to Myrddin or to any environmental trust that wasn't familiar to her.

Every speaker, every organisation, every stand in the exhibition hall was well known to her – except for one. The last session of the first day was simply headed *The Message not the Man*. No speaker was named and, unlike for all of the other sessions, there was no synopsis of the content.

Jane had returned to the website of that name and was reading it carefully. The impact was exactly as it had been when she had visited the site previously. The beautiful images and the gentle smooth flow of the text had an undeniable soothing effect. The text had a rhythm that was impossible to ignore. It compelled the reader to read at a slow pace, to linger on the words; and by refusing to allow the reader to rush, the meaning was absorbed.

And the message was not about saving the planet; it was about people saving people.

Jane's reading was interrupted by the telephone ringing. Arthur came into the room as she was finishing the call and he climbed onto her lap.

When she rang off, Arthur asked, "Who was it, Mummy?"

"It was Eppie. She was just mentioning a couple of things that she'd like us to take. She says Nudd has sprained an ankle."

"What's that?"

Jane explained and then said, doubtfully, "I wonder if we could find some crutches small enough."

"What are those?"

Jane explained again.

"So Nudd has a bad leg and Tegid has his poorly arm. The brothers aren't doing very well, are they? Maybe we can make them better. Have you finished working? Can I show you something I've found in the garden?"

CHAPTER 10

The odious Ronald Smith

There was the splintering crash of an expensive crystal decanter shattering against a wall. It was followed by a torrent of foul language and another series of destructive noises as a chair was hurled across a room. Then there was the unmistakeable sound of more glass disintegrating

In the next room sixty-year-old Patricia Jakes sat calmly at the antique desk in her perfectly-ordered office. The paintings that hung on the walls had been carefully chosen, not for their artistic merit, but for their commercial potential. Every one she had selected over the last twenty years had increased massively in value. Each time that the luxurious penthouse offices at the top of Smith Towers were re-furbished, two of the paintings were moved to the walls of her substantial Chelsea home, to be replaced by new acquisitions, the relatively low cost of which disappeared under the general heading of 'Office Refurbishment'.

Sitting straight-backed in the chair at her desk, with expertly manicured fingers she flicked a speck of dust from the sleeve of the jacket of her black suit and checked that the buttons of her cream shirt were correctly fastened. The string of pearls around her neck matched the simple pearl earrings. The cream of her short, tightly-curled hair matched that of her shirt.

On the desk lay Ronald Smith's appointments diary, a spiral notepad and a pen. The grey of the very expensive carpet matched the steely grey of her eyes. Those eyes were looking through platinum-framed spectacles with satisfaction at the most recently acquired paintings as she patiently waited for the call that she knew would come.

Patricia had been with Smith since he had recruited her to run his first travel agency when they were both twenty-three. As his business empire had grown she had stayed by his side acting as secretary, personal assistant and adviser. He made sure that she attended any meetings that were likely to be difficult. While he ranted and bullied she stayed calm and quietly observed. She was highly efficient at character analysis, ruthlessly identifying weakness.

After each meeting they held a debrief when he sought her input and advice. Smith knew how important she was to him and paid her accordingly.

There was a loud bang on the interconnecting door and a voice bawled.

"Trish! Get yourself in here!"

She picked up the diary, notepad and pen and walked briskly to the door.

*

Ronald Smith was born in an East End tenement, long since demolished. His accent told everyone where he was from and he made no attempt to disguise it. Very proud of his working-class roots, was Ronald Smith.

He had started out with a market stall and quickly moved on to corner shops. He had been astute enough to spot both the threat of the supermarkets and the potential of the new package-holiday industry. The corner shops were converted to travel agencies and Smith's empire-building was underway.

The travel agency became national with over one hundred branches. He spent so much money on publicity brochures that he bought the printing company and that, in turn, led him into publishing. Starting with holiday magazines he had expanded into glossy magazines devoted to cookery, cars, boats, property, photography, fashion and "celebrity". His current stable included thirty-seven titles. Each new magazine was launched with a blaze of publicity, but dropped the moment that profitability fell below target. He had moved on to launch a new Sunday newspaper and then a daily.

His interests had expanded into mobile phones, luxury hotels with golf courses, marinas, house building, luxury car dealerships, corporate event organisers, an independent television channel and, finally, an airline.

All of Smith's businesses were based in Britain. He didn't trust foreigners and he hated travelling abroad. Everywhere else was too hot, too cold, prone to extreme weather, full of insects that bit him, or had locals that didn't speak English and served food that didn't agree with him.

Not only were all his businesses in Britain, but they were all run from Smith Towers. The Smith Corporation was the holding company and all of the companies within the group were based within the thirty-three floors of offices that lay beneath his own top floor office suite.

Ronald Smith was Chairman of The Smith Corporation. Although there was a board of directors and a Chief Executive Officer, no-one doubted who was really in charge. Big Ron, as he was known with zero affection, ruled with a rod of iron and no-one, except for Patricia Jakes, felt that his or her job was safe.

Big Ron was aptly nicknamed. He stood six feet three inches tall and over the thirty-seven years that Patricia had known him he had steadily and remorselessly put on weight. He now tipped the scales at twenty-three stone.

Smith had a twenty-bedroomed mansion home in the stockbroker belt of Surrey, which was as far from London as he was prepared to live. The house came with a hundred acres of parkland, fifteen acres of woodland, stabling for ten horses, a lake (with boathouse), tennis courts and two swimming pools.

He travelled to work by helicopter, the pilot landing on the helipad on the roof of Smith Towers. If he had to travel by car, a liveried chauffeur drove him in a gold-coloured Bentley.

He had a sixty-foot yacht that he never used and his home had a one hundred thousand pounds kitchen that he'd never visited.

He had just about everything that money could buy, but it hadn't bought him what he most wanted. Ronald Smith wanted to be *Sir* Ronald Smith – but nowhere near as much as his wife wanted to be Lady Smith. It was the one thing he hadn't been able to give her and she was making his life a misery. It had been a bitter blow for her when in June the Queen's Birthday Honours list had been published and his name, once again, hadn't been there. He knew, of course, that it wouldn't be. He had been advised that if he was in line for such an award he would receive a discreet phone call well before publication of the list, but no phone call, discreet or otherwise, had been received.

Smith had done all of the obvious things. He had made large donations to the three main political parties and ostentatiously supported charities – particularly those with a member of the Royal Family as an enthusiastic patron. But somebody didn't like him. He wasn't surprised. There were a large number of public figures who had been the victims of attacks in his newspapers or on his television channel. Whether the stories were true or not, the public loved that sort of stuff. He had promised the ambitious Mrs Smith that he was a certainty for next time and was determined to increase the cash donations to a level that he thought would guarantee success.

But he had just come from the latest in a sequence of meetings that were indicating that he might not be able to carry out his plan. He had hurled the water decanter off his desk against the wall, thrown a couple of chairs about and kicked his brass wastepaper basket through the door of a display cabinet. He didn't feel much better, but he was ready to talk.

He banged on the door and bawled, "Trish! Get yourself in here!"

*

She closed the door behind her and as she walked to the desk on her four-inch heels she took note of the damage. She sat at the desk, crossed her legs and quickly made a shorthand record of the repairs that would have to be done before tomorrow.

Smith was standing with his back to her, looking out of the window. He turned and sat heavily in his enormous chair behind the enormous desk. Patricia thought that he wasn't looking too good. His hair, with the unnatural look of chemical blackness, was heavily oiled and brushed straight back from his forehead. That forehead, and the rest of his face, was a blotchy purple.

"I tell you, Trish, if one more of the cretins tells me 'it's all down to the weather', I'll rip his head off." He was breathing rapidly and there was the sheen of sweat on his brow.

He nodded at her notepad. "What did you make of them?"

She scanned her notes. "Sorry, Ron. I couldn't see much wrong with what they are doing or saying. They've made as many people redundant as they can without the marinas simply ceasing to function, and they're scared of losing their own jobs – but what else can they do? It *is* all down to the weather." She leaned forward over the desk. "Here – pull my head off if it makes you feel any better."

She waited a few seconds and then straightened up. She continued. "If people can't use their boats because of all the gales and rain they don't feel inclined to spend thousands of pounds a year on berthing fees – nor are they prepared to have a couple of hundred grand tied up in a boat they can't use. So they're selling their boats – or moving them to the med.

"It's time to get out of marinas, Ron."

Smith leaned back in his chair and looked at the ceiling for a few seconds before looking at her again.

"I know, Trish. I've been trying to sell them for the last two years – but this time I was too late seeing problems coming. So, this week we've had indicated half-year figures for marinas, golf courses and corporate events – and they're all down the tubes." He clenched his fists, his face turned a deeper shade of purple and he slammed both fists onto the desk. He swivelled his chair to glower out of the window.

"I'm going home. Find that bone-idle cretin of a pilot and tell him to get off his backside. I want that chopper taking off in five minutes or he's out of a job."

*

When the helicopter touched down Smith threw open the door, climbed out and stalked away standing upright, as if challenging the blades to touch his head. The pilot held his breath until his employer was clear.

Mrs Smith watched it all through a window. She could read the signs well enough; she put on hold the latest set of barbed comments she'd been preparing and made sure that she kept out of his way – which wasn't difficult in a house with twenty bedrooms.

Smith stormed in through the front door and came out again less than a minute later, still wearing his business clothes, but with Wellingtons on his feet and a shotgun under his arm. He didn't shut the door properly behind him and, after a few seconds of frantic scrabbling, a springer spaniel burst out and raced after him. Smith strode around to the back of the house heading for the stables. In one corner of the stable courtyard stood a dovecote and there was a row of the white birds lined up along the roof ridge of the stables. On his way past the building he casually raised the shotgun and fired. The bird on the end of the row exploded in a cloud of white feathers.

He walked on towards the woodland, the dog excitedly running in circles in front of him. As he crossed the neatly trimmed area of grass a cock pheasant ran across. The dog dashed after it, but before the bird could take off Smith blasted it. The dog picked up the shattered body and ran to Smith with it. He took the bird from the dog and booted the carcase into the air. As they approached the woodland Smith urged the dog into the trees. It charged about, head down, tail wagging furiously.

A rabbit flushed from the undergrowth ran a few feet from Smith and he gave it both barrels. More rabbits poured out onto the grass and he blazed away. He stopped. The last animal that had run from the wood had been the dog.

He turned on his heel and walked back towards the house. One of the gardeners was weeding a flowerbed.

"Oi! You! Get over here!"

The gardener had to hurry to catch up. Smith spoke without looking at him. "You'll find the wife's dog over by the trees. Bury it in the woods and keep your trap shut."

CHAPTER 11

The Scottish holiday

Bob was lucky twice over. First, he had been right about motor homes: the bad weather had left rental companies with vehicles on their hands. With some phoning around and negotiating he had secured a last-minute deal that they could afford. It was small, but adequate for the three of them. Secondly, he had been able to adjust his holiday dates so that they could all attend the Bristol conference on their way back from Scotland.

Jane would be listening to the Green Party speaker filling the second slot on the first morning and she would be one of the volunteers manning the Green Party stand. Bob and Arthur would wander around the stands and fill their time somehow while they waited to see if Myrddin contacted them.

They picked up the motor home on the evening before they set off for Scotland. Jane drove them in her car to Exeter; then Bob and a very excited Arthur travelled back to Chagford in the motor home with Jane following.

While Bob and Jane packed, Arthur explored every feature and corner of what would be their home for the next week. When it was time for him to go to bed, he insisted on sleeping in the little bed over the front seats.

They set out on their drive north at six o'clock in the morning. It was a long, long way, through frequent heavy showers and slowly moving traffic. Bob and Jane took turns at driving; they made frequent stops and when they finally reached the barrier at the estate entrance after ten o'clock at night, Arthur had been asleep for the last two hours.

Mr McDonald let them into the drive and they stopped briefly at the house before moving on down to park close to the wooden building that had been converted into the Dini's home.

They were tired and Bob and Jane still had their bed to make up, so after exchanging very brief greetings with the Dini, they lifted the still asleep Arthur into his bed and settled down for the night.

Next morning Bob was brought awake by Arthur tugging on his arm.

"Come on, Daddy! Get up! I want to show Enid our home on wheels – she can't believe how tall I am!"

Arthur climbed over him to open the curtains. Bob opened his eyes using a hand to shield them against the bright light. There was no sign of Jane.

"Where's Mummy?"

"Having breakfast. Come on, lazy bones!" Arthur scrambled back over him, pulling the duvet with him.

Bob looked out of the window. Enid was outside, waving up at him. Only seeing the Dini once a year, Bob never became accustomed to how small they were. Each time they met, it came as a surprise.

"All right. I give in." He swung his legs off the bed and pulled on T-shirt and shorts. He moved towards the door, but Arthur called him back.

"Can we put the bed away – please?"

Bob turned back. He quickly rolled up the bedding, put it in the storage cupboard below and converted the bed back into two seats.

"Thank you!"

Bob affectionately tousled his son's mop of blond hair and stepped out of the motor home.

"Good morning, Bob." Enid greeted him cheerfully in her high-pitched voice.

"Morning, Enid. I hear Arthur's keen to give you the tour." He bent and lifted her up onto the top step. "There you go!"

"Thank you. Hasn't our little boy grown?"

Bob chuckled. The top of Enid's head scarcely reached the middle of Arthur's chest. "He's grown bigger and you've grown prettier." Arthur and Enid both giggled. "I'm off to find some breakfast."

As Bob walked away he heard Arthur say, "My bed's right up there!"

He found that Jane had taken their folding chairs and picnic table inside and set them up at the end of the Dini's long low table. All of the Dini, except for Enid and Tegid, were in the room.

"Morning all." He sat opposite his wife. "How long have you been up?"

"Quite a while – Arthur stepped on my head climbing down from his bed." She pushed a bowl and a box of cereal towards Bob, who nodded towards a pile of papers in front of Jane.

"What have you got there?"

"We've been talking about Myrddin – of course. Coming up with all sorts of ideas about what he's been doing and why he should suddenly want the sword. I've been explaining about this strange website and the fact that whoever is behind it is going to be at the Bristol gathering. These are some of the pages from the website that I printed off."

"And what does everyone think of it?" Bob looked around the faces, but all he received was a variety of shrugs, baffled looks and muttered vague words.

"Issel came up with an interesting thought about the sword," Jane looked encouragingly along the table.

Issel was clearly embarrassed at being the centre of attention, but after a little hesitation she said, "Well, I just said that Gilda always had that little knife thing – she called it her athame. She would never be without it. Whenever she was brewing up her potions or saying the words at our ceremonies, she was always pointing with it. I only thought… well, maybe that great big sword is Myrddin's athame."

Bob stopped with his spoon half way to his mouth. "You could be on to something. After we met you all that first time, and we saw Gilda with her athame, we did some research into them. Practitioners of wicca magic use them to focus energies…You know, I still feel awkward talking about such things, despite everything."

"But what exactly is *everything*?" asked Bran. "Most of us never saw him actually *do* any magic. We heard The Droller's story about finding him in a lead box and restoring him and we heard the tale of the sword coming out of the sea. A good few years have gone by and it all seems so…unreal."

Bob and Jane exchanged looks. It was Bob who tried to answer.

"Well, we only spent a few days with him. We saw The Sword of Power, as he called it, come up from the sea; we saw the rate at which he was changing – in those few days he put on so much weight. You could almost see him getting bigger and stronger as you looked at him.

"But it's not so much what we saw him do – it's all the other strange stuff. Like he seemed to know that HRH would help to get you somewhere safe and that I would have the chance to meet him. And there are things that are hard to put into words: our house has *felt* different since the sword has been there; I feel strange when I touch it; it's very heavy and at first I struggled to lift it, but now I can handle it hardly feeling the weight."

"And there all the strange things involving Arthur," said Jane. "His being born for a start – we'd pretty much given up on having children. But he's not like other children – I've taught plenty of them. He seems old beyond his years. And he says the sword is his. And he told us that Myrddin would contact us before he did."

Bob chipped in. "Yes, and when Joe came for the sword he said he'd been hearing all about Arthur. Who could have been telling him? Myrddin, Gilda and Joe had disappeared from our lives before we even knew that Arthur was on the way."

Bob looked around the Dini's faces. They seemed uncertain and awkward.

"Carn, you spent time with him. Surely you haven't stopped believing?"

Carn glanced from Bob to Jane and sighed. "Right at the beginning I thought it was just one of The Droller's stories. Then I had to believe. I saw the sword come out of the sea; I saw the changes in him; I saw him call that raven down from the sky. I thought something wonderful was going to happen. Then you found us this safe place to live – maybe Myrddin had something to do with it, maybe not."

He looked around the others. "Here we are. We have somewhere comfortable to live. We feel safe. But we have no idea what has happened to The Droller or Gilda. And Myrddin hasn't been back to really help us. More than five years have passed. We are all five years older. We are five years closer to dying out.

"So, he's finally been in contact with you – but only to take his sword. I, *we*, don't want to get too excited about it. We'd rather wait and see what happens next."

Silence fell. Bob changed the subject. "How are you, Nudd? I hear you had an accident. How's the ankle?"

By way of answer Nudd raised his foot and rolled up his trouser leg to reveal a strapped ankle with purple and yellow bruising extending above the strapping and well up his calf. "I can't put any weight on it yet."

"Look what Mr McDonald made for him," said Eppie, reaching under Nudd's chair. With a rattle of wood she pulled out a very small crutch made from an old broom. The handle and the head had been cut down, the bristles removed and a piece of blanket bound around what was left of the head. On the other end the handle had been sanded down to take the rubber foot of a walking stick.

"How are you getting on with it?" asked Jane.

Nudd just shrugged.

Bob and Jane were relieved when Arthur appeared at the door. He had feathers in his hair.

"I've been to see the chickens! Come on! Let's go and see the ponies!"

Carn, Enid and Arthur led the way to the pony paddocks, Bob and Jane following.

"They all seem a bit sorry for themselves," said Bob quietly. "How were you getting on with them before I showed up?"

"All right. Eppie's lovely; she's always pleased to see us and happy to chat." Jane hesitated. "I did get the impression that although they're enjoying life here, as the years go by the lack of children is really getting to them. Eppie whispered to me that Enid keeps getting upset at the thought that she or Bran are likely to end up living here alone."

They walked in silence for a couple of minutes, then she added, "I really struggled with that website stuff. For a start they have no idea what a website is. When I got around that and read them some of the material it didn't have any impact on them at all. It only occurred to me afterwards that there were no surprises in it for them; it just describes how they've always lived. It only has impact for people living in the high-pressure modern world that we've managed to create.

"And you're right – they do seem a bit sorry for themselves. We need to talk it through with them. I have the feeling that there's some resentment. We think that Myrddin and the sword solved our big problem – they're wondering why he hasn't solved theirs."

"Aye, well, we've coped well enough, I suppose, but I do worry about them."

"I'm sure it's been a lot of extra responsibility for you, Mrs McDonald. Is there anything in particular that's worrying you? Is there anything we can do to help?"

"More tea, Jane?" Mrs McDonald re-filled Jane's cup without waiting for a reply. "And have another wee taste of shortbread.

"Now, don't get me wrong, we've loved having them here. They've really brightened up our lives. Rab has just loved being involved with sorting things out for them: the carts and the little tools – all that kind of thing. But I worry about them getting ill. Not that they ever seem to be ill; I suppose it's because they never mix with others so they don't catch anything. If we have the slightest wee sniffle, we keep away from them. But if one of them *did* get ill – or have an accident, like poor Nudd – what could we do? We can't call a doctor, can we? I thought of giving him painkillers, but they're so small. They're like tiny, wee bairns and the instructions on the packets say not to give them to young children. Your Arthur's only just turned five and he towers over them."

"Oh yes, I see. That must be a worry – for them as well as you."

"Aye, I'm sure it is. They tell me that one of their own, called Gilda, used to make them herbal remedies, but they don't know what she put in most of them and the ones they do know they say that they can't find the plants up here.

"Issel, now, she's getting on a bit. Some day soon I expect she'll be showing signs of growing old," Mrs McDonald unconsciously rubbed knuckles enlarged by arthritis as she spoke, "and I won't be able to do anything for her."

"But you do such a lot for them. They do appreciate it, you know."

"The other thing, y'ken," she looked over her shoulder to check that her husband hadn't come within hearing, "Rab's not getting any younger. He wouldn't admit it, but he's finding the work harder to manage. Not just looking after the wee folk, but the other work around the estate. If it hadn't been for the wee folk arriving, he'd probably have spoken to HRH about retiring afore now."

"Yes, I understand. Would you like Bob to mention it to the Prince? They usually have a little chat when he visits Dartmoor."

"Oh, no. Better not. I wouldn't like Rab to know we'd been talking about him behind his back."

"Do you think HRH will have someone that he trusts enough to take over here? You've done so well keeping their existence secret."

Mrs McDonald chuckled. "I wouldn't be so sure about that. Folks about here aren't foolish – or blind. They knew all about the conversion work on the old barn and they never see bairns coming or going. Some will also know that I buy a lot more things than I used to, and the bookshops in town know that I've developed some strange tastes in books. And everyone who drives by will have noticed the barrier at the end of the lane."

Jane looked alarmed. Mrs McDonald chuckled again and reached across to pat her on the arm. "Now, you mustn't mither y'sel on that score. Folks about here know how to mind their ain business – especially when it's anything to do with the Royal Family. Like Rab's, many of the families have worked for generations for the Royals and you'd have more joy squeezing a song out of a haggis than getting gossip out of them."

*

Back on Dartmoor, Nigel Sligo was finding gossip easier to come by.

He hadn't had much luck following up Ethel Clay's tales of pixies helping themselves from people's gardens and Alice Jackson had given him a flea in his ear when he'd tried to ask her about her accident in the snow – but he'd never thought that tales of Dartmoor pixies were anything other than useless nonsense. Nevertheless, his instincts told him that there was a story to be unearthed – or created.

He'd had to make changes to the way he usually worked. Normally, he used his non-descript appearance to good effect. He had a way of being such a faceless non-entity that people just didn't notice him. He could follow victims or listen in to conversations in pubs, cafés and shops without anyone being aware that he was there.

Now his rainbow-hued face made that impossible, so he was making use of it. Anyone who asked – and most people did – were told that he'd been injured in a fall that wasn't his fault. He'd been given time off work to recover and was confidently expecting a nice compensation payment; a payment that he was happy to spend on his new-found friends. It was costing him a few pounds buying rounds of drinks, but he was acquiring some interesting facts about the Johnsons.

The Ranger's relationship with HRH clearly rankled in some quarters. It had started six years ago when something happened during a routine Royal visit and the Prince had, without warning, made changes to his itinerary in order to visit the Johnsons' home.

They had had a child fairly late in life and Jane Johnson had given up her job as a teacher. She now had political ambitions with the Green Party.

Sligo felt a warm glow of anticipation; a story involving Royals and politicians – should be worth real money.

Apparently stray facts had a way of turning out to be significant and Sligo carefully filed away every scrap of information that came in his direction. For example, the Johnsons holidayed in Scotland every year – a habit that seemed to have formed after their meeting with HRH.

By accident, Sligo unearthed another stray fact. On several items in his rented cottage he had spotted stickers bearing the words, 'Supplied by Trader Joe'. He was in the packed bar of The Forest Inn at Hexworthy one lunchtime, when he overheard a conversation between two old farmers.

"How's the old rheumatics, Bill? I sees you'm limping a bit."

"Tiz dreadful. All this wind and rain don't help, neither. I used to get some stuff off Trader Joe. Wonderful that was. But I ran out years ago. If I'd knowed he weren't comin' back, I'd have got in a barrow load."

Sligo eased alongside. "Can I buy you gents a drink? It's thirsty weather."

"Well, won't say no. You'd better take it steady though – looks as if you had one too many the other night."

"Eh? Oh, no – I fell down some stairs – loose carpet. Not my fault. Should be getting a bit of a cash pay-out. Did I hear the name Trader Joe mentioned?"

"Bang on the head didn't affect your hearing then, boy."

Sligo managed a smile. "I just wondered who he was. Lot of stuff where I'm staying has his stickers on it."

"He does, or did, run a mobile shop. Welsh he was. His feyther ran it afore him. Came round once a month they did. Very useful, too. Sold all sorts of stuff. Suddenly stopped coming. No warning – just disappeared."

"I'd almost forgotten him," said Bill's friend. "Called on all the farms and most of the shops. Did you ever see inside that big van of his? Never seen anything like it. You wouldn't believe how much stuff you could get in one van."

"Yes," said Bill, "including those medicines of his."

"Can't you just buy it from Boots?" asked Sligo.

"No, I can't," said Bill. "Wasn't what you'd call proper medicine."

"Why don't you contact him and ask him where he got it from?"

"Wouldn't know how to."

"Well, what's his real name?"

The two farmers looked at each other, thought for a few seconds and then both shrugged and shook their heads.

"When did he disappear?"

"Oh, er, what, four or five years ago, would you say, Bill?"

"At least. All these questions make a man thirsty," he said, looking meaningfully at his empty whisky glass.

A couple of days later, Sligo's persistence paid off. He worked his way around the shops in Moretonhampstead and went into one for cigarettes. He casually asked, "I don't suppose you ladies remember Trader Joe?"

"Trader Joe? Oh, yes, of course. We used to get walking sticks and some lovely framed drawings from him. Whatever happened to him?"

"I don't know. I'm trying to get back in touch with him. You don't by any chance remember his real name?"

"Not off hand," one of the ladies replied, "but if you don't mind hanging on, I can probably find it for you."

"Thank you. That would be very kind."

She disappeared into the back room and re-appeared a minute later carrying a file. "Here you are!" she said, triumphantly. "I knew I'd find it. Very organised we are with our records. Always insist on receipts – unlike some."

She held in front of Sligo a receipt headed, 'Trader Joe'. Along the bottom was printed, 'Proprietor: Joe Morgan'. A Welsh address and telephone number followed.

*

Arthur woke early. He listened for a few seconds to the drumming only inches from his head. It was raining – raining hard. The noise on the motor home roof made it sound even worse than it actually was.

Arthur loved the motor home and he loved the visits to the Dini. He snuggled into his bed. The sound of the rain made it feel cosy being tucked up, nice and warm and dry. He thought about the day ahead with keen anticipation. Everything about the place was so much fun!

Everything seemed to be on his scale of size: the little tables and chairs, the sink he could reach, the showers with the low controls, the Shetland ponies and their foals – even the dexter cow appeared to be half normal size. And, of course, the tiny Dini were there. For once he wasn't looking up at adults, but down to friends who were smaller than he was.

What would they do today? He could help collect the eggs, help milk the cow, and pick raspberries and strawberries. Then he remembered: Mummy and Daddy were going into town to do shopping with Mr McDonald. They'd said he could stay behind with the Dini and Mrs McDonald – and Erbyn had said that they could go fishing.

Arthur pulled aside the curtain screening his bed and looked down. His parents were still sound asleep. He carefully climbed down, making sure that he didn't step on them. He pulled on some clothes, tugged on his Wellington boots and quietly let himself out of the motor home.

It wasn't raining as hard as he'd expected and it felt quite warm. No one else seemed to be up and about, but then movement down by the storage barns caught his eye and he set off in that direction. He saw Tegid open the door of the barn where the cart and harness were stored and disappear inside. He hurried to join him.

"Hello, Tegid."

Tegid jumped.

"Oh, it's you. What are you doing here?"

"I don't think anyone else is up."

102

"Why don't you go back to bed?"

"Not tired."

Tegid was trying to shrug off the rucksack on his back. Arthur stepped forward to help, but Tegid moved away. "I can manage." He eventually got it off and tucked it out of sight behind some bales of straw.

"What have you got in there?"

"Never you mind."

"We've hardly seen you since we've been here."

"So? Are we all supposed to stop what we're doing just because you lot choose to come?"

"Oh no. But it would be nice to do things with you."

"That's what you think."

Arthur smiled at the tiny man with the surly face.

"Why are you always so grumpy?"

Exasperated, Tegid thrust his stump under Arthur's nose. "Wouldn't you be *grumpy* with one of these?" If he was trying to frighten Arthur away, it didn't work.

Arthur moved his head back a little so that he could focus on the stump that was covered by a very dirty sock. "You were grumpy before that happened."

"Who says?"

"Everybody."

There was a hole in the sock and Arthur pulled open the hole to peer inside. "What does it look like?"

"You don't want to know."

"Yes, I do."

Tegid hesitated, then peeled off the sock. The stump beneath was none too clean. Arthur put both hands on Tegid's forearm to keep it still while he made a close inspection.

"Did you really cut off your own hand?"

"Yes."

Arthur looked really impressed. "You must be very brave. I don't think I could be as brave as that. Did you nearly die?"

"Yes. The others got me to Gilda and she saved me."

"I haven't met Gilda yet."

"Don't suppose you will. She was ancient when we last saw her and that was years ago."

Arthur smiled again. "I think I'll see her soon." He ran the fingers of his right hand over the stump. Tegid made to pull it away, but Arthur still had a firm hold on the forearm with his left hand. "It's very smooth." He let go of Tegid.

"I know why you're grumpy."

Tegid gave a derisive snort. "Just because you're bigger than me it doesn't mean you know anything. How old are you? Five isn't it? So tell me Mr five-year-old, why am I grumpy?"

"It's because you're different."

Tegid sat on a straw bale. "And how am I different?"

"All of the Dini are much smaller than Biguns, so they're all different. But you are a lot smaller than any of the others, so that makes you different to them. Did you always know you were the smallest?"

"Yes."

"You've been braver than the others to make up for it."

"Oh yes?"

"I've heard about the tricks you did on Biguns. The others wouldn't do that."

"Think you're clever don't you? Well, maybe you are – for a five-year-old. But you don't know much. I *played tricks* as you call it, because I hate the Biguns. I hate them because they killed my father in front of me with their dogs!"

This time Tegid's shock tactics worked. Arthur's eyes filled with tears.

"I didn't know that," he said quietly.

"There's more you don't know. When I cut my hand off, it wasn't because I was brave – it was because I was terrified! It was the only way I could avoid being caught by Biguns."

Arthur was quiet for a while. Then he said, "But you were brave to be there – to be doing things to that Bigun's car."

"You should tell the others that – all they say is that I was stupid."

There was another silence. Tegid sat on the bale swinging his legs. Arthur looked around the shed.

"It's not easy being different," said Arthur.

"How would you know?"

"Because *I'm* different."

Tegid looked at him sharply. "How are you different? You don't look different to me."

"I don't know – it's just how I feel. Mummy has taken me to play with a group of other children my age, but I just don't fit in.

I don't want to do the things that they want to do." He sighed. He looked up at the roof and listened. "I think it's stopped raining."

Arthur opened the door and went out. Tegid followed him.

"Yes, it's stopped." He looked back towards the house. There was still no sign of anybody else. "I think it's still very early. I'd like to go down to the river." He hesitated, "They wouldn't like me to go on my own – will you come with me?"

Tegid shook his head. "Waste of time." Then he saw the look on Arthur's face and added, "Why do you want to go to the river?"

Arthur frowned. "I don't know. It's a feeling I've had since I woke up. I just know that I ought to go there."

Tegid studied Arthur's face, then he groaned. "All right. Let's go. But don't forget, I've just walked miles carrying a heavy bag."

Side-by-side they walked in silence through the conifer plantation and down the next valley towards the river. Eventually they reached the end of the conifers and entered the strip of deciduous woodland along the river. On the river bank they stopped.

"Right. Here we are. Has your *funny feeling* gone?"

Arthur shook his head. He looked up and down the river and then he pointed upstream. "This way," he said, setting off walking in that direction.

After ten minutes Tegid had had enough. "That's it! Far enough! I'm been up most of the night and I'm ready for my breakfast."

"No. Please. It's just a little bit further."

"What is?"

"I don't know," said Arthur, continuing to walk.

Tegid swore under his breath but, after a brief hesitation, he followed.

Arthur soon stopped. He pointed to a group of boulders at the water's edge. "It's over there."

Tegid followed him to the boulders. They were high enough to stop Tegid seeing over and lay in a circle enclosing a small patch of ground that Tegid couldn't see.

Arthur could just see over. "There it is," he said, sounding both puzzled and satisfied.

An exasperated Tegid demanded, "What is it?"

Arthur lifted Tegid so that he could clamber onto the top of the boulder. "It's that plant with the pink flowers. What's it called?"

There were several clumps of comfrey growing within the circle of rock. Tegid looked down at Arthur.

"You brought us all this way and you didn't know what you were looking for?"

"No," said Arthur, "I just had a feeling that I had to come here. Is it any use?"

"Yes," said Tegid, "it is. This is just what we need to treat Nudd's ankle. We've searched all along these woods and not found any – not surprising with it hidden in here."

He gave Arthur a baffled look. "How did... never mind. Just find us a couple of sticks and climb over. We'll dig out a couple of clumps. I'll plant the roots of one up near the house, so it'll be easy next time we need it."

*

When Bob and Jane woke up and found Arthur missing they weren't at all concerned. But when they found that all of the Dini, except for Tegid, were in the house and that Arthur hadn't been seen, the first seeds of worry started to germinate.

After they had checked the henhouse, looked at the cow, been down to the pony paddocks and up to the McDonalds' house, the worry had grown to substantial proportions.

"Where else could he have gone?" Jane asked of no-one in particular.

"He was very excited about going fishing today. Maybe he's gone to the river," suggested Bob, already moving in that direction.

"Oh, God, I hope not. He knows he's not to go to the water on his own."

Bob, Jane, and all of the Dini, except for Nudd, hurried towards the river, with Bob and Jane running on ahead. As they hit the top of the down slope into the valley, Bob grabbed Jane's arm and pulled her to a stop.

"It's all right! Look!"

Plodding up the hill towards them were two small figures.

"Just hang on here, get our breath back and calm down," Jane gulped, trying not to be tearful. "If he's been to the river, then he didn't go alone. He hasn't been gone for long. Let's not make too much of it."

Bob turned, went back over the crest of the hill and shouted back to the others. "It's all right! He's here!"

He re-joined Jane and they waited while their son came up the slope towards them.

"What are they carrying?" Jane whispered.

"A bunch of flowers for you?"

The group of Dini arrived seconds before Arthur and Tegid reached them.

"Hello! Are you all going for a walk? Do you know what this is?" Arthur held out the clump he'd been clutching to his chest.

Bob and Jane looked at the plant and were both about to speak when several high-pitched voices shouted, "Comfrey!"

"Wherever did you find it?" asked Eppie, looking from Arthur to Tegid. "We searched all along the river and didn't find any!"

"He found it," said Tegid, nodding towards Arthur. "He didn't know what it was or why he wanted it – but he knew where to find it." Tegid raised his eyebrows and shrugged his shoulders.

"Shall I carry it?" asked Bob, bending down to take the two clumps.

As Arthur passed it over, he caught sight of the muddy patch staining the front of his shirt and his shorts. "Oops!"

"Don't worry," Jane reassured him, "it covers up the chocolate you spilled down there yesterday."

Back at the Dini's house while others prepared breakfast, Eppie and Issel worked on the comfrey. Eppie cut the roots from one of the clumps and gave it to Carn, who promptly disappeared to plant it in a corner of the vegetable patch. They carefully washed all the soil away and then finely chopped the leaves, stems and roots before mashing the whole lot together to make a thick paste. Then Eppie spread the paste over Nudd's foot, ankle and calf before binding it all in thin strips of a towel.

There was a cheerful atmosphere over breakfast, everyone feeling relieved to have been able to do something for their injured friend.

*

On the night before the Johnsons were due to leave, the three of them were having a meal with all of the Dini – even Tegid had joined them. Arthur was sitting at the low table with the Dini, while Bob and Jane sat at their picnic table. Once they'd all finished eating, Bob interrupted the conversations around the tables by tapping a spoon against his glass.

"Sorry, everyone, but we have to leave in the morning..." there were boos around the tables, the loudest from Arthur, "and there's something that I need to be absolutely clear about." He looked about to check that he had everyone's attention. "We will drive down to Bristol tomorrow, stay on a campsite overnight, and then we will go to the meeting where we think we may see Myrddin.

"*If* we see him, and it is only an if – none of us know what his plans are – what exactly do you want us to ask him. For all we know, he might disappear again for years, so, if he's there we have to grab the chance to find out as much as we can.

"So, I assume that you want to know what has happened to The Droller, Gilda and the Welsh Dini," he looked about the Dini faces seeking confirmation and got it. "And I expect, like us, you'd like to know what he's been up to for all these years?" Again there were nods around the low table.

"What else do you want us to be sure to ask him?" Bob sat back and waited. There were looks exchanged, a few mutterings, but no one spoke up for a while.

Then Carn said, "You two know our real problem well enough. If no new Dini are born, it won't be long before there are no Dini left." He hesitated for a few seconds. "At first we were just grateful to have been brought here – life on the moor was becoming impossible. But we thought, we hoped, that Myrddin would do something more to help us. Some of us thought that, if he's a great magician, we might make us grow to Bigun size." He looked embarrassed as he said it. "Then we wouldn't have to hide away; we could just live among the Biguns."

There was another long hesitation; it grew so long that Eppie took over.

"The trouble is...we've been watching your Biguns' television programmes. And now we know that we couldn't just live among them – there's just too much about your world that we don't understand. To be honest, we don't much like a lot of what we see. So, even if he somehow magicked us back to full size, we'd still have to hide away – or, at least, find somewhere to live well away from other people."

Enid joined in. "So, we don't know what we want. Stay small, live comfortably here – but die out; or be made bigger, maybe have children, but…where, and how, would we live?"

Bob found everyone looking at him, but he had no other ideas to suggest.

"All right, all we can do is make sure that he understands the problem and see if he has any plans or suggestions."

"Yes," said Carn, "I suppose all we want to know is whether he has any plans for our future – or do we just have to get on with sorting our own lives out and make the best of what we have?"

CHAPTER 12

The meeting

They made a really early start. Despite their pleas for the Dini and the McDonalds to stay in bed, everyone was up to wave them off. It was a drizzly, murky morning and the rain grew relentlessly heavier as they journeyed south. Bob was driving on the M6 approaching Birmingham when the traffic slowed to a crawl.

"Just how expensive does petrol have to get and how slow does road travel have to become before people stop using their cars?" Jane asked, more out of exasperation than wanting an answer. When she saw Bob about to reply, she said, "Don't say it! I know – we've driven to Scotland and back in a non-too-economical motor home. I've been telling myself off all week for not practising what I preach."

Arthur laughed out loud. "Go on, Mummy! Tell yourself off now – that will be very funny."

And so she did. Jocularly at first, putting on a stern voice, but as she continued the humour disappeared and the genuine strength of feeling showed through. Bob reached across to pat her on the leg. "Take it easy."

She broke off and bit her lip for a moment. "Sorry. Got a bit carried away there."

South of Birmingham the result of the heavy rain was easy to see. As they crossed the River Avon on the M5 they could see a line of boats that should have been along the riverbank, but now were isolated towards the middle of a stretch of water that was more than half-a-mile wide. Jane re-tuned the radio to a local station and they found that the programme had been given over to reports of the flooding. Summer floods that were supposed to be of a kind only to be expected once in a hundred years had now hit the area in three of the last four years.

"Has our house ever been flooded?" asked Arthur.

"No, we're safe enough. High up above the sea and with no rivers near us, there's no need to worry about our being flooded," said Jane seeking to reassure a worried-sounding Arthur.

"It must be sad to be flooded. Where do all the people go when their houses are full of water?"

Jane thought for a moment or two and was about to attempt an answer when Arthur continued. "We've got room for some of them."

"Er, well, yes. We have, but I expect they prefer to stay in the area where they live – they'll have schools and jobs to go to. And they'll want to get back into their own houses to sort out the damage as soon as the water goes away."

"Don't schools and job places get flooded?"

"Erm, I suppose they must do. That's a good idea of yours, but I've never heard of anyone asking people to come forward to offer places to stay."

There was a short silence, then Arthur said, "Do we have to wait to be asked?"

Jane twisted in her seat to look at her son. "What an amazing little boy you are!"

"Have you got the information on the campsite?" asked Bob. "I hope we haven't got too much farther to go – I think I saw that the reception office closes at nine."

Jane delved into her bag and pulled out an envelope.

"Yes, nine o'clock. Where are we?"

"Just passing Gloucester."

Jane checked the map and her directions. "About thirty miles to the M4 junction. We should just about make it – as long as I don't get us lost."

It was five minutes to nine when they pulled onto the site. Bob stopped outside the reception office and Jane hurried in through the rain. She apologised for their late arrival and commented on the weather. The man behind the counter looked truly miserable.

"Been like this for weeks. The site's nearly empty. Nobody stays more than a night or two," he said, "then they move on hoping to find better weather somewhere else. The lousy weather's been going on for so long I'm surprised that anybody still thinks of camping. This site won't be opening next year, I can tell you that."

111

They were relieved to find that the campsite had areas of hardstanding for motor homes and concrete pathways to the toilet blocks. The handful of tents pitched on muddy ground looked dismal under the darkening grey skies and relentless rain.

They got up early next morning, had quick showers, an even quicker breakfast and set out for the conference centre. The rain had eased to a thick drizzly mist so they didn't get too wet making their way from the vast car park to the main building. Jane went to find the registration desk while Bob and Arthur picked up leaflets in the foyer and sat on a bench to plan their morning.

They'd arrived so early that Jane was first in the queue to register and she had to wait while the two young women sorted out their record sheets and delegates' badges.

When they were ready to deal with her, Jane said, "Hello, I'm Jane Johnson, Green Party." While they searched for her name, Jane added, "Can you help me? I was only able to get one seat for the last session this afternoon. I don't suppose you've had anybody drop out? I really need two more seats."

The young woman in front of her was muttering, "Jane Johnson, Jane Johnson," as she scanned down the list of delegates and she didn't at first appear to have heard Jane's question. She suddenly stopped, looked up and smiled. "Of course, sorry – not thinking straight yet – bit early for me. I've got your tickets here somewhere – someone's sorted it all out for you." She searched among the papers on the desk, pulled out an envelope and handed it over.

"Oh, er, lovely, thank you," said Jane.

The envelope had *The Johnsons* written on it and Jane opened it as she walked back to Bob and Arthur. Inside were three delegates' badges with their names on and under each name it said *The Message not the Man*; there were also three tickets to the afternoon session in the lecture hall given over to the same organisation.

By the time she sat down next to Bob, there was a pink patch on each cheek. He could tell at a glance that something had disturbed her.

"What's up?" Bob asked and Arthur moved to stand at her knee.

"I just don't know what to make of all this."

"All what?"

"Look!" she showed them the contents of the envelope. "Three of us are expected. It's all got *The Message not the Man* on it."

Bob looked. "So, it looks as if you were right – it is Myrddin behind it."

"I'm part pleased that I was right; part excited and part furious!" she hissed. "For a start, I'm here representing the Green Party – I don't need his passes to get me around."

"And…" Bob prompted her.

"And I'm angry about his little games. I feel he's just playing with us. Why hasn't he just contacted us properly and told us what's going on? And how did he know that you two would be here? *I* didn't tell anybody. I just enquired about extra tickets as soon as we thought that we all wanted to come – I didn't tell anyone how many – but I was told that this was a very popular session and that they were up to the limit."

"Don't be upset, Mummy."

Jane looked into her son's big blue eyes and smiled, "I'm not upset – just a little bit confused. Anyway, I'd better try to stop thinking about all this and go and do what I'm suppose to be doing; I'm down to man the Green Party stand for the first hour and then I'm at our presentation. I'd better go and find the stand."

"We can show you where it is; we've found it on this plan of the place." Bob put a plan on Jane's lap and pointed. "There it is – which means it must be down there on the right," he pointed into the distance. They all walked in that direction until they found the stand.

"Right then," said Bob, "we'll leave you to it for a couple of hours. Shall we meet up in the coffee lounge we've just passed?"

"O.K. boys. Have a nice time – and try to be good."

Bob and Arthur looked at each other and then at Jane. They both shook their heads.

"What? Are you refusing to have a nice time, or refusing to be good?"

"We'll let you know," said Bob. He scooped up Arthur, placed him on his shoulders and passed up the plan of the exhibition. "Here you are; you're the navigator. Where do we go?"

Arthur pointed and they moved away.

113

They rejoined Jane two hours later. Arthur showed her the leaflets they had gathered, all urging them to save the planet in a host of different ways, most of them carrying detailed warnings of the fate of the planet if action wasn't taken on the emission of greenhouse gases and on various other forms of pollution.

Bob managed a rueful smile. "I don't doubt the sincerity of all these folks, but you end up with such a great big list of things you shouldn't do, and things you shouldn't buy, that life starts to feel impossible. It might be better if we could all agree on one simple, practical thing that people should do and only when we've got most people doing it, move on to the next simple thing."

They returned to the motor home to eat in order to avoid paying the high prices charged in the conference venue. As soon as he'd eaten, Arthur climbed up into his bed and went to sleep. His parents confidently stated that they were too wound up to sleep, settled back in their seats to listen to the radio and to look through the leaflets. Neither of them heard more than the first few minutes of the lunchtime news before they were breathing deeply, heads sunk onto chests.

Arthur woke them both as he climbed down, asking as he did so, "Is it time to go?"

Jane looked in panic at the clock as Bob struggled to rouse himself.

"Yes, it is! Thirty minutes to go before it starts – better get back."

They were back at the hall with twenty minutes to spare. People were already filing in through the open doors, but the queue stretched for sixty yards, going out of sight around a corner.

"We'll be lucky to find three seats together," Jane said as they joined the end of the queue.

The man in front turned to them with an enthusiastic smile. "I hear this has been playing to packed houses, as they say. Something very different, with a lot of impact. I'm really looking forward to it."

Bob politely returned the smile. "Let's hope it lives up to all our expectations." He winked at Jane and then re-assured her. "We only need two seats really, don't we? I expect Arthur will have to sit on my lap so that he can see."

The queue shuffled steadily forward. After a couple of minutes they turned the corner and could see the line of people stretching away to the open doors in the distance. There was a young woman moving along the queue towards them, apparently checking tickets.

When she reached the Johnsons she glanced at the name badges. "Ah, here you are!" She grinned down at Arthur. "If I'd known your group included such a young delegate, I'd have spotted you quicker." She glanced from Jane to Bob. "If you'd like to follow me, I'll show you to your seats."

Bob looked at his wife and raised his eyebrows, but said, "Sure, lead on!"

They followed their guide past the queue, into the hall and down an aisle. The hall was filling rapidly from the front. In the centre of the front row were three seats each bearing a small notice saying *Reserved*. As they were led along the front row they received curious glances from the people already seated.

"Here you are," said their guide, removing the notices. She bent to smile at Arthur. "I can see you're very special. I hope you enjoy it." The Johnsons thanked her and she walked briskly away.

Arthur sat between his parents who leaned towards each other.

Jane chuckled as she smiled down at her son. "So, that pretty lady thinks you're special." Arthur giggled.

"I never expected this. Actually, I had no idea what to expect," said Bob. "But it's rather exciting, isn't it." He ruffled his son's hair and then looked around the large hall.

It looked like a theatre. There were no windows, lighting being provided by a row of lights along the bare concrete block walls. The rows of seats rose slightly from front to back. Bob did a rough estimate and decided that there were about fifteen hundred seats. The stage was low, large, lit by spotlights and bare except for three big screens, one across the back and one along each side, linking to form half a hexagon.

Five minutes before the session was due to begin, every seat was occupied and the room was full of a sense of anticipation. At exactly three-thirty all of the lights went out and the hall was suddenly dark and silent. After a few seconds all three screens were filled with an image, a stunningly beautiful scene of sunrise over the sea. The sky and the sea were shining silver except at the horizon where there were bands of pale pink and yellow. At the centre of the scene was the black shape of an island silhouetted against the sky.

Bob gasped. That shape was burned into his memory. They were watching sunrise behind the islet of Great Arthur in the Isles of Scilly. As they watched, the yellows and pinks became more intense. From all around the hall came the gentle sound of waves rolling onto a shingle beach and the water draining back to the sea through the countless millions of shifting pebbles.

Arthur dug an elbow into each of his parents. When they looked down at him they could see by the light from the screens that he was pointing at the front right hand corner of the stage. A figure had silently appeared. No spotlights were on and the only light was from the screens. The figure was standing just to the right of the end screen in a position reached by very little light.

On the screens the sun could now be seen extending beyond the outline of Great Arthur. To the sound of the waves the plaintive cry of a seabird was added.

The centre screen continued to show the sunrise, but the side screens changed. The left-hand screen began to show a representation of the water cycle following a drop of water as it evaporated from the surface of the sea; rose through the air to join billions of others to form a cloud; chilled in the cold air over mountains until droplets re-formed and fell to the land to form tiny streams that joined to form rivers that flowed back to the sea. The right-hand screen began to show the life-cycle of a flowering plant from seed through germination and growth and back to seed.

The background sound reduced in volume and a voice spoke.

"Friends. Friends. When you entered this hall you may have known no-one, but you will all leave as friends."

It was a wonderful voice: warm, rich, soothing, gentle. The same words came again.

"Friends. Friends. When you entered this hall you may have known no-one, but you will all leave as friends."

It was the sound of a perfectly tuned musical instrument. It rolled over them like a gentle massage capable of soothing all their senses. Bob felt as if he had been lifted from his seat and was floating in warm honey.

"There are more stars in the universe than pebbles upon all the beaches of the Earth. The stars have planets. Our planet is one of countless billions. Friends, how fortunate we are to live upon a planet that has nurtured mankind. Nurtured a life form so complex that we have the sensitivity to appreciate the beauty of our own planet, Earth.

"Friends, we are not gathered together to save the Earth. She does not need us to save her. She existed for many millions of years before mankind lived upon her surface and she will exist for millions of years after mankind has gone.

"We are here because we are friends – and friends need each other. Friends care for each other, and care about each other. We are gathered together because we must care for each other by caring for the Earth. By caring for the Earth we do not ensure her survival, but we prolong our own survival."

The voice broke off and after a few seconds of the gentle background noises of waves breaking, streams flowing and birdsong, everyone in the hall was jolted by the sudden change of the images on the screens and the noise assaulting their ears.

The noise was the roar of heavy traffic, of aeroplanes taking off, of the scream of chainsaws and of children crying. Each image was shown for only a few seconds. They showed close-ups of black smoke belching from exhaust pipes; pedestrians on city streets wearing face masks as they walked past luxury cars stationary in traffic jams; giant trees crashed to the ground; stores full of luxury goods; forests disappearing in flames; multiple car pile-ups on motorways; beaches strewn with rubbish; dolphins drowning in fishing nets; cities deep in flood water.

Bob looked down at Arthur to see his reaction to the noise and the images. His son had a big smile on his face and was happily waving at the figure standing at the corner of the stage. The figure was waving back. Now that his eyes were adjusted to the light Bob could make out more details. The man had long hair, a long beard and was wearing what looked like a dark-coloured monk's habit tied at the waist by a light-coloured cord.

The jarring noise and the disturbing images stopped. After ten seconds of darkness and silence the gentle background sounds of the sea resumed and the screens were filled with stunning images of underwater creatures, woodland glades full of bluebells, deserts blooming with flowers after rare rain and young children collecting shells on the beach.

The wonderful voice, at once calming and soothing, began again. Bob heard seemingly disconnected, but somehow appropriate, fragments of verse and prose. Sometimes the same fragment would be repeated over and over again, a mantra of balm to the soul.

The central screen continued to show scenes of the sea, but the side screens began to show an unfolding story. A pair of semi-detached houses appeared, the back garden of one appearing on the right screen and the other on the left. The gardens were bare areas of decking, patios, lawns with tiny flowerbeds around the edges and high fences separating the gardens from neighbouring plots. Each garden had an identical shed. The sounds of the sea faded away and there was silence for a while as cameras panned around the gardens. Two men appeared, one walking from each of the houses into the garden and both began ripping up the decking. Then the patios disappeared and the lawns were dug over. Fruit trees and fruit bushes appeared. Strawberries grew among rows of vegetables; raspberry canes grew against the sheds. The gardens were alive with insects and birds; almost imperceptibly the silence was replaced by birdsong and the humming of bees.

The cameras zoomed in onto the men. Each was standing on their side of the fence with a large tin of timber treatment and a brush. They put their tins down and stood on them so that they could see each other over the fence. In the next scene the fence had disappeared and both men were working side-by-side. Then one of the sheds vanished and was replaced by a greenhouse. Finally, the camera moved to an overhead shot and zoomed out. All of the fences had disappeared from the back gardens of the circle of houses leaving one large intensively cultivated plot. In the centre of it was a communal seating area with a barbecue.

The scenes faded out. All three screens returned to showing the same sunrise over Great Arthur. The voice began again the gentle mantras of verse, prose and song.

Then it said, "Friends, you are not alone. You will go from here and find yourself surrounded by friends who will care for you as you care for them. And in caring properly for each other, you will care for Earth. And she will continue to provide for you."

The voice finished with a few lines of a song in a language that Bob could not speak, although he had an instinctive feeling that he knew its meaning.

The sounds of the sea faded away, the screens grew dark and after twenty seconds of total darkness the theatre lights slowly came on. The figure on the stage had gone.

118

Bob raised his hands to clap, but then realised that no-one else was clapping.

He looked at Jane and mouthed, "Do we clap?"

She shrugged and they both looked around. No member of the audience was moving. Not only was there no clapping, but there was movement, no sound at all. Bob looked at his watch. They had been in the hall for an hour, although it felt like no more than a few minutes.

A door near the stage opened and the young woman who had guided them to their seats came to them. She looked in obvious bewilderment at the silent audience. The silence made her feel obliged to whisper.

"If you'll please come with me, I'll take you to your meeting."

At the door she paused, looked again at the audience, and whispered, "What's going on?"

There was a slight crackle from the sound system and the voice spoke again.

"Friends, go to your homes and enjoy living your lives as you know they should be lived."

Instantly the hall came back to life, filled with animated chatter and good-humoured banter.

Their guide led them down a corridor. She didn't speak again until they reached a door. She tapped on it and pushed the door open for them. "Here you are."

It was a large room, empty except for a table at the far end at which stood two figures both wearing long brown habits pulled in at the waist with white cords. One was clearly Myrddin; the other was a tall, thin woman with long grey hair. As they moved towards Myrddin, she turned away and left via another door walking slowly and painfully as if every joint was affected by arthritis.

"Ah, the Johnson family! How very good to see you once more!"

Myrddin's handshake was firm; his eyes were bright and his smile of welcome clearly genuine. He looked down at Arthur and his face positively radiated pleasure.

"Arthur, my boy. It has been far too long. You are looking well. And me, how do you think I am looking?"

Arthur looked puzzled for a moment, but then he smiled. "You are looking very fine."

"Indeed I am – for someone of my age, eh?" He roared with laughter and Arthur joined in.

Bob, at last face-to-face with Myrddin, found that so many questions were jumbled in his head that he didn't know where to start. He looked at Jane who was staring at Myrddin, also speechless.

Myrddin looked at them both and then asked, "And what did you think of my little talk?"

Bob found his voice. "It was…unusual – I doubt if the audience had seen anything like it before."

Myrddin chuckled. "Yes, unusual, it is certainly that."

"The audience…they reacted strangely. It affected them in a way that it didn't affect us. They seemed, well, hypnotised, for want of a better word."

"That is not such a bad word to choose. You were not affected because you didn't need to be. They need something to help them remember the task ahead; something buried deep inside them that guides their actions. You have no need of such assistance." He looked down at Arthur and chuckled again. "For you have this fine young man to raise – a very special young man."

He bent, lifted Arthur and sat him on the table.

"I have so many questions that I hardly know where to start?" Jane suddenly blurted out. "Where have you been since you left us? What have you been doing? Why did you leave us with the sword? Why did you want it back? What happened to The Droller and…?"

Myrddin raised both hands to stop the flow. "Enough, enough. And you, Robert Edgar Johnson, you are no doubt bursting with many questions of your own?"

"I certainly am! For a start, why did you get us all fired up about playing some important part in your 'war', as you called it, and then disappear, leaving us not knowing what we were supposed to do?"

Myrddin looked shocked. "But you know your role! You have been fulfilling it!"

He found Bob and Jane looking at him blankly.

"My war, even if it is eventually successful, will be a long struggle. It will last many years and when it is over, if we have won, the world will be a very different place. The people will need new, different leaders to show them the way ahead." He turned to face Arthur, placed a hand upon his shoulder and then looked back at Bob and Jane. "You have the most important task of all. You are providing the people with the leader they will desperately need."

He looked back to Arthur. "You must be five years old."

Arthur nodded.

"And I have no doubt that you can read and write." Arthur nodded again. "And I have no doubt that you are very keen to learn."

"He starts school in September," Jane said.

Myrddin continued looking at Arthur while he said, quietly but firmly, "Arthur does not need to go to school."

"But he has to…" Bob started.

"He will not go to school. Why should he? Lady Jane, are you not a fine teacher of young minds?" He didn't seem to expect an answer. "Between the three of us we will teach him all that he needs to know – and far more than any school could ever achieve."

"But he has to go! We have no choice." Bob was definite.

"No, he doesn't have to go. There are procedures for legally teaching a child at home. My Lady, I'm sure that you know of these matters. Indeed, I am equally sure that you must have considered this."

Jane nodded. She had a relieved and satisfied smile on her face.

"Hang on!" said Bob. "You said 'between the three of us'."

"Arthur and I must spend time together. I would like to join you in your home – not all of the time, as I have many commitments, but for as much time as we can contrive to be together."

The door opened and the woman in the brown habit came back in. She moved slowly and painfully to Myrddin's side. She avoided looking at Bob and Jane and Myrddin made no attempt to introduce her. She leaned close to him and whispered in his ear.

"Ah, yes, thank you. I had forgotten." Myrddin turned to Jane. "Forgive me, Lady, but I wish to ask some personal questions."

He didn't wait for any response from Jane, but carried straight on. "When Arthur was born you were not, how shall I phrase it, in the first flush of youth. A first child at that age can be difficult. How were you through your pregnancy?"

121

The woman with the grey hair kept her head down, but Bob could see that she was watching Jane intently from eyes set in a curiously smooth face.

Jane raised her eyebrows. "I was well – very well indeed. None of the problems that everyone warned me about happened. I felt thoroughly well – and very happy – throughout. Why?"

Myrddin ignored the question and asked another of his own. "And the birth itself, did that go well?"

"Yes, thanks, very well indeed. As if I was born to it. Why?"

He again ignored her question. "Who was present at the birth?"

"A doctor, a midwife, a nurse – and Bob. Why?"

"Did you not see anyone else? Please think back carefully. Did you see anyone else? Someone you did not expect to see?"

"No, er, well. There was something – I'd just about forgotten it. I didn't tell anyone; I thought I'd had a bit too much of the gas and air and was seeing things."

"Yes," said Myrddin, encouragingly, "what was it?"

"I saw, or at least I thought I saw, a small figure in a brown cloak. I thought I was dreaming about Carn or one of his friends."

"Yes!" The hissed word came from the woman who looked up and for the first time Bob saw her extraordinary face clearly. The eyes were dark and deep set about a strong nose. Her face was totally smooth, the skin giving the impression of being stretched tight over her skull.

She exchanged looks with Myrddin, who said, "He came! We thought he would!"

Then she turned and made her painful way back out of the door.

"As I was saying, the three of us can…"

Bob interrupted. "Hang on! Let's get one thing absolutely straight. If, *if*, we agree to having you stay with us, there'll be no more of your little mysteries. We want straight answers to our questions – and if we don't understand, you'll have to find a way to make us understand. Right?"

Myrddin nodded gravely. "We will have all the time you need to receive the best answers I can give to your questions; all the ones you have now and any that you will have in the future."

"Good – so we can start now. What was all that stuff about Jane's pregnancy and Arthur's birth?"

122

"I will answer this one question now, but then I must take leave of you. I have another little talk to give in Birmingham this evening.

"The little figure that Jane saw was not a dream, neither was it one of your tiny Gododdin friends. It was Bes, worshipped by the Egyptians, among others, as the protector of pregnant women. We hoped that he would be aware of such an important event." As he said that, he poked Arthur in the ribs.

Arthur started to giggle, but then he remembered something and struggled to get his hand into a pocket of his shorts. After squirming about for a few seconds he pulled something from his pocket and offered it to Myrddin. "I brought you a present," he said.

Myrddin reached out and took the offered gift. He held it out and let the ancient strip of leather unfurl. Bob recognised it as the leather that Arthur had unwound from the hilt of The Sword of Power.

"Well, well," said Myrddin. "Thank you. I saw, of course, that it had been removed from the sword. When did you do it?"

"Not long ago. It was when I knew I'd be seeing you."

"Excellent! It is a fine gift. I will keep it safe. The sword is being returned to you. Joe has it in his car. You will find Joe waiting for you in the car park.

"And now I must go." He lifted Arthur from the table and hugged him briefly before lowering him to the floor. Then he gave a small formal bow in the direction of Bob and Jane and strode from the room.

Bob leaned against the table and scratched his head vigorously with both hands.

"What…?" he hesitated and tried again. "How…?" He gave up. He had so many confusing thoughts spinning in his head that he couldn't pull them into any sort of order. He shrugged helplessly at Jane and sighed.

"He's coming to live with us," said Arthur. "That'll be fun! Come on!" he reached up to take both of his parents by the hand and tugged them towards the door. "Let's go and see Joe. He's got my sword."

They allowed themselves to be led out of the room, out of the building and across the car park. They found Joe's car parked next to the motor home with Joe in the driver's seat fast asleep.

Jane tapped on the window and Joe slowly roused himself, got out and stretched his long frame.

"Prynhawn da, lovely people. Although what's good about it, I'd be hard pushed to say." A gust of wind swirled the drizzle about them and Joe zipped up his jacket. "Tell me, young Arthur, did some strange magic make me sleep till winter? I'm sure it was supposed to be summer when I fell asleep see, and this doesn't feel like summer to me, indeed it does not."

Arthur answered him seriously. "This is summer, Mr Morgan. Summer is like this."

Joe thought about that. "Well now, let me see. You are a fine big fellow of five, are you not?" Arthur nodded. "So, I expect you remember something of the last three summers. Hm…you're right! The last three summers *have* been like this." He turned up the collar on his jacket. "Best get you out of this weather. I have something of yours that I believe you would like back."

He opened the boot. One of the rear seats had been folded forward to take the length of the sword that lay wrapped in the old blanket that Jane had used when Joe had collected it. Jane opened the door of the motor home.

Joe looked a bit sheepish as he turned to Bob. "Perhaps you would like to help yourself. I seem to remember that you find it easier to lift."

Bob reached in and found the hilt through the blanket. He felt the familiar tingle through his arm and, after a moment's hesitation, with one hand he easily pulled the sword from Joe's car and then carefully carried it in his arms to slide it onto the floor of the motor home.

"It's relieved, I am, to see that go," said Joe. "I've been driving around terrified in case I was stopped by the police for any reason. How would I explain what it was or what I was doing with it?"

"Joe," Jane began, "what…?"

Joe interrupted her with a shake of his head. "Sorry, Jane. You know what it's like. If he didn't tell you something, the chances are that I'm not going to be able to. Have a safe trip home. It's scarcely stopped raining while you've been away. You'll find that the Somerset Levels are one huge lake." With that Joe got back into the car and drove silently away.

*

Back in Chagford, with the sword restored to its place on the chimneybreast and Arthur in bed, Bob and Jane were sitting at the kitchen table, mugs of coffee in front of them.

"So, what did you think of his talk?" Bob asked.

"It was very well put together. Top quality images, a very effective soundtrack, and his voice, well, it's simply amazing. You feel that you just want to go on hearing him talking to you. And it's an interesting slant – forget about saving the planet, instead concentrate the message on how to save the human race by being less selfishly focussed on ourselves and caring more about others. Very interesting.

"What was really weird was the effect on the audience. Fifteen hundred people absolutely mesmerised. I'd love to get together with some of them in a month's time and ask them what they remember of it and whether they've changed in any way because of it."

Bob nodded and after a gulp of coffee he asked, "Did you notice that the audience never really saw him? Not before, not after, not during. No one introduced him, no one to round it off and invite applause, no opportunity to ask questions. I was wondering why he needed to be there at all. It was obviously all scripted. Why not just record his voice, too?"

"Hmm…well, it's obvious why there was no chance to ask questions. Can you imagine it? What's your name? Where are you from? What's your background? As for his having to be there, there's clearly something psychological going on. Remember what Joe said about the mind control that Myrddin has? Maybe he has to be there to exercise it. Everyone in the room, except us, seemed to be under some sort of, well, spell. I was trying not to use that word, but it does seem appropriate for someone who thinks he's the re-incarnation of Merlin."

Bob shook his head. "No, he doesn't – he thinks he's the real, original Merlin, or Myrddin, who's just been through the odd form change. But his *spell* has the feel of mass hypnosis."

There was a pause while they both drained their coffee mugs.

"And what do we believe? There's all this strange stuff with Arthur – well before he was born we *knew* he was going to be a boy, without any test to prove it, and we both just *knew* that he had to be called Arthur. No other name was mentioned – there was never any doubt was there?"

Jane had to agree. "You're right. But when I sit down and try to think about all this in a rational way, the twenty-first century part of me just refuses to believe. If I don't try to analyse it, it feels comfortable. It's...*nice* to feel that there's someone around, with powers that we can't understand, who's going to pat us on the head and say don't worry, everything will be all right."

"Hmm," Bob didn't sound convinced. "You didn't raise any objections when he said Arthur shouldn't go to school."

"No. To be honest, I was delighted to hear someone else say it. I've been dreading him starting – missing out on all the time with him, watching him grow up. We waited so long for him, I don't want to hand him over to someone else to mould him. But I thought that might just have been me being selfish."

Bob stood, moved behind Jane and kissed the back of her neck. "Come on, let's go and sit somewhere comfortable."

They went through to the lounge. Jane waited until Bob sat on the settee and then sat next to him, in the same movement swinging her legs up to put her feet in his lap. Out of long habit he immediately started to give them a gentle massage.

Jane chuckled. "You realise he's done it to us again, don't you?"

"Done what?"

"Disappeared without answering any questions, leaving us not knowing what's going on. I've got to phone Eppie with a report on our meeting. All I can tell her is that he says he's coming to live with us and that we'll find out everything then."

"He did tell us one thing. It seems that our role in his war is to raise Arthur. I think I can cope with that. At one stage I had visions of charging about with that great sword lopping the heads of environmental villains."

"Are you sure you're up to it? We always knew he was special, but now we're told we're rearing a future world leader. He'll need to know more than the name of every insect crawling over Dartmoor."

"Very funny. I can also teach him that his mother can't bear to have her feet tickled." He grabbed one of Jane's ankles and tickled the sole of her foot while she laughed, screamed and lashed out with the other foot to try to break free. "And as a fully qualified chartered accountant, I can also show him how to fill in his tax return."

Bob let go of Jane's ankle as a new thought struck him.

126

"Tax returns; national insurance; all the rigmarole of officialdom – how has Myrddin been coping with all that? If the tale we heard from The Droller is true..."

Jane interrupted with a chuckle, "Don't tell me you still don't believe that Myrddin spent fifteen hundred years in a lead box."

"I had trouble with that bit when we first met him and he looked like a walking skeleton; now he looks so fit and full of life I just can't make him fit with that tale. Anyway, what I was saying was that if he's someone who officially doesn't exist, he can't do what he's doing without catching the eye of a bureaucrat somewhere."

CHAPTER 13

Sligo makes progress

Nigel Sligo, being of a generally miserable and malevolent nature, would never have admitted to being happy, but there were times when he felt a certain contentment with life. Those times usually meant trouble for someone else.

He had arrived in Princetown with only one objective in mind: he needed somewhere to hide away while his painful injuries healed. That somewhere had to be where no-one knew him, and where no-one would dream of looking for him, so that there would be no more unwelcome visitors to his door seeking retribution. So far, the plan was working. He had been very selective about answering calls to his mobile phone and had read, then deleted, all text messages. His battered face was no longer swollen and the bruising had faded to the extent that he was only left with a yellow tinge that made him look like a case of jaundice.

His initial impressions of Princetown had not been favourable, but his doubts about how he could possibly spend any length of time there without going mad had been dispelled. He was easily filling his time. Sligo had developed a routine. After his first two cigarettes and cup of coffee of the day, he strolled to the village shop for the morning papers. He varied his choice, but it was always one broadsheet, two tabloids and the local daily. He started reading them in one of the cafés until the need of a cigarette drove him to his car and he would either drive out onto the moor to park or sit in his car at a spot in Princetown where he had discovered an unprotected broadband connection that allowed him internet access via his laptop. He read through the papers with a pair of scissors to hand and cut out any articles that caught his eye. He looked for court cases, events and people where his own talents could discover an unsavoury element – an element that could be exaggerated and exploited to become a marketable commodity.

Most lunchtimes he spent in a pub and in the afternoons he gave some time to the pursuit of information on the Johnson family. He had investigated the firm of accountants that Bob had left in order to become a Dartmoor Ranger but, although it had cost him some expensive rounds of drinks at a wine bar in Exeter, and hard though he tried, he could detect no hint of anything in Bob's accountancy background, or in his reasons for leaving the firm, that suggested anything untoward. The lack of facts, of course, did not deter Sligo in the slightest. In his book, anyone who would give up a well-paid profession in order to dress up in a uniform and wander about the bleak wasteland of Dartmoor just had to be weird – and weirdness in itself could be built into a saleable story.

He had tracked down the school at which Jane had taught, but neither staff nor parents had come up with any trace of useful gossip.

On the face of it, to Sligo the Johnsons were a boring couple who looked an unlikely source of the material that was his stock in trade. But he *knew* that there was profit in them somewhere – his nose, trained by years of sniffing out dirt, told him so.

He was used to operating in the anonymous city where it was easy keep a watch on his targets, but in the country it was more difficult. It was impossible to park his car anywhere with a view of the Johnson house without being glaringly conspicuous, thanks to the narrow lane. With the help of a map he had spotted a public footpath that, with a decent pair of binoculars, gave a good view of the back of the house and the garden. He got a few soakings, and ruined a pair of trainers, for no reward. All he confirmed was that it was a big house for just a couple and one child. With only one modest salary coming in and a large, old house to maintain, Sligo thought of the money angle. Was there family money in the background? Could this be another case of a would-be politician telling everyone how they should live their lives, whilst enjoying the easy life, having been born with a silver spoon in her mouth?

On one occasion he spotted through his binoculars the Johnson woman shutting doors and windows and then walking off towards Chagford, where he had left his car. He followed her to the village and watched as she moved from shop to shop. It was easy to do – Chagford was so small that he could see most of the village from the square. She had her brat with her and he caught the brat giving him a funny look, but he ignored it. He saw her pause outside the post office and search through her handbag for some paperwork. When she went into the shop he followed and stood behind her in the queue. Sligo knew the brat was staring up at him.

She paid a couple of bills and chatted briefly at the counter. By the time that Sligo was being served with a postage stamp he had heard that the brat was not going to start school, but was to be taught at home, and he knew the name of the bank on her cheques.

Sligo paid well for information. He paid generously and he paid reliably. Over the years he had developed a range of contacts not averse to receiving sizeable cash sums. It cost him the promise of a three-hundred pounds payment, but within forty-eight hours he knew that the Johnsons had no source of income into their joint account, other than one salary, and that as far as that bank was concerned they held no significant investments, but had no debts.

One morning in Princetown, he was sitting in the Old Police Station Café with the papers unread on the table in front of him. On top of the papers lay his notebook opened at a page covered in his own personal form of shorthand. It was a summary of what he had learned about the Johnsons – and it didn't amount to much. There was no hint of scandal, financial or otherwise. At a glance, all he had set out on the page was the picture of a boring couple, living in a big old house, who had had one child fairly late in life and who were living a dull routine existence, except that they were not going to send the child to school – but as the mother was a qualified, and apparently highly-regarded, teacher there was nothing too surprising in that.

So what was it, Sligo asked himself, that was telling him that there was a story here? He underlined four points on his pad. The Johnsons seemed to have a connection with HRH The Duke of Cornwall; there had been 'incidents' that may, or may not, have involved some mysterious 'little people' and Bob Johnson had showed an interest in those incidents; a character known as Trader Joe, after years of regularly visiting the area had disappeared at about the same time as the 'incidents' had stopped; from that same time the Johnsons had developed a taste for holidaying in Scotland.

He stared at the list: what was it that was making his nose twitch?

Trader Joe? He had made some enquiries about Trader Joe and identified him as a Joe Morgan who had a police record for handling stolen goods. Didn't sound the most reliable of characters; the remarkable thing was not so much that he had disappeared, but that he had turned up regularly for years.

'Little people'? He had let it be known that he was a writer researching local folklore for a new book and this gave him cover for his questions about 'little people'. Following Ethel Clay's leads he had talked to various people in the area about fruit and vegetables being taken from gardens but, not surprisingly, most were reluctant to admit to any suspicions other than that the culprits had been rabbits or mischievous children.

He became aware of someone waving at him through the window. He groaned as Ethel Clay failed to take the hint of his curt nod, came into the café, put her shopping on the bench seat opposite and slid in to face him. He spoke through gritted teeth.

"Morning, Ethel. Cup of tea?"

"Proper job. What on earth you writing there, boy? Don't look like English."

"It's shorthand, Ethel. Just making some notes for the book."

"And that's just why I popped in. Something came to mind last night that you'll want to know."

"Biscuit with that tea?"

"Wouldn't say no. Although a bit of cake would be a treat."

Once Mrs Clay was settled with tea and cake in front of her, Sligo attempted to steer her conversation away from the state of her knees and the effect of the weather upon them.

"So, what have you remembered that I'll want to know?"

"Eh? Oh yes, well now, it's something as I heard about, oh, maybe five or six years ago. I heard the tale from a neighbour who worked in the Visitor Centre. Some old gentleman got lost on the moor – up in the Fox Tor mires it was – and he reckoned that one of the little people saved his life. Can't remember his name – not sure that I ever knew it – but Ranger Bob Johnson made sure he got home all right afterwards, so you can ask him."

Sligo had no intention of asking Bob Johnson, but as soon as he could get away he went to the Visitor Centre and struck lucky. One of the staff on duty had attended the school where

George Phillips had been head teacher and she remembered the incident well.

He had no trouble tracing George Phillips' house in Ashburton. The old boy was initially very abrupt and inclined to shut the door in his face, but when Sligo quickly said that he was writing a book about strange happenings on Dartmoor and that George's story was one of a number of similar occurrences that he was investigating, after a brief hesitation, Mr Phillips let him in.

The next day Sligo was back in the Visitor Centre appealing for information on any other such happenings, real or imagined. He was about to leave the centre when the phone rang and a member of staff answered it; he had reached the door when he heard her call out.

"Does anybody know if today's Fox Tor walk is still on? Brian's off ill, isn't he? Has it been cancelled or have we found another leader?"

He had the door open when a different voice said, "It's still on. Bob Johnson's leading it."

Sligo turned back to the counter.

*

Bob had made a busy start to the day. He'd had a full day planned before he took the early morning phone call about the walk and he'd had to do some last minute re-scheduling. It was close to the ten-thirty start time when he parked his Land Rover and hurried around to the front of the High Moorland Visitor Centre. During the drive there he had been telling himself that the chances were that no-one would turn up; the supposedly summer weather had been dreadful and the terrain around Fox Tor was notoriously tricky.

He smiled when he saw at least six walkers gathered on the steps. As he wished them, "Good morning," the door opened and three or four more came out to join the group.

He cast his eyes over them. They were all suitably dressed. Proper walking boots, some with gaiters, layers of clothing and rucksacks that suggested plenty of additional waterproofs and refreshments. Nevertheless, he issued his usual health and safety announcement and received assurances that everyone did indeed have clothing adequate for whatever weather Dartmoor had in store for them. As he spoke another figure came out of the centre and stood at the back of the group.

132

Most of the walkers had Ordnance Survey maps hanging around their necks in clear, plastic map-holders. To make sure that they would be able to follow the route Bob gave them a brief summary of the planned walk.

"We'll start off along the lane over there, marked in yellow on your maps, until just before it turns sharp left before it reaches Whiteworks. We'll leave the lane there and head for Siward's Cross on the green route known as the Abbot's Way. From there we head south-west towards Crane Hill; then we head south-east to cross the Plym at Plym Ford. At this time of year it should be no more than an inch or two deep, but we're likely to find it much deeper than that. If it's too deep to walk across we'll stay this side and follow the Plym to Plym Head. It would be easier on the other side, and certainly less boggy, but we'll manage. From Plym Head we'll go to find the letterbox at Duck's Pool. Can't guarantee any ducks, but there definitely will be water in it. Then we have to change our usual route for this walk. Normally, we head south back onto the Abbot's Way and head east to join the Two Moors Way, but if you check your maps you'll see that that would mean crossing five fords in the next two miles. That just wouldn't be sensible, so instead we'll head north over Crane Hill, head back to Siward's Cross and then head westwards along the green route that follows the Devonport Leat. We'll follow the leat all the way to where it meets the River Meavy and then follow the Meavy upstream to where the B3212 crosses it at Devil's Bridge. O.K? Sorry about the changes, but it can't be helped. At least it's not raining on us – yet."

They moved away from the centre heading to cross the road near the mini-roundabout. As the group broke up Bob got his first clear look at the late arrival. He was wearing a lightweight top, jeans and trainers and carried nothing except for an umbrella.

"Excuse me, sir," Bob called, "were you thinking of joining us on the walk?"

"Yeah, why not?"

Bob recognised the face of the man he'd first met when Bob had towed his car back onto solid ground. He'd seen the battered face around Princetown on a couple of occasions since. The injuries seemed to be improving, but not his manner.

"I'm sorry, but there's no way you can join us today – your clothing isn't suitable. It would be too dangerous to set out across the moor in trainers at any time, but particularly with the moor in its present state. And if it rains those jeans really aren't what's needed."

The man didn't seem at all put out, but neither did he show any sign of breaking off from the group.

They crossed the road and started up the lane. Bob tried again. "Excuse me! Did you hear what I said? You're not properly equipped to join us on this walk."

The man shrugged. "No problem. I'll just tag along until you leave this tarmac road and then I'll turn back."

Bob hesitated. There was something about this character that was very unappealing, but it was a public road and Bob could hardly order him off it.

*

Pompous prig, thought Sligo. *I don't know what you've been up to yet, but I'm gonna enjoy seeing your face splashed all over the tabloids.*

As they walked, the conversation in the group was mainly about the weather. Sligo looked them over. They were all wearing their fancy dress and a couple of them had produced long walking poles. *Where do they think they are? You old fools! This is Devon not the Antarctic!*

Most of them knew Johnson by name and were asking him pathetic questions. *Sickening bunch of teacher's pets.* They had all heard the exchange between him and Johnson and were studiously ignoring Sligo who cleared his throat and spat noisily, enjoying the reaction it provoked. He quickened his pace, manoeuvred alongside the Ranger and asked his first question.

"Is it right that most of the moor is owned by Royals?"

"All of Dartmoor is in private ownership and the Duchy of Cornwall is the biggest landowner."

"So, HRH is a regular visitor is he?"

"Yes."

"Have you met him? What's he like?"

"Yes, I've met him. He's a decent man and a decent landlord who is very interested in the problems of upland farmers."

"How many times have you met him?"

Sligo was an astute observer of people. Johnson was getting a bit edgy and hesitated before replying."

"Well, we're not on first name terms."

Sligo dropped back.

A little further on the Ranger stopped the group to point out the route of the Devonport Leat and to give a little of the two-hundred year history of the water-course built as the source of water for the developing Devonport dockyard.

Before they moved on, Sligo stood directly in front of the Ranger and asked, "Will we see any of the little people today?"

There were some sniggers from those grouped around, but the Ranger didn't laugh; he just turned away and walked on. Sligo had seen the tiny muscle reactions in the Ranger's face. He had seen enough. He turned back towards Princetown.

Back in the rented cottage he sat with his notepad on his knee. He didn't buy any of this pixie rubbish. For Sligo 'little people' meant children. There was something unsavoury going on here involving an ex-accountant, his would-be politician wife and a member of the Royal Family. This story could be bigger than he'd thought. Much bigger.

Sligo allowed himself a rare smile.

*

Bob was glad when the walk was over. The encounter with that unpleasant individual had unsettled him. On returning to Princetown he made a few enquiries; it seemed that everyone he spoke to had come into contact with the man who introduced himself as Nigel and said that he was a writer involved in researching a book. He quickly identified the cottage where Nigel was staying. A friendly contact in the Duchy office phoned the letting agent and obtained a surname, Sligo, and the added information that he'd booked the cottage for two months, but had said that he might stay longer.

Back home that evening Bob recounted his experience to Jane, who recognised the description.

"I've seen him in Chagford a few times in the last few weeks – could hardly miss him with the face he had."

"He's told anyone that asked that he fell down some stairs. Apart from his appearance, there's something really unpleasant about him."

"I remember now! He was behind us in the post office. Arthur said afterwards that he didn't like the man – and that's a very unusual reaction from Arthur."

"All I know about him is his name and he says he's a writer. Whatever he is I get the distinct impression that he's onto the Dini."

"Contact HRH. Better warn him."

"Just what I was thinking."

Bob made a phone call, but HRH was out of the country. He spoke to an aide that had had contact with Bob before. He, no doubt, didn't know the full story, but he knew that any request for help from Bob should not be ignored.

The aide phoned back a few minutes later. Bob hung up the phone and turned to Jane with a troubled look.

"Sligo is a freelance journalist who specialises in muck-raking. Apparently he pays well for information and then grossly distorts it to create a story he can sell to the tabloids."

"So, what can we do about him?"

"Nothing."

*

"TRISH!!!"

Patricia Jakes picked up the notepad, diary and pen and walked through the inter-connecting door into Ronald Smith's office. A chair hurled across the room had made a hole in the partition wall off which it had bounced and another wall featured a large purple stain where the port decanter had shattered. Port was still running down the wall onto the very expensive carpet.

Big Ron was sat behind his desk clutching a cut-glass tumbler that held the best part of half-a-pint of port. The colour of his face matched the drink in his glass. He didn't look up as he spoke.

"Well?"

She consulted her notes. "They did everything in the plan. They've implemented the cookery courses with celebrity chefs; held literary weekends with big-name authors; staged Murder Mystery events with top actors; had wildlife weekends with TV celebrities, made savings on the catering and property maintenance to the extent that complaints are rising rapidly. But, the problem is the same: why should people pay the premium rates to stay in hotels with golf courses, tennis courts and acres of immaculate gardens if the golf courses are often unplayable, the tennis courts are under water and the weather's so bad that a stroll around the gardens is not an attractive proposition?

"They can't charge enough for the indoor events to cover the cost of maintaining all the outside facilities. They looked like people resigned to losing their jobs. If they've got any sense they're looking for other employment."

"Yeah. Lucky them. They cut and run; I'm stuck with a chain of hotels costing me a packet."

She watched in quiet fascination as his grip on the glass tightened. As his knuckles turned white she waited to see if the glass would shatter. He was staring, without seeing, at the top of the desk. With his head down his several chins covered his shirt collar and she couldn't see the knot of his tie.

"I'm going home. I need to kill something."

After Big Ron had left, Patricia took the lift to the basement. She walked to the door bearing the impressive-sounding title 'Surveyor of the Fabric' and walked in without knocking.

A man in his fifties was sitting at a small desk that was covered in plans. He was holding a telephone to his right ear with one hand; his left elbow was on the desk and he was resting his head on his left hand. His eyes were closed. He looked a tired, harassed man. He didn't hear Patricia until she closed the door behind her.

When he saw who it was, he said, "I'll call you back," and hung up the phone. He stood up and adjusted the tie that had been hanging loose around his neck.

"Yes, Miss Jakes, what can I do for your?"

"The usual, Graham. One wall needs repairing; another wall is covered in port; there's glass all over the place and the carpet is a mess."

He sighed.

"Is there a difficulty, Graham?"

"That was one of our suppliers on the phone – we're very late settling their account."

"There are a lot of suppliers in London, Graham." The steely eyes glinted at him. "Get it done.

"And while you're at it, my room needs redecorating. There's coffee all over the walls."

"Oh, really? He doesn't usually throw stuff about in your room."

"No, he doesn't – and he hasn't. You won't actually see any coffee stains there – but I can put them there if you insist." She stared at him, raising one eyebrow.

"That won't be necessary."

"Good. It would have been a waste of good coffee. I want the walls pale pink this time." She showed him the colour chart she was holding. "That colour, in fact." She pointed at the shade she had circled.

"Yes, Miss Jakes."

Patricia walked back to the lift. She didn't like the way that things were going. There'd been tough times before, but nothing like this. It was time to take care of her own situation. She had seen a series of paintings by a promising young artist. They would look best hung against a pink background.

CHAPTER 14

Some questions answered

Sligo parked in Chagford and walked back out of the village towards the Johnson house. It was impossible to conceal himself as he walked along the narrow lane. He knew that his questions had rattled the Ranger and if either of the Johnsons drove by and saw him he reasoned that it would do no harm to shake them up a bit more; it might even spook them into some sort of panic reaction.

He left the lane and joined the public footpath that ran high across the back of the house. The path was muddy and his old trainers gave little grip. He slipped and slithered his way up the hill and was breathing heavily by the time he reached the spot he had found that gave him a clear view. He took a newspaper from his pocket and put it on the ground to give himself something dry to sit on and leaned back against a tree. Through his binoculars he could see the patio doors standing open. Sligo detected some movement and focussed on the vegetable patch where Johnson and his brat seemed to be planting something.

He swung back to the house as the wife came out with a tray of drinks. Her voice carried to him on the wind as she called the others to join her at the table.

Sligo lit a cigarette. As long as it didn't rain he would stay for most of the afternoon; he enjoyed spying on people. The Johnsons were still sat chatting at the table when he thought he heard the sound of a car moving onto their gravel drive, followed by the sound of two car doors closing. He watched as the wife went into the house. He thought he heard her call out and he watched the other two follow her into the house.

A few minutes later he heard a car door slam. He didn't hear any engine start, but he again heard the sound of a car being driven over the gravel.

The Johnsons returned to the back garden. Sligo sat bolt upright. He gave a near-silent whistle of pleasure. They were accompanied by the figure of an old man with long hair, a long beard and wearing a brown monk's habit. He pulled his camera from under his jacket and zoomed in. *This just keeps getting better and better*, he congratulated himself, *now we've got some sort of religious nutter added to the mix*. Mentally, he was rubbing his hands together, looking forward to the biggest payout he'd ever seen.

Suddenly Sligo was aware of someone coming down the path towards him. An old Staffordshire bull terrier was wheezing along the path closely followed by an old woman with white hair. Sligo went back to taking pictures, determined to ignore the intruders, but the old lady wasn't going to be ignored.

"Good afternoon. And what are you up to?"

"None of your business."

"My good man, in the country when we see strangers snooping around, we make it our business to know what they're doing."

Sligo put down the camera and gave the woman a contemptuous look. The dog moved between them. From deep within him a menacing growl rumbled and his top lip curled back to reveal an impressive set of teeth. Sligo was duly impressed and became more conciliatory. He held up his binoculars.

"Just doing a bit of birdwatching. Satisfied?"

"Possibly."

Sligo turned away from her and heard her start to walk on down the path. "Nosey old cow," he muttered. She may have been old, but there was nothing wrong with her hearing. She stopped and turned back towards him. The dog growled again, louder this time, and took some steps towards him.

"Good manners cost nothing, young man, but I suspect that it's too late for you to learn any. Come along, Winston – he's not worth one of your bites."

They started on down the path again and Sligo returned to his spying activities. He picked up the group on the patio, but found that the newly-arrived old man had moved a little away from the others. He concentrated on the old man and focussed his binoculars on the face. Suddenly, the striking face appeared to leap into focus at many times the size that Sligo was expecting and he had the feeling that he was staring straight into those deep-set eyes.

Sligo felt a sensation of discomfort. Just a slightly curious feeling in his head, but it rapidly increased until it felt as if his head was being squeezed in a vice. He staggered to his feet clutching his head in both hands and stumbled down the track, groaning as his head felt a terrible crushing pain.

As Sligo lurched towards the old woman, Winston sank his teeth into his calf and was dragged for fifty yards before the dog decided to release his hold. The pain in his head gradually subsided as he neared Chagford, but as that pain lessened the pain from his calf got worse. White as a sheet and soaked in sweat, Sligo limped into the pharmacy seeking treatment.

*

Jane was in the kitchen making a drink for Myrddin when she heard something on the radio that caught her attention. She went to the lounge and turned on the television selecting the news channel. She called the others in from the garden.

On the screen were pictures of a devastating earthquake in the Far East.

"I am surprised," said Myrddin, "I thought it would be San Francisco next."

When Bob and Jane looked at him quizzically, all he offered by way of explanation was, "The Great Goddess Anu is angry. Her patience is nearly exhausted. She sends floods, hurricanes, and shakes the Earth, but still mankind will not listen."

Bob raised his eyebrows at Jane. "I notice you didn't mention the Great Goddess Anu, or any other goddesses for that matter, in your presentation."

Myrddin gave a grim smile, his eyes not leaving the dreadful scenes appearing on the screen. "No, I did not. It would be foolish, would it not, to tell people something that they simply would not understand? What they hear from me are basic, self-evident truths; there is nothing that they are fundamentally unable to accept."

"But you tell us these things."

"You have seen enough to know that there are powers of which you were previously unaware."

Seeing Bob about to speak again, Jane said. "Hang on; I was getting Myrddin a drink. Let me get it and then we can talk."

141

When she got back from the kitchen she found the television turned off and Myrddin, Bob and Arthur all sitting staring up at the great sword. She joined Bob and Arthur on the settee.

"Right," said Bob, "well, we're pleased, not to say relieved, that you are here with us again. You said that once you joined us you would answer our questions. I know you've only just got here, but can we make a start?"

Myrddin smiled and nodded. "Ask your questions, Robert Edgar J…"

Bob interrupted him. "Just plain Bob has always been good enough for me – and it still is."

"If that's the name that you and the good lady Jane are happy with then so…"

"And Jane is happy with plain Jane."

"Ah, but Jane could never be plain I…"

"Look, you old rascal, stop flirting with my wife and let's get on."

Jane and Myrddin both laughed.

"Flirting," said Myrddin, "is a fine word that I have not previously had the occasion to use." He repeated the word a few times, savouring the feel of it. Then he saw the expression on Bob's face and held up a hand. "Forgive me. Bob and Jane, ask your questions."

"First," said Jane, "are you happy for Arthur to be here listening to this?"

"But of course." Myrddin smiled at Arthur and then looked from Jane to Bob. "Please do not be offended if I say that Arthur may well understand better than you do. His mind still has the flexibility of youth. He will not seek to analyse as you will; he will instinctively understand. Your analysis means that you will judge everything by your experiences of life. Those experiences mean that you have created your own rules; anything that appears to break those rules you find hard to accept. If all your questions are as simple, we will soon be done."

"Can we start at the beginning, or at least, at the beginning as far as we are concerned? I first met you in Trader Joe's van and I brought you, Joe and four of the Dini – Gododdin as you insisted we call them – back here. The Droller then told us the history of their people and described how they'd found you in a lead casket and restored you to life. Was that true? How could it be true?"

142

Myrddin looked at Bob for a few seconds before replying. "That is an example of why I warned you of your rules. Arthur would have no trouble believing, but you find it hard because you have rules based upon your own limited knowledge of the Earth." He got to his feet and walked out of the room.

Jane looked at Bob in concern, "Have we upset him already? Where's he going?"

They could hear Myrddin rattling crockery in the kitchen and then Arthur cried, "Look! He's in the garden!"

Bob stood up and looked out of the window. "He's gone into the shed. Whatever is he up to?"

A few seconds later Myrddin tapped on the glass and beckoned to them to go outside.

They found him at the patio table. He had placed a large, white dinner plate in the centre of the table.

"It is a pity to be inside on a rare dry afternoon," he said. "Please, be seated."

Bob and Jane sat down and Bob lifted Arthur up onto his lap.

Myrddin put on the table a packet of seeds he had found in the shed.

"We planted some of those yesterday, didn't we, Daddy? What are they called?"

"Proper name, *chaenorrhinum* – it's a sort of snapdragon."

Myrddin wet the end of his little finger and poked it into the packet. He examined what he'd extracted and seemed to carefully transfer something to the centre of the white plate. "Look," he said.

Bob and Jane looked, but could see nothing. They stood up; Arthur scrambled onto the table and crawled towards the plate tugging from his pocket his magnifying glass. When he leaned close to the plate, Bob could make out a tiny speck.

"Is that a single seed? Although we were sprinkling some onto seed trays I never really noticed how incredibly small they are."

Myrddin held up the packet of seeds so that they could see the picture of the striking blue flowers.

"Inside that speck of dust lies the Spirit of Life. It may lie sleeping for many years, but all it needs is a little water and warmth and the Spirit of Life, guided by the genetic make-up of the plant cells in which it finds itself, will cause this speck of dust to multiply and flourish until this beautiful flower emerges. And yet the flower is not the final objective. The Spirit of Life will drive that flower to produce a thousand specks of dust such as this.

"The Great Goddess Anu nurtures the Spirit of Life. She links the many strands of life on Earth: the bees that pollinate the flowers; the birds that spread the seed; the earthworms that eat the decaying plant and maintain the soil for future generations of plants.

"Within the specks of dust that lay in the bottom of the lead casket, the spirit of my own life waited. The Droller and his friends provided all that I needed to flourish into the fine figure you see before you." Myrddin roared with laughter and clapped Bob heartily on the back. "Jane, I have I confession to make. The tea that you made for me lies cold and untouched."

"I'll put the kettle on," said Bob, "I could do with a moment or two. Arthur, hot or cold drink?"

Bob returned after a few minutes with a tray of drinks and a plate of biscuits. He found Jane and Myrddin discussing the Dini.

"I asked Myrddin whether The Droller's Tale about their getting smaller because of a witch's spell could possibly be true."

"And in return I pointed out that I couldn't possibly know. When they rode with Artos they were as big and strong as any men alive. I was caught in a simple trap with no witchcraft involved. Fifteen hundred years later I found myself confronted by a tribe of tiny people. The Droller's Tale may well be true – it was certainly true in other aspects. But here your own rules can explain their position. Now you would not look for witchcraft, you would look for a genetic defect, its effect exaggerated by inbreeding."

Bob drank his tea and settled on his next question.

"Why did you disappear for so long without getting in touch with us?"

Myrddin shrugged. "I had a great deal to learn and a great deal to do. You didn't need me in your lives. You had Arthur to raise. And I knew that The Sword of Power would support you when you needed it."

"Where have you been for all these years?" asked Jane. "It's been a long time."

Myrddin didn't answer for so long that Jane was about to repeat the question when he finally spoke.

"I hardly knew you. My reading of your minds satisfied me that this was the family that Arthur should be born into, but I really didn't know how you would cope with having me around. I doubted if you could provide the secrecy I needed for what I had to do. If I wasn't here you could behave like a normal couple."

"So, where have you been?"

"Do you remember taking me to Axmouth and meeting me later in Lyme Regis?"

Bob and Jane both nodded and Bob said, "I also remember that you took a small spade and you were pretty muddy when we met you."

Myrddin chuckled. "I hadn't worked that hard in a very long time." He pointed a long bony finger. "You will enjoy this part, Arthur. I knew of the location of a hidden hoard of treasure."

"Treasure! How exciting!" Arthur's eyes lit up. "What is it? Where is it? Can we go and see it?"

"All in good time. It was a collection of Celtic and Roman artefacts hidden by the Romans when their legions were leaving Britain. On that and subsequent visits I removed a number of items. Joe arranged for me to meet with representatives of an international auction house. I knew nothing of how they operated, but at our meetings I have been able to, er, influence their thinking, so that they have no doubts as to my right to sell these items.

"Again with the assistance of Joe and a firm of solicitors, I formed a trust to receive the proceeds of the sales. As soon as the trust had sufficient resources, it bought the farm where the remainder of the treasure lay buried. We have continued to sell items to fund our projects. All the unsold treasures have been moved to a secure barn on the farm.

"And now, at last, the answer to your question – for most of the last few years I have been living at the farm."

"What? I just can't believe it!" Bob looked to be angry and bewildered. "Have you any idea how many hours, days, weeks of our lives we've spent discussing what might have happened to you? We've scoured newspapers and websites looking for any mention of any happening that might conceivably be related to you – and all the time you were living on a farm in Lyme Regis? I don't know whether to laugh or cry."

Arthur, who had been sitting on the table, scrambled across and jumped onto his father's lap.

"Don't cry, Daddy. We can go and see some treasure!"

145

Now that they finally had Myrddin in the right place and mood to answer their questions, Jane was keen to make sure that she asked all the important ones.

"What has happened to The Droller?"

"As soon as we could prepare the farm for them, we moved The Droller and his friends to the farm. They are well and reasonably content, I believe."

"I just can't take this in," Bob complained. "The Dini we took to Scotland are living in the middle of nowhere and we still worry about their being discovered, and yet you have a bigger group in Lyme Regis! That area swarms with tourists in the summer."

"Indeed it does, although the weather does seem to drive most of them away after a few days. However, we believe the farm to be secure."

"Did you not think that the Dini in Scotland would like to know that their Welsh cousins were safe?"

Myrddin nodded. "Yes, we were well aware that that must be so."

"But you did nothing?"

"His Royal Highness and I …"

"HRH! You are in contact with the Prince?"

"Yes. We could not be certain that the existence of either of the groups would remain secret. Nor could we know what would happen if their existence became known. We felt it wiser to keep the groups entirely apart. You have a saying about not keeping all one's eggs in a single basket."

"Does HRH know your, er, background?"

"He has heard The Droller's Tale, in full. He is a rare commodity – a modern man with an open mind."

"And Gilda, is she still alive? She seemed ancient when we met her."

"Oh, yes, Gilda is also at the farm."

"Trader Joe – has he been working for you all this time?"

"Yes. I am afraid that I have made over-large demands upon Joe's time. His services have been of great value. I knew almost nothing of how your world operates. Joe was essential in acquiring the farm, managing the work to create what was needed and initially handling all of our contact with the outside world.

"For many months, while I continued to build my strength, Joe instructed us in the ways of the world – not great philosophical debates, but the practicalities of daily life. He has been teaching more of the Gododdin to speak English and Gilda to understand Welsh. We do try to ensure that Joe gets home as often as possible, but he is well rewarded and, I fear, that probably means more to him than it should."

Bob had one question that was more important than any other, but he felt reluctant to ask it. He found Jane looking at him and he knew that she was hesitating over the same question. He decided to put off the moment and addressed a different issue.

"Carn and his friends want us to ask you about their problem."

Myrddin nodded. "I know of their problem."

"You do?"

"Of course. The Droller and his friends face the same difficulty – their tribe is dying out. We have lost one of our Welsh friends. He was kicked on the head by a pony and died instantly. We have lost none to illness – Gilda sees to that." Myrddin laughed. "It may be the efficacy of her potions, but I suspect that they are still too frightened of her to admit to being ill."

"Carn and the others never seem to get ill, either – and they don't have Gilda."

Myrddin raised his eyebrows. "How interesting."

"But, as you say they are dying out, I assume that no babies have been born."

"No, their tiny bodies remain infertile. We have been doing some investigating."

"What sort of investigating?" asked Jane.

"They thought that I was some great magician who would wave a magic wand, recite the words of an ancient spell, and they would be transformed. They would become the same size as the rest of mankind, living among them with no need to hide away – and would bear children. I have explained that I am no such magician – such powers that I have over others are more concerned with the control of minds rather than bodies. I fear that they are rather disappointed in me.

"Gilda, however, has refused to accept that increasing the size of their bodies is impossible. By working together we have found that I can use my own mental powers to increase the powers that she is able to focus into her own remedies, and we have had partial success – especially when she was able to use the unique forces of The Sword of Power as her athame.

147

"But, even if we were able to restore them, we have learned that they could not possibly survive among you Biguns, as they call you. Your society is just too complex, too hostile for them to fit in."

"The group in Scotland have reached the same conclusion – and that's just from watching our television programmes."

Myrddin nodded. "The Droller's group have no television now. They sampled it for a short while and then asked me to remove it.

"Gilda and I feel that their best chance of surviving as a tribe is for us to find a way of overcoming the infertility problem – which Gilda is working on – and introducing their existence to the world in such a way that they can continue to live separate lives, but without having to hide the fact of their existence – and we're working on that, too."

"When you say 'we', who exactly do you mean?"

"Me, Gilda, His Royal Highness and, of course, Joe.

"But it would be ironic, would it not, if we found the means of securing their future only to have it destroyed by the Great Goddess Anu. Our most pressing problem is to appease her before she wipes mankind from the face of the Earth. But before we begin to tackle all the questions you have about my plans in that direction, may I mention two things? Firstly, answering questions is a devilishly hungry business…"

Jane jumped to her feet. "I'm sorry, we haven't offered you a proper meal! We'll get something ready."

Myrddin held up a hand and smiled. "Thank you, but there is a second matter that I wanted to mention. Neither of you has asked the question that is most important to you." He waited for a few seconds while Bob and Jane looked at each other and at Arthur. Myrddin spoke again.

"There is no need to ask; I will tell you. Your fine son is a perfectly normal young man."

Bob and Jane looked at each again. Bob puffed out his cheeks and let out a long, slow breath. Jane was about to speak, when Myrddin continued.

"Except that he has some extraordinary abilities – abilities that my training will enhance. I told you before that, if mankind is to survive, your society must change. New leaders will arise, leaders with special talents.

"The spirit of Artos has again come to rescue his people from disaster. That spirit lives within Arthur. You didn't need me to tell you that. From the beginning, deep inside yourselves, you have known this to be true. That is why you named him Arthur."

*

Bob and Jane prepared the simple meal in silence. Bob gathered salad leaves, radishes and beetroot from the garden, tomatoes and a cucumber from the greenhouse and cleaned them in the kitchen. Jane boiled potatoes and eggs, made potato salad and grated some cheese.

They both laid the kitchen table. A couple of times Bob seemed about to speak, but remained silent. Jane was standing at the sink when she spoke quietly.

"Come and look at this."

Bob moved to stand next to her and they both watched through the window.

Myrddin and Arthur were sitting together on the old bench on the lawn. On the grass in front of them stood a robin, his head moving from side to side as he watched them. The robin hopped closer. Arthur slowly put out a hand towards the bird. The robin hopped closer still until he was close to Myrddin's feet. With a sudden flurry of wings the robin flew up and perched on Arthur's outstretched hand. Arthur turned towards Myrddin. His parents could see the joy on his face.

*

Later that night, after Arthur had gone to bed, the Johnsons were keen to hear of Myrddin's plans.

"The nature of the problem was clear to me. What baffled me was why your fellow beings seem unable to see it."

"Oh," said Jane, "I think they see it all right – but they all think that it's down to someone else to do something about it."

"For a while," said Myrddin, "I considered launching a new political party!" He began to laugh at the absurdity of the idea. "Can you see me as Prime Minister?" He laughed out loud and banged the table in delight.

"I am sorry to say this, Jane, but I only had to look at the Green Party to know that it would be a waste of time. Even now, as desperate as things are, you are making no impression."

"Oh, I wouldn't say that, we're…" Jane's protest petered out. She sighed. "You're right. We're fooling ourselves if we think we're making real headway. We'll be lucky if we have two or three MPs after the next election, but we need a hung Parliament and twenty to thirty members to have any effect."

"I reached the conclusion that the problem with politics is this strange system you've developed called democracy. It is utterly absurd – and yet you think that it is so wonderful that you are outraged if any other country does not wish to adopt it. I believe that your political leaders know what a handicap it is and are anxious to ensure that all other countries must struggle with the same burden."

"Sorry," said Bob, "I feel we're getting off the subject of your plans, but just what is wrong with government by the people for the people?"

Myrddin gave a derisive snort. "Leaders have to make decisions and take action. Sometimes the right action will not be popular and the leaders will be reviled – until they are proved right. How can leaders take unpopular actions if they have to rely on the goodwill of the people to re-elect them every few years? Democracy means a system where political parties compete to see who can create the most popular policies. Such a system will end in disaster.

"But you are correct, Bob, this is not answering your question about my plans. Mankind has but one chance. Attitudes must change. Your industrial revolution made the creation of wealth easier and quicker to achieve. Your sick society has become obsessed with the pursuit of money and the unnecessary trash that it can buy.

"My plan is to work on the minds of people; to change attitudes; to make people care more about others and in doing so we may stop them poisoning the planet. You have been to one of my presentations. I have a number that carry a similar message."

"But why don't you appear? Why hide away?"

"The title of the presentations and of the movement itself is *The Message not the Man*. The meaning is clear: it is the message that is important, not the messenger who brings it. No-one can challenge the simple truths in the message, but if I show them the messenger they will want to know who I am, what I am, where I come from, what right I have to deliver the message. But I cannot hope to convert enough followers to the message by my presentations. At each meeting there may be between one hundred and fifteen hundred. I planned to create a groundswell of support through the meetings before making use of television, radio and the press. If I cannot be in the presence of the listener, my influence on their thinking is much weaker. But the rate of progress is too slow. We must begin to make use of the mass media to get our message to the people.

"I started the presentations in the north and have covered most of the country, except for the south-west. I have some meetings planned for this region. I need your assistance, Jane. You have built up knowledge from your political activities of how to involve the media. We have three presentations planned in the south-west and I want to use them to get our message into the media."

There was silence while Bob and Jane considered what they had been told. Bob found himself staring up at the sword, as he so often did. He cleared his throat.

"Do you really believe it can work?"

"For the sake of mankind we must hope that it *does* work. I have used the power of the sword to call to Anu. I have told her that the spirit of Artos has returned and that we are changing the ways of mankind. I have pleaded with her to give us more time. But if we are not successful quickly, millions will die and mankind will be set back a thousand years.

"From the news of the earthquake, it seems that Anu is not convinced that our message will spread around the world quickly enough."

*

Nigel Sligo limped to his car, his laptop under one arm. He drove to the spot where he could get a broadband connection.

He had downloaded the photographs from the camera to the laptop. The pictures were not crystal clear, but he felt that the character was so distinctive that anyone who had seen him before would be certain to recognise the old man.

He emailed the photos to several photo agencies together with a request for help – with a promise of cash for anyone making the identification.

Sligo closed the laptop and made his painful way back to the cottage.

The banging on the bedroom door was so loud that, roused from a deep sleep, Bob sprang from the bed in a state of stunned confusion. He was still trying to work out what was happening when the banging stopped and Myrddin's cheerful voice rang out.

"Come on, you two! It's a wonderful morning and the pleasures of the Earth await us."

Bob heard the old stairs creaking an accompaniment to Myrddin's joyful singing.

"He said it's morning, but it feels like the middle of the night."

"What time is it?" Jane muttered, sleepily.

Bob peered across the dark room trying to focus his eyes on the red lights of the clock. "Half-past four," Bob groaned. "The last thing I remember is Myrddin putting his arms around the pair of us and telling us that we'd sleep like babes. Somebody ought to tell him that babes need more than four hours sleep. Have I got to go to work today?"

"No."

"Thank goodness for that." Bob lay back down on the bed and closed his eyes.

The door flew open. Arthur rushed into the room and jumped onto the bed. He clambered over Jane and turned on a bedside light. Bob and Jane quickly pulled the duvet over their heads.

"Come on! Up you get! We've made a picnic breakfast. We're going out for a walk." He crawled to the foot of the bed, rolled off onto the floor and yanked on the duvet as hard as he could. His parents covered their eyes with their hands.

Arthur climbed onto the chair near the door and turned on the main light. "If you don't get up, you know what you'll get! You'll get the cold flannel treatment!"

Bob could feel Jane chuckling beside him and he joined in. "We give in! Anything but the cold flannel treatment!" He stood up and headed for the ensuite.

"No time to wash!" Arthur cried. "We have to go!"

Bob splashed cold water on his face, which brought him more awake.

"Where are we going?" He heard Jane ask as she padded around the bed to join him.

"Don't know – but isn't it fun?" With a last urging of, "Please hurry up!" Arthur disappeared and they heard him charging down the stairs.

In the kitchen they found Myrddin and Arthur waiting impatiently for their arrival. Myrddin had discarded his monk's habit and sandals in favour of a checked cotton shirt, well-worn cord trousers and a pair of sturdy, if heavily scuffed, brown shoes.

"A different style of clothing today, Myrddin."

"I'm very proud of my robe – I'm not sure what else to call it. It was made entirely on the farm. We sheared the sheep, spun the yarn, wove the cloth, dyed it and created the garment. But I needed something more suitable for today, I felt."

Bob's rucksack was on the table. In it he could see bottles of water, fruit and plastic sandwich boxes.

As soon as they appeared Myrddin closed the rucksack, swung it onto his back and ushered then towards the front door. As Bob and Jane paused in the porch to put on walking boots, an excited Arthur asked a question.

"Would you like to hear our new song?"

"Yes, please," said Jane as she tugged on the bootlaces.

Arthur and Myrddin burst into an enthusiastic duet.

The house had a silly name.
It had rotten window frames
And woodworm in the doors
And mice beneath the floors.
But no-one was to blame
And they loved it just the same.

"That's very nice. Haven't heard that one before."

"No – we just made it up."

Arthur and Myrddin led the way along the drive and out onto the lane. At the gate Bob spotted the sign bearing the house name of Harrud, created by combining the first part of his father's name, Harry, with the last part of his mother's name, Maud, and the penny dropped.

"Hey, I'll have you two know – it hasn't got rotten window frames. We've just spent a fortune on new ones."

"I am sorry, Bob," Myrddin called back, "but in your downstairs lavatory I was able to push my finger deep into the wood."

"Oh, yes, well, we haven't had that little one done yet."

Myrddin, Jane, Arthur and Bob walked along the dark lane singing the song, hand-in-hand, arms swinging.

They crossed the Teign at Rushford Bridge and were about to leave the lane to join the Two Moors Way when Bob asked for a halt. To Myrddin's amusement he delved into his rucksack and pulled out two torches.

The sky was growing pale in the east as they joined the track and followed the Teign downstream. After a quarter of a mile they reached an area of woodland and Myrddin stopped level with a weir.

"This is a fine spot for breakfast," he announced.

They moved just off the track and settled down among the trees. Myrddin slipped off the rucksack. He opened it and passed around food and drink.

"Now we will enjoy some of the greatest delights that Earth has to offer."

They ate and drank without speaking, listening to the gentle sounds of the river. Around them the dawn chorus built as one after another the birds of the woodland joined in. Bob closed his eyes to concentrate. The birdsong was less intense than it was at the peak of the breeding season, but it was still a joy to hear. He focussed his attention on one song at a time, enjoying the cadences, identifying the bird, and then relaxing to take in their combined music.

A nudge from Jane made him open his eyes. The sun was rising and the light was improving rapidly. He looked at the sparkle of the water tumbling over the weir, but with another nudge and nod of the head Jane directed his attention to the pool below the weir. A small bow wave travelled across the water to the bank on their side and a large dog otter climbed up the bank. It bounded past them and was about to re-enter the river above the weir when it stopped. Its head turned and it looked back at them. The otter made one bound towards them and slowly looked along the row of four faces before turning away. It took a couple of leaps and then slid down the bank into the water. It plunged under the bank and reappeared with a wriggling eel in its mouth. The otter swam away upstream, looking for a quiet spot to enjoy its meal.

In a brilliant flash of electric blue a kingfisher sped by. The Johnsons all spoke at once.

"Wow!"

"Kingfisher!"

"How beautiful is that!"

But as they looked around at the scene revealed by the rapidly rising sun, their mood sobered up. They clearly weren't the first people to have had a picnic on that spot. Discarded cans and plastic bottles littered the area; wrappers from snack bars and crisps were pressed into holes in the bank.

"It is so very, very curious," said Myrddin, "that Earth is so full of beauty and mankind is the only creature that has developed the ability to appreciate that beauty, yet is the creature determined to destroy it."

Arthur got up to collect the rubbish and they all joined him. At the bottom of his rucksack Bob kept a plastic bin-liner in which to wrap any clothing soaked in a downpour. He took out the bag and they put in everything they collected.

Bob carried both the rucksack and the rubbish bag as they set out for home.

In daylight they could see the barbed wire fence that kept livestock from the river. The wire was festooned with the remains of plastic fertiliser bags that had snagged on the wire when the river was in spate; as it so often was.

CHAPTER 15

A visit to the farm

When they got back from the walk, Jane spoke to Eppie on the phone. Myrddin knew she was making the call and seemed relaxed about how much the Dini were told, so Jane passed on everything she could remember.

It took a long time as Eppie had to keep repeating Jane's news to Bran and Enid who were with her in the kitchen.

"The Droller used to tell us about that treasure hoard in his stories, but I don't think any of us really believed him. Do you think we can get to see The Droller and the others – or even just speak to him on the phone?"

"I don't know. I'll ask Myrddin. How are you all?"

"Oh, we're all right – except for Tegid, of course. For a day or two after you left he seemed a bit better, but he soon slipped back into his drinking. Sometimes he doesn't come in at night; he just sleeps it off somewhere. We do worry that he might wander off and be found."

"Oh dear, sorry to hear that. I expect Nudd gets into a real state over him."

"Yes. Poor Nudd. Tegid has always given him a hard time one way or another. Must go – I want to call the others together to tell them the news."

Jane had a lot of commitments in connection with her Green Party activities and for the next few days, while Bob was at work, Myrddin spent time with Arthur allowing Jane to get on. In the evening, after Arthur had gone to bed, the three of them made plans for Myrddin's Westcountry presentations. The dates and venues were already sorted out, so they discussed at great length the best way to introduce Myrddin and his message to the media.

It was also agreed that on Bob's next day off the Johnsons would visit the farm near Lyme Regis. Arthur's enthusiasm for seeing the remaining treasure hoard was only marginally greater than that of his parents.

*

Sligo drove to a supermarket in Tavistock to get in food supplies and then stayed in his cottage for a couple of days. His calf was swollen and painful. He eased the pain by conjuring up images of what he would do to that dog if he got the chance. The pain in his head had terrified him. It had been so intense that he'd thought he'd burst a blood vessel in his brain and was going to die. He'd spent the next two days worrying in case it returned.

When he checked his emails he was disappointed to find that none of the photo agencies had come up with an identity for the old man.

It's time for another look, he told himself, *and we'll see if the Johnsons have any more weird friends. The more the merrier – and the bigger the cheque.*

He needed a better spot from which to spy on them; somewhere that gave him a view of all the comings and goings. Google Earth provided the answer. When he used the website to zoom in on the Johnson house he found that on the opposite side of the lane was a large field. The gate was a good four hundred yards from the house. He could park by the gate, walk the length of the field and settle himself behind the thick hedge. He'd be well hidden, but should be able to get a good view straight up the drive to the front door.

With that planning completed he drove the Focus back to the cottage and then walked to the Visitor Centre. He still limped from the dog bite, but as he went in he emphasised it to make sure that the staff noticed. They knew him as a writer researching a book and had seen the signs of the injuries received, so they believed, when he had tumbled down some stairs. They had been on the receiving end of the oily charm that Sligo could display when he was seeking information. They were sympathetic about his further injury, especially when he pulled down the bandage to show the angry-looking holes left by the dog's teeth. He bought a walking stick and, although he didn't really need it, he used it as he hobbled home.

Back in the cottage he pulled off the rubber foot, sharpened the last one inch of the stick to a sharp point and pushed the foot back on.

I just hope that old bat is walking her damned dog again. I'll run it through. No-one could blame me – I'll say it attacked me again. He chuckled to himself. Revenge would be sweet.

The following morning Sligo got up at what was, for him, an unusually early hour. He had his cigarette and strong black coffee and then put more coffee in a vacuum flask and made some sandwiches – it could be a long day. He put his sandwiches, coffee, camera and binoculars in a carrier bag, picked up his walking stick and set off for Chagford.

He had no trouble finding the gateway and parked across it, but when he got out of his car and looked over the gate his heart sank. The field held a large number of cows. As a lifelong city-dweller, Sligo's knowledge of cows was limited to two facts: they gave milk and he hated them. They were just too big and he had the feeling that inside that vast body was a very small brain that meant the animal was quite likely to do something stupid. He always had the suspicion that lurking within any group of cows was a bull.

Sligo used his binoculars to convince himself that all of the animals standing up were obviously cows – even Sligo could recognise an udder when he saw one. But on the far side of the field a few of the beasts were lying down. He decided to take a chance, climbed over the gate and walked along the field, staying close to the hedge and keeping a close eye on the livestock. To his relief he attracted no more than the odd casual glance and the cows concentrated on their grazing.

As he approached where he thought the house was sited he checked every few yards by gently using his walking stick to ease the jungle of blackthorn, hawthorn and hazel stems apart to clear his view. Directly opposite the house he found a spot that gave him the view he wanted and saw that on the drive were the Johnsons' old Fiesta, the green Land Rover, plus a black car he hadn't seen before. Sligo set about making himself comfortable, wedging his body into a position where it was supported by the hedge.

Suddenly, he heard car doors slamming. He pushed his face painfully into the hedge to see what was happening. There was no sound of an engine starting, but the black car drove towards him off the drive and onto the road. As it swung past him he had a glimpse of the old man in the monk's habit in the front passenger seat and all three Johnsons in the back. His quarry seemed to have escaped – but at least he had the registration number and he quickly scribbled it on a cigarette packet.

This is costing me a fortune, he thought, as he dialled a number on his mobile phone.

"Ian, it's me, Nigel. Yeah, not bad. No, I haven't been around, but I'll be back soon. I need a trace. Yeah, yeah, same fee, in cash, as soon as I get back. It's a black Toyota; registration number is…" Sligo read out the number he'd written down. "No, I'll hang on."

He waited for no more than a few seconds. "Yeah, got it. Thanks, Ian. See ya."

Well, well, well. The disappeared Trader Joe Morgan re-appears. Is that the full set, I wonder? The would-be politician, the accountant that jumps out of a well-paid job, the religious nutcase, the mobile shop operator with the criminal record and a leading member of the Royal Family – could this possibly get any better?

Sligo had an unpleasant smile on his face. The smile remained even when he felt the blood from a scratch on his face trickle down his cheek. But the smile drained away when he pulled himself from the hedge and turned around. A semi-circle of cows stood no more than fifteen yards away. They were all regarding him with an unblinking stare, each mouth rhythmically working.

He inched his way back towards the gate keeping his back to the hedge and an anxious eye on the cattle. The end of the arc of cows was close to the hedge and Sligo realised that he would have to pass within touching distance of the nearest animal. The large beast calmly watched his slow approach. As he came close he started to talk, his voice coming out high-pitched and cracking.

"Nice cow, nice cow. You just stay there."

As Sligo came level the cow swung her head towards him and an enormous tongue slid out of her mouth and delivered a very wet, but abrasive, lick that travelled diagonally across his face. He stopped for a few seconds while he fought down a mixture of panic and disgust, then he turned abruptly and walked towards the gate as quickly as the wet, slippery ground would permit.

He glanced back over his shoulder and found the cows following him. With great relief he reached the gate and holding his carrier bag and walking stick in his left hand he scrambled up. He'd swung his right leg over the top bar before he became aware of the sound of a powerful engine.

A tractor pulling a trailer swung towards him; the lifting forks on the front passed either side of him and the machine stopped so close that there was insufficient space for him to get down. A young farmer climbed out of the cab, walked to the trailer and hefted a bale of hay onto his back. He walked to the gate, seemingly unaware of the intruder's presence, undid the catch and gave the gate a vigorous shove.

The gate swung open with Sligo clinging to the top bar. When the gate stopped abruptly Sligo toppled off onto the muddy ground, landing on the carrier bag.

The farmer stood over him as he pulled himself to his feet.

"What you doing in my field?"

"Having a pee. I was took short."

"Oh yes. And you had to walk to the other end of the field, taking your shopping with you. I suppose you rounded up my cows 'cos you thought they'd be impressed." He chuckled at his own joke. "Well, they're not so easily impressed." He laughed out loud.

Sligo was working out how to answer when a thought struck him. "Where's my car?"

"It was blocking my gate."

"So?"

"So now it isn't."

For a moment Sligo's fury almost got the better of him. The farmer sensed it and casually tossed the bale of hay away, a smile on his face. As he did so, Sligo caught sight of bulging biceps threatening to split the sleeves of the t-shirt that struggled to contain them. He controlled himself and walked around the farmer, through the open gate and out onto the lane.

Two parallel black lines ran off into the distance where Sligo could just see his car, left at the nearest point that the lane widened. As he stalked towards it, he heard a jovial call from the farmer.

"You might want to check those tyres. They looked a bit bald to me!"

Sligo reached into his bag to check on the condition of his camera and binoculars. They were all right, but when he shook the vacuum flask he heard the slushy sound of a shattered lining. Furiously he hurled it into the hedge.

At that moment he knew two things for certain: there was nothing, absolutely nothing, that he hated more than the English countryside; and someone was going to pay dearly for all of this.

*

As they drove down the lane away from the house, Bob caught sight of a silver Ford Focus parked across a gateway. The number plate was becoming familiar.

"Did you turn the alarm on?" he asked.

"Yes. Arthur went round checking that all the windows were shut. I checked the patio doors, the kitchen door and set the alarm as we came out. Why? You don't usually ask."

"I think that might have been the car of that nosey journalist."

"I do not think there is any need to go back, Bob." Myrddin spoke quietly.

Joe gave him a knowing look. "Have you set one of your specials?"

Myrddin simply smiled.

Joe directed his comments over his shoulder to the Johnsons. "We have all kinds of security at the farm, see. An electronically controlled gate, surveillance cameras everywhere – you'll be impressed, that you will. But before we had all that, Myrddin here had his own system. Worked very well, it did. Anyone who came too close developed a severe nose bleed and went away again."

Jane looked puzzled. "What? You punched them on the nose?"

Myrddin shook his head and tutted. "Jane, how could you suggest such a thing? Would the great Myrddin resort to anything so crude?"

"Oh no, nothing like that," said Joe. "Don't know how he does it. Don't like to ask in case he's tempted to demonstrate on me. These folks who came nosing around just suddenly started a nosebleed. Quite a sight it was. I thought of parking my van at the end of the drive so that I could sell them packets of tissues."

They all laughed.

Jane explained to Arthur. "Joe used to have a great big black van, fitted out like a shop and full of all sorts of things."

"Still got it, I have. Had to have a new engine and gearbox fitted. Mind you, I had driven it as far as the moon. But she comes

161

in useful sometimes, carting all the stuff around for Myrddin's talks. And we've slept in her on the odd occasion."

*

By the time Sligo got back to Princetown he was a sorry sight. Apart from his mud-stained clothing, the front of his shirt was crimson. His nose had stopped bleeding as soon as he drove off the drive and away from the Johnson house, but while it lasted it had been spectacular.

He was a worried man: first the excruciating headache; now a gushing nosebleed. There seemed to be something going on in his head that he didn't understand.

*

The entrance drive to the farm had the same electronically controlled barrier as was installed in the farm in Scotland. Arthur hung out of the car window to wave at the camera and the barrier swung open.

"Who's watching the screen?" asked Bob, "You haven't got your own version of the McDonalds, have you?"

"No, we look after ourselves," said Myrddin. "If we need to have outsiders onto our site, Joe or I make sure that we are here."

The barrier served to stop vehicles entering the drive. A few yards beyond was a tall gate, the width of the drive, set into a high fence. The gate opened as they drove towards it and closed behind them. A camera on a pole turned to follow their progress. The long drive curved through an area of woodland that screened the farmhouse from the road.

Joe pulled up in front of the house and after the others had got out, he drove the car out of sight around to the back. It was imposing; two stories high with four large windows on each floor. As they walked towards the central door, Bob spotted more cameras. Myrddin stopped at the door and was about to press a button when he paused and motioned to Arthur, inviting him to press another button that Bob now saw only eighteen inches from the ground. Arthur pressed it; there was an audible clunk and a very small door, little more than two feet high and set into the bottom of the main door, opened silently. Arthur stepped through and the door closed.

162

Myrddin pressed the other button and the main door opened. They walked into what looked to be a perfectly normal hall. A staircase lay directly ahead; the hall ran along the front of the house, brightly lit by the four windows.

Apparently full-sized doors led off into rooms that must have looked out onto the rear of the house.

"There is only one room of particular interest," said Myrddin, "but it won't take long to give you a tour, so let's look at all of it."

He walked to the door at the far end of the corridor. He noticed Arthur looking for buttons to press. "Just push," he said.

Arthur pushed the door and again a little door opened. Myrddin lifted the latch on the main door and they followed Arthur into what was a rather shabby kitchen, fitted out with full-size units that had clearly seen better days.

"The kitchen that Joe and I use – if we have to." He walked briskly out of the room and opened the next door along the corridor. It was a lounge, furnished with old, but comfortable-looking, leather settees and chairs arranged around an open fireplace. Bob thought that either Joe had bought them second-hand or they had been left by the previous owner. Vertical blinds screened the large window.

"On the rare occasions that we have visitors, they usually get no further than this room. You, however, may see rather more." He led them from the room. Passing the stairs he said, "Up there are four bedrooms and a bathroom." He walked past the next door, saying as they passed it, "Lavatory and sink in there." He looked down at Arthur, "You may prefer to use other facilities." He stepped back and looked Arthur up and down. "Although you may already be too big for them."

The next room was introduced as the 'work room'. It had two desks and a large table. Cupboards and shelves lined the walls. Books filled the shelves and stood in piles on all the surfaces. Amongst the general clutter Bob picked out two computers, printers and a telephone.

The next room also had a tiny inset door and Myrddin nudged it open with his foot before opening the main door so that they could follow Arthur into what was a very small kitchen. Everything in it was tiny and set low down. It looked like the kitchen in Scotland, but was very much smaller.

"I don't think I ever knew," said Jane "how many of the Gododdin there were in Wales."

"We have eighteen living on the farm."

"Eighteen! But this kitchen isn't big enough to cook for eighteen."

"No," Myrddin smiled, "I'm clearly not a very good guide. This is only used by whoever is on duty in the control room. There is a much bigger kitchen with the living quarters." He looked down at Arthur. "The small-scale facilities that I mentioned are through that door – but as you seem to be growing even as I look at you I am now sure that they are too small for you. And now for the control room."

As they walked towards the last door on the corridor, Bob noticed for the first time a camera on the wall that was clearly tracking them.

The control room was lined with screens, all set no more than two feet from the floor and on the shelf in front of each sat a panel of switches.

Two tiny figures were sitting on little swivel chairs and they both turned towards the visitors.

"Good morning, gentlemen," said Myrddin.

Two high-pitched voices said, "Bore da!"

"Now, I know that you've been having lessons from Joe and The Droller, so from now on, may we have it in English please?"

But they weren't listening to him. They were both staring at Arthur and he was looking at them with great interest.

"Beth yw eich enw chi?" one of them asked Arthur.

Myrddin was about to translate when Arthur said, "Fy enw I yw Arthur."

The Gododdin exchanged looks. "Croeso!" they both said.

"Diolch yn fawr iawn," said Arthur.

Bob and Jane were looking at each other in astonishment and Myrddin chuckled.

"Arthur, you constantly amaze your parents – but there is nothing mystical here. I taught him a handful of words while we have been together over the last few days.

"Allow me to introduce you. Brychan and Arfon, I'd like you to meet Bob and Jane Johnson, about whom you have heard much. Their son, Arthur, you seem to have already met.

"And now – a demonstration if you will." He pointed at the screens. "We have cameras that cover the entire perimeter fence and some of the buildings as well as the gates on the drive. They all take a turn in here – except for The Droller; he falls asleep within moments of sitting in front of a screen. Twenty-four hours a day there are two people on duty. Arfon, let us see the south-west corner."

Arfon's chair rolled easily on castors and he pushed it along the row of screens. He pressed a switch and the picture on the screen in front of him changed. He turned a knob and the camera zoomed in to show, in great detail, a point where two lengths of fence met at a right-angle.

"Excellent!" cried Myrddin. "But now we must press on, we have a lot to see."

He led them briskly from the room, back out of the front door and around the side of the house into a large cobbled farmyard, enclosed on all four sides. The farmhouse ran along one side. On the other three sides were buildings that had once been stables and outhouses, but looked to have been recently converted.

Myrddin pointed to the long side opposite the house where the former stables now had windows and tiny doors. "That is the living accommodation. And along that short side facing us are the communal living areas: the big kitchen and dining room, and next to that a room with plenty of seating. And here, along this side, is our secure barn."

"Is this where the treasure is?" asked Arthur.

"Indeed it is."

The barn had no windows and one very solid-looking metal door. Myrddin moved towards the door, but Bob hung back, looking around.

"Myrddin, you've had a great deal of work carried out here – structural and electronic."

"And there is much still to see: the barns where we make our cloth; our heating system; the sources of electricity."

"But who's done all the work for you? You must have had dozens of contractors in here. How have you kept what you were doing secret?"

"Before we moved our little friends here, it didn't really matter. Now outsiders are only allowed in when I am here. When they go I ensure that they remember nothing."

"What about the technology in your presentations?"

"Joe found an excellent production company. Either we go to their studios or we meet on location. They have never been here."

"Come on!" cried Arthur, running to the metal door. "Treasure!"

Myrddin went to an electronic keypad next to the door. "Ah, someone is already inside and I can guess who it is." He pulled on the heavy door. It opened silently and smoothly.

The barn was brightly lit by rows of spotlights along the apex of the roof. It felt cool and dry inside. Statues stood in a line down each side of the barn interspersed with display cabinets and cupboards.

They moved slowly along as Myrddin explained the significance of some of the gold and silver artefacts. "It is mainly the smaller items that we have sold so far, simply because they were so much easier to transport discreetly. If we need to go on spending, I can see that we shall be left with the statues and a few special pieces that we couldn't possibly sell."

"What else could you need to spend money on?" Jane asked. "You seem to have everything sorted out."

"There are our little friends in Scotland who may need to join us – and Joe has finally managed to regain contact with the Cumbrian part of the tribe. They have been hiding away avoiding all contact ever since they heard about you two discovering their existence, but they may yet require our assistance."

"How many are there in Cumbria?"

"About twenty we understand."

A movement caught Bob's eye and it registered with him that they were not alone. Two figures at the end of the barn were moving towards them; one small, the other relatively tall, both moving slowly at a speed apparently dictated by the taller one.

Bob realised that it was the woman with long grey hair that they had seen with Myrddin in Bristol. She still walked in a way that suggested that each step required an effort. Myrddin looked up from the golden dagger that he'd been showing to Arthur.

"Ah, there you are," he said and moved forwards to meet the strange pair.

Bob was again struck by the extraordinary face. It looked as smooth as china with well-defined cheekbones and a strong nose. It was the face of a young woman, but with old, old eyes and a body seemingly plagued with joint pain.

166

When he looked down at the smaller figure, Bob recognised The Droller. He had been old when Bob had last seen him, but now his face bore a spider's web of deep lines and he looked ancient. Jane beat him to the greeting.

"Droller! How are you? How good to see you again! And especially good to see you in such a pleasant, safe place."

The Droller gravely bent his head to Jane and Bob in turn and then fixed his gaze on Arthur. "And you, young man, must be Artos, sorry, Arthur, of whom we have heard much. Sut ydych chi?"

"Da iawn, diolch," said Arthur, "A chithau?"

The Droller looked at him in surprise and then laughed. "I have been trying to force a few words of English into the heads of some of my friends for years – and they still can't put two words together." He looked up at Myrddin. "How long did it take you to teach him that?"

"A matter of moments. It was as if he already knew it." The two old men smiled at each other.

When no-one made any attempt to introduce the woman, Jane said. "I'm sorry, but I don't think we've met. I didn't know that any other Biguns, as they call us, knew about all this."

There was a moment's silence, then The Droller cackled loudly. Shaking his head, he managed to say between more laughter, "Forgive me, but I must go and leave you to your tour." He looked at Arthur and said, "Hwyl fawr am nawr!"

Arthur replied, "Wela i chi!"

The Droller laughed again and walked away towards the door.

Bob and Jane looked at each other and then at Myrddin and the woman, awaiting an explanation of The Droller's behaviour. Eventually Myrddin spoke.

"Gilda had far too much useful knowledge to risk losing it by leaving it in such an old body."

"Sorry," said Jane, "I don't understand."

"The woman you see before you is the new Gilda."

"Sorry, it's not getting any clearer. What are you trying to tell us?"

Myrddin sighed and when he spoke again there was an irritated edge to his voice.

"This is the Gilda you knew. I told you that we had had some success with our attempts at increasing their size. This is the

167

result." He turned on his heel and walked to the door and out into the yard.

Gilda shrugged. "The great Myrddin does not like failure. It was not his fault; he didn't want to go ahead, but my researches told me it was possible. I thought that the forces within The Sword of Power would be sufficient."

"But," Jane protested, "It obviously *did* work. Just look at you! I can't believe it – you must be two-and-a-half times the height you used to be – and your face looks like that of a young woman. It's a miracle! How can it possibly be a failure?"

"The bones have stretched and that has simply stretched the skin tight, so the lines have disappeared. But the process is very painful and the internal organs have not adjusted to cope with the larger body. I may improve, but that appears unlikely. It is only the combination of my potions that I take every day that allows me to keep moving.

"But I was old anyway. I have been allowed more days than most. When Death comes for me I shall go content. But," she said with a smile that looked painful to produce, "I would rather not go just yet – not until I see my tribe's future settled. Shall we go?"

"But we haven't seen all the treasure yet," Arthur complained.

"I suggest that you let Myrddin show you the farm – that is something that he's proud of – and then come back here later. And then I will show you the special things; the things that the great Artos was so eager to possess. If we could learn their use, their power may be greater than that of the great sword itself."

Arthur happily agreed and they rejoined Myrddin. They left Gilda at the barn and Myrddin led them briskly out of the yard. As they went, as if in explanation of his display of irritation, he said, "The Gododdin knew of our experiment, of course. They were elated by the initial success, but then crushed by the failure."

The tour of the rest of the farm was impressive. Shetland ponies were used for pulling tiny ploughs and carts. When he saw them Arthur said, "Look! They're just like Carn's."

"Indeed they are," said Myrddin. "We buy all of the ponies that Carn breeds for sale – although he doesn't know it yet."

Close to the house were a large vegetable plot, a fruit garden, pigsties and a chicken run. Beyond that the stream that ran across the land had been used to create a lake covering more than half an acre and stocked with trout. Ten acres had been planted with willow to provide fuel. A high wire fence ran all around the perimeter with a strip of grass ten yards wide inside it. Then four ranks of fast-growing conifers had been planted to screen the farm from prying eyes. The fence and grass strip were covered by cameras.

Myrddin showed them a small group of dexter cattle and a flock of forty sheep.

"We make our own butter and cheese. We shear the sheep and weave our own cloth from which we make our clothing. Each year any surplus wool is used to improve the insulation in the buildings. One of the two small barns ahead of us is the dairy and the other is where we process the wool. We are dividing that one to set up a workshop to make use of the wood from the trees blown down by the gales."

As they walked around the farm they were introduced to the little people they found busily working.

"We produce all the electricity we need using photovoltaic roof tiles and wind turbines. Solar panels heat our water and we even installed a heat sink to warm the glasshouse." Myrddin beamed at them, clearly immensely proud of what they had achieved and his twenty-first century technical knowledge.

"How many acres do you have?" Bob asked.

"Close to two hundred. Ah, I see you have noticed the large area apparently unused. We actively farm about seventy acres. The rest we are encouraging to return to woodland and wild flower meadows." His face took on a sad expression. "This is not just their home, it is also their prison. They cannot leave this place, so they need some wild areas where they can feel the Earth and its riches."

Bob noticed that all the workers seemed to have disappeared and commented on it.

Myrddin looked about. "Excellent! It must be time to eat! My stomach is saying so – and my ears tell me that the others have gathered. Come!" he bent down and swept Arthur up onto his shoulders. "We must fly back to the farmhouse like swallows in spring."

With his arms outstretched and his brown robe flapping, he sped away, Arthur shrieking with delight as he clung to Myrddin's head.

Jane laughed and shook her head, "How old is he supposed to be?" She paused. "Can you hear music?"

"Yes! Come on! I'm starving and it sounds as if we're missing something."

They ran after Myrddin and arrived back at the cobbled farmyard laughing and out of breath.

Someone had decided to take advantage of the absence of rain to eat the midday meal outside. Two long, low tables, with benches either side, carried plates of food. At one end was a small chair facing down the length of the tables. The music stopped and Myrddin spoke.

"In case there are any among you who haven't yet met him, this is our guest of honour, Arthur."

There was an outburst of cheering, waving and the banging of cutlery on table. A pink-faced Arthur sat in the small chair at the head of the tables, where he found The Droller sitting next to him. Myrddin waved Bob and Jane forward. "And we are honoured by the presence of Robert Edgar Johnson, Guardian of the Earth, Companion of Kings, and the Good Lady Jane, mother of Arthur and a teacher of immense knowledge and wisdom."

There was another outburst of noise. Bob and Jane allowed themselves to be led, somewhat sheepishly, to the opposite end where a full-size table and five chairs stood. Joe and Gilda were already sitting there. Once the Johnsons had sat down, Myrddin stood at the head of the table. He raised his arms and spoke in a voice that rang around the yard.

"Great Goddess Anu, we thank you for the food that is ours only because you permit it. We thank you for your patience."

He sat down and the eating began. The food was simple: still warm, fried joints of rabbit, cheese, eggs, salads, fruit, bread, butter and jugs of water, milk and cider.

"Thanks for the embarrassing introduction, Myrddin," said Bob as he filled his plate.

Myrddin chuckled, "Don't worry! Most of them have learned such little English that they hardly understood a word I said."

As they ate, Jane kept an anxious eye on Arthur, but she needn't have been concerned. He was chattering away to the people on either side of him who were making sure that his plate remained full.

"You have all achieved something really remarkable here," said Bob.

"Thank you," said Myrddin, "we are proud of our community. But you have also achieved something remarkable." He was looking along the length of the tables at Arthur. "He is a fine boy."

"Well, we think so," said Jane, "but we may be biased. What am I eating?" she asked, looking at the mix of salad leaves. "This is delicious – so full of flavour."

It was Gilda who replied, "We have tried growing the salads that you seem to like, but after a lifetime of eating wild plants from the hedgerows the taste is too bland. Now we're growing the wild plants in our vegetable garden." She leaned forward and pointed with her knife. "Wild garlic, dandelion, catsear, water mint, orchid root, borage petals."

Bob was very hungry and ate with enthusiasm. He eventually became aware that conversation was dwindling. He looked up and down the tables and realised that he was the last person still eating. Everyone else seemed to be politely waiting for him to finish. He put down his knife and fork and pushed the plate away.

There was a flurry of activity and a number of fiddles, drums and pipes were produced from under the tables. The benches were moved back and the tables carried away. The musicians began to play and everyone clapped to the irresistible rhythm.

"Music," Myrddin explained, "has been missing from their lives for far too long. When they were hiding among the Welsh valleys and mountains they did not dare to sing or play instruments. It hasn't taken them long to re-discover the joy."

Joe was hauled to his feet and with very little reluctance was persuaded to sing. Bob and Jane understood nothing of the Welsh, but clapped along enthusiastically.

Then the dancing began and Joe pulled Jane into the throng, despite her protests.

"Of course you can do it, see. Just do what all the others are doing and if you don't know what that is, do whatever you like. No-one bothers, just enjoy yourself."

Arthur and Bob joined in. The only ones remaining seated were Myrddin and Gilda.

When a breathless Jane returned to her seat she said, "Carn, Eppie and the others would love it here."

Myrddin nodded. "Yes, they would. But one day we will be discovered. It is certain to happen. Helicopters fly overhead. A tree on a neighbouring farmer's land may blow down and bring down the fence; his animals may wander onto our land and he may, quite reasonably, come in to recover them. I don't know how it will happen – but it will. I would prefer to find a way of introducing their existence to the world and to have their existence accepted before I bring in the others."

As abruptly as it had started the music finished and efforts were made to clear away and return to work. Arthur came to persuade Gilda to show him the rest of the treasures, including the 'special things'. Bob, Jane and Myrddin went with them.

Gilda's special things turned out to be two golden salvers, each of them about two feet in diameter and covered in markings. Bob looked closely. Here and there the markings looked like letters, some Roman and some Greek; representations of horses, swords, axes and the outline of human heads were easy to see, but there were many other symbols that meant nothing to him and lines criss-crossed the surfaces.

"I thought at first that they were the same, but they aren't, are they?" Bob looked at Myrddin.

"No, one is the mirror image of the other. The symbol at the centre is the outline of the Isle of Anglesey. That was the main stronghold of the Druids, before the Romans destroyed it. The Celts had no written language; all learning was passed on verbally. I have seen nothing like these before. They are from well before my own time – perhaps close to three thousand years ago.

"The Druids were more powerful than the kings of the Celtic tribes. They understood the true meaning of life and death. Human sacrifice was important in their rites – that is why so many heads are shown." Myrddin paused to point out a number of them.

"The Celts were savage poets." He smiled at the curious looks that Bob and Jane gave him. "They loved nothing more than fighting and then composing stories telling of their triumphs. They beheaded their defeated enemies and displayed the heads on spears around their homes. They believed that all the strengths and virtues of a man rested in the brain and that whoever took that brain took those strengths. They didn't care who they fought and the Celtic tribes warred constantly with each other.

172

"The real achievement of the great Artos was to unite the Celtic tribes to defeat the Saxon invaders and then to live at peace with each other.

"The problem we now face is even greater. Now it is not tribe against tribe, but individual against individual. Everyone is competing against everyone else in the pursuit of money, status and possessions."

He looked down at Arthur. "The Spirit of Artos is needed to show mankind how to live together in peace."

He turned back to the gold salvers. "We do not yet know their purpose. I thought at first that they might be an astronomical device for calculating the times of sunrise and sunset." Gilda muttered when she heard this and shook her head. "But, as you see," Myrddin continued, "Gilda disagreed and now I think she is right. Why cover such an object in axes, spears and heads?"

The old woman spoke slowly but with force. "I know not what they are – yet. But I feel that they have great power. If we can solve their mystery and learn their use, we may have powers beyond even those of the great sword. Who knows what we may yet accomplish?"

"May I hold one?" asked Bob.

"Of course." Myrddin stood back to allow Gilda to swing open the door of the display cabinet.

Bob reached in and grasped the left-hand salver on opposite edges and braced himself to take the weight, but he found it surprisingly light. The gold was very thin and when he held it up to one of the spotlights, light shone through an intricate pattern of tiny holes. It was an extraordinary feeling to be holding such an ancient object, but Bob couldn't quite keep the disappointment from his face.

"No curious tingling? No sensation of power?" Myrddin smiled. "Try the other one."

Myrddin reached into the cabinet and passed Bob the second salver. He stood with one in each hand, but still felt nothing.

"Then, Bob, perhaps these, unlike the great sword, are not the weapon for you." Myrddin turned to Jane. "Maybe they require a lady's touch."

Very reluctantly Jane took the salvers from Bob. The yellow light reflecting from the golden surface lit up her face. She smiled with delight. "How beautiful they are!" Her expression

173

slowly changed. She looked from one salver to the other with a puzzled frown. Jane closed her eyes, breathing deeply. She spoke one word in a voice that didn't sound like her own.

"Eigra."

She opened her eyes, blinked a couple of times and passed the salvers back to Myrddin. "Sorry. They're beautiful, but I didn't feel anything either." Then she saw the looks on the faces that stared at her. "What?"

"It looked to us as if you felt something – you went a bit strange and you spoke in an odd voice." Bob gave his wife a concerned look. "Are you sure you're all right?"

"Of course I'm all right. What am I supposed to have said?"

"You said 'Eigra'," said Myrddin.

"Eigra? Is that all? That's not a word I know."

"It is a very old Celtic word. It means beautiful maiden."

Jane shrugged helplessly.

"It has also been used as a name."

"Oh, yes?"

"Yes. The mother of Artos was called Eigra."

CHAPTER 16

Early battles won

Jane dutifully phoned Eppie to report on their visit to the farm. At Myrddin's request she left out mention of Gilda's extraordinary increase in size. He didn't want to raise the little folks' hopes, when his own conviction was that the experiment hadn't worked.

Before making the call, she had a question that she wanted Myrddin to resolve.

"Look, can we sort something out? When we met Carn, Eppie, The Droller and Gilda for the first time, they called themselves Dini, short for Votadini, the Celtic tribe that they believed they are descended from. You then insisted that they call themselves the Gododdin. Now we're in the situation that the Welsh part of the tribe that you have at Lyme Regis call themselves Gododdin; Eppie and the others have slipped back into using Dini, but Mr McDonald, who seems to know his history, calls them Gododdin. So, which is correct?"

"Whatever they choose to believe is correct. The important fact is that they are fine people who have shown great resolve in surviving the way that they have. Their folklore has been passed down through their generations, with the droller of each generation making their own small amendments. That folklore began long before the time of Arthur. Both tribes existed, but the Gododdin became important many years after the Votadini – so both names could be correct. The Gododdin were fierce warriors who defended their lands valiantly against the Picts from the north and the Saxons from the east and were one of the tribes united by Artos.

"When I met them I found people who had grown timid from years of hiding away. They needed to have their courage restored, to be made aware of their own importance. Calling themselves Dini did not help. Tell me, which name do you prefer?"

175

Jane thought for a moment. "Somehow, Dini seems to fit."

Myrddin nodded. "And that is because it sounds like something small, timid, unassuming, unaggressive. Should I use the word 'sweet'?"

Jane opened her mouth to protest, but stopped and nodded. "You're right. It's impossible to look at them, at least when they're happy and enjoying themselves, without having the reaction, 'how sweet!' – they are just so tiny."

"Just so. But they are not kittens, they are fine people – and whatever the future holds for them, they will need courage and determination. Thinking of themselves as Gododdin might help a little."

"All right – Gododdin it is. And after I've made this call, we'd better press on with the arrangements."

The first of Myrddin's three scheduled presentations in the Westcountry was at a hall in Truro. They planned to make the introduction of the media a gradual process and Jane had persuaded a single newspaper reporter to attend. As well as covering health and tourism, she was the environment correspondent on the local evening paper. Jane knew her quite well after years of contact through the Green Party and had persuaded her to sit through all of Myrddin's presentation, rather than writing up a short piece based upon a press briefing.

In addition to the presence of a journalist, they were changing the end of the session. Myrddin would appear on the stage and invite questions. He would have to make unscripted public appearances sooner or later, so he might as well make a start.

Bob was at work on the day, but Jane and Arthur went. Jane helped Joe set up the equipment. She made a point of greeting the journalist and showing her to a seat in the front row, commenting only to the effect that she was about to enjoy a most unusual experience. Then Jane sat with Arthur at the back of the hall and waited anxiously for the reaction of the two hundred members of the audience.

In the event, she needn't have worried. The presentation went exactly like the one that she had attended in Bristol. Myrddin appearing on the stage produced no reaction and there were no questions – not even from the reporter.

The entire audience simply sat in silence, not responding to Myrddin's invitation to question him and then leaving the hall in a state of happy excitement once Myrddin suggested that it was time to leave.

The reporter sought out Jane. She rushed up to her with a big smile on her face and gushed, "That was amazing. I'm so glad you asked me to come. Thank you! Thank you! I can't wait to get back to the office and write it up."

As she hurried away, Jane looked down at Arthur. "She's never like that after a Green Party meeting."

Jane eagerly checked the next two editions of the evening paper. On the third evening there was a tiny piece, scarcely two inches of a single column, just giving the basic fact that there had been a presentation by the organisation calling itself, *The Message not the Man*. Jane phoned the reporter, who sounded both excited and annoyed.

"I haven't stopped talking about it. I wrote a great piece, but the editor wouldn't run it – he thinks I've lost my marbles."

Jane learned from that experience. She managed to get the editors of the two local evening papers and the regional daily to attend the next presentation given to four hundred people in Dartington. She thought about inviting a freelance photographer, but all they could have photographed was Myrddin – and that would have been against the basic principle that it was the message that was important, not the man delivering that message.

Instead, she gave each of the editors a compact disk loaded with a selection of the most effective still photographs from Myrddin's presentation.

The following day all three of the newspapers carried full-page coverage in prominent positions. Jane had pleaded for her own name not to be revealed and that had been respected. 'Members of the Green Party' were said to be involved in organising the event in all three publications. In two of them Myrddin was mentioned by name, but only described as 'the presenter'. In the regional daily the editor had retained sufficient presence of mind to give a little more detail, describing Myrddin as 'a self-effacing bearded figure wearing a simple robe'.

The tempo of Myrddin's war was accelerating.

*

Nigel Sligo walked to the Princetown shop for the morning papers and his cigarettes. Then he walked to the Fox Tor café, sat at a table tucked away where Ethel Clay wouldn't spot him, ordered a mug of black coffee and picked up the regional daily. He began his usual trawl for stories with a hint of the weird or the sordid, but he only reached page three.

At a glance it didn't look a likely source of his sort of material; he thought it was just another ridiculous environmental scare story, but the words 'Green Party' and Myrddin's description leapt out at him. His coffee arrived and stood untouched on the table as he read the whole article. When he'd finished he sat back and scratched his head.

Now this really is weird, he thought. It was pure claptrap, all wishy-washy, goody-goody nonsense about making the world a better place by caring for each other. Sligo gave a derisive laugh. His experience of human nature told him what rubbish that was. But what was weird was that it was the editor's name on the article. *Surely this sensible, staid, high-circulation regional rag can't be putting its name to all this junk. It's ludicrous!*

He went back to the first paragraph. 'The co-ordinator of this inspiring presentation is called Myrddin, a bearded figure wearing a simple robe, who is the driving force behind the *The Message not the Man* campaign that has been creating a stir across the country'. It also referred to the website www.themessagenottheman.com.

Myrddin, what sort of a name is that? Maybe he belongs to some crackpot religious order who refer to each other by single names only. This stuff isn't the usual junk about low-energy light bulbs and not wasting water. This garbage is waffling on about morality and personal relationships.

Sligo put the paper down and sipped his coffee. His digging out of dirt was moving too slowly for his liking. He knew the main characters in the story, but he hadn't dug out the key element – the element that would make him big money. Where did the kids fit in?

He knew kids were involved somewhere. He'd had the stories of Ethel Clay, Alice Jackson and George Phillips and, most importantly, he'd seen Johnson's reaction when he'd mentioned 'the little people' and HRH.

What had happened to the kids?

*

Jane was now dealing with the emails sent to the *The Message not the Man* website. She developed standard responses to most enquiries. Anyone asking for information about Myrddin received a reply saying that if they were asking the question, they hadn't understood the basis of the campaign.

After the newspaper coverage hundreds of emails arrived wanting to know the dates of future presentations. Only one more presentation had been arranged and it was clearly going to be a packed house. She had no problem moving the publicity to the next level. Someone from the BBC regional news team contacted her via the Green Party local office: there would be a BBC reporter at the presentation on Saturday afternoon in Plymouth; a camera team would be there to record the reactions of the reporter and other members of the audience as they came out.

Myrddin's powers over his audiences seemed to be increasing. As the crowds streamed out, Jane found a quiet spot in the foyer from which to watch the television team. There was no doubting the obvious enthusiasm of the reporter and the people passing her. The coverage finished with a few seconds of Myrddin talking to camera.

Myrddin was travelling back with Joe, and Jane hurried home to Chagford to get there in time to watch the local evening news with Bob.

It was the first item. The reporter was wide-eyed with excitement and all of the people that she seized on for comment seemed to have had the same uplifting experience.

Suddenly Myrddin's face filled the screen and Arthur stopped prodding Bob's leg with a plastic sword in an attempt to start a battle and laughed at the screen. "It's Myrddin!"

That strong face radiated serenity and a calm conviction. It was a very re-assuring face that managed to convey both strength and trustworthiness.

The three of them listened to Myrddin's brief statement in which he thanked those who had attended for the enthusiasm with which they had listened to his message.

There was a short winding-up comment from the reporter in which she mentioned that similar presentations around the country had been equally well received and that, 'We are seeing the rise of a movement that brings a fresh approach to saving the planet; an approach that focuses on saving ourselves and each other', and then coverage moved on to other items.

"Well, what do you think?" Jane asked.

"I think he's got a very nice face," Arthur said firmly.

Bob laughed. "Yes, he has. The average television viewer may not be too clear as to exactly what the presentation had been about, but the effect it had on everyone there was obvious. And I'll tell you something else: the effect on viewers will be so much greater because it came straight after the national news. I've never seen a news so full of doom and gloom; they showed the summer storms in the States that have killed over one hundred people, more about that earthquake, more floods across Europe and in Britain, and the cyclone that has ripped through Birmingham. The only non-weather items were those bits at the end about fishing stocks being depleted, record highs in oil prices and the giant turtle washed up on a Cornish beach and found to have a stomach full of plastic bags.

"After that lot, anyone watching will have been delighted to see all those smiles on the faces of the folks pouring out of the meeting and relieved to see Myrddin's reassuring face."

Jane nodded. "You know, I'm just starting to think that this might work. I thought the cynical British media would rip it apart, ridicule it. It's early days, of course, but as long as he can stick firmly to the rule that this is all about the message and that the messenger is not important, well, maybe the time is finally right for people to be ready to make changes."

Bob sounded doubtful. "I think that might be rather optimistic." He was looking up at The Sword of Power. "You know, it may be my imagination, but I've got the feeling that the glow is getting brighter."

Jane looked at the golden hilt. "You could be right."

Bob received a loud whack on the knee from Arthur's plastic sword. With a convincing roar of outrage he leapt from his seat and pursued a giggling Arthur from the room.

*

It seemed that newspaper editors and television producers agreed that their audiences were in need of some good news. The editors of all three of the local newspapers moved on from their coverage of the presentation they had seen and launched ongoing campaigns encouraging their readership to put into effect lifestyle changes based upon Myrddin's principles of cooperation rather than competition, and demonstrating the improvements in the quality of life that could be achieved by adopting a 'caring for each other' approach.

The item from the local news was picked up by the BBC on a national basis and given a few seconds at the end of the news. Two people who had attended the Plymouth presentation were instrumental in generating more publicity. One was a regular contributor to the *Thought for the Day* slot on Radio Four's *Today* programme. On the following Wednesday morning she was so enthusiastic in her account of the meeting and its message that, most unusually, the interviewers questioned her about it on air.

The other was the Bishop of Truro. Persuaded to attend by a member of his staff who had been to the Truro presentation, the Bishop liked what he heard and, as he was due to be a guest on a Sunday morning programme, he persuaded the producers to invite Myrddin to appear on the same programme.

In the meantime, Myrddin returned to work with the production company to prepare more material and Jane found a company that could stage a presentation at a football stadium at only two weeks notice.

On the Sunday morning the Johnsons gathered in front of the television. In Scotland the Gododdin had also gathered to watch.

It was the opening part of the programme. The presenters announced their important guest, the Bishop of Truro, and said that they were also delighted to welcome 'the man behind the *The Message not the Man* website and the movement that has been causing such a stir'.

"Bishop, I understand that you have attended one of Myrddin's meetings."

"Indeed I have," began the Bishop, and then launched into an enthusiastic commentary on what he had heard, the value of the message and the fact that the Church had been trying to preach a very similar message for a long time. The camera shot kept switching between the two men sat next to each other, both in robes, the Bishop's face animated and eager, Myrddin's serene, exuding a calm strength. The presenter turned to him.

"Myrddin – that's a Welsh name, I believe and I'm told that it is the only name that you use."

"It is a Celtic name, as you say, and it is sufficient."

"It seems to be a basic point in your message that it is the message that matters and that no-one should trouble to seek information about the bringer of that message."

181

"That is correct. No-one should waste time on me. I am merely the deliverer of the message. If the churches feel that they can deliver the message effectively then I will gladly disappear."

The presenter seemed about to ask another question but stumbled, looked at his script and hesitated. A momentary look of confusion passed across his face and the Bishop stepped in.

"No-one could argue against the basic tenets of Myrddin's message. They lie at the centre of all of the world's great religions. No, Myrddin, we do not want you to disappear. There is a sickness in modern society, a sickness that is spreading to the planet itself. For a reason that I do not understand, people are prepared to listen to the message when you deliver it. I do not need to understand. I simply urge you to continue with your work and I urge everyone watching to seek out your message."

The camera zoomed in on Myrddin's face. He calmly looked into the lens.

The presenter had recovered. "Now, before we move on to our next topic, we can hear comments from others who also attended that Plymouth meeting."

Viewers were shown the clip of the local news reporter enthusing about the presentation and getting equally positive comments from the audience as they passed. It finished with a shot that Jane hadn't seen before. The camera team had moved outside to the car park and filmed the crowd drifting away. As the camera panned around it swept over a big black van. Joe, getting ready to load the equipment, was standing talking to a figure in a brown robe. For a couple of seconds the cameraman zoomed in onto the face of that figure. It was a woman with long grey hair.

*

Nigel Sligo had a smirk of satisfaction on his face. Sunday morning television was not his usual source of entertainment, but he had seen a trail for the programme and made a point of watching it

His mobile kept ringing and there was the constant ping of an incoming text. He knew that when he next looked at his emails there would be a build-up in his inbox. The photo agencies that had been unable to put a name to the photo of Myrddin he'd sent them had now realised that he had taken a picture of Myrddin in the garden of a house. Photos of Myrddin were suddenly in demand and they wanted more.

182

He did want more photos, but he wouldn't be selling them just yet. He would wait until his story broke when he would get far more for them.

What Sligo also wanted was to know where Myrddin went when he wasn't at the Johnsons'. The obvious solution was to follow when Joe Morgan was driving Myrddin away from the Johnson house, but after the incidents of the headache, the nosebleed, the dog and the farmer his instinct for self-preservation was telling him not to get too close to the house. He took his mug of coffee out into the backyard, where he could sit with a good view of the prison, lit a cigarette and checked out his map.

To go almost anywhere from the Johnson place the easiest route would be to go via the middle of Chagford. He decided to spend more time hanging around the village in case he struck lucky with Joe's car or his van. He had invested in a more powerful telephoto lens. He was in no hurry. The story was getting bigger all the time.

*

The television coverage caused excitement and consternation in Scotland.

All of the Gododdin, including Tegid, were present, and from the start of the item a babble of confused voices threatened to drown out the sound from the television.

"Is that really Myrddin?"

"Hasn't he changed!"

"What's he wearing?"

"What's a bishop?

"What are they *both* wearing?"

"I like the purple one!"

It took a loud, "Quiet please!" from Carn to bring a little hush.

Apart from the occasional muttered, "What's he talking about?" the hush lasted until the last few seconds of the coverage of the Plymouth meeting.

"There's Trader Joe!"

"And his big black van!"

But a shriek from Issel silenced them all. "That's Gilda!"

They all looked at her and then back at the screen for a fleeting glimpse of the face of the woman in the long brown robe.

The item finished immediately after that and Carn turned off the television.

Issel was white, shaking, but determined. "I tell you, that was Gilda."

"How could that possibly be Gilda? You saw how tall she was."

"I may be getting old, but I'm not blind and I'm not mad. She may be bigger, but I recognise that face and hair. When I was a young girl, that was how Gilda looked. I don't care what the rest of you think – I *know* that was her."

"But," Eppie pointed out gently, "if Myrddin has somehow managed to make Gilda bigger…"

"And a lot younger, judging by her face!" Enid interrupted.

"…Jane would know about it, and she would have told us."

"I don't care about any of your 'buts' – I'm telling you, that was Gilda."

"Hmm, I have to agree," said Carn, "it *did* look like her. Her hair looked different, but that could be just because it's clean. You're right, Issel, there *was* something very familiar about the face – that nose and the dark eyes."

They sat in silence for a while, each of them thinking about the enormity of what they may just have seen.

Eventually, Bran asked, "What about the rest of it? Anyone have any idea what they were talking about?"

"It was a load of rubbish," said Tegid. "Typical Bigun nonsense."

Carn laughed. "For once, Tegid, I agree with you. Biguns do seem to make life complicated. But about this Gilda thing: either it is Gilda or it isn't…"

"And there, Carn, for once I have to agree with *you*."

"All right, Tegid, those may not have been the wisest words I've ever spoken. I was just trying to look at the two choices. If it *isn't* Gilda then nothing's changed – it just means that Myrddin and Joe have somebody helping them who just happens to look like our old friend."

Tegid snorted. "Friend! When was she our 'friend' – we were terrified of her!"

"She was our friend when she kept us healthy with her potions all those years." Eppie reminded him. "And she was being your friend when she saved your life."

"She needn't have bothered," Tegid muttered darkly.

"But, if that woman we saw *is* Gilda, what do we make of it?"

"Well," said Enid, "it would mean that Myrddin really is a great magician and he could do all sorts of things to help us."

"Yes," said Bran, "from the start we thought that his return meant that he would be on our side and that he would restore us to normal size and stop us having to hide away."

"And if we were back to normal size we could have children," said Enid, eagerly. "At least, that's what we hoped years ago when The Droller's group found him."

Nudd joined in, made nervous as usual by talk of change. "But, when we talked about this recently we agreed that just making us bigger wouldn't really help. We are so different that we just couldn't fit in with the Biguns and being bigger would just make it harder to keep hidden from them. So it *might* solve the children problem, but it gives us another one."

There was a general murmuring of agreement that encouraged Nudd to say something he was clearly reluctant to say.

"And the children problem probably only affects Enid and Bran, but the other problem affects us all." He went pink with embarrassment and made sure that he didn't look at Carn or Eppie.

"That may well be true," said Eppie, "as far as this group is concerned, but don't forget our cousins in Cumbria and The Droller's group."

"I've had a strange idea," said Erbyn. "Jane and Bob haven't said anything about Gilda being made bigger, but if she has been, then maybe *all* of The Droller's group have been made bigger. After all, we haven't seen them; all we've heard is that they're safe and living on a farm. If they chose not to tell us about Gilda, maybe they chose not to tell us about the others, either."

There was a silence, then Enid said, "It was the Welsh group that saved him. Maybe Myrddin thinks we don't deserve his help – some of us didn't even believe in him." She glared at Tegid.

There was an even longer silence that Eppie eventually broke. "From the night we met them, I've always thought that we could trust Bob and Jane. I don't like to think that they wouldn't tell us the truth."

Tegid gave another of his derisive snorts. "I don't know when you're going to learn. We've watched their television. The Biguns are always lying, cheating and fighting. I wouldn't trust any of them to look out of the window and tell me if it's raining. I need a drink." He walked out of the house slamming the door behind him.

*

The programme had ended, but in the studio an inquest was being conducted.

"I just don't understand. You had the questions on the pad in front of you and when I saw you struggling I gave you the next one through your earpiece. Why didn't you ask that Myrddin guy the questions we had agreed?"

"Sarah, I don't have an answer. All I can do is keep telling you that I don't know. I did have the questions in front of me; I could see them perfectly clearly. And I could hear you perfectly clearly as well, but I just couldn't ask the questions. I had them in my head, but I just couldn't bring them out.

"Sorry, but I can't tell you any more than that."

CHAPTER 17

The accident

Sligo had a stroke of luck. He was on his way to Chagford and had just driven over the humpback bridge at Postbridge when he realised that the old Ford Fiesta about to pass him going in the opposite direction was being driven by the Johnson woman. His quick glance revealed a front seat passenger that might have been Myrddin and the sprog might have been in the back.

He braked hard and did a u-turn over the forecourt of the East Dart Hotel. He was about to set off in pursuit when he saw the Fiesta's indicator flashing and realised that it was turning into the car park of the Postbridge Information Centre. Sligo stopped. He couldn't follow without being totally obvious. He waited for a couple of minutes, unsure of what to do; then the Fiesta re-appeared. The driver was turning right, heading towards Princetown. He grabbed his binoculars. As far as he could tell the Johnson woman was alone. He waited another minute and then drove along the road, over the bridge and turned into the car park. There were only two other cars and no sign of anyone about.

He waited in the car in case his targets should come out of the toilet block, but when they didn't, he walked to the Information Centre in the corner of the car park. There was a woman behind the counter, but otherwise the place was deserted. Sligo stood outside the door and looked about, baffled as to how his target had disappeared.

"Can I help you?" the woman called.

He turned back and gave her his oiliest smile. "Perhaps you can. I seem to have got separated from my two companions."

"An old man and a boy?"

"That's right."

"They walked past a little while ago, heading that way," she pointed. "If you go around the corner of the building you'll see a gate in the fence. I expect they're waiting for you there, or on the track. Would you like a guide to the walks around here?"

"No, th…on second thoughts, yes, that might be a good idea."

Clutching his leaflet Sligo hurried out of the shop, around the corner of the building and through the gate. A few yards from the gate the track crossed another, broader, track that ran perfectly straight for a quarter of a mile; he looked along it. Two or three hundred yards distant two figures were ambling away from him. He waited until they passed out of sight around a bend and then hastened after them.

Rain started to fall and he turned up his collar. His trainers provided little grip on the wet ground and he would never have kept up if his target hadn't been going so slowly. He was able to follow them as the track dropped down to a stream, using the many granite boulders as cover, but when they started climbing the slope of what the leaflet told him was Broad Down, he knew he had a problem. It was far too exposed. He pressed under an overhanging slab of rock where he could both keep out of the rain and keep his target in view. He didn't move again until they disappeared over the crest of the hill.

*

Arthur loved his excursions with Myrddin. His parents always made their walks interesting, telling him all sorts of stuff, but walks with Myrddin were different. For one thing, he didn't fuss. *By now*, he thought as they plodded up the hill, *with this little bit of rain they'd have made me put my hat and coat on and I would have been far too hot. Myrddin lets me decide for myself.*

And there was the singing. They constantly composed comic songs that they sang at the tops of their voices; nonsense songs about sheep, cows, ponies, birds and flowers. Myrddin knew a lot, too, but he always waited for Arthur to ask questions.

They sat on a rock on the slopes of Broad Down to catch their breath and admire the view. Myrddin had tucked his hair into a hat and was wearing a t-shirt, old trousers and walking boots. He swung a rucksack from his back, opened it and offered Arthur a bottle of water.

Arthur drank and passed the bottle back. At his feet he spotted a tiny yellow flower.

"I know what that's called," he said. "Daddy told me."

Myrddin nodded. "Your father knows many things."

"It has a funny name. And it's a strange plant."

Myrddin nodded gravely. "It has many names and can be useful for those in need."

"It's called tormentil," said Arthur. "It's strange because it usually only has four petals but sometimes, on the same plant, one of its flowers has five petals. We found one once." Arthur knelt on the wet ground and checked the tiny flowers. "These all have four. Why is it useful?"

"It treats many problems with the digestive system as well as fevers and infections. It's called tormentil because it eases many torments."

"Do you know any other names?"

"I know it as bloodroot. The roots are red inside."

"Can we sing a song about it?"

"Of course. We can do songs about anything." He paused briefly. "How about, 'Jill was ill so she took tormentil'?"

Arthur clapped his hands. "Good. My turn." He thought for few seconds. "The coot was a brute so they gave him bloodroot."

"Splendid! Let us go forth singing as bold warriors should!"

They marched up and over the top of Broad Down proudly singing their new song.

*

Their voices just carried on the wind to Sligo. *Mad as hatters. What sane person would wander about this desolate waste in the rain, singing?*

He eased himself out of his shelter and hesitated. He checked the leaflet. They seemed likely to be on a circular route that would take them back to their starting point. He turned back towards his car. He'd get a chance to take pictures later. He'd leave the nutcases to get wet.

*

Arthur and Myrddin lay face down on a slab of rock jutting out over the East Dart, looking down into the raging water below. The river, swollen to a level that was most unusual for summer, roared through Sandy Hole Pass. The shower had blown over and the hot summer sun was shining.

189

"Why don't all the little fish get washed out of the river?"

"The Great Goddess Anu shows them where to hide."

Arthur rolled over. "Look! We're on fire!" Steam was rising from the rocks and their clothes as the sun burned off the recent rain. "Come on! The waterfall will be great!"

Myrddin followed him along the river bank downstream and joined in with Arthur's latest song:

> *The river turns white at the waterfall*
> *The river turns white at the waterfall*
> *The river turns white at the waterfall*
> *And turns black again downstream.*

At the waterfall they settled on the rocks near the torrent. Myrddin pulled a couple of apples from the rucksack and as they ate them they watched the light play in the clouds of spray. Arthur shaded his eyes to help him see a group of birds swooping over the river a little further down the valley.

"Are they swifts or swallows?"

"Swallows."

"How can you tell?"

"The noise they are making. Swifts will be flying over your garden this evening. Listen to the swallows and listen to the swifts later."

"Daddy says that swallows fly to Africa for the winter."

Myrddin nodded.

"I don't know where Africa is."

"It lies a long, long way to the south. Where they go is more than ten times as far as you go when you visit Scotland."

"I asked Daddy how they find their way there, but he said no-one really knows."

"There is a simple answer: the Great Goddess Anu guides their flight."

Their walk back towards Postbridge was slow with many stops to look at beetles, slugs and lichen. They made a final stop at the point on the bank where the path left the river and they stood looking down the river to the bridge. Clouds were building in the west and it would rain again before the day was out.

Arthur was looking up at the clouds when he asked, "What was Artos's mother like?"

"Eigra was beautiful, wise and very proud of her son."

"Was she like Mummy?"

"Yes. The Sword of Power chose well."

Arthur pointed towards the bridge. "I was with Mummy when we saw a salmon down there." He wrinkled his brow. "Salmon are born in the river, then they swim thousands of miles across the sea. But they find their way back years later to lay their eggs where they were born. How do they do it?"

"The Great Goddess Anu guides their way."

"Why aren't there as many salmon as there used to be?"

"The Great Goddess Anu does not guide them around the nets of men."

Arthur gave Myrddin a knowing look and after a few seconds he said, "Can we go to the pub and wait for Mummy there?"

Myrddin and Arthur came out of the East Dart Hotel carrying their drinks, heading for a bench. Just before they reached it, Myrddin stumbled, went down on one knee and spilled a good part of his pint.

Arthur saw the irritated look on his face and offered some comfort. "I don't think the Great Goddess Anu wanted you to drink all that beer."

Myrddin stared at him for a moment and then the two of them burst out laughing.

*

Sligo had his photo. He had waited hours for it, but it would be worth it. He lowered his camera and moving out of the group of tourists standing on the bridge, he returned to his car.

*

On that same Monday morning Carn made his usual early start to the day. When he was troubled, as the news of Myrddin's return had left him, he sought the company of the ponies. He crept down the track towards the paddocks, but it never mattered how quietly he approached they always knew he was coming and were lined up waiting for him.

He made a brief fuss of the stallion, moved on to the mares, foals and geldings and then went to the fruit garden where he knew that the overnight winds would have produced windfall apples and pears. He gathered an armful and returned to feed them to the ponies. He felt like a ride. Erbyn and Nudd would be coming out before long to work with the geldings and the cart. He led one of the mares out of the paddock, her foal sticking like glue to its mother. Carn used the fence to climb onto the mare's back and rode down the track towards the stream with the foal trotting along behind. He didn't intend going too far and, anyway, it would soon be time for the mares and foals to run free.

The foal gained courage and started moving a few yards ahead of its mother before turning to run back, its overlong legs moving stiffly. As they neared the stream a red deer and its calf trotted across the track in front of them. The foal skidded to a halt, staring at the new sight.

The birds were singing and Carn was enjoying himself. At the bottom of the valley he turned upstream and they followed the course of the water to a ford. Across the stream he rode up the hill through the conifer plantation heading for the open ground at the top. It was what Trader Joe used to call a soft morning. He quickly thrust thoughts of Joe from his mind: he had come out to forget all about Joe, Gilda and Myrddin for a while.

He moved the mare to alongside a rock and slid off her back onto it. He left her to graze while he sat on the rock watching the foal with its wild bursts of energetic charging in circles mixed with periods of stillness spent staring at anything new – a leaf blowing across the ground or a magpie strutting through the grass.

He found himself thinking back to happy times on Dartmoor: the long rides with Eppie on Gog; the gatherings with their friends and The Droller at Beltaine and Samhain; his first exhilarating ride on Midnight; the moment when he called the wild stallion to him and realised the special power that he had with horses. They would go weeks without seeing Erbyn and when they met up he always had tales to tell about his fishing trips or the latest treasures he'd gathered; now they saw him everyday, knew just what he'd been doing and had little to talk about. They had been free to roam the moor. He stopped himself abruptly.

You're fooling yourself! What about all that time spent in the freezing waters of the Dartmoor rivers scraping together enough gold to buy what we needed; the rides back with Eppie trembling with cold; the day we were nearly burned alive; the days spent in our cold cave unable to light a fire to warm ourselves or our food because of the Biguns swarming through Wistman's Wood. We weren't free to roam; we were hiding away.

But the brief thoughts of their Samhain and Beltaine feasts had put thoughts of their old food in his head. On the way back he would check in the woods by the stream for burdock, silverweed and fathen; it would be autumn soon enough and that would bring the mushrooms and nuts. This year he would be sure to gather enough sweet chestnuts to make flour. He realised he was hungry.

He called the mare to him, swung up onto her back, checked that the foal was with them and pushed the mare into a trot.

Carn left the ponies drinking at the stream while he had a quick look for the plants. He was surprised in his task by a voice calling.

"Good morning, Carn. And how are you today?"

"Oh, hello Mrs McDonald. I'm fine thanks. Not a bad day."

"Indeed it is not. We are luckier than the poor folks down south. Rab's away all morning marking trees for felling on the far side of the estate. I thought I'd have a wee wander down here and pick a few brambles for a pie."

Carn had to think for a moment until he recalled that the McDonalds called blackberries 'brambles'. "I'm sorry, I don't think you'll find many around here. Enid picked a lot yesterday."

"Och, well, never mind, an apple pie will do us just as well."

"Always better with a few bla... brambles in, though. I can ride further up the stream and get some for you – better still, just call at the house on the way back. I think they are jam-making this morning, but they won't have done it yet. I'll walk back with you – if you're ready to go back."

She smiled down at him. "Oh, aye, this stream seems to get further away each year. I've had quite enough exercise for one morning."

Carn called the pony to him. Mrs McDonald patted the mare's neck. "That's quite a gift you have, Carn. I've seen Rab chasing these ponies for hours trying to get a halter on them, but you just call and up they tr..."

The foal, in one of its wild runs, and not quite in control of its legs, came charging back to its mother and knocked Mrs McDonald off her feet. She gave a startled gasp and crashed to the floor.

"Mrs McDonald! Mrs McDonald! Are you all right?" Carn looked anxiously into the old face. She wasn't moving; her eyes were half open. "Oh no!" Blood was appearing from beneath her head. Carn gingerly raised her head and could see that she had struck the edge of a rock leaving a deep gash above her ear. Blood poured out. Carn ripped up his shirt and pressed a pad of it to Mrs McDonald's head.

There was nothing he could do on his own. He could ride the pony back and get help, but he didn't want to leave her alone with nothing being done to stop the bleeding.

There was a chance, just a chance, that Nudd and Erbyn were with the geldings. Carn stared up the track. For the second time that morning he thought back to his silent call that had brought Midnight. He pictured the two geldings with their honey coats and cream manes. In his mind he stared into their eyes and directed all his energy into a silent call.

The mare skittered away: the foal stopped dead in its tracks. Erbyn and Nudd had harnessed the geldings to the cart and had just climbed up. Erbyn was reaching for the reins when the ponies shot forward. Erbyn cried in alarm, clutched at Nudd and the pair of them tumbled over backwards into the cart.

Nudd struggled to his knees as the cart bounced down the track. It was all he could do to cling to the side to avoid being thrown out. Erbyn did a little better. He hauled himself towards the bench seat and when one jarring bounce threw his legs into the air he managed to throw one leg over the seat and pulled himself onto it. There was no way that he could sit up; he just lay along the bench holding on with arms and legs. He could see that the reins were trailing along the ground, well out of his reach.

"Whoa, boys, whoa! Steady! Steady!" He did his best to call out, but the jarring made his voice breathless and shaky.

In the back, the ropes that they were used for securing their loads of logs were bouncing about and had wrapped themselves about Nudd's head. He had a sudden vision of the end of the rope becoming caught in the wheel and desperately tried to throw the ropes off. In his panic he didn't notice that the cart was slowing. It slewed from side to side and stopped. He lay in the back, wrapped in the ropes, gasping and trembling.

Erbyn eased himself upright. "By the great Cernunnos, what was that all about?"

"Sorry, boys! I needed help."

194

Erbyn wiped a hand across his face and blew out between pursed lips. "Next time can you just as...what's happened?" Erbyn had caught sight of Mrs McDonald lying on the ground. Carn was holding a blood-soaked pad to her head. The scarlet of the pad contrasted with the white of her face.

"The foal knocked her over and she banged her head. She's got a horrible gash."

"I'll go and get Mr McDonald," said Erbyn, jumping down and reaching for the reins.

"No good. He's not there. He's somewhere on the far side of the estate."

"We can phone him."

Carn shook his head. "They've only got one mobile phone – and here it is." He pulled a phone from Mrs McDonald's pocket. "I just tried to call the house, but there's no signal here."

"What do we do?"

"We have to get her off this wet ground and back to the house."

Erbyn looked at the prostrate body. "How are we going to do that? I know she's not very big for a Bigun, but we can't lift her."

"Have you got the ropes with you?"

"Yes, they're in the..." Erbyn suddenly realised something. "Where's Nudd? Did he fall out?" He took a couple of paces to one side and looked back up the track.

"No," said a voice, "he didn't fall out." Nudd's head, still with rope around the neck, slowly appeared above the sides of the cart.

"Come on, quick," Carn urged. "We need those ropes."

They tied one end of a rope around Mrs McDonald, passing it under her armpits, threw the other end over the tree branch above her head and then fashioned a loop in it that they placed around the mare's neck. As the sturdy pony leaned her weight into the rope and moved forwards, Mrs McDonald's body was raised from the floor. Carn, Nudd and Erbyn steadied her as best they could and Carn kept the pad pressed to the wound until he could no longer reach. They backed up the cart and then lowered the unconscious figure onto it. Her head and torso lay on the boards with her legs hanging over the end.

"Right boys, well done. Now let's get her back. I'll drive the geldings; Nudd, you sit with her, keep this pressed to her head and try to stop her rolling about; Erbyn, take the mare and get back to the house. Tell them what's happened and get everybody together."

Carn drove the cart to the house trying to go as quickly as he could while still avoiding the worst of the holes, stones and ruts.

When they got back to the house all of the others were waiting for them. Eppie and Issel climbed into the cart to check on the wound. The ponies were nervous and kept jerking the cart.

"Can we get her off this?" Eppie asked.

Carn nodded. "Tegid, grab the reins and walk them forward when I say. Everyone else hold onto her legs and take her weight as she slides off."

With the seven of them straining to take the weight they managed to lower Mrs McDonald to the ground and Eppie inspected the wound.

"Can you deal with it?" Carn asked anxiously. Eppie shook her head.

"It needs stitching. We could do that – but she's lost a lot of blood and I don't like the fact that she's still unconscious. It could be worse than just a cut. She needs a Bigun doctor – and quickly."

"What can we do?"

They all looked at other, but no-one had any ideas.

"I'll phone Jane," Eppie decided.

There was no reply at the Johnson house, so she phoned Jane's mobile.

*

Jane dropped Arthur and Myrddin in Postbridge and then drove on to Tavistock. She had arranged a meeting with some old teacher friends. It was now years since she had left the school and she was anxious that Arthur's education shouldn't suffer by his not attending. She wanted to bring herself up-to-date on what was happening inside the system.

She had no doubts that they were doing the right thing by keeping him at home. He was no ordinary boy and an ordinary education was not what was needed; she only had to see the enthusiasm with which Arthur greeted each new day to know that.

As she was getting out of her car, her mobile rang.

"Jane here. Oh, hi Eppie, how..." she stopped to listen to Eppie's worried voice. "Oh no! Hang on! Let me think." She

196

could only think of one thing to do. "I'll phone 999 for an ambulance. I'll tell them that Mrs McDonald has had an accident, phoned me and then passed out. You disappear when the ambulance arrives."

She made the call and relayed the address.

"What number are you on caller?"

Jane passed on her mobile number.

"And where are you phoning from?"

"Tavistock."

"Tavistock? That's in Devon, but the address of the accident is in Scotland?"

"Yes. I can only think that the bang on her head has confused Mrs McDonald and she phoned my number by mistake. Can you tell them to look for her at the end of the drive, not by the house?"

"All right, caller. The ambulance is on its way."

Jane phoned Eppie back. She didn't think she would be able to concentrate on her meeting, but it might keep her mind off thinking of possibilities.

*

Carn was angry with himself for not thinking ahead. "We should have got her off the cart up near the McDonalds' house, not down here."

"Can't worry about that now," said Eppie. "What's to be done?"

"Are you and Issel all right staying with her? As soon as you hear the ambulance coming, run into the woods and hide."

"We can do that. What about the rest of you?"

"Nudd and Tegid, you go to the McDonalds' house – the key's in her pocket with the phone. Wait until you hear the ambulance coming and press the button to raise the barrier." The brothers nodded at him and he added, "And, Nudd, keep your brother away from the whisky.

"The rest of us will get the cart out of sight and then take a pony each and ride to the far side of the estate. We'll search until we find Mr McDonald. Everybody clear? Good, let's get on."

*

Willie Clark was a waste of space. Even his mother said so.

He'd officially left school as soon as he could; although he'd played truant so much that he'd effectively left the year before. No-one at the school was sorry to see the back of him; a light-fingered individual, no-one's belongings were safe.

He'd hung around at home until his mother had thrown him out, tired of the frequent visits from the police and the fury of neighbours who had had car radios disappear. He now lived on benefits in a grotty bed-sit in the next village and still used theft as a means of boosting his spending money. He was banned from the five pubs nearest to where he lived.

Willie was driving his battered old red Astra. It was untaxed, uninsured and the MOT had long since expired. He'd bought it for twenty pounds from a scrapyard and he felt secure in driving it around the deserted lanes.

He felt a moment's panic when he heard a siren, but then he realised that it was an ambulance not a police car. It was coming towards him and just before they met it signalled a left turn and swung into a farm drive. Willie pulled up opposite the drive.

He knew this was part of the royal estates and he knew who lived there – everybody knew everybody else in that part of the world. It was an old couple called McDonald. On market days Rab McDonald would take a drink in Willie's local. He'd caught Willie going through the pockets of his coat and, old as he was, he'd nearly broken Willie's arm throwing him out of the pub – a pub from which Willie was now banned.

What made Willie stop was not a morbid interest, but the fact that he'd been driving along this lane late at night, taking home a young lady who should have known better, when something had shot across the road in front of the car. He'd jammed on the defective brakes, but felt sure that he'd hit whatever it was. He'd felt his stomach churn. He'd had a few drinks and he really didn't want the police involved. Driving a defective car was one thing, injuring someone with it while over the limit was a different proposition. Willie had had a quick look around and then driven off.

The image of what he'd seen that night hadn't left him. He'd had a very brief, but clear, view of what ran into his headlights. He'd kept it to himself – anyone else would think he was crazy.

That incident had happened just along the lane from the McDonald place – and there were only two properties anywhere near. The barrier hadn't come down behind the ambulance. Willie turned into the drive.

There was no sign of life as he drove slowly past the farmhouse. At the end of the drive he found the ambulance outside a large wooden outbuilding. He couldn't see anyone except two ambulance crew kneeling beside a body. He got out of the car and strolled over, having a good look around as he did so.

One of the ambulance men looked up and groaned. "Clear off, Willie."

"That's not nice, is it? Just being neighbourly, seeing if I can help."

"No-one needs your kind of help. Get away."

Willie looked down at the prostrate figure and sucked in his breath. "Looks nasty. Old boy whacked her, has he? Always was a quick-tempered old goat."

"Whatever's happened here is none of your business. I've told you twice. If you make me get up we'll need another ambulance for you."

"All right! Keep your hair on." Willie ignored them and wandering over to the building he pressed his face against the window. He was moving to the door when the other ambulance man tried another approach.

"When we get a call to a head injury, the police usually turn up. I expect they'll be here any minute."

Willie turned on his heel, jogged back to his car and drove quickly back up the drive and out onto the lane.

*

It was late that evening before Jane got the call she'd been waiting for. She put down the phone and turned to Bob, Arthur and Myrddin with a relieved smile.

"That was Mr McDonald. She's going to be fine. No fractures or other damage. She lost quite a bit of blood and they're keeping her in overnight with suspected concussion, but she'll probably be going home tomorrow."

CHAPTER 18

More successes

Myrddin was needed at a meeting with the production company to progress new images and soundtrack for his presentation at the football stadium and Joe had set out early from the farm to collect him; so early that he was able to join the Johnsons and Myrddin for a second breakfast. He came bearing gifts: a dozen eggs and a bag of the salad leaves that Jane had so enjoyed.

"Can we keep some chickens, Daddy? We've got plenty of room and chickens are so funny."

Jane saw Bob wavering and got her answer in first. "No! We've tried before, but we couldn't keep the foxes out. I think the foxes had more chickens than we had eggs."

Bob nodded his agreement. "You're right, Arthur, chickens *are* very funny. I find it impossible to watch them without a smile on my face. But that's the trouble: if you only have a few chickens you get to know them and you become very attached to them – which makes it all the more distressing when foxes kill them."

"Help yourself to coffee, Joe, and there's plenty of bread if you'd like more toast. I'll just go and check the emails in case there's anything we need to sort out with Myrddin before you go. Did you say you'll be back this evening or tomorrow?"

"Tomorrow, Jane. It will be best if Joe brings me back as far as Exeter; I'll meet you there for the magazine interview and come back here with you – if that is all right?"

"Of course. I need to go to the Green Party offices in Exeter, so I can do that first. It's Bob's day off tomorrow, and I've no doubt that he and Arthur can entertain themselves in their usual way– so everything fits in perfectly." Jane headed for the lounge and her laptop.

"So, young Arthur, what do you have planned for today?" Myrddin asked.

"Until Mummy's finished her work I'm going to carry on making the ladybird hotel."

"What might one of those be?" asked Joe.

"It's lots of little tubes all stuck together to give ladybirds and other insects somewhere to live." Arthur turned to his father. "I need some more glue."

"Really? You only started on that great big tube yesterday. I thought you'd have more than enough."

"Oh, well, I got a bit on my fingers."

"A bit," said Jane, coming back into the room with a sheet of paper, "I spent a lot of the day trying to separate stuck-together little fingers – and you had so many tubes stuck to your shirt you looked like a mobile ladybird hotel.

"Here's an interesting one, Myrddin. What do you think of this? It's from the vicar of a church in east Cornwall. As his bishop seems so enthusiastic about your message, he's wondering if you'd like to deliver a sermon to his congregation."

Myrddin chuckled. "I might be more at home with a group of druids, if you can find one – I believe that such people still exist." He was clearly thinking through the suggestion and they waited for his response. "No projected images, no soundtrack, just me, talking to them and having to make sure that it isn't me, but the message, that they are thinking about." He nodded. "It must be done – whenever and wherever the opportunity arises."

"Great!" said Bob, "But I think you'll have to brush up on the hymn singing – I don't think your comic songs will go down well. Right, I'm off to work. Enjoy yourselves!"

Arthur ran with his father to the front door and waved him off.

Bob was due to spend the day with a team of volunteers in the Burrator area re-painting signposts and putting up new ones. It was outside his usual patch, but the team would then be moving on to do the same around Fernworthy. The day wasn't looking promising when he set out and the weather worsened steadily as he drove across the moor. By the time he was passing through Princetown the rain was sweeping horizontally across the road, driven by strong gusty winds. It appeared to improve slightly as he dropped down off the moor.

He passed Sharpitor, crossed the cattle-grid and turned left, but as he passed the old railway line and drove down towards the meeting place at Norsworthy Bridge, the rain struck with renewed fury.

He turned onto the car park, stopped alongside the other green Land Rover that was already parked there, wound down the window and spoke to his fellow Ranger.

"Mornin' – lovely day."

"Hello, Bob. You'd think we'd be used to this by now, but I still start each day thinking it's going to be fine."

"You're not the only one by the looks of it – there are a few cars here." As he spoke another car pulled onto the car park.

"Yes – God bless the volunteers, I say. But even the keenest can't paint in this; not unless we've got some underwater paint. What do you think? Shall we give it twenty minutes and see if it eases?"

"O.K. I'll go round the cars and tell everybody."

"No, it's all right, I'll do it. I've already been around twice and got soaked – you stay in the dry."

"Cheers."

"But if it does ease off I can recommend having a look at the state of the river – it's spectacular. And drive back past the waterfall; the leat's over its banks. Regular Niagara we've got."

Bob wound his window up and settled back. The weather didn't improve. Rain hammered against the roof and streamed down windows that rapidly steamed up. Twenty minutes later, when he was pouring a coffee from his flask, there was a tap on the glass. He wound the window down.

"That's it. We're calling it a day here. Maybe the weather will be better in the winter and we can catch up on all the work then! Cheers, Bob. Say hello to Jane and Arthur for me."

Bob said goodbye to his fellow Ranger, finished his coffee, cleared the windows, started the engine and moved away. He stopped briefly to take a look at the torrent that was the River Meavy and then drove alongside the reservoir until he reached the spot where the water from the Devonport Leat cascaded down the hill to join the reservoir. It may not have been Niagara, but it bore little resemblance to the usual modest waterfall.

Bob drove on and stopped near the end of the dam. He smiled to see the ice cream van parked there in windswept isolation. He reached into the back for his waterproofs, pulled them on and then struggled to open his door against the buffeting wind and the deluge. The wind propelled him along the dam until he pulled himself into one of the insets in the parapet.

He peered over the top of the wall. Water gushed over the top of the dam and plunged into the gorge below. The spray mixed with the rain to form a swirling cloud of water so dense that Bob couldn't even see the tops of the trees in the valley below, let alone the River Meavy.

He moved to the other side of the road and looked out across the reservoir. He'd never seen it so full, not even in the depths of winter.

"Full, isn't it?"

Bob turned and it took him a few moments to recognise the man from the ice cream van. His face scarcely showed through the hood of the full-length waterproof cape that stretched practically to the floor.

Bob turned back towards the reservoir. "I've never seen Burrator like this. You need to come here to realise just how much water has been falling on the moor – and this only drains a small part.

"I don't think we'll be having a hosepipe ban this year."

The man managed a weak smile. "It's only a few years back that we had that drought and you could see the farm buildings at the bottom. Good year for ice cream, that was."

"I don't need to ask what sort of year you're having."

"No, it's dreadful. But I don't think it would make much difference if I were selling hot drinks and pasties; there are just no people around."

They re-crossed the road and looked down into the gorge. The water roared beneath their feet.

"And this is only the little Meavy. What else do we have taking water from the moor to the south? Plym, Dart, Teign – I expect I've forgotten some."

"Avon and the Erme," Bob suggested.

"I bet there are some worried people downstream. Only needs a high tide and wind in the right direction and there'll be a lot of places under water."

"I'm sure you're right."

"No doubt about it. But will they ever learn?"

Bob put a hand above his eyes so that he could turn into the driving rain to study the face alongside. "Learn what?"

"That it's their own fault. Mucking up the planet. Messing about with the weather." He paused. "Actually, I'm wrong. They *have* learned that – but what they haven't learned is that it's up to them to do something about it. Right, I've had enough of this. I'm off home. Fancy an ice cream – on the house?"

Bob hesitated. "You're on! But I'm going to pay, that way I won't feel guilty about asking for a flake."

The ice cream man pipped his horn as he pulled away.

Bob leaned against the Land Rover looking across the swollen reservoir. Lost in thought, white streams from his uneaten ice cream ran unnoticed over his hand and down his arm.

We've been blind and stupid for too long. Myrddin, you're thirty years too late.

*

Joe waved to Jane and Arthur and drove the Toyota out onto the lane heading for Chagford. The rain was keeping people off the village streets, but the roads were packed with traffic, mostly holidaymakers driven away from the beaches and passing the time driving aimlessly from village to village.

They made very slow progress until they reached the A30 dual carriageway and joined the solid flow of traffic heading towards Exeter. They were passing Tedburn St. Mary when Joe cleared his throat.

"I think we're being followed."

"Oh yes? How interesting." Myrddin moved so that he could see in the wing mirror. "And who do you think is following us?"

"The silver car, see: third one back. It joined the A30 at the same junction and no matter how fast or slow I go it stays the same distance behind."

"Ah! I wondered at the curious variation in our speed."

"What do I do about it?"

"Nothing at all. Just drive to the meeting as you would normally."

"I could try to lose him," Joe suggested wistfully.

"That will not be necessary, trust me."

Joe continued to keep an eye on the following car. When they joined the M5 and headed north he said, "He's still with us."

As they drove past the long slip road for junction twenty-nine, Myrddin turned in his seat to look back at the silver car.

As he continued along the motorway Joe said, "Oh, maybe I was imagining things – he's turned off."

"Yes, I thought he might."

*

Sligo thought he'd had a lucky break. He was still looking for somewhere to park in Chagford when he saw Joe Morgan and Myrddin drive by. He tucked in behind and followed, keeping the Toyota in view, and a couple of cars between them.

There was a lot of traffic on the roads. The rain grew heavier and it was so dark that all the other cars had their lights on.

Sligo was confident he hadn't been spotted.

He calmly watched the Toyota drive on up the motorway as he took the slip road at junction twenty-nine. He was only a couple of miles from Honiton before he realised what he'd done: he'd lapsed into some sort of daydream and let them get away. He heaped curses upon his own head and his initial reaction was to put his foot down and get back to the motorway as quickly as possible. But as he calmed down he knew that his chance had gone.

He slowed down and spent the rest of his journey back to Princetown reviewing the progress he'd made and trying to decide on his next step. There was one obvious move that he briefly considered.

Myrddin was in the news. He was receiving coverage in the press and on television and Sligo called himself a reporter. He could simply try for an interview and see what information he could wring out of the old man. But Sligo had a feeling that Myrddin was no ordinary old man and he had a vivid recollection of the pain in his head that had followed when he had looked into Myrddin's eyes – even though it had been a distant look through a pair of binoculars.

Then he'd had that peculiar nosebleed; and now this strange mental aberration. Added to that, the old goat seemed capable of playing mind games with the reporters that attended his meetings so that they enthused over his claptrap.

No, he'd do without an interview and continue his research from a safe distance, but what form could his research take? He'd spent money on this story, but it seemed to have got stuck. It wouldn't be long before other reporters tracked Myrddin to the

Johnson house and part of his advantage would be lost. On the other hand, the more publicity that the old man generated, the greater the impact that his own story would have when he broke the revelations about Myrddin, HRH, the would-be politician, the dubious ex-accountant, the trader with the criminal record and the disappearing children.

O.K. old man, while you're busy digging the big hole that I'm going to push you all into, I've got to find those kids so I'm ready to push the button.

He needed a breakthrough – and it wouldn't be long coming.

*

Being contacted by a magazine journalist had been a stroke of luck. It had guided Jane away from concentrating on the newspapers and television to the vast magazine market. Assuming that the first such interview in Exeter went well, Jane would set up more of the same. She spent most of the morning researching the market. Myrddin was keen to move everything along as quickly as possible, so from the initial long list of possible titles she discounted the quarterly magazines with their long lead-in times and prioritised the others by circulation figures. She would contact the top five as soon as she'd seen how the first interview went.

The daily flow of emails was bringing other opportunities. Radio Devon wanted Myrddin as a studio guest. That would be another first: no visual images, no eye contact with the listeners. She'd have to discuss it with Myrddin, but she felt sure he would agree. It may have taken him years to reach this stage in his plans, but he seemed possessed by an urgency, even a desperation, to make progress. Although when in Arthur's company he continued to radiate confidence and conviction, she could see that every day of bad weather, every news item covering the damage done by the elements, was increasing a restlessness in him. Only the previous evening he had told her that he would not be able to spend as much time with Arthur as he had hoped. His words had stuck in her mind and the expression on his face had chilled her.

"If we cannot quickly bring about the necessary change in people and begin the changes in the way that they live," he'd said, "there will be no people left for him to lead."

She shook her head and forced her attention back to the job in hand. The presentation in Bristol, forming part of an environmental conference, had been attended by members of a number of organisations and the enthusiasm of the attendees was now giving rise to enquiries from those organisations.

Friends of the Earth wanted to know if Myrddin would join a televised debate on the housing situation; a debate that would be focusing on how housing developments should be designed so as to give residents the highest quality of life compatible with minimal impact on the environment. The Green Party wanted a meeting to discuss how the key points of Myrddin's message could be written into a political party's manifesto.

Jane looked at her watch. She wanted to be finished by lunchtime so that she could spend the afternoon with Arthur. She set about dealing with the advertising for the football stadium meeting. Twenty minutes after she had arranged advertising on the local radio station, a reporter from the station's news desk phoned back. Tipped off about the forthcoming free event she wanted to know more about objectives, the speakers and the environmental trust picking up the bills. Intrigued by the answers that she received, she promised to arrange an interview with Myrddin to be broadcast on the day before the event. That, combined with the coverage in the local newspaper, a leaflet drop and the interest that Myrddin was already generating, should ensure a good attendance.

The national newspapers hadn't picked up on it yet. She had mixed feelings about it: yes, she would like the exposure that the press could bring, but she dreaded the thought of her home besieged by the tabloids.

*

The following morning arrived with weak, watery sunshine as if the skies had exhausted themselves with the torrential rain of the previous day. Jane left Bob and Arthur pulling on Wellington boots in readiness to go into the garden to tackle some of the damage done by the weather. She drove to Exeter to attend a meeting in the Green Party offices and then walked to the hotel where the magazine interview was to take place.

Jane was shown to the table she'd reserved in the coffee lounge. She ordered a coffee. Looking around the crowded room she was pleased that she'd had the foresight to ask for the reservation. She checked her watch. It was close to eleven o'clock. She still felt uncomfortable when Myrddin was on his own in the modern world: to her eyes he so clearly didn't fit in.

She checked her mobile for messages, but she needn't have worried, Myrddin arrived at the same time as her coffee.

She stood and waved as he came through the door. She couldn't help noticing that every pair of eyes in the room followed him as he walked to her table. Even this close to the cathedral, where men in religious garb were a common sight, Myrddin caught the attention.

And it's not just the long brown robe, sandals and long beard, is it? Jane mused as he approached. *There is something about you that just demands that people take notice.*

"Ah, Lady Jane, good morning." He spoke quietly, but in a rich warm voice that somehow carried around the room. He winked at her as he leaned forward to kiss her hand.

"Don't call me that," she whispered and gave him a gentle kick in the ankle as they sat down.

"A large glass of water, please," he said to the waiter who was still hovering after bringing Jane her coffee and who was looking from Jane to Myrddin with unconcealed curiosity.

"Certainly, sir, at once," the waiter said and started to move away.

Myrddin detained him for a moment with a hand on his arm. "There is no hurry, my friend. I am not dying of thirst."

The waiter looked baffled for a moment; then he nodded, smiled and walked away.

The room had gone quiet. All eyes were still on Myrddin, although most of the people were pretending to be looking elsewhere. He looked around and gave the room a serene smile before turning back to Jane.

"People today do not drink enough water."

Jane had the distinct impression that the water drinking of those in the room would undergo a sharp increase.

"Your meeting went well, I trust?" he asked.

"Yes, it did. And I had a good session yesterday – we have quite a few possible actions to discuss. How was your meeting yesterday?"

"Splendid. The boys and girls at the production company continue to work wonders. I had a little difficulty when we first met: they are so full of their own bright ideas that they were keen to share with me. But now that I have got them to see things my way, they produce exactly what I have in mind. It is uncanny, really." He winked again. "And they always make my work their top priority." He chuckled, clearly feeling very pleased with himself. "We will have a perfect presentation for the football stadium."

The door half-opened and a young woman struggled in. She was carrying a briefcase and an enormous handbag. Draped over one arm she had both a waterproof coat and a large knitted jacket. The waiter held the door fully open for her. Jane watched as she spoke to him and was then clearly directed to their table.

"Here comes our journalist," she said, quietly. "She's called Sophie Green of *The Way We Live* magazine. It comes out weekly and has a growing circulation; could be very useful to us."

The young woman made her way across the busy room, banging a coffee drinker on the head with her briefcase. When she turned to apologise she managed to sweep crockery onto the floor with her coat. When she eventually arrived at their table her somewhat plump face looked pink-cheeked and harassed. They stood to greet her but she began piling her belongings onto the spare chair and started speaking without looking at them.

"I could do with a double-strength Americano."

The waiter had followed her to the table and heard the request, but Myrddin caught the waiter's eye, shook his head and mouthed, "Another large water."

The young woman continued without pause. "Sorry I'm late. I don't know if I am. I usually am. The traffic was terrible and when I got here I couldn't find anywhere to park. Been driving round and round. Finally got on a meter and then found that I could only park for an hour. That's no use to man nor beast. We'll have to try and get through in time or I'll get another ticket. Then I didn't have the right change – you never do have, do you? You just don't know what to wear these days do you? I got drowned yesterday, so today I brought a choice of coats, but then the sun comes out and it's too hot." As she spoke she searched the briefcase for something that she'd clearly failed to find as she moved to searching the bulging handbag. "I know it's in here somewhere – I'm sure it is." She tipped the contents of the bag onto the chair and bent to pick up those items that cascaded to the floor. "Here it is. I knew I had it." She put a small voice recorder on the table. "The battery's nearly gone. I think I have a spare here somewhere. No, no, can't see it – have to do without. Now, where's my notepad. There it is." She pulled a notepad from the heap on the chair and half of the items returned to the floor. She groaned, but made no attempt to pick them up. She looked at her watch. "Oh no! That's fifteen minutes on the meter gone already and we haven't even started."

At last she looked at them and seemed to realise for the first time that they were standing.

"Sorry – bit of a shambles this morning. But then I'm a bit of a shambles every morning. Sophie Green, *The Way We Live* magazine." She broke off to search her briefcase and then the chair for a business card. "No cards; typical." Her face was bright pink and there was the sheen of perspiration on her forehead. She looked from one to the other.

"Mr Merdin and, er, Jane – oh, should that be Lady Jane?" she looked over her shoulder in the vague direction of the waiter. "He said something about…"

Myrddin reached across the table and took one of her hands in each of his. She looked at him, initially with one of the anxious quick glances that seemed to be part of her, but then she looked back to his face and into his eyes.

"Miss Green, everything is all right."

She held his gaze for a few seconds and then smiled. "Yes, everything is all right."

She didn't use the recorder or the notepad, but was delighted with the interview. They walked her back to her car with ten minutes to spare.

*

Sligo had followed Jane to Exeter, parked in the same multi-storey and trailed her to the Green Party offices. When Sligo was in pursuit of a good story he had the patience of any camouflaged predator waiting for prey to come within striking distance. And like many such predators, one good catch would feed him for a long time.

He had waited patiently for Jane to re-appear and then followed her to the hotel. He had watched Myrddin arrive and had smirked at the effect that the weird old man had on people he passed in the street. Sligo had walked past the window of the coffee lounge a couple of times and checked that he was watching the only exit.

He had seen them come out with a girl he didn't recognise and, safely concealed on Exeter's crowded streets, followed the three of them to the girl's car. He never got closer than a hundred yards and had used his binoculars to check the registration plate. He had also seen a sticker in the rear window promoting a magazine called *The Way We Live*.

After the car had pulled away, Sligo had followed Jane and Myrddin back to the multi-storey. He had only followed the old Fiesta for half a mile to be sure that they were heading back towards Chagford and had then let them go.

Later that day, back in Princetown, Sligo checked his emails and looked up *The Way We Live*.

He spoke out loud to his laptop screen. "Well, well – one of Big Ron's. Can't see one of *his* mags suddenly going holier-than-thou. Myrddin whatever-your-name-is, you're about to find that your easy ride is over."

*

Bob and Arthur had only been working in the garden for ten minutes before Bob called a halt. They had both built up big deposits of red Devon mud on their boots and wherever he stepped he was compacting the soil.

"Right, that's enough – we're doing more harm than good. Let's do something else with our day."

Arthur looked at him expectantly, but Bob didn't make any suggestions. "It actually looks as if it might be a fine day – what would you like to do?"

Arthur thought for a moment. "Let's catch the bus to Bovey Tracey! We can go to the marble place and the nature reserve and that place on the river with the nice things."

"The craft centre?"

"Yes. That's free as well. They've got a nice café, too." He hesitated. "But we don't have to buy anything."

Bob looked down fondly at his son. Arthur was busily engaged picking mud off his hands. They tried not to talk about money in front of him, but he clearly understood that there wasn't a lot of spare cash.

"Sounds good to me. I expect we can stretch to a bowl of soup and an ice cream. Come on! Let's go!"

They moved slowly from the fruit garden. Each step needed an effort to lift the boots and their muddy load.

Back on the patio, Bob said, "Hang on; let's clean these boots up a bit before we try to get them off." They moved to the hosepipe mounted on the wall where he unrolled a couple of yards and turned on the tap. The water came out steadily and Bob used his thumb over the end of the pipe to direct a high-pressure jet at Arthur's boots. As the last of the mud washed away, Bob moved his thumb slightly so that a fine spray hit Arthur in the face.

Arthur chuckled with his eyes tightly closed. "I knew you'd do that," he said.

"Oh dear; getting predictable am I?"

"Yes," said Arthur. "I'll do yours."

Bob passed him the end of the pipe and Arthur carefully washed the mud off his father's boots. Bob had a pretty good idea of what was coming.

As he moved around behind Bob to clean the back of the boots, Arthur reached out and gave the tap a couple of quick turns. A jet of cold water hit Bob in the small of the back. He gasped and started to turn, but Arthur wasn't finished. He jammed the end of the hosepipe down one of Bob's boots and then lay on the wet, muddy slabs helpless with laughter while Bob made a show of having difficulty turning the tap off, first turning it the wrong way so that water pumped out of his boot.

They had a great day out and returned in the early evening to find Jane eager to hear all about it and keen to tell them of the successful day that she'd had. The interview had gone well and an item should appear in the next edition of the weekly magazine; arrangements for the football stadium meeting were progressing nicely; an interview on local radio on the day before had been set up and, on the day following the stadium address, Myrddin would be appearing on a Radio 4 discussion programme.

They were all pleased with their day.

CHAPTER 19

The enemy

Sligo had placed an order for the next issue of *The Way We Live*. On the evening before it was due to arrive he went to The Plume of Feathers for a drink. He had made a point of telling anyone who would listen that he was a writer researching a book on the folklore of Dartmoor and that he was particularly interested in 'the little people'.

As the landlord poured his glass of red wine, he nodded in the direction of a man and a woman sitting at a table near the fireplace. "That's a man you should talk to. He can tell you a thing or two about the little people. Name's Dan Murphy."

Sligo moved over and fixed an oily smile on his face. "Excuse me. May I buy you folks a drink?"

Mr and Mrs Murphy looked at him suspiciously. "And why would you be after doing such a thing?"

"I'm a writer and I'm collecting material for my new book. It's about Devon folklore and what I really want to do is collect as many tales as I can about 'the little people'…"

Mrs Murphy interrupted him with a loud groan. "Who told you about that?" She turned and looked accusingly towards the bar. "Was it you?" The landlord shrugged apologetically and she turned back to Sligo. "He's not talking about it."

"Oh, I see. That's a pity. I can pay quite well for useful information. Still, never mind. Sorry to bother you." He started to turn away.

"How much?"

"Sorry?"

"How much will you pay?" Dan asked, ignoring the threatening looks from his wife.

"Well, that all depends on the information."

"Daniel Murphy, have you gone mad? I've only just managed to stop you talking all this rubbish, and now you're going to set it all off again."

"I saw one of the little people – and I saw him killed. I could have stopped it, but I didn't."

"When was this?"

"Five, six years ago, when I was in the army…"

"Right that's it! Either you shut up about this right now, or I'm off."

"I was a spotter on a live firing ex…"

Mrs Murphy slammed her glass down onto the table. "Give me the car keys." Dan meekly handed them over to his wife. "You can make your own way home. I'm leaving." Giving Sligo a glare that would have shrunk a more sensitive individual she stalked from the bar.

"Let me get you another pint of Guinness before we start." When he'd returned to the table, Sligo continued. "It's not easy talking about these things. You'd be surprised at how many people around here have seen something, but they don't have the courage to talk about it. Now, what exactly did you see?"

*

The next morning Sligo walked around the corner to pick up the magazine and a pack of cigarettes. He didn't bother with any other papers: he had a lot to think about. He crossed the road to the café and sat at a table towards the rear.

While he waited for his mug of black coffee, he sat with the magazine unopened looking at the shorthand notes on his pad. He didn't understand how there could be so many people in one small area who were all crazy enough to believe in pixies.

To him it was obvious: very small people equalled children. It couldn't possibly be anything else. The previous evening while he had listened to Murphy's tale, he had just about managed to keep an encouraging expression on his own face, but he had been struggling to prevent himself from shouting, "It was a child, you idiot! A sprog! Somebody's brat!"

Now he looked at his pad and shook his head in amazement. As if he couldn't quite believe it, he wrote the list out again so that it filled a page.

214

An ex-accountant who'd ducked out off his profession to take up a dead-end job.

An ambitious would-be MP keen to dip into the Westminster gravy train.

A senior member of the Royal Family.

A religious nutter telling us to save the planet by being nice to each other.

A Welshman with a mobile shop and a criminal record for handling stolen goods.

A child killed by the Army and the whole thing hushed up.

Sligo sat back in his chair. The satisfied smirk on his face showed that he was pleased with his thoughts.

I only came to this dump to get away for a bit and the fates have given me the story of the decade – no, longer. A hundred years from now they'll still be talking about this – and I'm the one who's going to break it.

He unconsciously reached into his pocket for a celebratory cigarette, but a voice from behind him said, "Sorry, no smoking." He gave an exasperated grunt and picked up the magazine.

If one of Smith's mags has started the press attack on this conman Myrddin, maybe I'll go to his group with the story.

*

The news report on the local radio station on the day before the football stadium meeting had generated so much reaction from listeners that the station had invited Myrddin to be interviewed on the morning of the event. Joe had been left at the stadium making sure that everything would be ready for the evening and Jane had driven Myrddin to the radio studios in the Toyota. The interview had gone very well, with all the questions asked being ones that Myrddin would have chosen himself.

As they got back into the car Jane congratulated him and passed him a copy of *The Way We Live* opened at Sophie Green's full-page article.

"I have to admit that I'm a bit nervous about tonight, but so far nothing could have gone better. Just look at that – it's perfect!"

Myrddin calmly read the article with a small smile on his face. He nodded. "Yes, rather good. In fact, I don't think I could have written it better myself."

As Sligo read his mouth fell open. When he'd finished he said aloud, "What the devil is this load of pap?"

He turned back to the cover, read the contents page and flicked through some of the pages. The rest of the magazine was exactly what he had expected: nothing but the thinly-disguised marketing of unnecessary goods and services aimed at the weak-minded, style-obsessed reader. Sixty-percent of the page area was covered with advertising.

The article entitled *The Message not the Man* stuck out like a sore thumb.

Sligo decided that it was time to make a phone call.

*

Ronald Smith's terrible year was getting worse week-by-week. The half-year figures from his hotels, marinas and corporate events companies had been bad, but those from the house builders were disastrous.

As the board had nervously reported, half of the land they had acquired for future building was currently under water, as were a sizeable proportion of the sites under development. Furthermore, their long-established practice of not employing any of their own labour, but using only sub-contractors screwed down to the lowest possible price, had back-fired. The shoddily built houses were not standing up to the extreme weather conditions and they were now finding it hard to obtain the industry-standard ten-year guarantee.

Smith's business empire was now dependent on the luxury car dealerships, publishing, the television channel and the airline.

Together with Patricia Jakes, he had just attended a meeting with the chief accountant of the holding company and he hadn't liked what he'd heard. As the other businesses had suffered Smith had demanded that the newspapers, magazines and television channel carry advertising for the struggling parts of his empire either free of charge or at much reduced rates. The more they had struggled, the more advertising he had demanded they run. This was having a significant impact on the profitability of the companies carrying the advertisements and the accountant claimed that analysts would now be querying the levels of advertising revenues.

The combined figures of all of the businesses within the holding company were so bad that the accountant had insisted that they must issue a profits warning to the City. No matter how Smith had ranted and railed against him, the accountant had quietly stuck to his guns. Not only that, but he wanted the warning issued before the rapidly approaching Annual General Meeting of the Smith Corporation.

For years Smith had enjoyed the AGM. It had given him the opportunity as Chairman to be the star of the occasion, boasting of the year-on-year increases in profitability and receiving the plaudits of investors grateful for the soaring share price and steadily increasing dividend stream. The last thing Smith wanted was to issue a profits warning before the meeting. Most of the shareholders at the meeting would be the harmless old duffers who liked their day out in the City because it made them feel important; but there would be the smart-aleck kids from the institutional investors and they would give him a hard time.

The accountant wanted him to issue the warning first and then use the meeting to address all the steps they were taking to improve the situation: which, he said, should include stopping all the contributions to charity and political parties. That, thought Smith, would be the end of his hopes of a title.

He was sitting at his desk, twisting a paper knife in his hands. When he thought of the hard time his wife would give him his twist on the knife snapped it and blood ran from a cut. He didn't notice. That wife of his: the last thing he needed was hassle from her. Maybe it was time to get rid of her. A divorce would be far too expensive: there was no way she'd be getting that sort of money out of him. No: an accident would be useful. A shooting accident? No: too obvious. Could he pay the pilot to push her out of the chopper? Unlikely – but he liked the thought. A robbery gone wrong? Yes: easy. He'd have to brief them on the security system and make sure it was when he was hundreds of miles away. Who should he use?

He was enjoying the planning process, but it was interrupted by a knock.

"What is it, Trish?"

She opened the door between their offices and poked her head into the room.

"Got a minute, Ron? There's something you should see."

He sighed and mentally filed away until later the planning of his wife's demise.

"Let's see it." He watched his personal assistant. approach his desk. She had a single file in one hand and the usual notepad and pen in the other. She put them on the desk, took the paper knife from his hands, dropped it in the brass wastepaper bin, came around to his side of the desk, opened one of the drawers, took out a pad of tissues, pressed it against the cut on his hand, went back to the other side of the desk, sat down and crossed her legs.

"I should have married you, Trish."

She raised an eyebrow. "Yeah, you've said that before, Ron. Nigel Sligo phoned…"

"Who? Oh, yeah, that cretin – how could I forget? That story of his we ran last year cost us a hundred grand in damages." He paused and an unpleasant smile spread across his fat face. "Worth it, though. That idiot had ideas of becoming Prime Minister – no chance now. Anyway, what's scumbag Sligo phoning me for? If he's got dirt on somebody he goes to the editors; he doesn't bother me with his muckraking."

"He phoned yesterday, but I wanted to do a bit of research before I bothered you with it. He says he's onto the biggest story ever: so big that the whole world will want to hear it. It involves all of these:" she looked down at her pad and read off, "a senior member of the Royal Family; a would-be MP with the Green Party; an accountant who left his profession under strange circumstances to take up a dead-end job; a Welsh mobile shop owner with a criminal record for handling stolen goods; a child killed by the Army, who hushed it up; and a religious nutcase who calls himself Myrddin. That's Welsh: it's spelt M-Y-R-D-D-I-N, but it's pronounced Merthin."

Smith raised his eyebrows. "And knowing Sligo, he'll be digging up every speck of dirt he can find, but why did he come to me with it?"

She opened the file and passed Smith an opened copy of a magazine. "He wondered if you knew that one of your mags is carrying this sort of stuff."

Smith started reading. After a couple of paragraphs he glanced up to see the name Sophie Green as the by-line. Halfway through, with his face already as black as thunder, Smith turned to look at the cover and check the contents page. When he'd finished reading he looked up at Patricia Jakes.

"Madness!" He shook his head. "Black bag job. No," he turned to look at the editorial page and found the name of the editor, "two black bags. Call security."

"Will do – but you'll have to be quick, Ron. There's more."

"More!!" He looked back at the magazine.

"It mentions in there a meeting at a football stadium. That was yesterday evening. It was arranged at only two weeks' notice and it was a sell-out – no, that's the wrong term, it was free. Anyway, over ten thousand people turned up. There are rave reviews on local radio, in the local press, and in one of the broadsheets – its editor was there."

Smith's face was purple and had developed a twitch affecting one eye.

"And that's not all: you may have noticed that the BBC's staging an 'environmental week' with a lot of 'special' programmes. There's a discussion programme starting in twenty minutes. This Myrddin character is a 'special' guest. I think you should listen to it."

Four minutes later Patricia Jakes ushered the editor of *The Way We Live* into Smith's office. She'd never been in the room before. There wasn't time to take in any details other than that the bloated figure of Smith was sitting behind an enormous desk and there was an atmosphere that she could have cut with a knife. Smith didn't look at her; he stared at a copy of her magazine that lay on the desk in front of him.

The door opened again and two uniformed security men moved to stand behind the editor. One of them carried a black, plastic bin-liner.

Smith spoke without looking up.

"Is Sophie Green at her desk?"

"Er, yes, I think so."

"You will tell her that she is instantly dismissed."

"Yes, Mr Smith, on, er, what grounds?"

"On the grounds that she is insane. These two gentlemen will go with you. One will take her car keys and security pass and will then accompany Miss Green from the premises. You will then put any of her personal possessions in the black bag and the other gentleman will take it outside to her. Is that clear?"

"Yes, Mr Smith."

"Good." He finally looked up at her. "You will be back here within eight minutes. Is that also clear?"

She nodded. Patricia opened the door for the editor and the security men to leave.

Seven minutes later, the editor was shown back in. She wasn't invited to sit down.

"Tell me, whatever your name is…"

"It's…"

"…what are the sources of income for your magazine?"

"The cover price and the advertising revenue."

"Quite. And what percentage comes from advertising?"

"Last year, seventy percent; it will be lower this year because of the low cost ads we're running for other companies in the group."

"Quite so. And why do our client advertisers choose to pay us to advertise in this magazine?"

"Because our readership reflects their target market."

"Exactly – we tell the gullible fools that they will be socially inadequate unless they buy the sort of useless junk that is advertised on all the pages." Smith paused and opened the magazine. "So why did we print this article that tells the readers that in order to be happy they needn't buy any of the stuff that is advertised in the magazine."

"Oh, but that's not what it says, it…"

"That is exactly what it says." The door opened and the two security men stepped back into the room. "You're fired. One of these gentlemen will escort you from the building: give him your car keys and security pass. Miss Jakes will clear your desk of all your personal possessions. They will be passed to you outside the front door."

He looked at his watch and at Patricia. "Ten minutes."

She was back with two minutes to spare.

Smith used the remote controls on his desk to turn on the wall-mounted flat-screen system and selected Radio 4. Patricia went to the drinks cabinet. She took a cut glass tumbler and a bottle of thirty-year-old single malt to his desk before settling herself with her notepad on her lap. For the hour of the programme the only sound in the room, apart from the radio, was the sound of her pen scribbling rapid shorthand.

The programme took the form of a panel answering and discussing questions put to them. The panel comprised a cabinet minister, two scientists, representatives of Friends of the Earth and the Green Party, the Bishop of Truro and Myrddin. It always seemed to be Myrddin who had the final word on each topic. He waited until everyone who wished to speak on a topic had done so and then he delivered his own comment in his rich, deep, reassuring voice. After he'd spoken, no-one challenged, or sought to add, to what he had said.

On housing they heard him say it was time to stop building new houses where the purchaser would have to use a car to get to places of work, shops, schools, hospitals, restaurants and leisure centres: that the priority was to build communities, not houses, and that the each community needed, not just gardens, but areas for the cultivation of food and social interaction.

On air travel he said that an efficient rail system, sensibly priced, would remove the need for internal flights; that politicians and business people were failing to grasp the potential of video-conferencing to remove the need for travel and that people had come to believe that they needed their foreign holidays 'to get away from it all' when all they needed to do was to make adjustments to their daily lives so that the need to get away evaporated.

On consumerism he pointed out that people had allowed themselves to be brainwashed by commercial interests into believing that they needed to keep buying goods to give them satisfaction and that the more they bought, the greater the pressure on them to earn the necessary money, and the greater the pressure, the more things they bought as a release.

On gas-guzzling cars he commented that high taxes on fuel hit everyone and that the best weapon against the selfish rich with their massive cars was ridicule. "Laugh at them in the street and as it is envy that they are seeking, they will soon change their misguided ways."

At the end of the programme they heard the chairman congratulate Myrddin on the previous evening's highly successful presentation. He confirmed that a much larger gathering was now being planned for Wembley Stadium when he would share the platform with HRH The Duke of Cornwall.

Patricia was scribbling the last of her notes when she heard a crunch. Smith was pointing at his mouth and she realised that he'd bitten a piece out of his glass. She carefully removed the bite-sized fragment from between his lips.

As soon as he felt safe he said, "What's going on, Trish? We've heard all that claptrap before. There's nothing new – so why are people listening this time?"

"I don't know, Ron. He *has* got a wonderful voice. If they'd shut the others up and just let him talk, he'd have convinced the million or so people listening."

Smith snorted. "Right – let's sort this conman out and get this lot nipped in the bud. I don't know what his angle is, but I do know he's got one. Call a meeting for this afternoon in the staff restaurant at three o'clock. I want the editor and deputy editor of both the papers and all the mags there – plus the three senior members of the board of SmithTV. Tell them that if they want to keep their jobs, they'll be there.

"And phone Sligo. Tell the creep that whatever his story is, we want it – and we want it now. Where is he, anyway?"

"Dartmoor."

"Dartmoor? How come he's working on a story in Dartmoor? What's he in for – I didn't hear anything about it."

"No, Ron, he's not in the nick, he phoned from some village on the moor. Most of it's owned by HRH The Duke of Cornwall, apparently."

*

When Sligo's phone rang he checked the number of the caller before answering.

"Hello, Trish; took your time."

"Miss Jakes, to you, scumbag."

"No, Trish, it's whatever I want to call you: I've got something you need, remember, Trish? And with every insult the price goes up."

"Big Ron says he wants the story and he wants it now."

"No."

"What do you mean, no? You know he'll pay top price – and that's why you phoned isn't it?"

"Yes, but I'm not ready to sell yet; there's one more element of the story that I need to get a grip on."

"He won't like it."

"No, I don't suppose he will, but tell him he'll like the story even more with the last piece of the jigsaw in place. There's one thing you can do for me."

"Oh yes?"

"Ask your news offices for anything they've got connecting the Duke of Cornwall, children and Scotland over the last five or six years."

"Scotland? I thought the story was in Devon."

"Most of it is. I can take care of this end, but I need a hand with Scotland. Anything at all involving kids."

"Ron'll go mad."

"You can handle him, Trish, you always have."

*

"That cretin's got the nerve of the devil. Expects me to pay him for a story and wants us to get it for him. It better be as good as he says it is."

It was three o'clock and they were walking to the staff restaurant. Smith's bulk moved along the corridors like a steamroller, any staff seeing him coming dived for cover. As Smith pushed the double swing doors open the buzz of conversation immediately stopped.

He didn't waste time with preamble.

"We have a problem: a problem that threatens everybody working for the Smith Corporation. If you want to keep your jobs, listen to me and take the necessary action.

"We've had the lunatic fringe of the environment lobby after parts of our business for years and we've fought them off – or bought them off.

"Now we're up against something new. All the different bands of loons may be uniting behind one figurehead – a Welsh conman who calls himself by the sole name of Myrddin and who runs an organisation called *The Message not the Man*. He calls it that because he doesn't want anybody looking into his background – and we know what that means, don't we? His message seems as much religious as environmental."

One of the television channel team made a noise and half waved a hand. Smith nodded at her. "Yes?"

"I've heard of him. There's a whisper going around that he's impossible to interview. Interviewers on air don't seem able to ask their questions. They end up letting him control the interview."

"Interesting. So we seem to be dealing with a religious environmentalist who is either a complete fruitcake or a clever

223

conman capable of playing mind games. Whichever it is, we're going to stop him.

"You are not, repeat not, to run anything on him yet. You are just to do the research. I want to know everything about this creep that there is to know. Then, when I'm ready, we blitz him. Every one of you, and I don't care if your mag is devoted entirely to motor bikes or cooking tea-cakes, will then run stories ridiculing him and dishing the dirt on him and his crazy ideas. No matter how big he's grown, we'll wipe him out in a week.

"Understood? Good. But there's another thing. For some reason His Royal Highness, the Duke of Cornwall, is aligning himself with this Myrddin character – so we go for him as well. I know some newspaper proprietors lay off the royals 'cos they want a knighthood – well not me. We go for the throat and I want to see blue blood spilled. I want the whole country convinced that the buffoon should be locked-up.

"So direct your research at HRH, too. Particularly to any of his activities in Scotland that involve children. Got that? Scotland and children: but anything else as well – as long as it makes him sound unsavoury or ridiculous.

"Pull together all the stuff you get on a daily basis and email it to Miss Jakes.

"One more thing: we are co-operating on this one with Nigel Sligo." There was a murmur in the room. "Yes, I know he lives in the sewers, but he reckons he's already onto something, so if he wants anything on the Scottish angle, give it to him.

"Any questions? No? Good – get on with it."

Smith swung around and steered his bulk from the room.

*

In the Johnson house, the atmosphere could hardly have been more different. Jane and Myrddin had got back late the previous night from the football stadium where Myrddin had been delayed after his presentation by members of the press keen to arrange interviews.

Early that morning they had driven to Exeter to catch the train to London for the BBC radio programme. They had taken Arthur with them for his first visit to the capital and after the programme Jane had taken them on a quick tour before catching the train back to Exeter.

224

Now they were all gathered at the kitchen table where Jane, pink-cheeked with the excitement of their successful week, was telling Bob all about their day, while Arthur, equally excited, chipped in with comments about riding on the underground and seeing Big Ben and Buckingham Palace.

"You know," Jane said, beaming around the table, "it just couldn't be going any better. I thought we'd hit problems before now, but everyone we meet is just *so* supportive."

"You'll have to be careful, Myrddin, with all this travelling they'll be having a go at you about your carbon footprint." Bob was joking but Myrddin appeared to take it seriously and nodded.

"Yes, I have thought about that. The train is not a problem. The train is going there anyway, so I may as well get on it. But all this driving around is not good. Perhaps I should fly."

Jane and Bob gave him a puzzled look and Bob said, "But that would be worse, surely."

"Not necessarily," said Myrddin, winking at Arthur.

Still puzzled, Bob changed the subject. "You two may have been too busy to notice, but today was the eighth day in a row that it hasn't rained. We've had a whole week that has really felt like summer."

Jane looked at him. "You're right – I've been too busy to notice, but now that you've pointed it out, you're right, aren't you – I haven't worn a coat or put up an umbrella for days. We're making progress with our campaign and the weather's better. The world suddenly feels a better place."

"You may well be right," said Myrddin. "Perhaps someone has noticed what we are doing."

Bob and Jane exchanged looks and Jane turned to Myrddin. "You don't mean…" she broke off, not sure as to what question she was asking.

"Perhaps," said Myrddin, "the Great Goddess Anu is giving us a little more time."

CHAPTER 20

Snatched!

Sligo only had to wait two days.

When he looked at the batch of emails from Patricia Jakes, one leapt out at him.

It was from a Scottish news office of Smith's Sunday paper. Someone had contacted them wanting to sell them a story about strange goings-on on one of the royal estates. Five or six years ago an outbuilding had been converted, supposedly as a holiday home for handicapped children, but none of the locals had ever seen children, handicapped or otherwise, anywhere near the place. It wasn't much, but Sligo's instincts told him that this could be his missing jigsaw piece. He phoned the news office.

"Haven't got much more than we put in the email," a broad Scottish voice told him. "It was me that took the call, but the laddie sounded drunk and he was rambling on about something he saw one night and a security barrier. Didn't seem worth following up. I thought that by the time he was sober, the story would have disappeared."

"Did you get any contact details?"

"Oh, yes, I typed them into the log while he was on the phone."

"Good – I'm on my way."

Sligo packed his battered old suitcase, got into the Focus and drove through the night, stopping only to grab a couple of hours sleep at a motorway service station. He walked into the news office at eight-thirty with black circles under his red eyes, unshaven and wearing clothes that had clearly been slept in.

"My, my – there must be more to this than I thought," said the reporter, looking him up and down.

"Let's hope so," said Sligo. "Have you got the details for me?"

"Sure. Here you are." He handed Sligo a slip of paper bearing the name Willie Clark, a mobile phone number and an address – not one word of which meant anything to Sligo. "He said the mobile isn't usually on as he can't usually afford to put any credits on it."

"Is this address anywhere near here?"

"Oh no, it's a good forty or fifty miles away." When Sligo groaned he added. "I'll just get on the internet and print you a map, but you look as if you could do with a wee bit of shuteye."

On his way back to the car, Sligo bought an Ordnance Survey map covering the area around Willie Clark's village, then he drove a little way out of town in the right direction and pulled into a lay-by where a hot food caravan was parked. After a bacon sandwich, a mug of coffee and a couple of cigarettes he tried to sleep, but the caffeine and the nicotine had his head buzzing. He gave up and drove on to Willie's village. When he got close he tried the mobile number without success. He eventually found his way to the rundown property that had been loosely converted into bedsits. Picking his way through ripped bags of rubbish and piles of dog mess, he got to a front door that seemed to be painted with pink undercoat, but at least it bore the number he was looking for, albeit scrawled in pencil.

There was no bell, so he banged on the door with his fist. The door opened and an unshaven individual in a vest and torn jeans peered at him warily.

"Willie Clark?"

"Who wants to know?"

Sligo waved a press card bearing the name David Fox. "Press. You contacted my paper about a story." Clark looked uncertain so Sligo added, "There could be good money in it."

Clark walked away from the door, leaving it open. Sligo followed him in, his feet sticking to the lino floor. "What a dump," he said, looking around the hovel of a kitchen.

"You're not looking too special yoursel'", said Willie, looking Sligo over. "How much money?"

"That depends on the story. What have you got for me?" When Clark hesitated, Sligo said, "Just tell me everything. I can guess that some of it might sound weird, but weird stuff's just what I want – and it pays best."

So Willie told him everything he knew: about the estate owned by the Duke of Cornwall that was mainly forestry; about

227

how Willie knew a builder who had worked on the conversion of an outbuilding, supposedly for handicapped children, but no children had ever been seen coming or going; about the security barrier and camera; and about the accident he had had in his car.

"You hit a child?"

"Didnae say it were a bairn."

"You said a tiny figure ran out in front of you and you hit it. How tiny?"

Willie put out a hand to indicate height.

Sligo looked at him. "Looks like a *bairn* to me."

Willie shook his head. "I saw its face."

Sligo sighed. For a moment he wondered how the country survived with so many weak-minded fools in the population.

"What do you know about the McDonalds?"

Willie shrugged. He said that he didn't know Mrs McDonald, but said that the old man had a mean temper and warned Sligo not to underestimate him. He went on to tell Sligo about the day he saw the ambulance go into the estate and how he'd seen Mrs McDonald lying on the ground with a head injury. Word was that she had had a fall, but Willie suspected the old man.

"O.K. – show me the estate on this map." He unfolded the large sheet of paper and had to wait while Willie cleared the kitchen table. "Can you wipe it?" he asked nodding at the deposits of margarine and jam. Willie used a towel and then Sligo spread the map on the table.

Willie clearly wasn't the sharpest tool in the box and Sligo could barely control his impatience until Willie, after much muttering, head scratching and running a dirty finger along the roads, eventually stabbed at the map. "There."

As Sligo was putting a mark on the map, Willie made a suggestion.

"Tomorrow's market day. Old McDonald usually takes a dram or two in the Rutting Stag about twelve o'clock, if you'd like a look at him."

"Oh, yeah, I saw that place on the way here. O.K. meet me in there at twelve and you can point him out."

Willie shook his head. "Canna do that – McDonald got me banned."

Sligo sighed. "O.K. Outside will do. Where can I get a room around here?"

Willie shrugged. "The Rutting Stag."

As Sligo left, he handed over a twenty-pound note with a promise of more to follow.

The Rutting Stag was an attractive pub in the neighbouring market town, but Sligo was in no mood to appreciate its finer points; he could hardly keep awake. His eyes, red from lack of sleep, felt full of grit.

Sligo and the landlord looked each other up and down: neither was impressed by what they saw. Sligo saw a giant of a man towering over him and looking like a caricature of a Scotsman: masses of ginger curls on top of his head merging with an even bigger mass of curly ginger beard that reached to the barrel chest. As he stood with his hands on his kilted hips, he looked a yard wide.

The pale blue eyes looked Sligo over: yes, they had a room, but Sligo would have to pay in advance, in cash. He paid for two nights and was shown to his room.

It was clean, tidy, well equipped and, to Sligo's surprise, came with a wireless broadband connection. He dumped his battered suitcase on the floor, placed his laptop on the dressing table and collapsed onto the bed, where he slept for six hours.

When he woke up he shaved, showered, dressed in slightly less rumpled clothes and, feeling rather more human than when he had arrived, he went in search of something to eat. After a steak that he'd ruined by insisting that it was cooked until it was very well done, he sat at a table in the bar where he would have stayed all evening but, unsettled by the baleful looks that the landlord was throwing in his direction, Sligo went back up to his room and spent a couple of hours doing some useful internet research.

*

"No, Rab, don't be silly. Of course I'll be all right. It was just a wee bang on the head and it was a while ago. You go to the market. You know you like a wee bit craich with your pals. I'll be as right as rain."

With those words Mrs McDonald shooed her husband out of the kitchen and into the estate pick-up.

She waved him off and then turned to Eppie who was sat on a stool wiping eggs at the kitchen table.

"Och!" she said with a smile, "he doesn't do so bad for an old'un."

When she next saw Rab he wasn't looking so good.

Sligo scornfully declined the porridge, the kippers and the bacon and eggs. He had his usual breakfast of several cups of coffee and an equal number of cigarettes.

Afterwards he drove to check out the royal estate. There was nothing to see and he wasn't yet ready to be spotted by the McDonalds so he returned to the town, parked back at the Rutting Stag and walked to the market. It was a warm day and the smell of the livestock market was too much for his city nose. He gave up in disgust and went back to the pub. He sat on a bench near the front door, with his cigarettes and a glass of red wine in front of him.

It was busy and he soon gave up trying to guess which of the many old men was McDonald. Just after twelve o'clock he saw Willie frantically gesturing at him from the other side of the road. Sligo beckoned him across and a clearly reluctant Willie came.

"That was him that was going in when I waved at you."

"Well, come in and point him out."

Willie shook his head. "I'm not going in there. I told you – I'm banned. McDonald's wearing a brown tweed jacket, brown trousers and a McDonald tartan tammy shanter."

"All these old farmers are wearing brown tweed jackets and brown trousers – and how do you expect me to recognise McDonald tartan? You haven't got to stay for a drink, just look through the door and point him out."

Willie shook his head. "Have you not seen McTavish? When McTavish bans a man, only a fool goes anywhere near his pub. I shouldn't be he…"

Sligo grabbed Willie's arm and dragged him to the door, to the amusement of some onlookers. Willie pointed to an old man just sitting down at a small table. "That's him!"

As soon as Sligo let go of his arm Willie ran off. Sligo called after him, "Stick around – I might need you!"

He went in and as he worked his way to the bar between the crowded tables he took from his pocket a small notebook and a fountain pen. McDonald was sat on his own at a tiny table and Sligo wanted to join him before anyone else did. Before the girl behind the bar could serve him, the giant form of McTavish appeared from the other bar and stood before him. As he'd been made to pay cash, rather than with his credit card, Sligo had booked in under the name of David Fox and there was something about the way that McTavish looked at him that made him feel guilty.

"Tell me, Mr McTavish, is there anyone called McDonald in today?"

There was a silence. The pale blue eyes stared down at him. "And why would you need to know that?"

"I'm doing research on the McDonald clan and I'm always interested in chatting to any members."

"There's a McDonald over there; but he's not one for idle chat."

"Excellent! May I have two of whatever Mr McDonald is drinking?"

Two large single malts and a small jug of water appeared in front of him. When McTavish turned his back to use the till, Sligo squirted a few drops of a clear liquid from the fountain pen into one of the glasses. He moved across to the table where Mr McDonald was sitting with both hands resting on the handle of a walking stick.

"Do you mind if I join you, Mr McDonald?" Sligo put the glasses on the table and slid one towards the old man.

The look he received made it clear that Mr McDonald would mind very much.

"I don't know you."

"No, Mr McDonald, you don't, but I hope we'll soon be friends." Sligo slid into a seat as he spoke.

"I have friends enough. How do you know my name?"

"Mr McTavish told me. He knows that I'm researching the McDonald clan and he thought we should have a chat." Sligo smoothly rolled on. "My grandmother was Scots, a MacDonald in fact, although her family spelled it with the 'a' in Mac. It is confusing to someone like me: these different spellings. I see the current clan chief spells it with the m-a-c, but he uses a small d.

"I'm not even sure what to call the clan. Should it be the McDonald Clan or the Clan Donald? What do you think?"

Mr McDonald didn't reply, but Sligo managed to keep a smile on his face as he carried on.

"Have you been to Armadale Castle? I haven't, but I hope to get there on this trip. That's the real centre of the Clan Donald, isn't it? Although it's called something else now: the Museum of the Isles, or something like that."

Sligo raised his glass. "Slainte!"

Mr McDonald hesitated, but then he raised his own glass. "Slainte!"

Sligo pushed his luck. "May the best ye've ever seen."

Mr McDonald smiled. "Be the worst ye'll ever see."

This time Sligo's smile was genuine. *Isn't it wonderful the rubbish you can learn with a little bit of time, a laptop and access to the internet.*

Mr McDonald had drunk the first malt that Sligo had given him and was well down the second. His drinking companion was just starting to think that the drug hadn't worked when he spotted the first signs. The old man was peering intently at the glass in his hand and seemed to be having trouble focussing.

"My old Gran reckoned she could trace her side of the family right back to the first Lord of the Isles. I hear that the current Lord of the Isles owns land around here."

Mr McDonald opened his eyes wide and then nearly closed them as he still tried to focus on his glass. "I work for the Lord of the Isles," he mumbled.

"Do you really?" Sligo suddenly thought he might have given his victim too much. "What about the children you have at the farm?"

Mr McDonald made a noise that was probably a slurred chuckle. He muttered words that Sligo couldn't understand. It sounded something like 'god o'thin car nappy fine people'. Before he could press the old man further, a large shape behind him cut off most of the light from the window and Sligo felt a heavy weight on his shoulder.

He glanced down and found that the weight was a very large hand covered with coarse tufts of ginger hair. He looked further up and found the hand attached to a forearm the size of a leg of pork.

A voice from behind and above him said, "Are ye all right, McDonald?"

Sligo twisted around. "He's fine – just had a bit too much to drink." He tried to rise, but the hand held him down.

"McDonald never tak's a dram too much."

The hand left Sligo's shoulder and he felt his neck seized in a vice-like grip.

McTavish called out. "Janet, tak care of Mr McDonald."

Sligo rose vertically and was carried across the room with his feet six inches from the floor. McTavish used Sligo's head to push open the door and then hurled him over the steps into the street. He put up his hands to protect his face, but the concrete pavement did a lot of damage to his knees and elbows.

The area was still busy and an unsympathetic group of onlookers gathered around as Sligo tentatively tried moving his head to see if his neck was broken. He realised that Willie was one of the crowd and he held out a hand for Willie to help him up.

Suddenly an upstairs window flew open and the crowd scattered as Sligo's suitcase flew out and burst open on the pavement near his head.

The crowd cautiously moved in again. Someone said, "Think yoursel' lucky, laddie: it could have been you coming out of yon window."

The window opened again and something black skimmed out. "Catch it!!" Sligo screamed.

Willie took three quick paces backwards and caught Sligo's laptop above his head, then he moved forward to haul Sligo to his feet. His shirt was torn at both elbows where blood oozed from the painful-looking scrapes. His trousers were torn at both knees and more copious amounts of blood could be seen running down his legs. He limped slowly to his car parked at the back of the pub, while Willie stuffed laptop and clothes back into the ruined suitcase and then hurried to catch up.

Sligo gingerly lowered himself into the passenger seat. Willie dropped the suitcase in the hatchback, took the keys from Sligo and drove him to his mother's where his deeply suspicious parent was very reluctantly persuaded to provide first aid. She would go as far as patching him up, but she flatly refused to let him stay the night.

All Sligo wanted was to rest for the remainder of the day and the night to come. He had a choice: the floor of Willie's flat, or the car. He chose the car.

*

When Mr McDonald became aware of where he was, he found himself lying on the settee in McTavish's sitting room with the doctor standing over him. He heard the doctor speaking.

"Nothing's wrong with his heart or his blood pressure and his temperature's fine. I've no idea what he's taken, but I've got a blood sample and that might tell us. The chances are that he'll sleep off whatever it was and be fine in the morning. You can take him home."

He drifted in and out of consciousness as McTavish drove him home in the estate pick-up.

*

Mrs McDonald was getting worried. Rab wasn't usually as late as this coming home after market day. She busied herself in the kitchen while keeping an anxious eye on the screen. When the camera finally showed her Rab's pick-up turning into the drive, she pressed the button to open the barrier with a smile of relief. It was only when the pick-up pulled up outside the window that she realised that Rab wasn't driving. She pushed the alarm button for a few seconds and then hurried out.

She found McTavish helping Rab from the cab.

"Whatever's happened?" she said, rushing to Rab's side.

"Dinna fash yoursel', Margaret," McTavish reassured her, "Some Sassenach idiot slipped a wee something into his drink. The doctor's checked him over – says he'll be fine in the morning."

McTavish scooped up Mr McDonald and carried him into the kitchen. "I could tak' him up to bed, but he seems to be coming around. I expect he'd like a drop of tea."

Mr McDonald was indeed coming around, sitting upright on the kitchen chair. "McTavish is right. A cup of tea is what I need. I have a taste in my mouth that I wouldn't like to describe. Will you stop for tea, McTavish?"

"No thank you, McDonald. Janet'll be here in a moment to pick me up and we'd best be getting back."

Mrs McDonald walked with McTavish up to the barrier.

"Tell me, Margaret. What was that loud ringing from the woods when we arrived?"

"Just something Rab rigged up to scare the birds off his fruit patch."

A car pulled up. McTavish got in and the car swung around and headed back.

Back in the kitchen Mrs McDonald sounded the alarm bell briefly and then thought she'd better walk down to tell the Gododdin what had happened.

When she got back to the farmhouse she found her husband asleep in an armchair in the sitting room.

*

Sligo woke early. He lay motionless in the fully-reclined front passenger seat while he mentally examined the various sources of pain. His left knee hurt marginally more than his right; the same applied to his elbows; the sensation in his neck was more stiffness than pain, but he had the impression that would change when he moved his head; the new pain was an ache in the small of his back.

He very slowly returned the seat to the upright position and found that he couldn't light his first cigarette of the day without the slight movement increasing the pain in his elbows. He sucked the smoke deep into his lungs and the racking cough that followed caused explosions of pain in his neck.

Sligo sat quietly for an hour gently moving his head from side to side, up and down, until he could move it freely enough to allow him to drive. He gingerly clambered out of the car, hobbled around it a few times to free up his knees and then did some stretches against it to ease his back.

Willie had driven the car to a lay-by outside his village and left Sligo there. It was a beautiful morning; the sun was shining in a cloudless blue sky; birds sang in the trees over his head. But Sligo didn't notice any of it: blind to everything except the anger inside him. He'd had enough of being treated like dirt. It was time to make someone, anyone, pay for everything he'd suffered in recent weeks. He was tired of pussy-footing around: it was time for action.

He limped to the hatchback and looked in his suitcase for his camera: it was missing. He slammed the hatch down and got into the driver's seat. Now the pain of his movements drove his anger. He went to the bedsit and banged on the pink door. He had to bang on the door several times before a bleary-eyed Willie, hair standing on end and wearing a vest and baggy boxer shorts, cautiously opened it.

Willie looked relieved. "Oh, it's you." He headed for the kitchen, leaving Sligo to follow him, and put the kettle on.

He looked enquiringly at Sligo who said, "Black coffee, large, strong, two sugars." He looked at the grubby plastic-covered seat next to him, realised that his clothes were in such a state that a bit more dirt wouldn't matter, and sat down

235

Willie rummaged in the heap of dirty pots in the sink and pulled out two mugs and a spoon that he rinsed under the cold tap and wiped on his vest. He waited for the kettle to boil, yawning and scratching one armpit. He opened the filthy fridge door, took out a plastic milk container, took the top off, sniffed the contents, wrinkled his nose and put it back into the fridge.

Two black coffees made, Willie sat down at the kitchen table opposite Sligo and slurped noisily at his mug.

"Have you seen my camera?"

Willie had a mouthful of hot coffee and didn't reply, but Sligo saw his eyes flick in the direction of a kitchen drawer. Sligo opened the drawer and removed his camera.

"Charming. We're supposed to be on the same side, remember? I'm paying you for help and information."

Willie shrugged. "You haven't paid me much and I didn't know if you were coming back." He nodded at the camera. "That was just in case."

Sligo took out his wallet. He flicked through a wad of twenty-pound notes that Willie stared at with intense interest. "You'll get paid all right: but you have to earn it. I'm going to the McDonald place – and you're coming with me." Willie shook his head, but Sligo ignored it. "You're coming with me. You're going to show me the converted outbuilding that you saw. We're going to have a good look around and I'm going to take lots of pictures." Willie was still shaking his head. "If you don't come you don't get paid."

Willie licked his lips nervously. "They'll call the police."

"So what? What offence are we committing? Trespass? As long as we don't do any criminal damage all the police can do is ask us to leave – and by then I'll have what I want. Let's go." He stood up.

Willie sighed. "All right. Gimme a minute to get some clothes on."

*

The doctor had been right: Mr McDonald slept off the effects of the drug. He felt fine when he woke up, except for a trace of light-headedness. A twenty-minute walk cleared that and by the time they sat down for breakfast he was feeling his usual self and dismissed his wife's concerns over his health.

They did, however, have other concerns over the incident. Who was this character who had booked into the Rutting Stag under the name of David Fox? Why had he slipped a drug into the drink? Was he just a stupid prankster or was there a purpose to his actions?

The fact that Fox had been seen driving off with Willie Clark was not reassuring. They had been warned that the light-fingered Clark had been snooping around when Mrs McDonald had had her accident.

"I don't like the feel of all this, Rab." She put a hand on her husband's forearm and gave it an anxious squeeze.

"Nor me, Meg. We'd best get the Gododdin together and tell them exactly what's happened: warn them to be extra careful. And I'll phone HRH: he should know about this."

*

Carn was sitting on the top rail of the pony paddock fence talking to the foals and fondling their soft muzzles when he heard his name being called. Bran was calling from the track and waving at him. There was clearly something wrong and he hurried back to the house where he found the McDonalds and all his friends, except for Tegid, gathered in the kitchen.

Carn really didn't know what to make of the McDonalds' story. After they had left, he walked with Eppie back to the ponies where he groomed the stallion as they tried to make sense of what was going on.

"We've lived our whole lives hiding away, terrified of what might happen if the Biguns found us. But when Bob and Jane found us, nothing horrible happened. Then we met HRH and all he did was help us. Now we know the McDonalds – and they couldn't have been kinder. So why are Joe, Bob, Jane and HRH so desperate to keep us hidden away? What do they think the other Biguns would do to us?"

Carn stopped brushing and shook his head. "I just don't know. We've tried asking Bob and Jane, but I never understand their answers. It sounds so vague to me: just talk about intrusion and pressure and interference. I can't picture what they're talking about, but we've watched their television programmes and we know that we couldn't live the way that most Biguns seem to." He was silent for a few seconds and resumed brushing the pony. "We

237

could always go back to living the way we used to. It was hard at times, but we managed to survive."

Eppie shook her head. "I'm not sure how well we'd do now. We had Trader Joe coming once a month. Without him…" Eppie shrugged.

Carn stopped the grooming and moved to sit beside Eppie. He put an arm around her. "This will probably turn out to be nothing to worry about. Whatever happens, we'll get by somehow."

*

Back in the farmhouse Mr McDonald tried phoning HRH. As usual, a royal engagement meant that HRH wasn't carrying his mobile phone. An aide answered, took a message and Mr McDonald returned to the kitchen.

"Meg, I missed a couple of meals yesterday. I'm fancying one of your rabbit pies." He unlocked the gun cabinet and the ammunition drawer. With the shotgun broken open over one arm and a pocketful of cartridges, Mr McDonald walked up the drive heading for the meadow that ran alongside the lane. The gate to the meadow lay just before the barrier. As he reached the gate, a silver car that he didn't recognise pulled into the drive and stopped at the barrier.

He recognised the passenger – Willie Clark.

The driver's door swung open and he also recognised the man who got out and limped towards the barrier. Willie also got out, but stayed by the open door of the car.

In the kitchen Mrs McDonald stopped her pastry preparations and watched the screen.

"Fox – or whatever your name really is – you have no business here."

"That's where you're wrong, old man. I have plenty of business here."

Sligo put a hand on the barrier. Mr McDonald slipped two cartridges into the shotgun and snapped it shut.

"Who are you trying to fool? You know you're not going to use that."

"I wouldn't be so sure about that!" Willie shouted.

Sligo ignored him and ducked to get under the barrier. Mr McDonald fired the shotgun. The pellets whistled over Sligo's head and removed the driver's wing mirror of the Focus. That was too much for Willie who fled down the lane.

Mrs McDonald pressed the alarm button.

Sligo changed his mind about passing the barrier and straightened up, still on the other side. "You stupid old goat! I've a good mind to…" He stopped, distracted by a noise from the hedge.

Tegid, returning from another raid on the cider farm, had drunk rather too much on his way back. Tumbling into the hedge, he had found himself in an acceptably comfortable position to sleep it off. Now, woken by the shotgun blast and the raised voices, he groaned and stirred.

The slight movement caught Sligo's eye and he moved towards it. When he realised that he was looking at a tiny body in the hedge, a body clad in t-shirt, shorts and tiny Wellington boots, his eyes lit up. He had found his missing link!

Sligo grabbed what he thought was a child by the arm and hoisted it triumphantly into the air. When he saw Tegid's face, his mouth dropped open, his eyes opened wide in astonishment and he froze.

He regained the ability to move when two things happened simultaneously: Tegid lashed out with a foot, kicking him in the mouth and Mr McDonald stepped up to the barrier, thrust the shotgun into Sligo's midriff and said, "Put him down."

Sligo smirked at him. "No way, old man. Do you want all this to come out in a police enquiry into a shooting on a royal estate? I don't think so."

Tegid twisted around and sank his teeth into Sligo's hand.

"Ow! You little toad!" He grabbed one of Tegid's legs with his other hand and moved quickly to the back of the car. With Tegid hanging upside down by one leg, Sligo opened the hatchback, swung Tegid on top of the suitcase and slammed the hatch shut.

Mr McDonald ducked under the barrier and headed for the car intending to use the shotgun as a club to shatter the windscreen, but he wasn't quick enough. Sligo gave him a violent shove. Mr McDonald fell, with the shotgun clattering to the ground alongside him. Sligo picked up the shotgun, pointed it briefly at its owner and then swung the gun away to blast the camera. He tossed the shotgun over the hedge.

"Bye, old man. Thanks for the story." He got into the Focus and drove away.

*

Carn and Eppie were still sitting by the pony paddock when they heard the sound of a gun being fired, followed instantly by the alarm bell.

They jumped to their feet and Eppie started to move towards the trees.

"Wait," said Carn, "that could be trouble. We can't just hide from it – let's go and see what's happening."

As they passed the woodshed, Erbyn called to them, "Where are you two going? That was the alarm!"

Carn hesitated. A second gunshot rang out. "I want to see what's going on," he called and moved forward, keeping close to the edge of the track. Erbyn and Nudd came out of the shed and joined them. As they passed their house, Carn saw a curtain twitch and a moment later Bran, Enid and Issel appeared at the door.

"What's happening?" Bran called.

"No idea, but we're going to take a look."

They all moved on in single file, ready to rush into hiding if they had to.

When they turned the last bend and could see up to the farmhouse and beyond to the barrier, they saw Mr McDonald get into the pick-up, drive under the barrier as it swung up and turn out into the lane.

They hurried up to the farmhouse where they found a distraught Mrs McDonald.

She pointed at the flickering screen. "I saw it all. I thought he was going to shoot my Rab – but he shot the camera instead." With tears in her eyes, she sat down at the kitchen table. "It was the man who drugged Rab yesterday. I'm sorry – he's got Tegid."

*

Mr McDonald drove to the Rutting Stag where he found McTavish stocking shelves.

"Good day, McTavish. I thank you for your assistance yesterday."

"Good day, McDonald. Ah can't be having regulars getting drugged in ma pub. Ye were lookin' awfa peely-wally. Are ye quite recovered?"

"I am indeed, McTavish. Do you happen to know where that bampot Willie Clark lives? I feel he may have something that disna belong to him."

"Ah know it well. Ah've had occasion to visit there masel' afore now."

With McTavish sitting next to him in the pick-up it leaned to one side to the extent that Mr McDonald had some difficulty steering a straight course as he followed his passenger's instructions.

When they reached the bedsit McTavish simply put his shoulder to the pink door and gradually increased the pressure until the screws pulled out of the wooden frame sufficiently for the door to open. They were in without making a sound. McTavish moved along the short corridor with his arms brushing the walls on each side. When he stepped through the open kitchen door, Willie fell off his chair and then scrambled to his feet.

In a high-pitched voice he gabbled, "What d'ye want? I hav'na anything of yours."

Mr McDonald eased into the kitchen to stand alongside McTavish.

"We're looking for your friend, Mr Fox."

Willie shook his head. "He's no friend of mine – and I don't know where he is."

McTavish took a pace forward and Willie's voice went even higher. "Wait! Wait!" He scrabbled in a pile of twenty-pound notes on the table.

"We're no after the man's money," growled McTavish. "That's his, no doubt."

"No, no – it's mine. He owed it me." Willie was still scrabbling among the notes. "Look! Look! His name's not Fox. When I took the notes from his wallet, this came with them." He held out a piece of card.

Mr McDonald took it and read out loud. "Nigel Sligo. Freelance journalist." At the bottom of the card he found a mobile phone number and a landline number with a London code.

241

CHAPTER 21

Re-grouping

The clattering of the helicopter was deafening. The fierce downdraught as it descended turned the farmyard into a bowl of swirling dust.

Arthur, with his hands over his ears, turned his face away and pressed it into Jane's legs. Jane picked him up and together with the other onlookers retreated into the shelter of the surrounding buildings.

Bob watched through the kitchen window and the dust storm as the aircraft in the red, white and blue livery of No. 32 (The Royal) Squadron made a smooth landing. Three uniformed men jumped down, slid a large wooden crate out through the opened doors and lowered it to the floor. A few seconds later the roaring clatter intensified and the windows shook as the helicopter took off. Moments later it was out of sight. Calm returned and the dust began to settle.

Doors around the yard swung open and people, large and small, poured into the yard and hurried to gather around the crate.

Bob used a hammer to knock off the clips that kept the end in place. Then Joe joined him in lowering the wooden crate end panel to the ground. The crowd pressed forward. It was a very sorry sight that presented itself. Inside the crate, seven tiny people sat with their hands over their ears and their eyes tightly closed.

The Droller stepped up to the crate opening and said, "My friends, welcome to your new home."

Still no-one in the crate moved. Arthur moved around The Droller and into the crate. He came back out gently leading Issel and Erbyn by the hand. Three times he returned to the crate until Carn, Eppie, Bran, Enid, Issel, Erbyn and Nudd were standing in a white-faced group looking traumatised and clearly incapable of grasping what was happening to them.

Myrddin announced, "Our newly-arrived friends need a little time to recover from their journey." He nodded to Arthur and then turned and walked slowly to the farmhouse. Arthur took Eppie and Carn by the hand and led them after Myrddin. Bob knelt and looked into Enid's face; she looked a greenish white, swayed slightly and was clinging to Bran's arm.

Bob spoke quietly. "Hello, Enid, Bran. Let's get you inside and you'll soon be feeling better." He picked one up in each arm and carried them. Joe and Jane brought along the other three.

Inside the farmhouse Myrddin calmed them and they steadily revived. It wasn't long before Eppie was recounting what had happened to them.

"Mr and Mrs McDonald told us that we had to leave as soon as possible – and that we would be flying back to the south-west by helicopter. We had to hide when the helicopter arrived with that big box. Then the McDonalds sealed us inside with just some blankets to sit on and some bottles of water. They told us that we had to be very quiet.

"Then the helicopter came back. The noise was terrifying and most of us felt sick with the swaying about. It was very dark in there – there were just a few little holes in the top of the crate. We landed three times. Each time we thought that we must have got here, but then we took off again. It was awful – I thought it was never going to end."

Eppie started to cry. "We have nothing. Our clothes; my pens, brushes, paints and paper: everything was left behind."

Carn put an arm around her, gave her a hug, but he couldn't think of anything encouraging to say.

As Bob looked along the line, he felt that he could tell what thoughts lay behind each of the troubled faces. He would have bet a lot of money that Carn was thinking of the ponies he'd left behind.

Issel was thinking of the kitchen she'd lost; Erbyn of the all the work they'd put into the vegetable and fruit gardens. Nudd was worrying about his lost brother. But Bran and Enid looked as if they were rapidly getting over the physical discomforts of the flight and, with the resilience of youth, were starting to look around and take an interest in their new surroundings.

Now that he thought that they had recovered sufficiently to take in what he was saying, Myrddin explained.

"I am sorry for the haste and the disturbance. We know the man who has taken Tegid. We know that he is a singularly unpleasant individual who will, no doubt, attempt to make as much money as possible from his discovery. But we do not know how he will attempt to do it. Before he had a chance to return, we thought it wise to remove you from the estate that simply wasn't secure. We are also removing any trace of you're having been there.

"But do not despair! Let me give you the good news! There is plenty of room for you here and The Droller, together with your Welsh cousins, is waiting to welcome you.

"Carn, the ponies from Scotland are being transported here – and on this farm you will find all of the foals you have reared over the last few years." Carn visibly brightened.

"All of your belongings have already been packed and are on their way, together with the pony carts and the furniture from your former home. By this evening that building will have been stripped bare."

From out in the yard came the sound of music and laughter.

"I think the celebration of your arrival is beginning. When you feel ready, you will find food, drink and good company."

There was a general stirring and a move to go outside into the warm sunshine, but Nudd had a question. "What can we do about Tegid?"

Myrddin looked at him and smiled sympathetically. "Your brother is in our thoughts. I trust that he will rejoin us soon."

Arthur led the arrivals outside. Myrddin remained at the window. "I believe that you did not tell them about Gilda."

Jane shook her head. "No, we didn't."

"They will hear soon enough."

The door opened and Gilda came in. Myrddin turned from the window and spoke to them all.

"The timing is unfortunate. We cannot afford to let this interfere with our campaign. We have a number of television, radio and magazine interviews arranged and we must have more yet. I believe that we have what is known as momentum – and that must not be lost.

"I am indebted to The Droller and his tribe. They are fine people – but they are few and we are seeking to save many.

244

"But we cannot undo what has been done. Not only is their existence now known to someone outside our little group, but that someone is holding Tegid and we can only assume that he will be seeking to gain maximum publicity. I was hoping to keep their existence a secret for another year, or two. Now it seems that we will have to bring forward introducing the world to them. After all, Mr Sligo only has one." He looked out of the window. "We have so many more. Perhaps the public interest that we can arouse will drown out Mr Sligo's effort.

"How much does Tegid know about this farm, I wonder."

"As much as Carn, Eppie and the others, I should think," said Jane. "They must have discussed all the news we gave them about our visit here."

Myrddin nodded. "So he will know about our little trinkets," he said, looking towards the secure barn.

"I expect so, yes – I think they were all fascinated to find the treasure hoard part of The Droller's stories was true."

Myrddin was silent for a while before continuing. "Tegid is one of the strongest characters among them: although, unfortunately, he has his weaknesses. Depending upon how he is handled, he may choose to tell Sligo everything, or nothing. I hope that Sligo does not resort to his drug approach. With a body as tiny as Tegid's, any dose could be fatal.

"I wonder what Tegid will say about me?" There was another brief silence. "I think I'd better bring our little friend back to his ever-anxious brother."

*

As Sligo drove away from Mr McDonald he felt triumphant. He didn't know what it was that was now kicking at the parcel shelf, but whatever it was, it was the basis of a massive story. It wasn't the story that he'd thought he was onto; no tale of the mistreatment of children; in fact, at the moment he couldn't think of any unsavoury acts by any of the characters involved. So, it may not have been his usual sort of story, but the whole world was going to want to hear it. A rare smile of satisfaction started to form, but the kick in the mouth had split his lip and it made smiling hurt.

The kicking of the parcel shelf didn't slacken off. Every time that Sligo yelled at the creature to stop, the kicking intensified. He stopped the car to check. There was no way that the parcel shelf could come off when the hatchback was closed, but an opening was beginning to appear in one corner. If it got much bigger and a small hand happened to press the button, the back seat would come forward and his captive would be out.

Sligo drove slowly through the town, glowering at the Rutting Stag as he passed it. In the main street he spotted a pet shop. He decided to take a chance, parked on the double yellow lines outside the shop and hurried in. He snatched a large pet carrier from a shelf and pulled out his wallet to pay for it. All of his cash had gone.

It took him less than a second to work out the likely culprit. He fumed at the delay as he paid by credit card. He risked leaving the car while he hurried to a nearby bank and took five hundred pounds from the cash point. Back at the car he found two old women peering curiously through the window at the jumping parcel shelf. He ignored them; threw the pet carrier onto the back seat and made his escape.

A mile out of town he pulled into a lay-by and stood by the hatchback with the pet carrier open at his feet. The unceasing hammering on the parcel shelf meant that he knew where the creature was. He waited until he was certain that there was no passing traffic and whipped the hatch up. The creature was lying on its back on top of the remains of Sligo's suitcase, kicking at the parcel shelf above. It was so startled that Sligo was able to grab it by an arm, thrust into the pet carrier and shut the door before it had time to react.

"Excellent!" said Sligo aloud. He moved the suitcase slightly and put the carrier into the car, using the suitcase to jam the door shut. He spread clothes over the cage to muffle any noise. "That should keep you nice and safe. You can kick those bars as much as you like, but you might as well stop struggling and relax."

He got back into the driver's seat. He had two more problems to consider before he could set out for London. The first was Willie Clark: Sligo was strongly tempted to go after his money. He checked his watch. It wasn't all that long since he'd driven away from the estate. Clark was on foot and, even if he'd headed straight home, he might not be there yet. Sligo decided that it wasn't worth the risk. He was going to be a rich man on the strength of his story – and his captured exhibit. He reluctantly decided to leave Willie Clark with his loot.

His other problem was the wing mirror blasted by the shotgun. There were a lot of miles between him and his London home and that meant a reasonable chance that a police car would be behind him at some stage. The last thing he needed was to be pulled over by the police: he'd better get the wing mirror repaired – and keep below the speed limit all the way home.

At the next town he spotted the familiar blue oval and pulled into the Ford dealership. Yes, they did have the wing mirror in stock: no, they couldn't do it there and then; he would have to book it in. Sligo offered to pay for the work by credit card, with one hundred pounds cash for the service manager, and was on his way again in thirty minutes.

It was going to be a long drive home, but he had a lot of planning to do and pleasant thoughts of money to keep him occupied. It occurred to him that it was a lovely, sunny summer day.

He stopped for fuel near Perth. As he was eating a sandwich he realised that he ought to be keeping his captive in good health. He had no idea what it ate, so he bought a pack of two sausage rolls, an apple and a bottle of water. Parked in the most remote corner of the service area he opened the pet carrier door a fraction and pushed the food and water through the gap. He checked that his cargo was secure and set off again.

As Sligo drove south his initial elation at the big story that he'd captured began to dwindle and was partially replaced by doubt and concern. He had never been in this sort of position before. His way of operating was to negotiate the sale of a story, pass over everything he had by way of information and photographs, and then let the newspaper editor decide on whether all of the story appeared at once or was put out a little at a time.

Now Sligo wanted to be in control of a story that he wanted to run and run, but when he thought about it he realised that he had a problem. He had captured something that, for want of a better name, he would call a pixie. That in itself was a stunning story that the whole world would want to see or read about, but it wasn't the story that Ronald Smith wanted him to come up with. Sligo had told Smith to expect a story involving a massive scandal that would involve HRH and the nutcase, Myrddin. That it would also involve a would-be MP, an ex-accountant and a mobile shop owner was almost irrelevant to Smith who was expecting something that would protect his business interests by destroying the reputations of HRH and Myrddin.

Smith had some very unpleasant connections and he didn't take well to being let down.

Sligo would offer Smith's newspapers and television channel exclusive rights to the story. He could provide background information, such as the pixies saving Alice Jackson and George Phillips, to keep the story going, but while a story that would boost Smith's readership might placate Smith a little, it really wasn't what Smith was looking for.

Sligo could tie-in HRH to the story, but the fact that HRH had apparently been trying to provide a safe home for the creatures was just the opposite of what Smith wanted. And, although there might be a weak connection between HRH and Myrddin as they were both to appear at the same environmental rally, Sligo couldn't connect Myrddin to the pixie story at all: even if he did, it was quite possible that, like HRH, Myrddin would come out of it with his reputation enhanced, not destroyed.

He decided that he would just have to avoid contact with Smith while he got a grip on the pixie story and worked out how to handle it.

It had been a long day after a night of disturbed sleep in his car and he yawned uncontrollably as he negotiated the traffic jams of the M1. Eventually, he had to pull off into Toddington Services, sleep for an hour, have two coffees and several cigarettes before finishing his journey. He was lucky: as he drove slowly along the street of terraced houses looking for somewhere to park, one of his neighbours pulled away leaving a space only thirty yards from Sligo's front door.

He stuffed his clothes, camera and laptop into his ruined suitcase and carried it to his house. There was a mountain of accumulated post behind the door and he quickly kicked it aside before hurrying back for the pet carrier.

He put his captive on the kitchen table and then took time to look around. The place was a mess. He winced at the memory of his hasty departure and couldn't help checking the walls in the hall for bloodstains.

Sligo had left the kitchen blinds down and he checked all the downstairs curtains were drawn before pouring himself a glass of Scotch and sitting at the kitchen table. He raised his glass to the pet carrier.

"Cheers! Whatever you are. Here's to all the money!"

There was no sound. He knew from the weight that his captive was still in there and he had a sudden panic as the thought that his victim may have suffocated crossed his mind. The slits in the sides were too narrow for a clear view. Sligo cleared everything off the table apart from his glass and the pet carrier, checked that both doors from the kitchen were firmly closed and tentatively opened the door of the carrier.

Sligo could see a small body inside and he moved his face nearer for a better look. An apple core flew out and struck him in the eye.

"Ow!"

"Serves you right!"

"You speak English!"

"What did you expect, you Bigun fool?"

Sligo hadn't stopped to think about language and it came as shock to find that the creature spoke at all, let alone English. The voice was high and grating; it had a curious accent, but was understandable.

"What did you call me?"

"A fool, fool!"

"No, before fool. You said a *something* fool."

"Bigun."

"What's that?"

"It's what we call all the big fools like you."

"Ah. Not just fools, then. You little people call us Biguns." Sligo liked the sound of that. It added charm to the story he was bringing to the world. "Would you like to come out? It's quite safe."

"I'm not sure I can move, I'm so stiff."

"Oh, sorry. Hang on, I'll take the top off." Sligo undid the catches and lifted the top half away. "Take your time." The little creature stirred painfully and eased up to a sitting position from which it glared at Sligo.

Sligo realised that he was going to have to take this gently: his story would be so much easier to present if he and the creature were on good terms. "Have you got a name?"

"Of course I've got a name."

"Sorry, yes of course you have. What are you called?"

"Tegid."

"Tegid?"

"Yes."

"Hello, Tegid. I'm Nigel." Tegid just glared at him.

"Tegid, er, what are you, if you don't mind my asking?"

"Isn't it obvious what I am?"

"Well, you look like a very, very small man."

Tegid gingerly raised himself to his feet and stretched, arching his back. "Well done. What do you want? A prize?"

"Well, there are all sorts of men. I just wondered, if you call us Biguns, what do you call yourselves?"

"Dini – although that old fraud Myrddin said we were Gododdin and tried to make us use that name."

Sligo smirked. *Bullseye! That's involved Myrddin.* "Really? How interesting."

Tegid starting walking around the table, getting feeling back into his legs. Sligo watched in astonishment: the world was going to love this tiny creature – even if it did seem rather bad-tempered.

You are entitled to be bad-tempered my little friend: snatched from your home; stuck in a pet cage and locked in the back of a car for hours. Never mind: Nigel will calm you down.

Tegid sat on the upturned lid of the pet carrier and stared at Sligo. "Where's the toilet?"

"Eh? Oh, right. Sorry. Never thought."

"I assume you have a toilet?"

"Of course. It's upstairs."

Tegid looked interested. "We didn't have stairs." He jumped off the table onto a chair and then swung down onto the floor. "Come on, then. I'm bursting."

As Sligo moved to open the kitchen door he asked, "How would you like to take a bath and I'll get you some clean clothes? If you don't mind my saying so, the ones you have on look rather grubby and you'll feel better in clean clothes with some decent food inside you."

Tegid shrugged.

Sligo opened the door and led the way to the bottom of the stairs. "It's up there. Can you manage?"

Tegid gave him a scathing look and swarmed nimbly up the stairs. As Sligo followed him he tried to make an assessment of the sizes of Tegid's clothes and shoes.

At the top of the stairs Sligo opened the bathroom door. He turned on the hot water tap and heard the boiler fire up. "Hang on. I'll just run a bit of this and get some cold in. Can't have you scalding yourself." He checked that the window was locked and removed the key. "Here's a towel. Soap's in the dish. Right: I'll leave you to it." He left the bathroom, shut the door behind him and then grabbing his dressing gown from his bedroom he tied one sleeve to the bathroom door handle and the other to the banister.

He hurried away to the supermarket three hundred yards down the road and got back as soon as he could, carrying a selection of clothes, bread, milk, cheese, eggs, fruit and a mincemeat and onion pie.

When he came back into the house he could hear a rhythmic banging on the bathroom door. He opened the bathroom door a fraction, passed in the new clothes and said, "Here you are. Try some of these on for size. I'll be downstairs getting food ready."

Down in the kitchen he put the oven on to warm the pie. It wasn't long before Tegid appeared, his long hair still very wet. The t-shirt was far too big, but the trousers were a reasonable fit and, from the way he kept looking at them, he seemed impressed with the tiny trainers.

"Why don't you climb back up onto the table and we can have a chat?"

Tegid did as suggested and sat down on the pet carrier again.

"What would you like to drink?"

Tegid looked at Sligo's glass. "Whisky – or cider."

Sligo laughed. "I wasn't expecting you to say that. I haven't got any cider – I'll get some tomorrow." He looked through a cupboard, found a small port glass and half-filled it with whisky. "Water?"

Tegid nodded and Sligo topped the glass up with water before handing it to Tegid, who grasped it by the slim stem.

"Cheers!" Sligo raised his glass.

Tegid ignored the gesture. "Where am I?"

"In my house, in London."

"Why have you brought me here?"

"Why do you think?"

"From what I know of Biguns, you think you can make money out of me."

He's no fool, thought Sligo.

"Partly right. I do think that there is a lot of money to be made…"

"Yeah. We were warned about what the Biguns would do if they found out about us: shut us up in cages," Tegid kicked the other half of the pet carrier across the table, "make our lives miserable with something called the media." He took a swallow of his whisky and water.

You'll have to be careful with this one.

"Well, as I was saying, there *is* a lot of money to be made – but it's money for us both to make. Yes, we will make the money out of the media, but we can control it. The world will want to see you – and the world will pay a lot of money for the privilege. What happened to your hand?"

"I cut it off."

Sligo stared at Tegid. "You cut off your own hand! How…why?"

"It was trapped under a car wheel. The only way I could avoid getting caught by Biguns was to cut it off."

Sligo looked at him, speechless. *He's not only smart, he's got guts – but if he was capable of cutting his own hand off to escape, he's capable of cutting my throat.* Sligo looked nervously around the kitchen, checking that there were no knives within Tegid's reach.

"Who told you about the media?"

"Trader Joe, when we used to ask him about the Biguns. Then the Johnsons and the McDonalds said the same."

"Ah, but they don't really understand the media. I do – I work in it. I know how to manipulate it so that you and I make a lot of money, but stay in control of our own lives."

"You're not letting me go, then?" Tegid drained his glass and held it out for a re-fill.

"Well, er, no – not yet. But I think that by the time you understand what your life can be like, you won't want to go."

"So, I'm not free to go – so you're in control. And you're part of this media business – so I'm a prisoner of the media. That must have been what they were warning us about."

Sligo was feeling his grip on the situation slipping away. "There's a meat pie in the oven. Are you hungry?"

Tegid shrugged.

Sligo turned the oven off, pulled the pie out and then, after a slight hesitation, used a spoon to put a little on a small plate and passed the plate and teaspoon to his reluctant guest.

Tegid balanced the plate on his knees, tasted the pie, pulled a face and put the plate down on the table. "It's cold and it tastes disgusting – all greasy and slimy. Did you make it?" he asked, accusingly.

"Er, no, I didn't. I bought it when I went out."

"No wonder you Biguns are miserable all the time if you have to eat that muck."

"You won't have to eat food like this when the money comes rolling in. You can have the best food in the world; stay in the finest hotels; be driven around in the best cars; buy whatever house you want, wherever you want to live."

"Oh yes," growled Tegid, clearly not impressed, "and I expect you will, too."

"Well, that would be good, yes. But I can't do anything without you. You are the star that everyone will want to see. They will see that you're smart and brave: that tale of you cutting off your own hand will make you a hero the world over."

Sligo took a big bite of pie. It seemed all right to him, but he was used to such food. "This doesn't seem too bad, but would you like some cheese instead?"

Tegid nodded and there was a brief pause in their conversation while Sligo put bread and cheese onto a small plate: a pause that both used to gather their thoughts.

"What about the others?" Tegid asked, holding out his glass.

As Sligo poured the whisky, he did some rough calculations. He was only pouring tiny amounts, but based upon their relative sizes, by the time Tegid had drunk this latest measure it would be roughly the equivalent of Sligo drinking a bottle of Scotch. Sligo was impressed, although he did detect a slight slurring of the words in Tegid's last question.

"What others?"

"My brother and my friends in Scotland?"

"How many are there?"

Tegid took a drink before replying. "Seven."

"What would you like to do about them?"

Tegid shrugged. "Doan know: but my brother will be worried – he always is."

"I'll get a message to him and tell him you're all right. What's his name?"

"Nudd."

Sligo reached for a pad and pen. "Nudd? How do I spell that? Come to think of it, how do I spell Tegid?"

"Dunno – Carn's the only one of us that can read and write."

Sligo made a guess at the spellings. "What are the others called?"

"Eppie, Enid, Issel, Bran and …" Tegid frowned in concentration and took another drink. "I've mished shumbody. Who've you got so far?"

Sligo read the names back off his pad.

"Oh, yesh, forgot Erbyn."

"If you want, you'll have enough money to buy a place big enough for all of them. I expect we'll have to tell the world about them, as well. But you'll be the star. I'm sure the others aren't as interesting, smart or brave as you."

Tegid thought about that for a few seconds and then nodded.

"Tell me, when you cut your hand off, how come you didn't bleed to death or die of some infection? Did a doctor treat you?"

Tegid shook his head, drained his glass. Sligo immediately topped it up.

"No, Gilda sewed it up and wrapped it up in shtuff."

Sligo checked his list. "Who's Gilda? I don't have a Gilda?"

Tegid shook his head again. He tried to focus on the cheese and bread on his lap, but had difficulty as it was a moving target. Sligo caught the plate as it slipped from Tegid's knees and put it on the table next to the uneaten morsel of pie.

"Gilda?" he prompted.

"She's not with us anymore. She went off with Myrddin. They say she's…" Tegid broke off, gave Sligo a sly look and tapped the side of his nose.

"You called Myrddin a fraud earlier. Where does he fit in?"

"The Droller turned up with him."

"Who?"

"The Droller. Said they'd found him in some hole in the ground in Wales. Said he's the great magician that was with Artosh when they fought the Saxons. Jusht another of The

254

Droller's silly stories. I never believed it, but the others did. Fools."

Sligo was struggling to get to grips with what he'd just heard.

"So, The Droller, he's one of you..." Sligo searched his pad, "Dini?"

Tegid nodded and took another drink.

"And he's from Wales. So there are more of you there?"

Tegid shook his head. "Not any more. Myrddin moved them to a farm he bought."

Sligo was scribbling. "Artosh? Who's Artosh?"

Tegid peered at him in disbelief. "Everyone knows who he was – even you Biguns."

Artosh, Saxons, Myrddin, magician.

"You don't mean Arthur, King Arthur, and Merlin the Magician?"

Tegid shrugged. "If that's what you want to call them?"

Sligo whistled. "So, this Myrddin character thinks he's a re-incarnation of Merlin?" He chuckled.

Tegid shook his head. "No, no re-intar, re-incat, re-inshun, what you said. He says he's the real one. He's jusht been sleeping and The Droller woke him up. Oh, yeah – and he's got a magic sword." Tegid cackled briefly.

Sligo sat back in his chair and scratched his head. He looked at his pad and laughed out loud.

"Hang on. You said he'd bought a farm. How did this nutcase get the money to buy a farm? Is that where HRH came in? Did he believe this rubbish and buy the farm?"

There was no reply. Tegid's head had tipped forward onto his chest and his eyes had closed. Sligo leaned forward and shook him.

Tegid's eyes opened and he drained his glass.

"How did Myrddin get the money to buy a farm?"

"Tresher. He's been selling gold and silver things from a load of buried tresher."

"What sort of things?"

"Old, old things. Celtic tresher from Roman ti..." Tegid's eyes closed again. He slid off his seat onto the table and immediately began to snore, his face resting in cold meat pie.

Sligo stood and walked around the table, too excited to sit still any longer. His big story had just got bigger. It had got bigger and now it was also the story that Ronald Smith wanted.

He picked up his glass from the table and toasted himself. "Nigel Sligo, you've got it made."

He looked at his watch. Far too late to catch Smith at his office and he didn't have Smith's home number. It would have to be first thing in the morning. He gave the snoring Tegid a look of revulsion. "You may be an obnoxious, deformed, drunken lump of something scarcely human, but you're worth a lot of money. What shall we do with you?"

He put an old hand towel into the bottom half of the pet carrier, put Tegid, none too gently, on top and fastened the other half of the pet carrier in place. "You're staying at the foot of my bed."

CHAPTER 22

Problems

"He's not in the office yet, Sligo. He shouldn't be long. I'm sure I heard the helicopter a few minutes ago."

"Do me a favour, Trish, when I speak to him can you stick it on the loudspeaker and listen in. I've got a feeling he'll need calming down."

"That doesn't sound too promising. Here he comes."

The door to his office opened and Ronald Smith rolled in, red-faced, sweating and complaining. "Lousy weather for months; hotels and golf courses down the tubes; marinas down the tubes; building sites under water – and suddenly it's summer." He caught sight of Patricia Jakes waving his phone at him. "What's going on?"

"It's Sligo. Says he's got news. Wants me to listen in."

Smith nodded; peeled his jacket off, let it fall onto the floor and dropped into his chair that groaned in protest. "O.K Trish."

She pressed a button and turned up the volume.

"Right, cretin, I'm listening – and I'm long overdue some good news."

As Sligo spoke, Smith's face changed from red to purple. After only twenty seconds he interrupted. "Sligo, you useless heap of excrement, who do you think you're messing with! Either this is a very unfunny joke, or you've been drinking, or you've completely lost your marbles – or all three."

They listened for a few more seconds, but Smith could stand no more. "If you say one more word about pixies I'll tear your arms out of their sockets and beat you over the head with them! I've heard enough Trish. Get rid of the lunatic."

His P.A. held up a hand. "Hang on, Ron. He knew what he was going to say would make you react like this. He warned me to expect it. He doesn't sound drunk or deranged to me. I think you should hear him out."

Smith gave her an exasperated look, but nodded.

"Start again, Sligo," she urged.

"Thanks, Trish. I was wrong. I thought this story involved children, but it doesn't. It involves pixies – or at least, it involves a tribe of very tiny people who were living wild on Dartmoor. I know it sounds crazy, but it's true. Honest to God. I brought one back with me – he's here in my house in London. He's about eighteen inches high and he's a normal human being – he just happens to be very, very small."

Trish interrupted. "You're telling us that you have one of 'the little people' in your house?"

"Well, yes – and no."

Smith was describing circles with a finger around his ear and rolling his eyes.

"When I say that, I mean yes, I have a very little person in my house. But when you say 'one of the little people', or when I used the word 'pixies' it suggests something magical or supernatural – like the Irish and their tales of leprechauns. But there's nothing supernatural about these people – they're perfectly normal; they're just tiny."

"How many are there?" Trish asked.

"There are seven more on the Prince's Scottish estate. The one I've got here was telling me over breakfast that they're dying out. There haven't been any young ones born for years."

"So what are they doing in Scotland? I thought you said they were living on Dartmoor."

"Yes, Trish, they were, but Dartmoor got so busy with people tramping about all over the place that they were finding it hard to stay hidden. HRH found out about them, took pity on them and moved them up to a remote estate he has in Scotland. That was five or six years ago."

Smith had been calming down, but now Trish could see from the colour of his face that his blood pressure was increasing again.

"Look, you moron, you were supposed to have a story for me that would ruin the reputations of HRH and this Myrddin character. Even if this ludicrous story of yours were true – and I don't for one moment believe that it is – how is it supposed to help me? What have we got? A tribe of tiny people, dying out, and HRH nobly saves them and keeps them hidden in some safe spot. You're making the man out to be some sort of hero. That's not the deranged imbecile image that I'm looking for!" Smith's voice had risen throughout that little speech until the last sentence was bellowed into the phone from spittle-flecked lips.

"Hang on!" said Sligo. "Look, I know just what you want – and I've got it. But we're not going to get anywhere until I've got you believing the first part of this – and then we can move on. What's your mobile number, Trish? I'll take a couple of photos, send them to you, and then I'll ring back."

A few minutes later Smith and Patricia were staring open-mouthed at the images on her phone. One showed a tiny man standing on a table with a wine bottle alongside him to show his size. The other showed the same little man sitting on the edge of the table, his legs hanging down and Sligo crouched down beside him with an inane grin on his face.

The mobile rang and Trish answered it to hear Sligo say, "Just in case you're still not convinced I'm sending you a video clip of him climbing the stairs."

After seeing the clip, Smith heaved himself up and moved to stare out of the window. He said nothing out loud, but he kept shaking his head and muttering to himself.

The phone on his desk rang and Smith returned to his seat.

"Right, I assume that you now know I'm not bonkers."

"I'm almost convinced," said Smith, "but I'll have to see it for myself before I really believe it. I still suspect that it's a child with some sort of mask on – and if you're giving me the run-around, Sligo, I'll have you fed to the pigs on my farm."

"It's got a hand missing; what happened to it?" Trish asked.

"Believe it or not, he got his hand trapped under a car wheel and, to avoid being caught when the driver came back, he cut his own hand off."

Smith groaned. "All right, enough of the drama, let's move on. I can see that this story will run and run in my publications and on my channel. Good for circulation and advertising, but that's chicken feed. I've spent a lifetime building the businesses in the Smith Corporation and the whole lot is under threat. The weather has pushed us to the edge and now these environmental crackpots are threatening to push us over.

"How do we turn your 'little people' into a terminal punch in the face for Myrddin and HRH?"

"Ah! Now we come to the best bit. That Myrddin character is completely off his trolley. He thinks he's Merlin the Magician: the Arthurian legends and all that stuff."

"What? So he's one of these mindless cretins believing in re-incarnation and he thinks he was Merlin in an earlier life?"

"No, no, it's much better than that. He says he's the original Merlin. He reckons he's been around for over fifteen hundred years! Not only that, but he thinks he's got Excalibur and that it's a magic sword!

"And there's more. The group of little people in Scotland aren't the only ones. There's another group of about twenty that Myrddin has on a big farm in the Westcountry. He paid for that farm using money obtained by the sale of historical artefacts that he had no right to sell. He's been helped in all this by a Joe Morgan who has a criminal record for handling stolen goods."

There was a pause while Smith digested all this. Then his fat face split into a smile and he ran his tongue over already-wet rubbery lips.

"And HRH is in on all this?"

"Yes."

"Perfect!"

"I thought you'd think so." Sligo paused. "It's cost me a lot to put this story together."

"All right, Sligo. You'll get your money. Plenty of it."

"Excellent. I have some ideas on how we move this along."

"Go on."

"Well, this story is just too big to let anyone else in on it without it leaking out. I need somewhere secluded to keep my little captive. I need to take lots of still photos, and a camera that I can use for recordings that will be of TV quality. Plus I need the lighting to shoot it properly. So, can we keep him at your place and can you have some of your bods set up a room as a studio?"

Smith thought for a moment and then nodded at Trish. "All right, Sligo, take it to my place. I want to see it for myself, anyhow. Trish'll give you the address. She'll also tell my wife and the housekeeper to expect you and a top-secret guest that no-one is allowed to see. You and it can have adjacent rooms and we'll turn the next one into a studio with all the kit. It'll be done by, say, two o'clock.

"I won't be there until tomorrow afternoon. I'm flying to Manchester to try to sell a bunch of hotels."

"That's great, Ron. You'll be delighted with all this."

"It's Mr Smith to you, Sligo – and one more thing."

"Yes, Mr Smith?"

"Keep your grubby hands off the pictures and the ornaments. I know exactly what's there."

*

Sligo wrote down the address on his notepad and then went on to write a brief shopping list. He'd never seen the Smith mansion, but he had the feeling that it wasn't the sort of place where he ought to turn up with his clothes in a carrier bag, so the first item on his list was a suitcase. He added shirts, trousers, cider, and chocolate. As an afterthought, he added a first aid kit; the bandages and plasters on his elbows and knees would soon need replacing. Then he wrote down 'something small and lightweight for him to drink out of'.

When Tegid was in the bathroom, Sligo again used a dressing gown to secure the door and set off on his shopping trip. Although he was as quick as he could manage it, an hour had slipped by before he returned to open his front door. He could immediately hear the regular kicking on the bathroom door that was becoming irritatingly familiar.

He bawled up the stairs, "All right! All right! I'll be there in a minute!"

The kicking didn't stop. Sligo ignored it. He went into the kitchen, shut the door behind him, put the kettle on and unpacked his shopping while the kettle boiled. He had a leisurely cup of coffee and two cigarettes, before going upstairs to release Tegid.

The infuriating kicking of the door continued as he untied the dressing gown from the handle. He turned the handle and was about to give the door a violent shove when he controlled himself at the last moment.

Don't let him get to you. The last thing you need is to break his skinny little legs.

He tapped on the door. "I've got things sorted out now. Do you fancy a drink? I've got cider."

The kicking stopped. Sligo waited a few seconds before gently opening the door.

261

Tegid was glaring up at him. "Why do you keep shutting me in here? You said this morning that we were partners."

"Yes, we certainly are. Sorry about shutting you in. I was as quick as I could be, but when I'm not here it seems safer for you to be in here – you're far too important to risk you injuring yourself in a strange house. What if you fell down the stairs?"

"Oh yes? Well, what if the house caught fire with me trapped in it? It smells as if it's on fire now."

Tegid brushed past Sligo's legs and went nimbly down the stairs using his one hand to steady himself as he jumped from one to the next. Sligo followed him down and into the kitchen.

"It stinks in here," Tegid complained. "It's those things you burn. Why do you keep setting fire to things and sucking in the smoke?"

Sligo shrugged, started to answer, "Makes me feel good. They…" but Tegid interrupted.

"Don't bother. I expect it's just another of the crazy things you Biguns do all the time. Where's that drink?"

"Hang on," said Sligo, "I'll get you something more comfortable to sit on." He went to the lounge and came back with two large, square cushions from his armchairs. He put one on top of the other on the kitchen table. Tegid climbed up and sat down.

Sligo produced two of his purchases: a bottle of cider and a small plastic mug. He passed the half-filled mug to Tegid and then placed his laptop on the table. Patricia Jakes had not just given him the address of Smith's place, but also told him where he could find pictures of it on the internet.

"You, my friend, are going to be a famous TV star – possibly the most famous TV star in the world. You are going to stay at the home of one of the richest, most important men in the country, Ronald Smith. He owns newspapers and has his own television channel. Everyone in the world is going to see you and hear what you have to say – and they will pay you a lot of money for the privilege." As he spoke, Sligo was tapping at the keys of the laptop.

"There! What do you think of that? That's the house you'll be staying in." He turned the laptop so that Tegid could see the images of the imposing mansion that filled the screen. Every few seconds Sligo tapped a key to move to the next image. They looked at views of all four sides of the house, the stables, the grounds, and various shots of the interior with its swimming pool and grand staircase.

"So," Sligo prompted, "what do you think of going to live in a place like that? And it's the sort of place that you could own soon, with all the money you're going to earn."

"How many of his friends live there with him?"

"Er, none. He lives there with his wife." Sligo clicked back to an image of Smith, his wife and the recently departed dog: the three of them standing in front of the imposing front entrance.

"He eats too much."

"Yes, I expect you're right."

"Why do they need such a big house for just two of them?"

"They can have friends come to stay – like we are going to do."

"What do they keep on all that grass? Ponies? Sheep? Cows?"

"I think they've got some fields for the animals. That grass is just kept cut short to look nice."

Tegid snorted. "Grass? Looks nice? It's just grass!"

"So what would you do with it when you have a house like that?"

"Don't want a house like that – everything's too big. And I wouldn't waste land on grass – I'd plant apple trees." Tegid looked meaningfully at the cider bottle and winked at Sligo; then he held out his mug for a re-fill.

"Look, you're going to have to travel to Mr Smith's house in that box again. We just can't take the chance of you being spotted. But it should only take an hour and you can have this to keep you company." Sligo passed Tegid a hip flask. "It's full of whisky."

Just after one o'clock, adequately bribed, Tegid allowed himself to be shut in the pet carrier and carried out to the car where he joined Sligo's new suitcase.

It was two-fifteen when Sligo drove up to the high wrought-iron gates. He pulled alongside an intercom mounted on a smart black and gold post and pressed the button. There was a crackle and a voice said only, "Yes?"

"Nigel Sligo; I'm here by arrangement with Mr Smith."

"Yes, Mr Sligo, we are expecting you."

The gates swung open and Sligo drove down the long, sweeping drive, immaculately edged between lawns mown in neat, shaded bands. He pulled up at the foot of the steps leading to the front door. As he did so, a middle-aged lady in a navy blue suit came out and waited for him at the door.

"Mr Sligo, follow me please." She led the way up the staircase to the second floor and along a corridor until she stopped at the last door.

"Mr Sligo, we have our instructions, delivered most forcibly. The gentlemen were here this morning and have set this out to your requirements, I trust." She opened the door and stepped back.

Sligo walked past her into the room. A camera mounted on a tripod stood in the middle of the floor. A row of lights clamped to a metal stand was directed at a settee. A selection of microphones lay on a table. Someone had left an instruction booklet for the camera there too – and a mobile phone. He picked it up and looked enquiringly at his guide.

"There is only one number in the address book and that is mine. If you require anything at all, just call."

"Excellent! Mrs Nicholls isn't it? I was told that you are the housekeeper."

"That is correct, Mr Sligo. We have prepared two bedrooms." She nodded at the doors on either side of the corridor. She caught Sligo looking and said, "Yes, the locks have keys. I was told that was a requirement. I am afraid that the rooms on this floor do not have ensuite facilities, but the next door along is a bathroom. My other instructions are that the identity of the other guest is to remain secret and that no member of staff is to see them." She paused. "I did not notice anyone in the car with you."

"He is there, Mrs Nicholls. He is concealed in the boot."

She raised her eyebrows.

"If you could make sure that there are no members of staff around to see him, I'll bring him in."

"Certainly. We should do that at once, it must be very hot and uncomfortable for him."

As they walked back along the corridor she said, "As soon as you are both inside, we will place a screen across this end of the corridor. No member of staff will pass the screen. That means that your rooms will not be cleaned and any meals that you request will be left on a table outside the screen."

"That's just perfect, Mrs Nicholls."

"When you've finished with your car, do you mind moving it to the garages at the rear? Mr Smith likes to keep the front of the house clear."

With the pet carrier and his suitcase safely moved into the house and the car put away, Sligo checked out the bedrooms. One looked out over the front of the house and the other was at the rear. He decided that he preferred the view to the front and unpacked his suitcase. It was a pity that Smith wasn't staying away for longer: Sligo rather fancied the idea of a few days holiday with his meals being prepared for him. But he knew that Smith would be looking for rapid progress.

Tegid seemed unusually quiet. When Sligo opened the pet carrier he found his captive clutching an empty hip flask, sound asleep and snoring gently. Sligo put the open pet carrier on the bed, closed the curtains and left the room, locking the door behind him. He glanced down the corridor to see that the screen was in place and went into the makeshift studio where he passed the time familiarising himself with the camera and the microphones, and planning exactly how he intended making use of Tegid.

It was two hours before he heard Tegid banging on his bedroom door and calling out. When Sligo opened the door it was a very grumpy Tegid that glared up at him. He was clearly hungover from his lunchtime whisky consumption; black circles underlined the red eyes in an otherwise very pale face.

"Stop locking me in! I'm hungry; I need some water and I want some fresh air."

He didn't look like the subject that Sligo needed: he wanted one that the audience would warm to; someone who would be the innocent victim that would generate sympathy and affection in all who saw him.

"Of course, of course. You are such an important person that you can have whatever you want. First things first: water." Sligo went into his room for the bottle of water that he had in his suitcase and returned with it and the plastic mug. He filled the mug and passed it to Tegid, who noisily drained it, belched loudly and held his hand out for a re-fill.

"Right," said Sligo, attempting, not altogether successfully, to sound cheerful. "Food – what would you like to eat. I'm sure you can have whatever you'd like."

"Good. I'll have rabbit pie made with chestnut flour pastry, roast silverweed root, fried puffball – and a bowl of dried whortleberries."

Sligo clenched his teeth and with a big effort managed to refrain from kicking Tegid back into his room. The temptation became even stronger when he found Tegid smirking up at him.

Sligo forced what was supposed to be a smile onto his face. "I'll tell you what, I'll order something really nice and while it's being prepared we can have a little chat about making the recording for television – the one that will make you famous."

He phoned Mrs Nicholls and then pointed at the settee. "Let's sit here and have a drink and a chat while we wait."

When Tegid had climbed up, Sligo asked him, "Now, what's it to be? Would you like whisky in that water, or would you prefer cider?"

Sligo had a difficult evening. He confirmed what he had already suspected: he needed alcohol to control Tegid. There was a brief period in between recovering from a hangover and being impossibly drunk again, when Tegid's demeanour was suitable for filming. In the stages either side he was able to take some still photos that conveyed Tegid's size, but the rate of progress was too slow and when Smith returned the following day, Sligo had a feeling that he wouldn't be happy.

He wasn't the only one who thought he had problems.

*

Bob came in from work to be greeted by an excited Jane with news of a development.

"Myrddin asked me to get in touch with the local BBC unit and arrange for live coverage of an event at the farm. I couldn't tell them anything other than it would be a sensational news story that the national news, and all of the networks, would be after straight away. I was giving them the chance of a really major scoop. We're not even telling them exactly where it is until fifteen minutes before they can start broadcasting. All I've said that it is just west of Lyme Regis, near the coast.

"I really didn't think I could pull it off – but I did! There's been so much local publicity about Myrddin that they couldn't resist it. I suppose they're bound to have other stuff ready in case this doesn't work out, but they'll have a reporter and camera crew from *Spotlight* ready to be at the gates at six-thirty-five."

266

She was hanging on to Bob's arm, cheeks pink and eyes sparkling, but Jane instantly saw that Bob didn't share her excitement.

"What's the matter?"

Bob squeezed her arm and kissed her on the cheek. "We need to talk about all this." Arthur had realised that his father was home and came rushing in from the garden. "We'll have a chat later," Bob said, bending to sweep his son up into his arms. "Hello, Arthur, my boy! What have you been up to?"

"Come and see!" Arthur wriggled to be put down and then led Bob out into the garden, leaving Jane staring after them with a puzzled look on her face.

Bob seemed pre-occupied through their evening meal. As soon as Arthur was in bed he said, "Let's have that chat."

"I really don't like the sound of this. Is something wrong at work?"

Bob shook his head. "No, nothing to do with work. I'm having a beer – do you want one?"

"I think I better had."

Bob opened a couple of cans, poured the beers and carried them through to the lounge. He put them on the coffee table, sat on the settee and patted the seat next to him. Jane sat, swung her legs up and looked at his serious profile.

"You've really got me worried now. What's this all about? Are you ill?"

Bob shook his head and reached forward for his beer.

"I've been wanting to say this for a while, but things have rushed along at such a pace since Myrddin re-appeared that there just doesn't seem to have been the opportunity." He took a large swallow of his beer before continuing. "I know I'm not going to make a very good job of putting this into words." He turned to look at her, "Just remember how much you mean to me and hear me out. O.K.?"

Jane nodded. "O.K."

"We were happy together before Arthur came along, weren't we?"

Jane nodded again.

"Kids were the only thing missing from our lives. Then I came across Myrddin, Joe, Carn and the others – and our lives were turned upside down. For a few weeks everything was just chaotically exciting, until Myrddin disappeared and we moved the

Dini to Scotland. Then things calmed down a little and returned towards normal – except for two things: we had that sword on the wall, and Myrddin had left us convinced that we had a part to play in his war to save the planet from the destruction that mankind is causing." He looked at Jane who nodded.

"Yes. I can't argue with any of that – but nor can I see any problem."

"I'm getting to it. Then you found that, after almost giving up hope, you were pregnant. Arthur arrived and, as far as I was concerned, my life was complete. I had you, a son, a job I loved and I was living where I wanted to live. I didn't need anything else."

He took another mouthful of beer and there was silence while he clearly struggled to control his emotions.

"But there *was* something else in my life – there was that sword." He nodded at the Sword of Power. "It *does* have a power – I can feel it. Like you, I thought that we had a part to play in Myrddin's war and whenever I doubted it, I only had to touch the sword. But I was content to wait to see what the future had in store. It seems to have affected you differently." He looked at Jane who raised her eyebrows and shrugged.

"It seems to have fuelled your passion for your environmental campaigning. You were getting involved before Arthur arrived but, since then, it has taken over our lives." Jane was about to speak, but Bob held his hand up. "Please, just let me finish this bit.

"You didn't want to return to work after Arthur was born – and I was certain that you were right. We had waited too long, and he meant too much to us, for us to hand him over to child-minders. I wanted him to be with you all day.

"But year-by-year all this environmental stuff has taken over. It's all got too intense and I don't think we've been as happy as we should have been.

"The trouble was that there was never a point at which I could object to what you were doing. You sincerely believed in it and it was impossible for me to say that you were wrong. Although there have been times when it's been hard to stay quiet."

"Such as?"

"Well, the fact is that we haven't been practising what you've been preaching. Just look at the size of this house: far too big for the three of us. All the really serious energy-saving measures, we couldn't afford to install. Then there's the location – too much fuel wasted getting about. And your old car belching out fumes."

The expression on Jane's face was hardening.

"When you wanted to become a Green Party candidate, I went along with it. There was no harm in it..."

Jane swung her legs off the settee and jumped up. She stood in front of the fireplace with her hands on her hips, a furious expression on her face. "How dare you! How dare you patronise me and try to belittle what our Party stands for and what we could achieve!"

Bob put down his glass and held up both hands. "I'm sorry – but when I said that there was no harm in it, I meant it literally. There *is* no harm in it. In fact, if only people would listen and act upon what they hear, only good could result. So, there is no harm in it – unlike the present situation."

"What do you mean? What present situation?"

"I mean what Myrddin is up to."

"What do you think he's *up to*? All he's been doing is telling people what we've been telling them for years – but now they're listening."

"Yes – but why are they listening? Why do they listen to him when they haven't listened to anyone else saying the same things?"

Jane took her hands off her hips and put them in her pockets. "You know the answer to that as well as I do. He seems able to exercise some extraordinary control over people's minds – to bend them to his way of thinking."

"Quite. So, is he convincing them by his arguments or just controlling what they do by some sort of mass hypnotism?"

Jane shrugged and didn't answer.

Bob pressed her. "He can't hypnotise the whole world, can he?"

"No, but maybe he doesn't have to. If he just gets a movement going, maybe it will have the momentum to carry the message around the world. He's doing all right so far."

Bob patted the settee next to him. "Please?" Jane gave him a hard look, but then returned to her seat.

"You may not be agreeing with much of what I'm saying, but hear me out – I've nearly finished." He took a deep breath.

"We don't really know who he is. We don't really know anything about him. We have The Droller's story about how they found him in a lead box. But, The Droller *is* a storyteller – that's what he's all about. It may be true: it may be a complete fabrication made up by The Droller and Myrddin – or it may be another example of Myrddin's mind control games with The Droller saying what Myrddin has planted in his mind."

Jane was shaking her head with an exasperated expression on her face. "But what about the sword? *You* pulled it out of the sea – I saw you do it. And there's Arthur – the strange goings on: you held him up to take that leather cover off the sword; he knew that Myrddin was coming back; there's definitely a very close relationship between them. And...we called him Arthur. Myrddin wasn't even around."

The expression on Bob's face was bleak. "I don't have the answers – I'm just telling you my concerns. I can't explain Gilda, if that is Gilda, or the treasure hoard. We have a strange old man who tells us that he's Merlin and that he's in touch with the spirit of Arthur who, by tradition, will return when the Celtic people are in danger. He says that that spirit is now in our son and that the danger threatening the people is environmental catastrophe and that his task is to save us from it. And we know that he has an extraordinary ability to influence people's minds.

"So, if he's been influencing the minds of all these people, what has he been doing with ours – and that of our son?" He let that question hang in the air for a full minute.

"He's got you doing whatever he wants you to do, without question. Maybe this whole business about the sword is just something that he's planted in us?" He let that one hang, as well.

"I don't doubt his sincerity. I don't doubt his conviction that he can make all this work. But maybe, just maybe, we should doubt his sanity."

His speech finished, Bob reached for his beer and drained the glass.

Jane had a question. "If he's controlling our thinking, how come you're saying this?"

Bob shrugged. "I told you I didn't have the answers. Maybe he's stretching his powers so thinly that he's losing control. All I'm really trying to say is that I'm worried about how this whole thing is going to end. And I can't shake off the feeling that it's going to end badly – for all of us. "

There was a silence that stretched into five minutes, then Bob said, "I'm sorry if anything I've said upset you. You know I wouldn't want to do that." He stretched out an arm towards Jane.

She eased along the settee to snuggle up to him and said, "I can't say I wasn't shocked by some of the things you said. You know what I'm like, I'll have to take time to slowly digest and analyse what you said. But if that's been on your mind, you were right to tell me."

Bob sighed. "I'll tell you just one more thing: something that I can be certain about: there is absolutely no way that he will be able to control the media hysteria that will follow his public unveiling tomorrow night. He has no idea of the storm that is going to hit them. I pity Carn and all the others."

He looked down at her. "You're not planning on being there, I hope."

She shook her head. "No, I'll be here, watching on TV."

"Good. If we can keep ourselves out of this, we'll be very lucky."

CHAPTER 23

The secret is out

Myrddin and Joe left Lyme Regis in the early hours of the morning and drove to London. Given his landline number, it had not been difficult to trace Sligo's home address. It was barely light as Joe double-parked the Toyota directly outside the house.

Myrddin got out, walked to the front door and rang the bell. After he had rung it twice more without any response he nodded to Joe who took a large sledgehammer from the boot, strode to the door and with one blow burst it open.

They stepped inside and pushed the door nearly closed behind them. Joe stood at the door, keeping a watchful eye on the car while Myrddin checked the rooms, first downstairs and then up. He was soon back downstairs.

"Nobody here, Joe. Our bird has flown."

"But was he ever here?"

"Oh, yes." Myrddin held up Tegid's old Wellington boots. "He's been here all right, but where, I wonder, has he gone?"

Myrddin looked around the mess in the kitchen. The kitchen table held a large plate and a very small plate, both holding a congealed mass that might have been a meat pie. There was a large supermarket carrier bag on the floor and Myrddin picked it up. It was empty except for three pieces of paper: a till receipt, a credit card payment slip and a shopping list.

"It looks as if our Mr Sligo is off on his holidays. He's treated himself to a suitcase, some shirts, chocolate, cider, a first aid kit and a child's drinking mug."

"Very interesting, I'm sure; but is that any help to us?"

"I believe that it is. Mr Sligo kindly wrote his list underneath this."

Myrddin held up the slip of paper so that Joe could see the name Smith, a Surrey address and the words *Mrs Nicholls housekeeper.*

"Most considerate, don't you think? Let us go and seek out the Smith residence."

*

Sligo was up unusually early for him, but he needed to make progress before Smith returned. He showered, dressed and went to find Tegid, determined to have him in a presentable condition for a filming session.

He unlocked Tegid's door and went into the room. The heavy curtains let little light in and Sligo had to turn the light on. He half-expected a complaint from Tegid, but there was no sound. The tiny body wasn't on the bed or in the pet carrier that stood on the floor. In a rising panic Sligo looked under the bed, inside the wardrobe and even in the chest of drawers.

His precious captive had disappeared – but the door had definitely been locked and the room was on the second floor. Desperately he looked around the room checking for places that he might have missed. The curtains were still drawn and stopped just below the window ledge, so that wasn't a hiding place. As he was looking at the curtains he saw them stir slightly and a breath of wind wafted into the room. Sligo crept towards the window and very gently moved a curtain aside so that he could see out.

The sash window had been pushed up and Tegid was sitting on the window ledge, his legs dangling in space. His eyes were closed and he appeared to be enjoying the morning sun on his face. Sligo moved behind Tegid, grabbed him by both arms, jerked him back into the room and threw him across to the bed. He bounced once and crashed onto the floor. Sligo slammed the window shut and made sure that the curtains were fully drawn closed.

Tegid was picking himself up from the floor when Sligo pounced on him, lifted him into the air and shook him violently.

"You idiot! You stupid, stupid, little idiot!"

Tegid lashed out with his feet, but Sligo had been caught like that before and was holding Tegid at arms' length. When the shaking stopped, a startled Tegid complained, "What's the problem? I was perfectly safe – just getting a breath of fresh air."

"Anybody could have seen you! And if they have, I'll sling you out of that window myself."

"What's got into you this morning?"

273

"I'm sick of you and your lack of co-operation. I'm trying to do you a favour here. I'm trying to make you rich and famous. Now, we're going next door and you're going to sit on that settee and answer the questions exactly as I told you last night."

"Not until I've had some breakfast, I'm not."

Sligo reached for Tegid's throat, but stopped himself just in time.

"I need a cigarette," he said and stormed back into his bedroom and then into the studio where he snatched up the phone. He dialled a number. "Mrs Nicholls, please send up some cigarettes – any sort will do."

"I'm sorry, Mr Sligo, since Mr Smith gave up smoking two years ago he hasn't allowed any tobacco products into the house. He's very particular about it."

Sligo rang off and groaned. He had already smoked a full packet in the house. He knew that the three rooms would smell strongly of stale cigarette smoke and there were discarded cigarette ends littering the floor.

He went back into Tegid's room with a bottle of cider. "Here's your breakfast. You seem to prefer it to food. I'm going out. You go anywhere near that window and I'll pull you inside out!" He slammed the door behind him, locked it and strode off along the corridor and down the stairs.

He was crossing the hall to the front door when a voice called, "Ah! Mr Sligo isn't it?"

He turned to see a tall, slim, blonde woman moving towards him with a well-practised poise. He recognised her from the image on the internet. She was at least twenty years younger than her husband and she managed to look elegant even in jogging suit and trainers.

Sligo gave her his oiliest smile as he shook the perfectly-manicured hand offered to him. "Mrs Smith. How kind of you to have us here."

"Don't thank me, Mr Sligo. Ronald said you would be here and here you are – together with a degree of intriguing secrecy." She raised an eyebrow at him in an undisguised enquiry.

"Yes: sorry about that – but it won't be for long, I promise you. You'll understand the need for secrecy very soon."

"How fascinating! I knew that something unusual was going on: Ronald has been looking at me and smiling in a strange way over the last few days. Are you going out?"

"Er, yes. I need some cigarettes; although I understand that this is a non-smoking house."

"Yes, I'm afraid so. I finally bullied him into giving up his foul-smelling cigars, but if Ronald can't smoke, neither can anyone else."

Sligo was stunned to think of anyone bullying Smith and the surprise must have shown on his face.

"I can be very persuasive, Mr Sligo. Now, your cigarettes: the village shop is less than two miles away. I was about to go for my morning run. I usually run around the estate, but the village shop and back will do nicely. Shall we go?"

"Er, I'm not really equipped for jogging."

She laughed, revealing a lot of perfect teeth. "No, Mr Sligo, we don't have to run. A brisk walk will do just as well." She put an arm through Sligo's and led him to the door. "Let's not be so formal. I'm Lavinia."

"Nigel."

"Nigel. How charming."

*

Joe pulled up at the wrought iron gates. "Now what? I don't think the sledgehammer will open these."

"Don't worry, Joe, your sledgehammer will not be necessary."

Myrddin got out of the car and pressed the button on the intercom. After a short delay there was a slight crackle and a woman said, "Yes?"

Myrddin closed his eyes and spoke in his richest, warmest voice. "Good morning. Do I have the pleasure of speaking to Mrs Nicholls?"

"I am Mrs Nicholls. Who is this?"

"We are friends of Mr Sligo. Mr Smith has arranged for us to call. You may open the gates." After a brief pause he repeated. "You may open the gates."

"Yes, I may open the gates."

The gates swung open, Joe drove through and Myrddin got back into the car. Joe whistled as they moved silently along the drive.

"This bloke Smith aristocracy, is he then?"

"Far from it, Joe. I believe that his connection with Sligo is that he owns a number of newspapers and magazines, plus a television channel. He is the chairman of the Smith Corporation – of which you have no doubt heard."

"Indeed I have. It's strange how many ways there are of being in business. There was me with my mobile shop and little terraced house – and there's Smith with all this. How much do you know about him?"

"If my campaign is to succeed, it is people like Smith that I need to support it. But I know enough about to him to know that that will never happen. There is no basic goodness in the man with which I could work."

They reached the entrance and Joe pulled up at the foot of the steps. As they got out a woman appeared at the front door. If she was surprised at the sight of Myrddin in his long robe, she didn't show it.

"I'm afraid that Mr Sligo has gone out."

"Ah. Did he go alone?"

"No. He went with Mrs Smith, but as they were walking they cannot have gone far."

"Thank you, Mrs Nicholls. Is he the only guest you have?"

"There is another, but I have not seen him."

"Excellent. You may show us to their rooms and we will wait for them there."

After only the slightest hesitation, Mrs Nicholls led them up two flights of stairs and then pointed at a screen.

"You will find their rooms at the end of the corridor."

"Thank you, Mrs Nicholls. You have done well. Everything is as it should be."

She nodded gravely and went back down the stairs.

They moved the screen aside and Joe began to hurry along the short corridor. "Come on – they could be back any minute!"

"Oh, but I think that I would rather like to meet Mr Sligo."

"But what about Mrs Smith – and there must be other staff in the house. Plus, I saw at least two gardeners outside."

They looked in Sligo's bedroom first; then the studio, where Myrddin gazed at the camera set-up; finally, Joe tried the other door that was locked. He turned the key and looked around the door before opening it wide and turning on the light.

Tegid was lying on the bed, sound asleep, with a half-empty cider bottle beside him. They stood either side of the bed looking down, but when Joe put out an arm to shake him, Myrddin stopped him.

"Let him sleep." He lifted up the pet carrier. "It looks as if he's accustomed to travelling in this."

Joe gently lifted Tegid and placed him carefully in the pet carrier. He wriggled slightly, but didn't wake. Joe fastened the top half in place and they left the room to walk out to the car.

No-one challenged them as they drove back to the gates that swung open automatically on their approach.

*

Mrs Lavinia Smith could be very persuasive and as Sligo walked with her back towards the house he had the uncomfortable feeling that he'd said far too much. His feeling of discomfort increased considerably as they turned the last corner just in time to see a black car turn out of the gates and drive along the lane away from them.

"Any idea who that was, Lavinia?"

"No idea at all. But you can be certain that Mrs Nicholls would not have let them in, unless they had a very good reason for being there. Fortunately, I have the PIN number, otherwise I suspect that she might not let *me* in." She smiled at the joke she'd clearly made many times before, but Sligo wasn't re-assured and quickened his pace.

He ran the last hundred yards, bounded up the steps and tried to run up the stairs. His lack of fitness defeated him and he walked up the last few stairs wheezing and coughing. The screen had been moved. He found the door to Tegid's room standing wide open. There was no sign of Tegid and the pet carrier had gone.

Sligo hastily packed his suitcase and carried it downstairs where he found Lavinia talking to a very confused Mrs Nicholls.

"Nigel, what's going on? This poor woman doesn't seem able to answer simple questions."

Sligo hurried past them heading for his car. He knew that Smith would have some questions when he arrived and Sligo had no intention of being there to answer them.

*

Sligo had almost reached Princetown before his phone rang. He let it go to his message service and waited until he was back in the cottage before he listened to Smith's apoplectic ranting.

He drank a mug of strong black coffee and smoked a couple of cigarettes before phoning back. Smith resumed his rant and Sligo let him carry on until he appeared to be running out of steam.

"There was nothing I could do about it Mr Smith. He was safely locked in when I left him for a few minutes. But Myrddin turned up, your housekeeper let him in and he's snatched Tegid. Yes, I'm sure it was him – I saw the car pulling away and he used his mind games to get in.

"No, I assure you that I'm not messing you about…Yes, I know that I'm the only one who's seen Tegid – but that's what we agreed…You'll find some footage on the camera that proves he was there…I'm back in Devon…Yes, sorry about the carpet and the mess."

Smith's last comment was interesting.

"While you've been messing everything up, you moron, I've got some information. Our SmithTV people have had a tip-off. The BBC local news programme down your way is running a special live feature in the six-thirty edition. It's been set up with this Myrddin character. I suppose even a cretin like you can manage to watch the television."

*

Bob, Jane and Arthur were lined up on the settee. The six-thirty local news programme started with a few minutes of headlines and then came the announcement.

"In recent weeks you may have seen or heard the publicity concerning the mysterious individual who calls himself Myrddin and his *The Message not the Man* campaign. You may even have been at one of his meetings to hear his message that he hopes will protect the environment by getting us to fundamentally change the way we live. Well, Myrddin has invited us to send a camera to a secret location in Dorset where he has promised that we will be the first to see a sight that the whole world will wish to see.

"We have absolutely no idea what this is all about, but we couldn't turn down an invitation like that, so Julia is at that secret location and we can go to her, live, right now. Julia, what more can you tell us?"

"The answer at the moment is: not much. We were told to be here with a camera unit by six-thirty-five, which is only seconds away. The secret location turns out to be a farm near Lyme Regis. The driveway into the farm is blocked by this barrier behind me and a just a few yards further on is a high metal gate. There is no sign of anyone ar...

"Oh, here it goes: the barrier is going up. Come on! Let's go in!

"Now the big gate is swinging open. I have to say that this feels like a Willy Wonka moment."

The camera followed Julia as she walked along the drive, constantly looking back over her shoulder into the lens and keeping up a commentary.

"As you can see, the drive is quite a long one and is swinging around behind this patch of woodland. I can just make out that there is a building appearing: a building that I suppose is the farmhouse. It's big and imposing, with lots of windows and a gravelled area in front of it. And, as I expect you can see, there are people waiting for us. Now, I recognise the man in the centre: that's Myrddin. Probably a lot of you will recognise his distinctive beard and long robe. Around him there is a group of very young children.

"Let's get there and see what they're going to show..." Julia skidded to a halt on the gravel and the camera moved from her stunned face to the small figures at which she was pointing.

Arthur jumped off the settee and rushed to sit next to the television.

"They aren't children!" The camera showed Julia bending over, peering into the faces. She straightened up and looked into the camera. "I...I...I just don't know what to say. I promise you, there's no trick – I am surrounded by tiny people, no more than two feet high and, as you can see, most of them are wearing robes that look like those worn by Myrddin." The camera kept moving off her to go from face to face in the crowd. Arthur pointed to the faces and shouted out the names.

Julia turned to Myrddin and the camera focussed on his face. "Myrddin, what's going on? Who are these people? Where have they come from?"

Myrddin smiled into the lens. "These fine people are the last survivors of an ancient Celtic tribe. Hundreds of years ago, to escape the torments inflicted upon them by those of normal size, they left their homes and sought out the wild places. There they have lived ever since; living at peace – there is no conflict within their tribe – and making such little impact on the environment that the rest of you have failed to notice their existence. Some of this group lived on Dartmoor, the others among the mountains of Wales."

Julia was standing with one hand clutching the hair on the top of her head. Another woman moved into camera shot. The director couldn't bring herself to stay back; she asked Myrddin, "Do they speak English?"

"Some speak only English, some only Welsh and a handful can manage a conversation in both." He looked around. "Carn and Eppie, would you care to say a few words?"

The group parted and, with obvious reluctance, Carn and Eppie moved to the front. They were wearing their usual modern clothing.

Julia bent down. "Hello. Who are you two?"

"I'm Carn, and this is Eppie."

The Johnsons were accustomed to the voice, but anyone hearing it for the first time would find it as strange as his appearance.

"And, er, Eppie, do you live on this farm?"

Eppie nodded. "Yes, but we lived on Dartmoor for many years." Her voice was lighter, sweeter and easier to listen to.

"But where on Dartmoor? Did you have houses?"

"No; most of us lived in the old mineshafts."

Myrddin interrupted. "Julia, that must be all for today. Walk with me back to the gate."

The camera stayed on the tiny figures as they began to go into the house through the small door set into the main door, but then swung back to Myrddin and Julia. The cameraman hurried to get in front of them and kept them in shot as they walked to the gate.

"I brought them to this farm because it was becoming impossible for them to remain undiscovered. The wild places of Britain are not as remote as they once were. Indeed, I am sure that there will be people watching who have seen these little folk, but who have remained silent, either because they doubt their own sanity or because they fear the ridicule that would follow if they spoke of their experiences.

"Beginning tomorrow, I invite you to come each day for a short visit. We will show you around our farm and you will see how we live: how we grow our own food; produce our own electricity; make our own clothing. They are almost entirely self-sufficient. You will see where they eat, sleep and join us in song and dance.

"They are gentle and charming people and we need to introduce them to the world in a way that causes them as little distress as possible.

"I trust that everyone watching will respect that."

They had reached the gates that swung open for them. As soon as the television crew had passed through, the gates closed and Myrddin walked away towards the house leaving Julia looking at the camera in a state of bewildered excitement.

"I can't believe that has just happened – and I don't know what else to say. I think I'll just pass you back to the studio."

The image on the screen changed to the two presenters in the studio who were looking smilingly bemused.

"Well, Julia's not the only one who can't believe what they've just seen. It's not the first of April is it?"

"No, no, I don't think it is. But if we're going back there tomorrow, I can hardly wait. But now we'll have to turn our attention to the day's other events in our region."

Bob used the remote control to turn off the television.

"What did we think of that?"

"I thought it was fun," said Arthur. "I like seeing them on the television."

Jane nodded to her son. "You're right! It was fun." She looked at Bob. "I think it went fine. Given that Myrddin wanted to get this done quickly before Sligo puts out his stuff, what else could he have done?"

Another voice butted in and they all turned towards the tiny figure looking lost in an armchair.

"I still don't know why I'm here and not with the others," said Tegid grumpily.

Bob chuckled. "What's the matter, Tegid, sulking because you missed being on the telly? You know why you're here – you've been told several times already. Myrddin asked us to bring you over here because you can't be trusted to behave yourself. You've been drinking far too much and with or without alcohol you'd make life difficult for everyone at the farm – especially poor Nudd. And that's the last thing they need right now."

Bob looked at Jane, "I didn't ask, how was it driving the Toyota back?"

"Weird. It'll take some getting used to, this driving along silently with the engine cutting in and out. Nice of Myrddin to lend it to me, though."

"I did tell Joe that your Fiesta is going into the garage in a few days and that might be the end of it. I don't suppose Myrddin is going anywhere for a while, he's going to have his hands full."

"Why's that?" asked Tegid. "There doesn't seem to be much going on to me?"

"By tomorrow the place will be over-run."

"What with?"

"The media – in all its forms."

"Ah! The dreaded media," said Tegid with a sneer. "Are we going to see what you lot have been on about all these years?"

"Yes," said Bob, "I'm afraid so."

*

Within the hour the BBC news channel was running the item obtained by the local news and it was run again in its entirety on the ten o'clock news. At ten-thirty Sligo's phone rang. He saw that it was Smith calling and answered it.

"Sligo."

Smith didn't waste time on preamble. "I take it you've been watching."

"Yes."

"Did you spot your escaped prisoner among them?"

"No, I didn't. I got the impression that they were all that bit taller than he is."

"One of our outside broadcast units will be there first thing in the morning. Get yourself over there. Now the big secret is out you can start briefing a production team on your own stuff, so we're ready to go…"

"Yes, M…"

"I haven't finished. I've seen what you recorded and the stills in the camera and the notes you left when you hurried off. It's good – but it's not enough. I want our little star back."

"But…"

"No buts, Sligo. Just get him."

Myrddin and Joe had arranged for a company that provided security teams to send ten uniformed men at seven o'clock and they turned up just as Julia left.

The first photographers, professional and amateur, had tracked down the farm by eight o'clock and found security in place on the gates. The most energetic set off to follow the high fence around the perimeter of the farm. It was after dark by the time they got back, muddy to the knees and showing the signs of encounters with several hedges, to report that there were no other gates, that more security men were patrolling within the fence and that the whole length of the fence was covered by CCTV cameras.

The next BBC visit had been arranged for eleven o'clock in the morning and was to be screened live on BBC 1 and on the BBC news channel. By eight o'clock there were more than twenty photographers gathered between the barrier and the gates. Their cars were blocking the roads and the police were there in force.

Myrddin agreed to an appeal for more manpower from the security staff and a further twenty, including dog-handlers, were requested to get there as soon as possible.

By ten o'clock the farmer who owned the field opposite the farm entrance had opened the field gate and was charging photographers, reporters and outside broadcast units a hefty fee to park in there.

By the time that the BBC crew arrived for their scheduled session the crowd in front of the gate had grown to more than fifty. Their rival news gatherers were not inclined to be co-operative and there was no way that Julia and her colleagues could get to the gate until the additional security staff arrived in a coach and forced a pathway through the crowd.

At the scheduled time for the broadcast to start, Myrddin watched the unpleasant scenes on television. The guard dogs, barking furiously, lunged and snapped at the crowd. The pictures became a chaotic mix of out-of-focus bodies as the crowd surged around the BBC cameraman. Eventually, a dishevelled and out of breath Julia made it to the gates. As the gates swung open the security men attempted to get only the BBC crew through, but the surge forward was so great that three photographers were through the opening before six hefty members of the security team were able to force the gates closed aided by two dogs snapping at anyone venturing into the reducing opening.

"Well," said Julia to camera, "extraordinary scenes here this morning contrast sharply with the peace and quiet of yesterday. But at last we are inside and now we're going as quickly as we can to the farmhouse where I understand that we will be met by our guides for an hour-long tour of the farm.

"Oh, yes, now we can see Myrddin just coming out of the front door. He has with him only one of the group of little people that we saw yesterday. Here they come to greet us. Good morning, Myrddin. What do you think of the interest that you are generating? That's quite a crowd at the gate."

"Good morning, Julia. And good morning to everyone watching on television. I am sorry for the difficult time you had getting in to see us. I have just been speaking to the police and, hopefully, by the time that you leave us, everything should be under rather greater control.

"I would like to introduce one of my friends. He is known by his title, The Droller. The position of storyteller has long been one of great importance within Celtic tribes. The Droller not only provides entertainment by the eloquent telling of tales, but has the responsibility of preserving and passing on knowledge of the tribe's history."

The camera focussed on the old, lined face of The Droller, who bowed gravely both to Julia and the camera.

Myrddin continued, "You will find The Droller particularly helpful as he speaks Welsh and English with equal fluency and so will be able to act as translator as well as guide."

"Oh, are you not being our guide?"

"Alas, no. I hope to join you for a good part of the time, but other matters are currently demanding my attention. You are in safe hands, however."

"If you would care to come this way, madam, we will first visit our living quarters." The Droller led the way around to the side of the house, heading for the yard at the rear. The cameraman hurried ahead so that he could capture Julia and The Droller walking towards him.

As soon as they were out of sight, Myrddin turned towards the area of trees in front of the house. The CCTV cameras had shown him that the three photographers who had got in through the gate had fled into the trees. He could feel them looking at him;

could sense the cameras clicking. One by one he sought them out. His icy stare lingered on each for a few seconds before moving on. Three figures blundered from the trees and staggered back towards the gate. Two were trying to stem profuse nosebleeds, while the other clutched his head, the victim of a sudden fierce migraine attack.

The gates were opened a fraction and the three bundled into the throng outside. The three casualties became the focus of attention as their fellow photographers jostled to capture shots of blood-stained shirts and the pain-racked face. The camera crew from SmithTV paid particular attention.

Sligo, hanging around on the edge of the crowd, recognised the symptoms.

Myrddin returned to the house and went to the control room with its banks of screens. The head of the security team was there.

"Mr Andrews, how is everything?"

"For the moment, sir, just about under control. But some of these men have now been on duty for sixteen hours and they are long overdue a break. As soon as we get the BBC people back out of the gate, I'll have to re-distribute my men to allow some to rest.

"It's the gate that's the obvious problem. Believe me, you will have people coming over, under and through the fence. The gate is the only place that we can eject them – and you could see the problem we have opening and closing it. We need the police to push them all back to the barrier and keep them behind that; then we'll be able to open and close the gate without any problem."

Myrddin resumed his earlier conversation with the police and was assured that two police vans and a minibus full of officers were on their way, but their progress was slow along the blocked roads. The crowd outside was growing by the minute as more media teams arrived together with large numbers of the general public. Locals and holidaymakers alike were swarming to the area, most of them carrying cameras, all curious to see what was going on.

Myrddin crossed the yard to rejoin Julia and The Droller. She was on her knees in the communal kitchen and eating area, clearly delighted with the tiny furniture and fittings. She was eventually persuaded to move out to see some of the farm.

*

285

Tegid was in a bad mood. He needed a drink. He had refused to get up for breakfast and had eventually come downstairs only after Jane told him that if he didn't come down of his own accord, she would set up a baby chair, carry him downstairs and force him into it.

He was now sitting at the kitchen table on a cushion on a high stool.

"I want to go out."

"You're not a prisoner. The door's open. The secret is out: as of last night the world knows that the Gododdin exist."

"Dini," he muttered.

"What?"

"We're the Dini, not the Gododdin – it's only Myrddin who calls us anything else. We know who we are – why should he decide we're something different?"

"All right; the world knows that the *Dini* exist, so go out and let the world see you if you want. But before you do, come and see this. Come on!"

Muttering under his breath and casting baleful looks in Jane's direction, he climbed down from his seat and followed Jane into the lounge where Arthur was watching events unfold on television.

"Hello, Tegid! Look at all this!" Arthur was sat on the floor near the television and he patted the floor at his side.

Tegid joined Arthur on the floor.

Jane explained what was going on. "One BBC camera crew is inside and we keep getting shots of the farm, the buildings and the Go- the Dini. But they've got another camera outside, filming the crush at the gate. Look at that! Myrddin has made the farm secure enough to keep them out, but they're all desperate to catch a glimpse of your friends.

"Go out if you want to, but if you're spotted all that interest will be focussed on you and we have no way of keeping them out. Try the other channels, Arthur."

As Arthur pressed the buttons on the remote control, most of the channels were showing similar scenes. One channel had a camera in a helicopter and was showing the field that had rapidly filled with parked vehicles, the crowd at the gate and the convoy of police vehicles trapped in the road congestion.

The helicopter followed the farm drive, passed over the farmhouse and the yard, before hovering over the fields. It descended until the noise and the downdraught forced Myrddin, Julia and The Droller to take shelter in an outbuilding. The helicopter may well have landed if it hadn't been for the presence of the security guards and their dogs.

Back on the BBC their camera captured the distress on the old face of The Droller and Myrddin's anger.

Tegid had stopped complaining. "So that's 'the media' that Joe, and then you, warned us about."

Jane nodded and sighed. "Yes, I'm afraid so. But the media's appetite only remains at this level for a week or two. After that, well, the world certainly won't lose interest in you, but, with a bit of luck and Myrddin's planning, the interest should settle down at a tolerable level – I hope.

"In the meantime, if you want some fresh air, the garden should be safe enough."

*

The police abandoned their trapped vehicles and made their way on foot. Some set about clearing the traffic congestion; others reached the gate and, after three arrests for public order offences, succeeded in moving the crowd back from the gate to the barrier.

After a visit that had lasted an hour longer than planned, the BBC crew went back through the gate and at least reached the barrier before they were caught in the crush and the barrage of questions shouted at them.

As the afternoon wore into evening, the crowd reduced as the police efforts at clearing the roads took effect and the onlookers from the general public decided that they were likely to be seeing more at home on the television.

As darkness set in, the intrusions began. A local window cleaner had cheerfully sold his ladders for five times what it would cost him to replace them and the first reporter successfully scaled the fence. In a neighbouring field a group of reporters worked together to move hay bales up to the fence and built themselves a ladder. Through the night more ladders, wire-cutters and ropes were all used to gain access to the site. All of the intruders were apprehended and ejected through the gate.

At dawn an exhausted security chief had a suggestion to make.

"Why not let a BBC camera crew stay on site, rather than restrict them to short visits? As I understand it, you're happy for them to see everything and having them here all the time would have two advantages. For one thing, they could be filming all these intrusions – and that might just help stop them happening. For another, giving out a lot more coverage that you can control might just satisfy the public's demand."

Myrddin nodded. "You know far more of these situations than I, Mr Andrews. I am content to take your advice."

The BBC eagerly accepted the offer and by lunchtime their camera team was in place.

Lunchtime also brought a suggestion that was less welcome, but was hard to resist.

The senior police officer present pointed out that restricting access to just the BBC was causing a lot of ill-feeling within the other media teams, particularly the overseas news teams that were now turning up, resulting in a hostile atmosphere outside. He requested that Myrddin allow in other reporters, in groups of no more than ten at a time, for a series of 'press conferences'. Reluctantly, Myrddin agreed.

Sligo managed to get himself into the first group. After Myrddin and The Droller had spent ten minutes answering some particularly inane questions, during which Sligo kept a very low profile, the reporters and cameramen were allowed twenty minutes with the little folk – and as none of the press people spoke Welsh, it was Carn and his friends who were in demand.

Sligo managed to corner Nudd and Erbyn, although he didn't know who they were.

"Perhaps you would be kind enough to help me? I've made a note of all of the names mentioned and I'm trying to put faces to the names. Who are you two?"

After the pair had introduced themselves, Sligo went on. "Excellent! Now I think I've met all of the Dartmoor group except for…" he made a show of consulting his notepad, "Tegid."

Nudd and Erbyn exchanged startled looks, but said nothing.

"Tegid," Sligo persisted, "have I got the name right?"

"Er, yes, but you can't see him," Nudd stumbled.

"Oh, that's a pity. Is he inside?"

"No, that is, he's not…" Nudd's voice tailed away as Erbyn shook his head at him.

Out of the corner of his eye Sligo spotted Myrddin approaching and he quickly moved on after giving them a big, oily smile and a, "Charmed to meet you, I'm sure." His place in front of Nudd and Erbyn was quickly filled by another reporter and Myrddin's advance was halted by his having to assist with a question delivered with a trans-Atlantic twang.

"Hey! Do you guys have tiny johns?"

Sligo made his way back through the gate, through the crowd and back to his car. He was sure Tegid wasn't at the farm. And there was only one other place that Sligo believed he could be.

CHAPTER 24

How many dead?

Sligo drove to the cottage in Princetown to make sure that he had everything needed for a lengthy stake-out in Chagford. He needed fully-charged mobile phone, radio and mini TV together with his camera, binoculars, food and drink.

He felt more comfortable about watching the Johnson house knowing that Myrddin wasn't there. Nor, with the spell of settled weather, did he have to worry about getting soaked.

He was almost ready to leave when Smith phoned.

"Any progress?"

"I'm sure Tegid isn't at the farm – which means that he's probably at the Johnson place. I've finished briefing your production team, so they've got everything they need when you decide to go with it."

"Yeah, I know – but as I told you before Sligo, what you have isn't enough. Get your little friend back in front of a camera or you won't get a penny out of me."

Sligo didn't like the sound of that. He was well out of pocket on this story and he'd fully expected it to be a big payer; plus he wanted compensation for the injuries and rough treatment he'd received.

Before he left for Chagford he spent an hour on the phone contacting editors desperate for material on 'the little people' to sell what he knew of the stories of Alice Jackson, George Phillips and Dan Murphy, together with the photos he'd taken without their knowledge.

He eventually reached Chagford in the early evening and drove slowly past the Johnson house. He was surprised and alarmed to see the black Toyota parked on the drive alongside the NPA Land Rover and the Fiesta.

That Joe Morgan, with or without Myrddin, must have driven over here. That was bad news as far as Sligo was concerned. He didn't fancy tangling with Myrddin and Joe Morgan was a big man. Sligo had been picturing seizing his chance when Jane Johnson was on her own.

He parked in Chagford and switched on the tiny portable television. The image on the five-inch screen wasn't clear enough to identify individual faces, but from the commentary he knew that another 'press conference' was in progress and Myrddin was there.

So he had the Johnsons and Morgan to deal with. *Let's hope that Morgan hasn't turned up to take the little beast back to the farm.*

Sligo hurried back along the lane towards the house. He turned onto the public footpath just before the house and walked briskly up the hill to the vantage point that he had used previously. He settled into the hedge with his back against the tree and took out his binoculars. The garden and patio were deserted but the double doors were open.

He couldn't make out any movement in the house, but it seemed likely that they were all watching the television coverage. He turned on his mini television and played with the channels. He was amused to find a panel discussion taking place involving a survival expert describing the diet that he thought 'the little people' had lived on, and a geneticist venturing opinions on how their size had come about. *Typical television – if you don't know the facts, fill the time with wild guesses,* he thought, the direct comparison with his own style of reporting escaping him.

He caught the occasional glimpse of the Johnsons in their kitchen, but no-one came outside until the last of the evening sunshine was all but spent. Bob Johnson came out onto the patio with a mug in his hand. He was followed by his son who carried a bowl. Sligo watched as the boy turned and called into the house.

A smirk of satisfaction lodged on Sligo's face as he saw Tegid come outside. The boy was intent on picking fruit and appeared to be trying to persuade Tegid to join him. He was finally successful and the two of them moved into the fruit patch, heading towards the hedge that ran alongside the public footpath. Sligo eased to his feet and walked slowly and quietly down the path. He pulled out of his pocket his hip flask and unscrewed the top: he had the bait to draw Tegid to him.

He moved silently, peering through the hedge for a sight of his target. He needed a spot where he could whisper to Tegid, draw him close with the proffered flask and then grab him and yank him through. *He'll pick up a few scratches, but he owes me that.*

Sligo reached a spot where the hedge was thin enough for him to see the two small figures. He was in luck – Tegid was the nearer and not far from the hedge. He just needed the boy to move away a little.

Sligo heard a noise on the track and looked back up the hill. An old woman was walking towards him and just behind her he could see her dog.

Then he heard her say, "Come along, Winston. Nearly home."

The marks on his calf stabbed with pain. He swore under his breath and retreated to his car. Tegid would have to wait until tomorrow.

*

Sligo was driving back towards Chagford early the following morning when Smith rang again.

"We're going with it today. The fool has played right into our hands. We thought we'd have to sit on it for a couple of weeks as no story would knock his little morons off the front pages, but he's been so miserly with access and information that all the papers and broadcasters are desperate for anything even vaguely related. They're also furious about the way he's favoured the BBC. We're going to set it up for mid-afternoon and put out more stuff afterwards. Everyone else will latch onto it – it'll be everywhere! We're keeping some back for tomorrow." Smith sounded exultant, but then the tone of his voice changed.

"But I warn you, Sligo, we need more material – and I'm looking to you to get it. It's the AGM tomorrow afternoon and I want to make sure that we have this wrapped up before the meeting starts. Get on with it! Catch your little freak and get him to us by tomorrow morning at the latest – or you don't get a penny from me. Not now: not ever."

Sligo drove slowly past the house and cursed when he saw that there were still three vehicles parked on the drive. He parked in Chagford and was walking towards the house when he saw the nose of the Land Rover slowly appearing from the drive. Sligo jumped into the ditch and pressed himself into the hedge. Bob Johnson didn't notice him as he drove by on his way to work.

292

Sligo climbed out of the ditch and stood in the middle of the lane, undecided. He could go up the public footpath to his usual spot or risk the cows and go into the field opposite the house. Sligo decided to risk the cows. The crucial factor was the presence of Joe Morgan: by watching the front of the house he would know the moment that Morgan left.

Luck was on his side: the cattle had gone, although proof of their recent presence was scattered all over the field. He picked his way between the cowpats staying close to the hedge until he was directly opposite the entrance to the drive. He wriggled into the hedge, settled into a reasonably comfortable position and gently moved some stems aside. Both cars were clearly in view. He hoped that he wouldn't have long to wait. Sligo had already spent hours trying to come up with a workable plan – and failed. Now he had nothing to do but rack his brains looking for some idea that he might have missed.

*

To Jane's relief, Tegid had got up without argument; had even eaten a sensible breakfast and had joined Arthur in front of the television. However, he didn't stay there long. The only thing new from the previous evening was film of a couple of intruders being detained and ejected. The BBC presenters were happy to condemn the irresponsibility of the intruders and quote the angry reactions of their viewers who, like everyone else in the country, were entranced by 'the little people'.

Arthur took Tegid into the garden and encouraged him to look through the magnifying glass at insects, worms and flowers. It was sufficiently interesting to keep him occupied for an hour, but then his attention wavered.

Tegid went back into the house, looked at the television for a couple of minutes and then wandered back upstairs. Jane had put out a pile of Arthur's old clothes for Tegid to check through to see if anything fitted him. He idly picked up a couple of items and dropped them back onto the heap. He was bored.

Despite Jane's warnings, Tegid moved to the window and eased the drawn curtains aside. He looked out over the hedge opposite and across the fields. He needed to be outside: not in the garden, but free to roam. He thought back to the times when he and Nudd roved the moor looking for the chance to relieve unwary Biguns of small possessions. He had a smile on his face. He had enjoyed those times; although he didn't think that Nudd had shared his enjoyment. The smile left Tegid's face for a moment as he thought about his brother. Poor, anxious Nudd: Tegid was not the sort of brother that Nudd needed – nor deserved.

Tegid put those thoughts aside. He wanted to go back to those days of freedom; days of relying on his wits and cunning to survive. Taking fish from the streams; birds' eggs, in season, from the hedges. His eyes scanned the hedge opposite – and caught a tiny, unnatural, movement. He checked the trees for wind: there was none at all. Yet part of the hedge had moved. Tegid focussed on the spot and waited with the patience of a hunter.

Sure enough, there was the same movement, and when it happened there was a brief glimpse of a colour that had no place in the hedge. Tegid called out.

"There's someone watching the house."

Jane's voice came up the stairs. "Sorry, Tegid. What did you say?"

"There's someone in the hedge opposite, watching the house."

Jane and Arthur rushed upstairs and into the room. Tegid gestured to them to be cautious. Arthur squeezed up against Tegid to look through the same opening that he'd created. Jane stood over them and gently moved another part of the curtain aside.

"Where are they?"

"Look straight over the black car into the hedge. Close to the ground. I think they're sitting down."

"Can't see anything," said Jane.

"Nor me," said Arthur.

"Just watch carefully. Every few minutes they move a bit of the hedge."

Jane went to get her binoculars and then stood in her own bedroom. The curtains were fully open, but the bright sun was not shining into the room and she doubted if anyone could see through the hedge and to the back of the bedroom. She focussed on the spot that Tegid had described and called.

"I'm watching from in here. Shout out when you see something."

A full ten minutes passed and Jane had put down the binoculars when Tegid called, "Now!"

Jane brought the binoculars up just in time to see the ends of two fingers pushing aside some grass stems. She caught sight of a chin and a flash of blue shirt before the grasses moved back together.

"Did you see it, Mummy?" Arthur shouted, in an excited voice. "I did!"

"Yes, I saw it!" *But what do I do about it?*

She went downstairs to phone Bob and launched straight in. "There's somebody watching us. They're hiding in the hedge opposite the house."

"Any idea who it is?"

"No – well, I can't *see* who it is, but I can make a guess. I bet it's that Sligo, still snooping around."

"Didn't Tegid think he caught a glimpse of him on television at the farm yesterday?"

"Yes."

"I bet he was looking for Tegid, decided he's not at the farm and worked out that he's probably with us."

"Probably – but what do I do about it? I can't ignore it – he'll be looking for a chance to snatch Tegid again."

"For a start, make sure all the doors and windows are properly shut."

"All right. But I still won't feel safe – what sort of a man is he? Could he be violent?"

"I doubt it, or he would have tried something before now. I'm a good forty minutes walk from the Land Rover and a twenty-minute drive away – plus I'm tied up in something with a group of volunteers. I'll get back as soon as I can. Phone the police."

"I was just thinking of that. But they're bound to come to the house and they'll think it very strange if I don't invite them in."

"Ask them in, then."

"I don't trust Tegid to keep out of the way."

There was a brief pause, then Bob suggested, "Phone Tony."

Jane hesitated. "Are you sure? You know what Tony's like?"

"I know exactly what Tony's like – and he's just what you need. It is his field after all."

"O.K. – if you're sure." Jane glanced at her watch. "But he'll be out around the farm somewhere."

"That's all right – I've got his mobile number. Do you want me to ring him?"

"No, give me the number, I'll do it."

Jane dialled the number. "Hello, Tony. Jane Johnson here."

"Hi, Jane. How are you?"

"O.K. – but I've got a bit of a problem."

"If it's anything I can help with, you know you only have to say."

"Thanks, Tony. There's someone hiding in the hedge in your field, watching our house." Jane heard the noise of a tractor engine starting.

"He doesn't by any chance drive a silver car, does he?"

"If it's who I think it is, yes he does. Why?"

"In that case, I've met him before. He was probably doing what he's doing now, although I didn't realise it at the time. Leave it with me. Be right there."

The phone went dead and Jane made her way back upstairs.

"We've just seen them again," said Arthur. "Was that Daddy you phoned? Is he coming?"

"Daddy's a long way away. Tony's coming."

*

Sligo was getting desperate. Time was slipping away and no plan had suggested itself. There was no movement from the house: no sign of Morgan leaving. Sligo had reached the conclusion that Morgan must be there as a sort of bodyguard for Tegid – and that was going to make life very difficult. He was just considering setting fire to the house in the hope of grabbing Tegid in the confusion, when he was surprised by a tap on his shoulder.

Sligo looked up into the face of the young farmer who had towed his car down the lane.

The farmer said just one word, "Out!" and accompanied it with a jerk of the thumb.

Sligo sighed. "Look, why don't you just go away and mind your own business? Go and wash some cows, or whatever you d…"

A hand shot out, grabbed him by the shirt and hauled him to his feet. The farmer smiled at him. Disconcerted, Sligo started to smile back, until he realised what the farmer was saying.

"We know how to deal with perverts around here."

Sligo didn't see the uppercut coming. It caught him neatly on the point of his chin. His head snapped back and he toppled to the ground.

Tony took one of Sligo's ankles in each hand and walked back to the gate dragging Sligo along the ground. He didn't bother to avoid the cowpats. At the water trough near the gate he pulled Sligo up and stuck his head under the water. Revived by the shock of the cold water, Sligo spluttered back to consciousness.

Tony propelled Sligo from the field, past the tractor and into the lane. There he turned Sligo to face him.

"Listen very carefully. If I see you around here again, I'll keep your head under that water and then bury you in my slurry pit." Tony turned Sligo and gave him a violent shove that sent him staggering away from the Johnson house.

As he watched the filthy figure stumbling away, Tony picked up his mobile phone and dialled.

"Hi, Jane. Problem sorted. He won't be bothering you again."

But Tony was wrong. Very wrong.

*

Sligo walked back to his car in a blind rage. He had promised himself before that somebody was going to pay for all the pain and humiliation that he'd suffered in pursuit of this story. He'd promised himself – but still nothing had worked out. No-one, but him, had yet paid in money or anguish. That was going to change.

But first he had to change something else. His shirt was stuck to his back by foul-smelling glue and he was attracting a cloud of flies. He looked at his watch. He would go back to Princetown, shower, get into clean clothing, have something to eat and then sit in front of the television. He could watch, and enjoy, Smith's opening blast against Myrddin. Maybe that would shake things up in the Johnson house. Maybe Morgan would clear off back to Lyme Regis.

Whatever happened, Sligo was going back to the Johnson house, after dark, and he was going to get inside.

At his car, Sligo peeled off his shirt and with a look of disgust he dropped it into the gutter. He drove back to Princetown in a very angry mood.

Later, in relatively clean clothes, and surrounded by sandwiches, cigarettes, beer and whisky, he settled in front of the television with a sense of anticipation. Now, at last, he'd start to see justice done.

*

Myrddin was at the latest so-called press conference. The questioning of 'the little people' was becoming increasingly intrusive and bizarre. The session ended and as the reporters were being shepherded towards the gate, he felt a tug on his sleeve.

"Excuse me, Myrddin, sir, may I have quick word."

He looked down into a pair of pretty green eyes, set into a slightly freckled face that was surrounded by long red hair. "Yes, young lady, you may."

"This may sound strange, but I'm not really interested in these little people that you've found. They're very charming, I'm sure, but we're getting feedback from our viewers that what they really want to hear about is your *The Message not the Man* campaign. We all feel that the campaign is much more important, but it's being over-shadowed by all this."

"The campaign has not been forgotten, but you are correct – this is an unfortunate distraction."

"I wonder, would it possible to fit in a short interview now that we can broadcast to our viewers? Just a few minutes, so that you can re-assure them that your campaign will continue."

"That should indeed be possible."

"Perhaps inside the house? Somewhere where the viewers won't be distracted by having all this going on in the background?"

Myrddin glanced at the camera crew behind her and nodded. "Follow me."

He led them into the farmhouse lounge. The young reporter was on her mobile phone and sounding very excited. "Yes, yes. Myrddin has agreed to an interview. Yes, yes, great isn't it? Oh, really?" She turned to Myrddin. "They're so pleased! They are going to interrupt the programme to carry it live!"

Myrddin sat in an armchair and patiently waited while the lights and microphone were set up.

"I'll just turn the TV around so that the crew can see the picture on screen when we go live, but so that it isn't facing you and being a distraction."

There was a brief pause and then she said, "We'll be going live in thirty seconds."

Myrddin indicated the seat facing him. "Perhaps you should sit down and get comfortable before you start on your questions."

"Oh, no, I won't be asking the questions. I'm just a junior reporter; they wouldn't let me do that. The presenter in the studio will ask the questions. That's all right isn't it? He's a big fan of yours." She gave him a big bright smile and, after a moment's hesitation, Myrddin nodded.

"That's lovely! You'll hear the questions through the television. O.K. everybody, here we go."

"And now, as promised, we can go live to Lyme Regis where we can join Myrddin, who has agreed to answer a few questions. Myrddin is the mystery man behind the *The Message not the Man* campaign; a rather surprising campaign aimed at saving the planet by having us all be nice to each other. That campaign was attracting a lot of publicity, but has been lost in the hysteria over Myrddin's revelation that he has discovered a tribe of tiny people living wild in Britain.

"You are a man full of surprises, Myrddin."

Myrddin nodded. "And I may have bigger surprises for you yet to come."

"Indeed? How fascinating! The really strange thing, Myrddin, is that we know so little about you. The whole basis of your campaign is that we should listen to your message and not enquire about you. The problem is that to have faith in a message, we really need to know whether the messenger is trustworthy. Wouldn't you agree?"

"Many people appear to have accepted my message with enthusiasm, without troubling themselves over who I am."

"Yes, they do don't they? Strange that. What is also strange is that in none of your interviews has the interviewer asked the obvious questions; like 'who are you?', 'where do you come from?', 'what have you been doing up until now?' Don't you think that is odd?"

Myrddin smiled, although the smile was looking a little forced. "Perhaps you should ask the interviewers about their questions."

"Oh, but I already have. Do you know what they told me? They said that they were prepared with exactly that sort of question, but found themselves physically incapable of asking them! What do you think of that?"

Myrddin shrugged. "I answer the questions that I am asked."

"Excellent! Well, I have a question for you. You are a man with a very special talent. You are able to exercise some control over the minds of people in your presence. That is why previous interviewers could not ask their questions; but I am many miles away in our studios and you cannot control me. Your talent is such that the people who have attended your meetings have come away with their thinking distorted. They have accepted your nonsensical message, not through any rational thought, but because you have cleverly and cynically subjected them to mass hypnosis. So here is my question: is that true?"

Myrddin turned slightly and looked out of the window at the blue sky. "Tell me, young man, what channel is this?"

"You are being interviewed live on SmithTV."

"I thought so. SmithTV, one of the many companies controlled by Ronald Smith. I feel I have made a mistake. I should have taken care of Smith and his ilk before starting my campaign."

*

Smith banged his desk and roared with rage. "Take care of me! Take care of me! Who does this cretin think he is?"

"We know who he thinks he is," said Patricia Jakes, "we'll be getting to that next."

*

"I don't think Mr Smith will be worried by your threats. I'd like to return to my original point – who are you? You didn't answer my last question. Let's try a really easy one: do you have a National Insurance Number?"

Myrddin laughed out loud. "That is priceless, young man. What a truly perceptive interviewer you are."

"Myrddin: is that the Welsh equivalent of Merlin, by any chance? Merlin the Magician. Merlin Companion of King Arthur."

"He wasn't a king."

"What was that?"

"I said that Arthur, who was actually known as Artos, was not a king."

"And, of course, you'd know all about that wouldn't you? We have it on good authority that you actually believe that you are the real Merlin – still alive after fifteen hundred years! Either that, or you have brainwashed all around you into believing it. Oh, and of course, you think you have a magic sword." The interviewer broke off to give a loud derisive laugh.

"Let's move on to money. I expect that many people watching the coverage over the last few days, seeing the farm that you bought, the facilities you have there, the security you have hired, will be wondering how much it all cost. There is also the funding of your public meetings: you recently hired a football stadium and staged a free brain-washing presentation. Where has the money come from, Myrddin, Merlin, or whatever your name really is?"

Myrddin looked steadily at the camera, unshaken, but with a look of sadness on his face. "Why don't you go ahead and tell your viewers where you think the money came from?"

"Certainly. The money has come from the sale of valuable historical artefacts that you had no right to sell. You have been helped in this exercise by your assistant, Joe Morgan, who has a criminal record for handling stolen property. I don't think you'll have your expensive security for much longer, do you? Once the police have frozen the accounts of your trust and the security people realise that they aren't going to get paid, I think they'll disappear. Now, that *will* be magic."

Myrddin rose from his seat and left the room.

"It seems that Myrddin, or whatever his name is, has had enough of our questions. But keep watching SmithTV! We have a lot more for you yet. And tomorrow we have some startling revelations that link the Royal Family to this sorry affair."

*

Myrddin hurried from the room and went to the security room. "Mr Andrews, would you kindly make sure that all members of the press, including those currently in the lounge, are off this farm within the next two minutes – if not quicker."

Myrddin called Gilda downstairs and they went in search of Joe.

"Joe, we have a major problem. It is time to use the emergency quarters. Round everyone together and get them there as quick as you possibly can.

301

"Gilda, get your 'special' items from the treasury and take them with you into hiding."

Shortly after the farm had been bought, the remaining treasure hoard had been removed from the cave and placed in the secure barn. The cave had then been adapted to form an emergency shelter more than capable of housing the total number of occupants of the farm. Sufficient supplies of food and drink were stored to last for several weeks. To people accustomed to living in caves, it would be like going home.

The entrance was a slit in a vertical bank, hidden behind a tree. A long, slim slab of rock had been balanced at the top of the bank. Once Myrddin was assured that Joe, Gilda and all of the little folk were inside, he pushed on the rock and it slid down between the bank and the tree, forming an effective seal.

Back at the farmhouse he found Andrews had called his men together. "I'm sorry, sir, but there seems to be a problem. I've had instructions to get all of our personnel off site."

"I quite understand, Mr Andrews. Thank you for your help. You've done a wonderful job for us."

From his respectful demeanour, Myrddin gathered that Andrews had only had a phone call giving him instructions and had not yet heard about the latest TV coverage. He watched as the men and their dogs walked away from the farmhouse to collect their colleagues at the gate on their way out.

Myrddin watched the scenes on the CCTV screens with wry amusement. It was obvious that the reporters and cameramen who still besieged the gate were receiving calls on their mobile phones. Through the open window Myrddin could hear the clamour. He shut the window and then quickly checked all the other downstairs doors and windows.

As they watched the security team approach the gate the crowd fell silent, unsure as to what was happening. Myrddin pressed the button to open the gate and they walked through, heading for the barrier. The last men hadn't passed through the gate when the members of the press spotted their opportunity and surged forward.

The police, distracted by all the talk they'd been hearing about deception and fraud, only made a half-hearted attempt to stop them.

Myrddin pressed the button to close the gates, but one reporter, who had been sitting on a folding chair, grabbed it and thrust it between the gates to stop them closing. Myrddin watched the stampede coming down the drive; some carried small cameras; some had large TV cameras over their shoulders; others carried just notebooks. Someone fell and was trampled in the rush. The herd separated: a few individuals headed for the front door; most rushed headlong down the side and into the yard. When those at the front found the door firmly closed and that all the windows only looked onto an empty corridor, they hurried around to the back and joined the others in kicking open doors in the sleeping quarters and the communal kitchen.

The scenes were being broadcast on three channels simultaneously and hundreds of photographs were being taken.

It only took moments to discover that the former stables were empty of people. That left the secure barn and the farmhouse. The barn with its solid metal door and no windows defeated them.

Most of them focussed on the kitchen door.

Myrddin left the security room and climbed the stairs to the first floor. He heard the splintering of glass and the sound of people tumbling into the kitchen. Instantly the ground floor seemed to fill with a vile stench. Those already in the kitchen fought desperately to get back outside, but the crush kept them trapped. Myrddin smiled at the sound of vomiting. In a few minutes, noise from inside ceased and he looked out of the window. Of the crowd standing about the yard, some were looking green and ill, but most were merely angry and frustrated, glaring around the yard seeking a target.

Suddenly, a helicopter flew over with a deafening clatter and dropped towards the fields.

Someone shouted, "There are barns and outbuildings over there!" and the crowd, every one of them desperate to ensure that they missed nothing, ran from the yard towards the distant buildings.

It took an hour before they were all convinced that the only places on the farm that could possibly be concealing their main targets, Myrddin and Joe, plus all twenty-five of the little folk, were the secure barn or the farmhouse. They all gathered back in the yard. Myrddin watched with amusement from his window vantage point. The first intruders into the kitchen had left the door open. Each time that the group encouraged one of their number to have another go at getting in, a fresh wave of the appalling smell drifted out.

The red-haired reporter was speaking to camera. "Are we witnessing a dreadful tragedy? Confronted by the SmithTV exposure of his fraudulent activities, the con-man calling himself Myrddin, has disappeared along with the tribe of little folk that had so endeared themselves to us. The evidence is pointing to a horror story. The farm has been searched and the only place they could possibly be is in the farmhouse behind me. But there is the terrible smell of poison gas coming out. In one last vicious act of defiance, has the con-man killed everyone, including himself? We will have to wait for the police and the fire-service with breathing apparatus to confirm the terrible truth."

*

Bob got home just in time to hear the end of that last piece to camera. He had found Jane and Arthur in tears and Tegid ranting hysterically at the television.

Jane didn't know where to start in describing developments, she just sobbed, "It's all over."

"Look, I've heard all about the SmithTV disclosures and everything that's happened since, on the radio on the way home. Tegid, calm down, Myrddin hasn't killed everybody."

"How do you know?" Tegid shouted bitterly, "He's just a crazy old man – he could do anything!"

Before Bob could say anything else, the telephone rang and he answered it. A familiar voice sounded in his ear.

"Good afternoon, Bob. You are well I trust."

"Myrddin! What's happening?"

Three faces stared at Bob's trying to read his expression.

"Ah, you may have seen this afternoon's theatre staged by SmithTV and its repercussions."

"I didn't see it, but I've heard all about it. How is everybody?"

"I thought that you might be concerned, which is why I am calling. All is as well as could be expected. Do not believe what you hear on SmithTV – or any other broadcaster, for that matter."

"So where is everyone?"

"Everyone, except myself, is safely concealed in an underground hiding place with a good supply of food and water."

Bob broke off to repeat the news to his audience.

"Tell Tegid not to worry – his brother does enough worrying for both of them."

304

Bob repeated that message as well.

"But what's all this about a poisonous gas?"

Myrddin chuckled. "Just a little device of mine to keep them out of the house."

"What happens next?"

"I do not know – yet. I must resume the campaign as quickly as possible, even if it has to take a different form. Perhaps now I have to let the message speak for itself and exercise a little less control."

*

Jane, Arthur and Tegid had been among many watching developments on SmithTV. Few had watched with more enthusiasm than Sligo. He had punched the air and shouted with delight to see Myrddin discomfited and the scenes of chaos that had followed.

His enjoyment was ended by a phone call.

His attempts at congratulating Smith were cut off.

"You are not supposed to be sitting on your backside watching TV. This Myrddin character's got bottle. I don't believe for one moment that he's topped himself. Where's your little friend, Sligo? I told you: we need him by tomorrow or not one penny – not one bent penny!"

The phone went dead.

Sligo sighed. He thought that with Myrddin gone he'd be off the hook. Maybe Smith was wrong. He wasn't going to risk breaking into a house for no reason. He'd stay where he was and watch events unfold. If they were all dead, he'd crack another bottle of whisky.

*

The police were soon all over the farm, rounding up reporters and escorting them from the property. There were police everywhere: manning the barrier and the gates and standing at all points around the yard. Talk of mass murder, fraud and treasure hoards meant that the farm was potentially the scene of major crime and the Chief Inspector in charge meant to protect the evidence.

Myrddin watched with interested amusement as a fire engine pulled into the yard and two firemen began getting into breathing apparatus. He made his way downstairs.

The firemen cautiously entered the kitchen and then moved out of the Chief Inspector's sight as they went into the corridor.

Two minutes later, one of them re-appeared without his breathing apparatus. He called, "Chief Inspector, you'd better come in."

The police officer moved to the kitchen door. He couldn't smell anything and stepped into the kitchen. "What have you found?"

"Not a lot. Come and see."

The Chief Inspector followed him out of the kitchen, along the corridor and into the lounge. There he found the other fireman talking to Myrddin, who was sat in an armchair with a glass of beer. He stood up to greet the police officer with a relaxed smile.

"Good evening."

The two firemen both shuffled out of the room, grinning.

"Er, good evening. Chief Inspector Hawkins, sir. You are, er, Myrddin, I believe."

"That is so."

"Yes, I recognised you from the television."

"What can I do for you, Chief Inspector?"

"We had reports of poisonous gas in the house, and a lot of people missing."

"Unfortunately, when your officers allowed the press to stampede onto the farm, my little friends fled in panic. They are hiding in the fields and the woods. They are very good at hiding – they've been doing it all their lives. It is pointless me going to look for them. I expect they'll drift back over the next few days – as long as they don't receive another scare."

"Ah, yes, sorry about that, sir. We'll try not to let it happen again. And the poisonous gas?"

"Mass hysteria, I'm afraid. When the pack of newshounds broke into the house a whole mass of them tumbled into the kitchen. One of them must have turned the gas on. I have since turned it off and it seems to have cleared." He breathed in deeply through his nose. "I can't smell anything; can you?"

"No, sir, I can't. One other thing; there were some allegations made on television concerning the source of funds for your environmental trust. The Fraud Squad may well investigate. Do you keep the trust records here?"

"No, Chief Inspector, I do not. The trust is, of course, administered by trustees. The trustees are partners in a firm of solicitors."

"Can you give the name and address of the firm?"

"Of course, if you'd care to come into the office, I'll give you one of their cards."

The Chief Inspector took his leave of Myrddin and stepped back into the yard just as the fire engine was pulling away. He beckoned the sergeant to him.

"I want one officer on the back door and one on the front door, all night. Six more on that barrier outside the gate. Get the rest of this lot back to doing something useful."

When he walked out of the gate the press crowd surged forward against the barrier, shouting questions.

"How many dead?"

"What was the gas?"

"Can we have a full statement?"

He answered the last one. "Yes, ladies and gentlemen of the press, you may have a statement. Get all those TV cameras on me. I want everyone to hear this. No questions – just my statement.

"There are no dead bodies. There was no poisonous gas. What we had was a disgraceful display of unruly behaviour by members of the press. You literally stormed these premises en masse. The little folk were terrified and have run away to hide. And they are very good at hiding – they've done it all their lives.

"If any of you put so much as a finger end across this barrier, you will be arrested."

*

Sligo swore loudly when he heard the statement. He would have to go to Chagford, after all. But now he'd had too much to drink. He decided to sleep the worst of it off. He went to bed after setting his alarm for two o'clock in the morning.

CHAPTER 25

Disaster

Jane was in the kitchen making a milky drink that she hoped would help her to get to sleep. Bob joined her.

"Arthur's sound asleep. So is Tegid – although he's on the lounge floor."

Jane had been in tears throughout the evening; sometimes sitting silently with tears trickling down her cheeks; occasionally letting out an uncontrollable wail of anguish. Bob and Arthur had been unable to do or say anything to comfort her. Now Bob put his arms around his wife and hugged her.

"How are you doing?"

She pushed away from him, too wound up to stand still. "What a terrible, terrible day. I'd really started to believe that his campaign was going to work, but now it's all over. I thought it was our chance to change the world, but it's Smith and his kind who are going to win."

Jane turned on Bob accusingly. "How can you be so calm about it?"

Bob poured himself a glass of fruit juice and sat down, trying to make the situation less face-to-face confrontational.

"Ever since Sligo got hold of Tegid we've known that something like this was going to happen – it was just a matter of when."

"But doesn't it bother you that it's all over?"

Bob sighed. "I haven't been as involved with it as you have. And being a bit more on the outside, I never believed that it could work. Something like this was bound to happen. If it wasn't Smith it would have been someone else: someone else with a vested interest in keeping things the way they are."

There was a pause and Jane sat down.

"On the phone Myrddin said something to you about trying to carry on. Something about making changes to his campaign."

"That's what he said."

"But you don't think that will be possible, do you?"

Bob shook his head. "Absolutely no chance. He thinks he finished the day all right. That the stuff at the end about the journos terrifying the Dini – or the Gododdin, thanks to Tegid I'm back to not knowing what to call them – I suspect he thinks that got the public back on his side. He just doesn't understand how it works.

"This is only the beginning. We know that SmithTV won't let it drop. They've been telling people all evening not to miss their breakfast programme. The rest of the media will pick up on it. They're going to rip him apart. By the time they've finished, half the country will be laughing at him; the other half will want to see him in jail.

"I suppose he could disappear for a few years and come back with a completely different approach, but, for now, it's definitely all over.

"It's Carn and the others that I feel sorry for. This is all nothing to do with them, really: it's just something they've been caught up in."

There was another silence during which they both finished their drinks. When Bob spoke again it was of something more practical.

"Your car's booked into the garage in the morning. I'll take it in before I go to work."

Jane looked at him incredulously. "How can you be thinking of little things like that when there's all this going on?"

Bob shrugged. "Somehow we just have to get through it. Life will go on – and you need a car. Joe might ask for the Toyota back any moment. I'm going to bed – it's been a long day. Coming?"

"Not yet. I won't be able to get to sleep, so I may as well stay up."

"O.K. but do yourself a favour: don't watch any more telly. Put some music on."

"All right." She managed to raise a smile on her puffy, tear-stained face. "I might just snuggle up on the floor with Tegid."

"Are you trying to make me jealous, Mrs Johnson?"

*

309

At two a.m. the alarm penetrated Sligo's deep, alcohol-induced sleep just sufficiently for him to reach out a hand and turn it off. He resumed snoring almost immediately.

*

For a while Bob thought that the Fiesta wasn't going to start, but eventually the engine caught and he was able to drive it to the garage, albeit with a certain amount of misfiring and in a cloud of smoke. Terry, the owner, was just opening up and watched him pull onto the forecourt.

"Mornin' Bob. There's a skip around the back – just take it straight there."

"Yes, thanks Terry: just the expert advice I wanted to hear."

"Leave it with us. We'll see if it's beyond hope. I take it you've been watching the telly, along with everybody else in the country?"

Bob nodded.

"Pity you didn't spot those little folk on the moor. Could have made your fortune, that could. I could have been flogging you a nice new motor instead of putting sticking plaster on the old one."

If only you knew, thought Bob.

He went to the newsagent and found himself at the end of a queue for the morning papers. He bought the last three in the shop and looked at them as he walked home. It was exactly as he had feared it would be. There was no mention of the press invasion of the farm, but there was page after page devoted to the mind control/mass hypnosis, the sale of the historic artefacts and Myrddin's conviction that he was Merlin the Magician.

Different papers gave most space to different aspects, but all were salivating over the revelations still to come. The mention of the royal connection had been seized upon and all three had made the link between some of the little folk living on Dartmoor and HRH The Duke of Cornwall owning large areas of the moor.

Back home, Bob was reluctant to show Jane the newspapers, but she already knew.

"I've just seen the bit on the news where they look at what's in the papers. The coverage is just what you said it would be. Oh, SmithTV keeps saying that they are broadcasting their next load of revelations at nine o'clock. They sound very excited about it."

"Don't they always? I can't hang about for it. I've got a nine o'clock meeting. Let me know what they have to say. I'm off."

Bob Johnson kissed his wife and son for the last time.

*

Sligo opened one eye. The room was bright with morning sunshine. He opened the other eye and focussed on the clock. He threw the bedclothes off and rolled out of bed. Standing in the middle of the floor he threw back his head and screamed curses towards the ceiling. The cursing continued as he dressed and ran downstairs. He had to pause in the kitchen to drink several glasses of water. His whisky consumption had kept him asleep for ten hours and now he had very little time to grab his target.

His phone rang. It was probably Smith hounding him again. He answered it.

"I'm on the case, all right."

"Nige, is that you? Micky here."

It took a few seconds for Sligo to realise that it was his next-door neighbour in London.

"Yeah, Micky, it's me. Can't talk now."

"O.K. I'll keep it short. You've got squatters in your house. Just met one of them outside. Says they found the door open, nobody around and just moved in. The lock's been smashed, but the squatters say it was like that when they found it – so you've probably been robbed."

With a scream of rage Sligo hurled his phone against the wall. He stood with both hands on the kitchen table, head down, breathing deeply.

I'm going to get that little creep if it kills me. And the amount that Smith is going to pay for him has just gone up.

He needed weapons and looked around the kitchen. There wasn't much to choose from. He took a knife and a hefty metal meat tenderiser. He went into the back yard and cut down the washing line. On his way back through the kitchen he picked up the plastic tub of pepper. Sligo put the whole lot into a plastic bag and hurried out to the car.

Near the Warren House Inn he passed Bob Johnson going the other way. For a second their eyes met.

311

Bob pulled up at the side of the road and phoned home.

"I've just seen Sligo. He was driving very quickly along the B3212 towards Moretonhampstead, but he could be heading for Chagford again."

Jane hesitated. "He could be going anywhere. Probably heading for Lyme Regis where the story is. I don't think he'd have the nerve to come around here again."

"I think I'd better come home, just in case."

"No, no. As you said last night, life has to go on. You go to your meeting. We'll be fine. If I catch sight of him I'll phone you – and Tony."

Reluctantly, Bob drove on towards Princetown.

*

Sligo drove slowly past the house. The Toyota was the only car on the drive. That meant that Morgan was on his own, guarding Tegid. Sligo paused. He couldn't just pull onto the drive as that would give Morgan too much warning. But the lane was narrow and he couldn't risk leaving the car near the house, blocking the lane: someone was bound to come along and kick up a fuss.

He finally parked in the nearest spot where the lane was wide enough for two cars to pass, and walked back towards the house.

*

Just before nine o'clock, with an overwhelming sense of trepidation, Jane sat on the settee to watch the SmithTV broadcast. Arthur and Tegid joined her.

The usual few strident chords jarred the ears and the camera slowly zoomed in on the thirty-year-old male presenter wearing a shiny suit, a lot of hair gel and a fake tan. He beamed an unnaturally white smile at the viewers.

*

"Good morning and welcome to this special SmithTV broadcast. Yesterday we were delighted to expose the conman who calls himself Myrddin. We told you about his cynical mind control tricks that have influenced audiences at his *The Message not the*

Man meetings. He didn't want anybody to look at him too closely – and now we know why, don't we?

"We exposed his environmental trust as a sham – a sham funded by the illegal sale of historic artefacts. In this he was aided and abetted by Joe Morgan, a former mobile shop operator with a criminal record.

"We exposed his madness. This truly weird, weird individual really believes that he is Merlin the Magician." He broke off to chuckle. "Yes, priceless isn't it?

"We promised you more revelations today – and we are not going to disappoint you.

"He has showed the world a group of tiny people that he claims he found living wild in Wales and on Dartmoor. He says that the big fence around the farm where he keeps them is for their security. But that isn't true. The fence is to keep them in – not to keep the rest of us out.

"What harm would we possibly do to them? They have endeared themselves to all of us. No, the fence is to keep them in. To keep control of them so that he can exploit them for his own ends.

"Now, here is our big surprise for you. We have one of the little folk under our care and protection. We rescued him from Myrddin's captivity – and now you can hear what he has to say. His name is Tegid. Here's some of what he had to tell us. And just in case you have trouble making out what he's saying, we've subtitled it."

*

The image on the screen changed to a shot of Tegid looking tiny on a large settee

"It's you, Tegid! You're on the television!" Arthur shouted in excitement.

Tegid stared glumly at the screen. Jane watched in horrified fascination with one hand over her mouth.

A voice started speaking and Tegid said, "That's Sligo."

*

The voice said, "Tegid, would you mind just standing and holding that stick. I'd like people to see how tall you are."

Tegid climbed to his feet on the settee and held a measuring stick alongside him. The camera zoomed in to show the viewers that he was just eighteen inches tall.

"Thank you, Tegid. Please sit down and make yourself comfortable again. Now, Tegid, I know that you don't like talking about this, but the viewers will have noticed that one of your hands is missing. What happened to it?"

"I got it trapped under a car wheel and I cut it off so that I could get away before the driver returned."

"You cut your own hand off?"

"Yes."

"You must have been terrified of being caught."

"Yes."

"Why?"

"Because of what the Biguns would do to us if they caught us."

"Biguns? Is that what you call us people of normal size?"

"Yes."

"Who told you that the Biguns would do bad things to you?"

"Trader Joe."

"Trader Joe? Is that what you call Joe Morgan?"

"It's what everybody calls him."

"When did he tell you this?"

"When he came to the moor once a month to trade with us."

"Ah. So it was Joe Morgan who discovered you, not the old man who calls himself Myrddin?"

"I suppose so."

"Did you want to leave the moor?"

"No I didn't."

"So you didn't want to go to Myrddin's farm?"

"I didn't go there."

"You didn't go from the moor to Myrddin's farm?"

"No."

"Where did you go?"

"Scotland."

"Whereabouts in Scotland?"

"Don't know."

"So you were moved to Scotland until Myrddin had his farm secure enough to hold you?"

314

Tegid shrugged.

"Who owned the place where you stayed in Scotland?"

"The Duke of Cornwall."

"Really! Who arranged for you to stay there?"

"Bob Johnson."

The scene cut back to the presenter in the studio.

"Bob Johnson is now a Dartmoor Ranger. Under mysterious circumstances he gave up his lucrative career as a partner in a substantial firm of Chartered Accountants. Despite only having one modest income, Johnson and his wife live in this imposing house on the outskirts of property hot-spot Chagford, on the fringes of Dartmoor."

An image of the Johnsons' house appeared on the screen.

"We will have another special broadcast tomorrow, at the same time, when we will be taking a closer look at Mr Bob Johnson, his would-be MP wife, Jane, and HRH, The Duke of Cornwall.

"Oh, one other piece of news. Myrddin really is a magician and his favourite trick is making pints of beer disappear. Here he is, pictured outside a Dartmoor pub, when he's clearly done his favourite trick too many times."

Sligo's photograph of Myrddin stumbling outside the East Dart Hotel appeared on the screen.

*

Jane pulled two large suitcases and one small one from the cupboard under the stairs. Shouting at Arthur to follow her, she struggled up the stairs with the cases. She told Arthur to pack some clothes and toys in the small case.

"Where are we going, Mummy? What's happening?"

"We're going to stay with Auntie Louise and Uncle Mike for a while."

"Oh, good. Has he still got his boat? Can we go out on it?"

"We'll see. Just pack as quickly as you can."

In the bedroom Jane began stuffing clothes into the cases with one hand while she tried to phone Bob with the other. His mobile was turned off, so she phoned the office.

"Hi, Jane. Bob's in a meeting. Shall I get him to call you?"

Bob phoned back a few minutes later. Jane started to speak, but he interrupted her. "I know all about it. The phones here are red-hot. I've been told to clear off out of the way. They reckon this place will be besieged by the press within the hour. They'll be heading for the house, too. What are you doing?"

"Packing. I'm not going to be trapped in here. Let's go to Louise's house. I'll be ready to go in a couple of minutes. I'll pick you up."

"Great. Don't come through Princetown, we'll be spotted. Take the Tavistock road. I'll park in that first parking area, opposite the pump house."

"Fine. See you there. Love you."

"Love you too."

*

Myrddin watched the same television programme. When it finished he climbed the stairs to one of the bedrooms, opened a dormer window and climbed out onto the roof. He walked up the slates to the ridge and along the ridge to the highest point of the gable end. There he stood motionless, gazing into the far west. He cried into the west wind.

"I have failed Artos. You sent your spirit in the time of need, but I have failed you this time. You understand the ways of men better than I. I needed you by my side."

*

Sligo reached the public footpath and walked up it far enough for him to be able to see the back of the house. He was desperate to find a door or window open. He needed a way of taking Morgan by surprise.

Both patio doors opened and then closed again. It was the Johnson woman making sure that the place was secure. He was close enough to hear her shout.

"Get in the car, you two. We have to go."

Sligo was disorientated for a few seconds. He was so convinced that it was Morgan that he had to deal with that he struggled to come to terms with the change.

Get in the car, you two. Which two?

He heard a car door slam and ran down the track. Before he reached the bottom, the Toyota passed along the lane heading towards Chagford. He was close enough to be sure of one thing:

there was only one adult visible in the car. He knew who the two must be.

Sligo ran along the lane after the car. In the distance he saw it stop. A herd of cows was crossing the lane. Sligo was still seventy yards short when the last cow moved slowly out of the way. He was close enough to see the Johnson woman wave at someone, but then the car rolled away from him and gathered pace down the lane.

He stopped, wheezing for breath and coughing.

"Not you again! Some people never learn."

Sligo saw the young farmer stepping towards him. He flipped the lid off the tub of pepper and flung it into the farmer's eyes.

Then he ran down the lane, not stopping again until he reached his car.

He reckoned she had three or four minutes start on him. If she didn't know he was after her he could make that up – provided he had guessed right and that she was heading across the moor. Sligo emptied his weapons and the length of washing line onto the passenger seat next to him and set off.

He took crazy chances going around the tight bends in the narrow lanes, but luck was on his side. When he hit the B3212 he caught sight of the Toyota, scarcely three hundred yards ahead. On the relatively open road, Sligo put his foot down and the Focus roared up through forty, fifty, sixty, seventy, eighty miles an hour. He floated around a bend, crested the brow of a hill – and found the Toyota stationary in front of him, stopped by a group of ponies wandering across the road.

Sligo slammed on the brakes.

*

Jane was glad to be on the road. After the fraught days in front of the television it was good to be out of the house. At least after all the television coverage, Louise wasn't going to be too astonished by one of her unexpected guests.

It was a beautiful, sunny morning and the moor looked stunning spread out before her. She came over the crest of a hill to find a group of ponies gathered at the side of the road. She cautiously moved to the centre of the road to ease past, but the little black stallion led his mares across in front of her. She stopped and waited.

"Look, Mummy! Do you think that's Midnight that Carn talks about?"

Although he'd been told to stay hidden, Tegid pushed the coat off and stood to have a look at the moor. He wound down the window.

There was the squeal of tyres on the road. Jane glanced into the rear view mirror and saw the silver car hurtling towards them. She took her foot off the brake and tried to move to one side to give the other car room to pass, but she was too late.

There was a loud crash and the Toyota lurched forward. For a moment it teetered on the edge and then Jane screamed as it toppled off the road. It cartwheeled down the steep slope before turning in the air and landing on its roof on the jagged granite boulders at the foot of the slope.

*

Sligo glared down on the car below. *Not my fault you stupid cow! You shouldn't have stopped there!*

It didn't look as if he'd be getting any money out of Smith. Not even Smith paid for dead bodies. He angrily kicked a small stone from the edge of the road.

He checked the Focus. One light cluster had gone and the wing was crumpled, but he was able to pull the bodywork away from the tyre. It looked driveable – and there didn't seem to be anyone in sight.

Sligo got back in the car and drove to Princetown, pulling onto the small parking space in front of the cottage and stopping with the damaged wing tight to the wall.

*

Bob's phone rang. "Hello."

"Bob. Tony here. I thought you should know, that creep who was hanging around the house, he was back today. Jane was driving that black car along the lane and he was running after her. I tried to stop him, but he threw pepper in my face. Shouldn't think there's anything to worry about: she was driving and he was on foot."

"O.K. Tony, thanks for the tip-off. She should be all right. She wasn't planning on stopping anywhere."

"Bob, if you see him around here again, be sure to tell me."

"O.K. Tony, I will. Thanks for the call."

Bob didn't like the sound of that. He knew that Jane wouldn't answer while she was driving, but he called her anyway. When it switched to the answering service, he left a message. "It's me. I'm where we agreed. See you soon. Give me a ring if there's any problem. Look out for Sligo."

After half-an-hour he was getting concerned. Jane knew the road well, she'd driven it every day when she'd been a teacher in Tavistock, it was fine weather and she was in a nearly-new car: there shouldn't be a problem. He phoned again and left another message.

After another fifteen minutes, he was pacing around the Land Rover going through the possibilities. She couldn't have stopped for petrol; she wouldn't be passing any filling stations. Maybe she was waiting for him somewhere else – but she would have returned his message. Maybe she forgot to pick up her mobile phone in the panic to get away quickly. That would explain the lack of phone calls, but not her non-arrival. Maybe she went through Princetown by mistake and had been blocked in by the press; it didn't seem likely that they could be there in such numbers, so quickly.

In the distance he saw the police helicopter, followed shortly afterwards by the air ambulance.

He checked his watch every minute. When he'd been waiting an hour he phoned again. This time it was answered.

"Thank goodness! I was worried. Where are you?"

A voice he didn't recognise spoke. "Who's calling?"

"I'm sorry. I was phoning my wife. I must have rung the wrong number."

"Is that Mr Johnson?"

"Yes – who is this?"

"It's the police, Mr Johnson. I'm afraid there's been an accident."

*

A fire engine, ambulance and four police cars lined the road that had been closed to traffic.

Bob stood at the top of the slope looking down at the wreckage. He stood with his arms hanging limply at his sides, his head down. Lines were deeply etched in his deathly pale face.

Tears ran down his cheeks unnoticed and dripped from his chin. His breath came in long, choking sobs.

Someone in uniform came to stand by his side. Bob didn't look at him. "We have recovered both bodies Mr Johnson. Rather than try to carry them up this slope, they'll be taken to Derriford by the helicopter."

"I want to see them."

"Maybe at the hospital, Mr Johnson, but you really don't want to see them as they are now. Best to remember them as they were."

At last, Bob turned to face him. "But I must see…"

Bob was vaguely aware of movement on his other side and a waft of breeze moved his hair. He saw shock on the police officer's face and the man stumbled back a couple of paces. He felt a hand on his shoulder and he turned.

"Leave them, Bob. Jane and Arthur are not in this place. What you would see now, is not your wife and son."

Bob looked into Myrddin's face. He hardly recognised it. The eyes blazed with a fierce anger and the muscles of his face were working with a scarcely controlled rage.

"Come," said Myrddin, "we have someone to see."

Bob still hesitated, reluctant to leave, but below him the air ambulance was taking off. They both watched it swing away towards Plymouth.

Myrddin spoke bitterly. "Twice. Not once, but twice, the stupidity of mankind has robbed me of him."

"How did you hear? How did you get here?"

"I didn't have to hear – I felt his passing. It doesn't matter how I got here; all that matters is that I am with you – and we have someone to see."

"Who?"

"Sligo. He is responsible for this."

"Are you certain?"

"Yes. Tegid told me."

"Tegid? But I thought…" Bob gestured down the slope.

"He jumped out of the car window as the car toppled over the edge. He is now in the back of your vehicle. Come!"

Bob allowed himself to be led to the Land Rover.

"You know where Sligo may be found?"

Bob nodded.

"Then take us there."

As his anger cooled, Sligo's mood changed to one of desperate self-preservation. His first instinct had been to keep driving and get as far away as possible. But he couldn't expect to get far in the damaged Focus before the police stopped him.

Back in the cottage, he smoked cigarette after cigarette as he considered his options. If anybody had seen the accident and described his car, the police would soon pick him up. But, with any luck, no-one had seen it. He was half inclined to sit it out. Maybe he could wait a couple of weeks and then get his car repaired. But commonsense told him that the skid marks at the scene and the broken glass lying about would not be missed by the police. He ought to get away, but how?

He didn't want to do anything to draw attention to himself. He phoned Plymouth airport and found that there was a seat on the afternoon flight to Gatwick. He booked it.

He could get a taxi, but the local taxi driver was bound to remember.

Sligo decided that the most anonymous way to get there was to catch the next bus. He packed his suitcase and left it just inside the front door. He took two old blankets and spread them over the front of the car, covering the damage. Then he went to the café. From his seat in the window he could watch the front of the cottage.

He had another hour to wait for the bus and he passed the time deciding where to go from Gatwick. He fancied a spell a long way away; somewhere warm, with cheap booze. He phoned his solicitor and told him to start the process of getting rid of the squatters. Ten minutes before the bus was due, he walked across to collect his suitcase.

As he was backing out of the door, he felt something blocking his way. He turned and looked into Myrddin's eyes. After a moment's hesitation he dropped the case and ran for the back door. He was struggling to undo the bolts when a searing, skull-crushing pain hit his brain. He dropped to the filthy floor and lay whimpering in the grease and cigarette ash.

Myrddin, Bob and Tegid followed him into the kitchen.

None of them spoke. The pain must have eased, because his whimpering reduced and he looked up at Myrddin.

"Please! Please, it wasn't my fault!"

"Who's fault was it Sligo?"

"Smith; Ronald Smith. He made me do it."

"Who was driving the car, Sligo?"

"Me – but Smith was forcing me to get him."   Sligo pointed at Tegid.

"Sligo, you are an utterly worthless, contemptible creature. Yet you have destroyed something beyond value."   Myrddin pointed a long, bony finger at Sligo's face.

"Die, Sligo! Die in the dirt where you have lived all your life!"

Sligo clutched his head and screamed. Blood spurted from his nose and ears. He writhed onto his back and the screaming faded to a whimper. The noise stopped altogether and his hands fell away from his face. Blood oozed from beneath his eyelids.

Myrddin stared at the lifeless body, the expression on his face one of despair rather than anger. Then he turned away.

"Come!"

They walked from the cottage, making no attempt to conceal Tegid.

As they walked to the Land Rover they were spotted by the mob of press around the Visitor Centre. The mob surged after them, but stopped ten yards short. There was an aura about the strange threesome that no-one dared violate.

Bob sat behind the wheel of the Land Rover, his face, pale and strained.

"That doesn't make me feel any better."

"No, Bob, that was for my benefit, not yours. Drive us home."

Bob sat there, unmoving. "Bob, drive us home."

He drove steadily back to Chagford. None of them spoke on the journey.

Fifty yards behind them trailed a convoy of press vehicles. Only on one occasion did anyone try to get close.

A motorbike with a photographer riding pillion pulled alongside. With a nod of his head, Myrddin sent them careering off the road into the moor.

There was another horde of press at the house. A police car was on the drive and two officers were keeping the gate closed.

When the Land Rover was recognised the photographers attempted to slow it by standing in front, but Bob didn't seem to see them. He simply drove on and they were forced to leap out of the way. The police opened the gate and Bob drove to the front door. The police were struggling to close the gate, but Myrddin walked to it and the crowd fell back.

Bob was in the hall. "I don't want to be here. It isn't the same. The house is dead."

Myrddin gently guided him into the lounge. Bob looked up at the great sword. The hilt was still golden, but the glow that had warmed the room was gone.

Myrddin took the sword down from the chimneybreast. "Hold it. It will help."

Bob gripped the hilt. He felt the familiar tingling in his arm and a surge of power through his body. He felt anger growing within him and the need for revenge. But as quickly as it had appeared the power drained away. Once more all he felt was the sensation of iced water in his veins: a cold, cold feeling of loss.

"Come, Robert Edgar Johnson, you have a journey to complete – one that you will be glad that you made."

Myrddin folded the Sword of Power into his cloak and led Bob back to the Land Rover. "The next stage of your journey is to Lyme Regis, Bob. And we need to be there quickly."

The Land Rover swept out of the drive scattering photographers and reporters and headed for Lyme Regis at the head of an even longer convoy.

There were a dozen members of the press still gathered at the farm entrance. Bob drove straight through them and stopped at the barrier. Myrddin wound down his window. The police officer looked confused.

"Oh, sorry, sir, didn't recognise you for a moment. We thought you were still in the farmhouse."

"Clearly not, officer. May I enter my farm?"

"Of course, sir." He signalled to a colleague behind the gate. The barrier swung up and the gates opened.

Bob drove through and followed Myrddin's directions across the farm and backed up to the tree that hid the entrance to the cave. Myrddin got out and took the tow-rope from the back of the Land Rover. He looped one end around the rock and dropped the loop in the other end over the tow-bar.

"Drive, Bob, drive."

As the vehicle moved forward the rock slid over and toppled to the ground. Myrddin put his head into the entrance and called. "Joe! Gilda!"

The large figure of Joe soon appeared and squeezed through the narrow opening. Gilda hobbled out behind him.

Myrddin spoke to them quietly and urgently. A look of shock and horror settled on Joe's face and he made a move towards Bob, who hadn't left the Land Rover.

Myrddin put a hand on his arm and stopped him. "Leave him, Joe. He is beyond our comfort. Bring the van over here.

"Tegid, get down into the cave and tell your friends that they must leave this place. Tell them to start carrying up the supplies of food and drink."

Joe quickly returned with the van. He opened the rear doors and pulled out the ramp. As the little figures poured out of the cave with the supplies, Joe stacked it into the van.

Gilda looked up at the sky. "Look."

In the west, something extraordinary was happening. It looked as if a black veil was being slowly drawn across the sky.

Myrddin drew Gilda aside. "Anu's patience is exhausted. It is time."

The extraordinary face looked enquiringly at Myrddin. She spoke only one word.

"Cumbria?"

Myrddin shook his head. "They will not move. They trust no-one. And I doubt if you have time."

"Joe?"

"Give him the choice: go with you, or return to his family. I doubt that he will understand the implications of what you tell him. He is a good man: even if he understood, I believe he would choose to be with his family." Myrddin turned away. "Droller! Leave that work for younger folk. I need to speak with you."

When The Droller came to him, Myrddin said, "When the van is fully-loaded I need to speak with you all. If you would kindly translate for the Welsh speakers, it will save me having to repeat myself."

Within twenty minutes the van was packed as full as Joe could manage, while leaving room for its living cargo. Myrddin called everyone to him.

"Some of you may have heard this news from Tegid," he looked enquiringly at Tegid, who shook his head. "It seems not, so I will tell you all of the sad developments. Today, Jane Johnson and Arthur were killed." There were gasps of consternation and cries of grief.

324

"Bob Johnson is in the Land Rover, so deep in shock and so filled with despair that he is beyond our comfort."

"No! No!" cried Eppie, running for the Land Rover with Carn, Eppie, Enid and Bran close behind. Carn lifted Bran so that he could pull down the door handle and they swung the door open. He dropped Bran to the floor and then lifted Eppie and Enid so that they could clamber in. They climbed onto Bob's lap, but he didn't stir. He just sat with his head on his chest. They didn't know what to say and buried their faces in his neck and sobbed.

Myrddin walked slowly across and gently lifted them down to the ground. "I know how you feel, my friends, but I meant it. His grief is such that he is unaware of anything else. Come, re-join the others." When they were all back in one group, he continued.

"They were killed by the greed and stupidity of mankind. Look to the western sky. You will see that the gods themselves are tired of the selfish actions of mankind and will seek to wash their poison from the face of the Earth.

"Into the van now, my friends. Your journey will be long and uncomfortable, but at its end you will be in a place of safety. A place where your greatest problem may yet be solved. Go in peace, my friends."

They filed up the ramp into the van, some still sobbing from the awful news, others looking fearfully back over their shoulders at the extraordinary sky. Tegid and Nudd went up the ramp together, Tegid comforting his anxious brother.

Joe raised the ramp and closed the back doors.

Myrddin passed him a piece of paper. "Your destination. We will be there before you. On your journey, Gilda has to explain something to you, and you will have a choice to make. Travel safely, Joseph Morgan. All life passes. With the years allotted to you, you have achieved more than most. Your kindness to these little people will be remembered."

As Joe climbed into the cab, Myrddin turned to Gilda. "Well, sister, you have all that you need?"

Gilda nodded. "All, except for the sword."

"You will have that before the day is out." He smiled down at her. "The gods have seen fit to grant you many years, sister. The gods are wise."

She smiled back. "Or forgetful." The smile faded. "You have taught me much. The practitioners of the old magic are brothers and sisters who should be together. Will we meet again?"

"If the gods wish it." He helped her up into the cab. "Farewell."

Back in the Land Rover, Myrddin held the sword hilt against Bob's hand. "Start the engine Bob Johnson and drive. Follow that van."

Bob did as he was told. The van was bumping and swaying across the fields heading for the fence. Joe pulled up a few yards short of it and jumped out. He reached up and undid some catches holding one of the fence panels in place and then let the panel fall to the ground. Then he drove the van over the panel to join a farm track. They followed the track until it reached the road, a full half-a-mile along from where the press were gathered at the farm gate. Joe stopped the van and waved Bob past.

For the next two-and-a-half hours Bob followed Myrddin's directions. Myrddin kept some part of the sword in contact with Bob and the energy flow was sufficient to keep Bob functioning.

They stopped outside a conference centre on the banks of the Thames. Myrddin got out and opened Bob's door. "Come."

"I can't park here," said Bob, vaguely aware of the lines along the road.

"You can, and you have. Come!"

The old bearded man in the long brown robe and the man in the green Ranger uniform attracted some curious glances as they approached the gleaming stainless steel and glass structure – but only brief glances as most people's attention was on the strange effect overhead where the black veil now covered more than a third of the sky and under the blackness forked lightning could be seen.

There was a uniformed security woman on the door. "We are expected," said Myrddin.

"Of course, sir," she said, opening the door for them.

Myrddin glanced at an information board and steered Bob into a lift. On the twelfth floor two more security people were standing at a pair of closed double doors.

Myrddin looked from one to the other. "We are expected."

One of the men nodded and opened a door. Myrddin slipped through and pulled Bob after him.

It was a large room seating several hundred people, all looking towards a low stage. On the stage was a table. There were four men seated at the table and one grossly fat man standing. Behind them tall French windows stretched the width of the room giving views over London and providing access to a wide balcony.

Ronald Smith was clearly in good form. Most of the audience were laughing at some wisecrack. Myrddin stood pressed against the wall at the back of the hall. He breathed deeply and his eyes were closed.

Bob looked around the room, unclear as to what was happening; his senses deadened by the crushing weight of grief.

The room gradually fell quiet. Smith was on his feet at the table, giving the most positive slant that he could to some disastrous results set out on the papers he was holding. He became aware of the silence and looked about curiously. He saw walking towards him down the central aisle, two figures. He had his reading glasses on and had to take them off to see who it was.

As soon as he recognised Myrddin, he said, "What are you doing here? How did you get in?"

Myrddin neither replied nor stopped and Smith called, "Security! Throw these two out!"

No-one moved in the room, except for Myrddin and Bob slowly approaching the stage. "Security! Security! Where are you, you morons? Do what you're paid to do!"

Myrddin climbed the three steps to the stage and walked towards Smith. When he found no security coming to his aid, Smith tried to move away, but his legs felt numb and they wouldn't move. He tried bluster instead.

"What do you want, cretin? Irritated that we've blown the lid off your little cons?"

"I've come to take care of you. You may have heard me say that I should have taken care of you and your type a long time ago."

"Security!" Smith bellowed. The noise bounced around the room, but no-one moved. Smith turned as far as his frozen legs would permit and shook the man next to him at the table. "George! George! You fool! Do something!"

Myrddin stopped in front of Smith. He slipped the Sword of Power out of his robe.

"What...what...what you gonna do?" Smith gibbered.

Myrddin raised the sword and ran the edge of the blade across Smith's purple, sweating forehead. He wiped the blade on Smith's very expensive suit.

Myrddin turned to Bob who was standing alongside and offered him the sword. Bob took it and for a moment anger flared within him and he drew the weapon back.

"No!!" roared Smith.

The anger melted away. Bob shook his head and passed back the sword.

Myrddin took it and held it in front of Smith's face. "This sword was forged for the greatest leader of men this country has ever known. He destroyed many enemies with it – all of them better men than you. I am reluctant to foul the blade with your blood.

"But it must be done."

The blade sang through the air. Bob felt the splatter of warm droplets on his arms, but for a moment nothing seemed to have changed. Smith still had the same expression on his face.

Slowly the large head toppled from the body and landed with a thud on the table. Blood pumped from the neck as the body crashed to the floor.

Myrddin took Bob's arm and led him onto the balcony. Far below was a paved area and beyond that the River Thames. The Tower of London stood across the river, but what caught Bob's attention for a few seconds was the extraordinary sky. He turned away from it to stare into Myrddin's eyes.

"Who are you?"

"You know you I am."

"I know who The Droller says you are."

Myrddin frowned, but nodded. "He tells a fine tale."

Bob glanced at the sword. "I thought I pulled that from the sea and felt its power. But now I'm wondering if you put those thoughts in my head."

Myrddin passed him the sword. Bob grasped the hilt, but when the old man took his hands away, he couldn't take the weight and the sword clattered to the floor.

In one movement Myrddin swept it up and flung the sword from the balcony. "Others need its power." He turned back to Bob and said fiercely, "Now, more than ever, you must believe."

Bob watched the sword fall until it plunged into a flowerbed. Still looking down, with tears in his eyes, he whispered, "My son, he *was* special, wasn't he?"

Myrddin put a hand on Bob's shoulder. "He was very, very special – and he needs you now as much as he did when he lived."

Bob stared again into the old, old eyes.

"They are waiting for you, Bob."

There was a noise in the conference room and Bob turned towards it. He noticed the blood on his arms and tried to wipe it off. There was a movement and a flapping to his side: Bob looked around. Myrddin had gone.

"Myrddin?"

Bob looked around the balcony and then looked down at the ground. All he saw was a raven that flew up level with his face, looked him in the eye and when wheeled away across the Thames. Bob watched the raven cross the river and then circle over the Tower of London. He counted seven ravens, flying awkwardly, spiralling up to join the circling bird. Then the flock flew away, heading south.

A scream rang out in the hall and he could hear a babble of voices.

Something moving on the river caught his eye. Bob stared. Two figures were rising from the water. They waved to him: they were smiling and beckoned him to join them. Bob climbed onto the balcony rail.

Uniformed guards rushed across the balcony towards him. Hands grabbed at his clothing, but with a smile on his face, Bob stepped off.

He had no wish to keep his family waiting.

*

A shocked crowd gathered around the broken body. Among them was a figure in a long brown robe. She eased away from the others, drew an old sword from a flowerbed, folded it into her robe and hobbled away.

CHAPTER 26

An end and a beginning

The black veil covered the sky.

The low pressure area that settled over Britain was the lowest ever recorded. It drew in the sea and combined with the gales to create two tidal surges. One travelled down the North Sea and the other along the English Channel. Coastal towns along the east and south coasts disappeared under water as the surges overwhelmed inadequate defences.

Torrential rain began to fall and didn't stop. The violence of the thunder and lightning took roofs from buildings. The storm-force winds blew down power cables: fallen trees blocked roads. The storms raged overhead for days that stretched into weeks. The weeks stretched into months. Reservoirs overflowed; dams collapsed.

Rivers seized their flood plains and hungrily ate more and more land, consuming crops, homes, businesses, roads and railways.

A tidal surge travelling up the Thames estuary met the torrents of rainwater coming down the river and central London disappeared beneath the water. The foul water poured into the underground, into the Houses of Parliament and into all properties within half-a-mile of the riverbank.

Lightning strikes caused terrifying eruptions of sparks. Cables melted, fires broke out – even in the areas under water. The power lines remained down.

Water treatment plants failed and untreated water got into the system.

Trains stopped running. Roads were impassable. No-one travelled to work. Shops didn't open. Hospitals could no longer care for the sick and injured.

Food shortages led to lawlessness.

Disease broke out and, untreated, spread quickly.

The dead were left to rot among the living.

And still the storms raged.

*

The old black van, with no name on the sides, had headed for the south coast, fleeing just ahead of the black veil.

The driver, with a smooth, smooth face, but old, old eyes had caught one of the last ferries to cross the channel.

She had headed south down the length of France. Whenever the pain in her joints had become too great, she had seized the great sword by her side and drawn strength from it.

Ever southwards she had driven, staying ahead of the black veil darkening the sky behind her.

She had crossed into Spain and driven into the High Pyrenees. There she left the black veil behind. In a remote valley, high in the mountains she had stopped.

The people had made them welcome. She had known that they would.

Thousands of years before, when their Lyonesse home was disappearing beneath the sea, the Votadini had built a fleet of ships and divided themselves into three groups. Two groups had settled in Britain and their descendents had fought with Artos against the invading Saxons.

The third group had sailed south and landed on the northern coast of Spain. The fertile coastal lands were already heavily settled and they'd had to keep moving inland to an area in the Pyrenees where the terrain was harsh and unoccupied. They had settled there and thrived in their isolated valley.

Two hundred of their descendents still lived there. They had not fought with Artos and had avoided the effects of Demetia's spell. They were a strong and hardy people who had never abandoned the old religion.

They were practitioners of the old magic – a magic that had kept their valley undisturbed. Gilda knew that with their help and the Sword of Power, she would release the powers of the two golden salvers.

*

Carn, Eppie, Bran and Enid had gathered, as they often did, to drink a glass of red wine and watch the sun go down.

From behind them came the sounds of music, laughter, the crackle of fires and the aromas of food cooking.

It was not yet full summer, the last of the spring flowers warmly coloured the steep slopes, but as the sun began to slide behind the mountains, the air took on a slight chill.

Enid shivered and said, "Let's join the others."

"Shall we wait for Tegid?" Eppie suggested. "Here he comes."

With the steady, patient tread of its kind, one of Carn's donkeys was coming up the track towards them. On its back rode Tegid, his arms wrapped around his Welsh wife.

"Time to call the children back," said Bran.

Carn put a hand to his mouth and the call of a nightjar rolled down the valley.

The sound that had once brought Gog, carried to the four children. They stopped arranging flowers on Gilda's grave and waved.

The oldest was seven. Robert was already taller than his parents.

Extracts from readers' letters and emails in response to Dartmoor ...The Saving

- Finished it, enthralled and tearful, at 1.30 a.m. this morning

- I am a huge fan

- I so enjoyed it I cannot wait for the sequel

- I'm all in a dither!

- It was humorous, exciting and thought provoking in turn

- One of the best books that I have ever read

- Excellent

- Thoroughly enjoyed it

- I had to shake myself back into the real world

- Half-way through first chapter was gripped and couldn't put it down

- Enjoyed it very much and really looking forward to the sequel

- Wonderful story-telling

- So engrossed I could hardly put it down

- The test of a good book is if it remains with you afterwards and this one certainly did

Further comments overleaf…

Extracts from readers' letters and emails in response to **Dartmoor** ...The Saving

- What a great book

- Already read it several times

- Enjoyed every page

- This original tale is one of the best!

- More than once I felt a lump in my throat

- I was amazed at the effect it had on me

- What a great book – I bought it as Christmas presents for all my family

- As I read I felt I was actually there (reader aged 80)

- Best book I've ever read (reader aged 12)

- Just wanted to say what a brilliant book

- Read it avidly from cover to cover

- I hope someone has the sense to make the film

- Now I can't walk on the moor without looking over my shoulder

- What a great storyteller!

Further comments overleaf…